W9-BSN-138

THE WHIRLING GIRL

Barbara Lambert

THE WHIRLING GIRL

a novel

Cormorant Books

Copyright © 2012 Barbara Lambert
This edition copyright © 2012 Cormorant Books Inc.
This is a first edition.

No part of this publication may be reproduced, stored in a retrieval system or transmit-
ted, in any form or by any means, without the prior written consent of the publisher or a
licence from The Canadian Copyright Licensing Agency (Access Copyright). For an Access
Copyright licence, visit www.accesscopyright.ca or call toll free 1.800.893.5777.

The publisher gratefully acknowledges the support of the Canada Council for the Arts
and the Ontario Arts Council for its publishing program. We acknowledge the
financial support of the Government of Canada through the Canada Book Fund (CBF)
for our publishing activities, and the Government of Ontario through the
Ontario Media Development Corporation, an agency of the Ontario Ministry of Culture,
and the Ontario Book Publishing Tax Credit Program.

LIBRARY AND ARCHIVES CANADA CATALOGUING IN PUBLICATION

Lambert, Barbara
The whirling girl / Barbara Lambert.

Issued also in electronic formats.
ISBN 978-1-77086-093-3

1. Title.

PS8573.A38494W55 2012   C813'.54   C2012-900258-5

Cover design: Angel Guerra/Archetype
Cover art: Detail, "The Party," acrylic and inkjet on canvas,
© Charles Pachter, 2001. Used by permission of the artist.
Interior text design: Tannice Goddard, Soul Oasis Networking
Printer: Transcontinental

Printed and bound in Canada.

The interior of this book is printed on 100% post-consumer waste recycled paper.

CORMORANT BOOKS INC.
390 Steelcase Road East, Markham, Ontario, L3R 1G2
www.cormorantbooks.com

For Douglas

"Never have I seen her so pale. She is like the shadow of a white rose in a mirror of silver."

Salome, OSCAR WILDE

ONE

THE GARDEN'S KEEPER SEES a flash of a silver-dotted under-wing, then another and another, as sun breaks through the ruined wall. The butterflies skim in, a drift of mirrors. Soon, as spring warms the Tuscan woods, more endangered ones will arrive, perhaps even a shimmering False Apollo such as last year was blown from distant shores to rest its frayed transparent wings in his sanctuary. But what is he to do with such a blow of beauty, so alone? The young man hungers to shelter something rarer still, culled from the half-remembered, the forgotten, what never was.

⁓

With Second-Best Regrets

CLARE LIVINGSTON HAD KNOWN nothing about her uncle's obituary: not that it had been published internationally (even in the *Frankfurter Allgemeine Zeitung* and *Corriere della Sera)* nor that — most hurtfully to her aunt — it had also appeared in the local weeklies. Only when a lawyer tracked Clare down in Vancouver and summoned her to the family farm in western Washington did she learn the scandal-making nature of her uncle's bequest. Later, when she read the obituary, Clare realized her uncle had written it himself.

Noted ETRUSCAN SCHOLAR GEOFFREY KANE DIES AT SIXTY, IN SEATTLE, RAN THE HEADER IN THE *SKAGIT VALLEY HERALD*.

Born in Oxford, England, Geoffrey Kane (a.k.a. "Fufluns") travelled to Anacortes, Washington as a graduate student to assist the retired historian Perseus Livingston in compiling his research papers. Kane stayed on for fifteen years after marrying Livingston's only daughter, before an abrupt departure for Italy where he found employment with the Rome bureau of *The New York Times.*

Etruscan archaeology was Kane's passion. During his twenty years in Rome, he spent his leisure time travelling around

Etruria, exploring the remains of Etruscan cities and cemeteries, and publishing a series of articles under the pen name "Fufluns." On returning to the States to undergo treatment for what turned out to be his final illness, Kane let it be known that a forthcoming book would release spectacular information about a hitherto unknown Etruscan site.

Unlikely to be missed, Geoffrey Kane is survived by his niece Chiara Livingston to whom, with forgiveness, he leaves his Tuscan property, and by his wife Marion Livingston Kane, to whom he leaves his second-best regrets.

Clare's aunt met her at the farm gate holding the shotgun she'd been using to keep back the local press. Clare had not seen her aunt in twenty years. Now the long braid was grey. Clare remembered it as yellow like her own. She remembered how it twitched back and forth like a lion's tail; the feline beauty was still there, as was the ice-blue glare that could maul her from yards away.

The old farmhouse had gone grey as well, the paint finally giving a cracked and stony look to the fake Italian tower.

In a show of family backbone, Clare's aunt had turned this occasion into an ironic wake. She invited selected relatives to drink sherry in the cavernous *salotto* (as generations had insisted the room be called), where the air was thick with dust motes and speculation. For surely (the murmuring suggested as they waited for the lawyer) the obituary had got it wrong. Surely the will itself would make clear that if Geoffrey Kane had managed to acquire substantial property — if he'd managed to make a prosperous life for himself after decamping all those years ago — he would not have left everything to Clare.

In the wind-rush of dropped jaws as the bequest was confirmed, Clare took the sealed envelope the lawyer handed her and fled up the spiral stairs to the tower.

She stood for a long time looking out across the acres that had been tulip fields when her great-grandfather built the folly of an

Italianate villa for his bride; the fields were horse pasture now, sodden in the rain. This tower room had been the retreat of her grandfather Perseus, later her uncle's study. Now there was some old lumber, the smell of mice. She slit the envelope with a rusty knife from the sill. There was nothing personal inside. Just the command — typewritten by a lawyer in Cortona — for Clare to carry with her, to Italy, "the bodily remains of the most lamented Signor Geoffrey Kane, to be disposed of as you will see fit, once you have arrived."

Two weeks later, she was driving north from the airport at Rome with the disturbing cargo concealed in a plastic makeup case. Who knew what the strictures might be about bringing someone's ashes across international borders?

Clare. Or as the obituary might have put it, *a.k.a. Chiara.*
(In Italian: *clear, bright, light-filled, fair.*)

GEOFFREY HAD HELD HER on his knee when she was little and told her tales of distant lands; she'd known she was the light of her uncle's life. Such imaginary travels they'd escaped on — to the great lost cities of the Amazon, now overgrown with trees so tall that if you were a jaguar, stalking, you would move through constant deep and leafy gloom. He'd promised he would take her there. He would take her to far-off Italy too, to the lands of the powerful Etruscans who had left behind incomparable treasure in their lavish tombs. Safe on his knee, safe and loved, the lost civilizations rose again and beckoned, conjured by his words.

The Italian hill town of Cortona was older than Troy. That was another of his stories. Long ago, the local ruler's wife had borne the child of Zeus, and the scandal had driven the boy to seek his fortune in Asia Minor. When he lost his hat in battle, on that spot he founded Troy.

The autostrada rolled under the rented jeep's wheels no matter how Clare sped or slowed. Somewhere to the north, behind that ancient city of Cortona, her uncle had bought a house and olive grove, where he made a life that she'd known nothing of.

Castled towns rose and fell in the near distance. Red ploughed fields glistened against other fields that were not parched and umber, as she had expected, but a wild lush green. The wind held a hothouse softness too, though mixed with freeway fumes. After the dreary week of her stopover for research in London, this late spring fullness was a hopeful sign. She sped past exit signs for Tarquinia, Tuscania, Orvieto, hilltop cities where once those great Etruscan strongholds loomed.

To my niece Chiara Livingston, with forgiveness, the will had read. Not just the immense and shaming gift — a gift clearly designed to shock — but the twisted offer of forgiveness.

She had been left a house, a *Tuscan* house, a piece of Tuscan property, *the stuff that dreams are made on.* She would not allow ancient grief to spoil this. She forced her concentration back to the work she planned, the research she'd already undertaken during her week in London; she had in mind a lavish book that would delve into folk witchcraft, the so-called "old religion," rumoured to have survived from Etruscan times. It would be illustrated with her botanical paintings, giving it the same scientific imprimatur that had garnered praise for her Amazonia book — and this time it would be a piece of work that no one could possibly look askance at if they peered too closely. Perhaps this would be the one to make her moderately solvent. She would be able to hang on to the Tuscan property, hire wily Italian solicitors to outsmart her uncle's widow's lawyers.

She took her eyes from the perils of the autostrada long enough to steal a glimpse of her reflection in the rear-view mirror. A young woman in a serious hat, entering a new chapter of her life. She tugged the brim of the hat lower. An Italian tour bus swooshed past. Her rented jeep shuddered in the rush of wind. Clare Livingston, reputed Amazonian explorer, tried to pull a lightly spangled veil over the dark matter of the journey, the bequest, even the druggy sense, as the road pulled her closer to his house, that he would meet her there.

The exit sign for Chiusi flashed by. "Choosy," she said aloud; big mistake. A shutter in her head flew open and there it was, his voice: *No no, Chiara, it's pronounced Keee-oo-see with a k-sound, as in your own name. We will go there. We will hunt for the lost tomb of Lars Porsenna! We will look for scarabs in the jeweller's field.*

She skidded onto the verge, blind with sudden tears, spraying gravel, choking back all she'd been holding off, an ache so deep that she was again tainted and helpless, exactly what she had been to make him flee.

Traffic buffeted the jeep. You were not supposed to stop here. Then the crunch of gravel as a car pulled in behind. She thought of the Carabinieri at the airport with their shining boots and tidy submachine guns. They would find the ashes. She would be lost in the great jungle of Italian rules and regulations, maybe carted off to prison, maybe never seen again.

She looked up to see a 1950s model cream-coloured Mercedes. A young man was getting out, his profile reflected in her side-view mirror like a face on a coin — grand high-bridged nose, determined chin. Now he was coming forward as if she knew him, as if she would be glad, his hair blowing and then falling straight in the wind of passing cars, his linen jacket hunching up around his shoulders with the urgency of what he had to say. She felt a rush of recognition, of idiotic joy, even of rescue, as her eyes locked with this unknown person in the mirror.

She rolled down the window.

She shoved the stick shift into gear, rammed her foot to the floor; and when she saw his startled look, she tore off her hat and hurled it up over the top of the car. In the mirror she saw it hovering for a moment, flapping, before a gust from another passing tour bus sent it soaring towards the roadside field. Her hair fizzed out around her, spun the mirror full of gold.

"Italy is Dangerous"

ALONG THE NARROW TWISTING road that led from the autostrada, Clare passed olive groves, meadows, red fields with shadowed furrows. A stretch of umbrella pines floated like obedient clouds. No further sight of the cream-coloured Mercedes. What cheap force had flooded up in her back there? She felt another light-headed rush and then another.

Italy was dangerous. She'd been warned of that by jealous friends before she left. The place was rife with handsome roadside mashers. She'd been quite right to flee. But what an idiotic thing to throw away her hat, which she had rediscovered in a trunk and decided would be a talisman of sorts; it had belonged to the dear old relative in Vancouver who'd taken her in as a runaway when she was just thirteen. She brushed back her wild hair. What had she imagined — that an eagle would swoop down and restore the hat, heralding her triumphal entry into a new exalted state of being, the way the first Tarquin had entered Rome?

Rough purple mountains appeared in the distance. On a nearer slope a vast rocky patch appeared, disappeared with a bend in the road, swung into view again, and became three-dimensional. A whole city pulling itself up into massive walls and ochre buildings and towers, like a child's pop-up book.

Cortona. The city older than Troy.

She rummaged in her bag for the directions the Italian solici-tor had sent along with the key. The house was on a farther slope, behind the town. When she found it, would it be heartbreaking and lovely? Or would the walls ooze a toxic mix of forgiveness and guilt? Sometimes, in the weeks before she'd left Vancouver, the amazement of the bequest had opened before her like a reprieve. Sometimes it snapped shut like a trap.

She circled the base of the hill, wound through a maze of lanes, turned up onto a steep dirt track where the jeep had to straddle washed-out ruts. She peered at the notes again: "Just past some newly planted hectares of the olive, one must turn into the lane to one's left. One is home."

THE LANE WIDENED INTO an area of rugged grass. Geraniums in terracotta pots perched along the edge. Treetops reached from below. The house seemed to grow right out of the slope, a house of lichen-covered stone with a side arbour of wisteria. It was ancient, weathered — the stone steps that led up to the arbour, too. One large window on the upper level scattered the setting sun from its many panes. Green shutters covered the others. Clare parked under a great gnarled oak. The air was thick with the scent of wisteria, and the sound of bees.

She was shaking. She let her gaze escape across the wide sweep of the valley, towards some distant cone-shaped hills half-lost in mist. She took out the big iron key, hefted out the plastic case that held the ashes. Her clothes had gone on to some other destination, but the suitcase with her art materials had made it. She dragged it to the double door on the lower level, and into a shuttered area where the space was divided by a ladder stairway. Was this one of those old farmhouses where the lower floor had once been a cattle barn? A scorpion skittered into a dark corner. She dropped the cases, and made her way up the ladder stairs.

THE ROOM SHE STEPPED into was striking and unexpected, yet for a moment seemed foretold. She experienced the same feeling she'd had on the freeway when the young man had come striding up.

Light poured through the great window, pooled on the uneven terracotta floor. A smoky mirror caught the view of distant hills settling in a froth of golden mist. At one end of the room a great stone fireplace rose, big enough to roast a calf in; doors of heavy wood and glass led out to the wisteria arbour at the other. Down a set of shallow steps she glimpsed copper pots above a black enamel stove.

One is home.

She stretched out her arms, turned slowly, faster, whirled, catching her reflection again and again in the cloudy mirror. Dizzy, she braced herself on the heavy sideboard that held the mirror, studied the woman with the wild shining hair as if this were an illustration in an old-fashioned book where the heart of the heroine was gold and pure.

In that mirrored land, the distant olive groves on the back slope of the hill that held Cortona looked close enough to touch. A ruined fortress loomed at the top, against a sky turning amethyst. A bell rang in Cortona. Perhaps the bell from the basilica of Santa Margherita, a saint whose story began like a fairytale — an innocent country girl, barely a teen, seduced to live with her noble lover in one of those distant hilltop towns that now glimmered across the plain in the last evening glow.

But real dusk was seeping in, reflections jittering in the warped panes of windows and doors. The wrought-iron lantern above the trestle table cast the merest slick of light. Catching a flash of movement, Clare whirled around. A lizard clung to a ceiling beam, its jewelled scales attracting the lantern light, its bright eyes sharp. Then with a tiny flick, it was gone, leaving a ripple of unease. Probably Italy was dangerous. Her helpful friends had warned her of the gangs of wandering gypsies or Calabrians, and the famous Butcher of Florence who slit the throats of lovers in the woods.

Were the doors all locked? She started to check, first the small oak door beside the fireplace. It scraped on the tiles as she eased it open. She stood with her hand on the door frame. Her uncle's room. In the shuttered gloom, the dark outline of a bed. She retreated.

Back down the ladder stairs, she twisted the iron key firmly in the lock. With the light on, she discovered it was a fine space. Not a trace of a former barn, the walls lined with books, a mellow brick floor.

Above a desk, though, hung the ugliest oil painting she'd ever seen, a paint-by-numbers stream gushing diagonally down a slope between brooding trees, lumpy striped rocks breaking the flow. Worse, on a shelf below, a purple hand mirror popped into view, the back stamped with a motto in fake gothic writing: "Seek and ye shall find."

Her heart stopped.

So many innocent games he'd devised when she was little, because she had no playmates on the farm. Treasure hunts and paper chases, even a wooden puzzle-box that had required Zen-like patience, till she worked out how to spring the lock.

Seek and ye shall find.

Hadn't the obituary said that he'd been working on a book that would tell of some remarkable Etruscan find? Could these odd objects be clues in one last puzzle he'd set for her — this was why he'd brought her here? He must have left behind notes and papers — a true paper chase, giving further clues?

She started pulling books from the shelves, tearing open the desk drawers, checking out the alcove behind the staircase where she found a great luxurious tiled bath — then racing up the stairs, searching through the rest of the house, shying past the door into his bedroom, to pull open every drawer and cupboard.

Nothing. Except to discover that the great beautiful room upstairs was badly lit. How would she do her work? She spied the top of an angle-poise lamp poking up behind a big fireplace chair, but this turned out to have a tiny lemon-sized bulb, and worse, the lamp was wired to an almost unmoveable bronze statue of Romulus and Remus suckling the she-wolf, the whole contraption so extraordinarily tacky that she could only shake her head. The low table this sat on was covered with a beautiful shawl of heavy silk, fringed with coloured crystal beads. The beads made a tiny tinkling music when she reached down and fingered them, before she worked up the courage to push open the bedroom door again and fumble for a light switch.

BESIDE THE BED THERE were three books.

Absurd to imagine he had made sure exactly those three books would be in that position, certain to catch her eye.

The two Everyman volumes were on top, worn gilt print on the spine, above a pattern of flowers. *Cities and Cemeteries of Etruria.* So many times she'd seen him pull one or the other from his pocket. She knew exactly where the art nouveau design on the frontispiece of Volume One would be stained because a child had spilled cocoa on it. She knew the page she should turn to, in order to find, in the upper left corner, a small black-and-white illustration: *Etruscan Dancing-Girl.* She knew how either of those compact little books would feel if she were to pick it up and open it at random: *Sutri, Nepi, Norchia, Pitigliano, Tarquinii.* The names of places that had held queerness and splendour. She had learned to read by spelling out those names, often pronouncing them wrong.

And under the top volumes? Without coming a step closer she recognized the book he had kept on a shelf in his study in that other farmhouse in western Washington, never knowing (she had thought then) how she had crept in there almost from the time she could read, to sound her way through the true grownup versions of the stories he had told her ever since she was very little. Ovid's *Metamorphoses,* the Oxford edition, on the cover the helpless form of the young god of war, asleep, pinkly draped across the lap of a Venus who smiled a creamy smile.

A whistle broke the silence.

Just a bird?

She remembered a stout burled stick in a copper stand by the kitchen door. When she went to get it, foolish or not, she noticed a hunting coat hanging on a hook by the door, an old green coat with cargo pockets and cartridge loops.

She took the coat down. She buried her face in the quilted lining, caught the smell of once-familiar tobacco. Finally, a whiff of him. She sank down at the kitchen table, and stared through the glass-paned door to where the kitchen light shone on a flowering quince. A pinkish-white petal floated down, and then another. Watching this, waiting for another petal to fall, breathing the smell that the old coat released, she understood how absurd all this other caution was, how it hardly mattered about the thieving gypsies and the strangling Calabrians.

After a while, she turned the pages of a loose-leaf binder on the table. It held information about the house, the pages yellowed, typed with an old machine where the c and the g struck above the line of type. "If you hear noises in the night, they will be these: a wild boar (*cinghiale*) rooting in the woods beside the house or among the olive trees; a porcupine grubbing out the arum lilies along the drive; a screech owl. There is nothing to fear."

But there's always something to fear, Clare thought.

It comes creeping up from inside if nowhere else.

IN RAINFORESTS OF THE upper Rio Negro, Clare, the imaginary traveller, had not been afraid. She had watched the ruby eyes of caimans gliding by, as her guide poled the dugout through dark waters. She had eased past giant anacondas on the trail. She had calmly gathered up her painting materials and slipped back to camp, when she heard the crashing of a jaguar in the brush.

Where the Bull Was Kept

HUDDLED INSIDE HER UNCLE's hunting coat, on his dark bed, Clare listened to a little wind slipping through some unfamiliar Italian trees. She heard the rushing of a stream. In the rafters, night thoughts roosted. She tried to concentrate on just the whispers of air as they played through twigs and leaves, pretending this could be a new discipline, identifying growing things not just by leaf and bract and stem but by the sounds they made as the wind played through.

Then the moon reached in and said, *Hush now little Clare. Your mother's name was Selene, another name for the moon. You will never be an orphan, Chiara, because your mother will always be shining down on you.*

On nights when she couldn't sleep, he used to comfort her with these words.

To the sound of the stream, Clare began drifting back and back to the true place, the good place, and darkness gave way to the full rich green of a coastal morning rising, where a man and a little girl were heading to a stream full of cutthroat, the man carrying his own rod and the girl's new one as he helped her through the fence into the field where the bull was staked, below the folly of a west coast farmhouse with an Italian tower. The bull was raising its head, shaking its chain. The man said, "Stand tall; show him that you are not afraid."

"Are you afraid?"

"I would be. But he's staked, Chiara."

They were playing hooky from a long list of chores. In his pocket were two hard buns with slabs of cheese, and in his other pocket was Volume One of *Cities and Cemeteries of Etruria*. They had only just started on these travels, which he would take her on whenever they managed to escape for the next brief years, Volume One illustrating the map of a city with its ancient gates and streets and ruins and the cemetery that held tombs like small brilliant houses, and such paintings on the walls. All this was described in a way so grownup that Clare let a lot of it flow over her. Bit by bit the pictures formed. Her uncle said they would go there together.

This was the prelude. Now, to inhabit the crucial moment that exploded some days later, to be truly there, she needed to summon up the smell of burning sun on clay, the glitter of Oregon grape against the cliff that dropped from the farmhouse to the field. And then little Chiara, digging, digging — in danger and hot young jealousy and fury — into that steep cracked wall of clay.

If she is quick — but has left enough clues — he will come and find her.

It turns out she is nothing in that house. He doesn't care that she did the drawing of the foxgloves just for him. She signed the drawing with the tiny upright fork shape he'd explained made a *k* sound in the Etruscan alphabet, "as in your name, Chiara," signed it with the symbol only he would understand, to show how she absorbed everything he said. But he had left her picture on the table where her aunt could come and crumple it and throw it on the fire. Now Clare has the butcher knife and she is carving a place to disappear.

"Oh, what our Etruscans could have done with this cliff face, Chiara," he'd said when they came back across the field the week before, his face lighting up in that way that made her feel peculiar power. "We'll pretend the cliff is limestone, shall we? Its location would have been ideal for our Etruscan friends to carve tombs."

Excited now, pointing out how the horseshoe shape of the cliff brought it into perfect view of the house above. "That is the essential element for an Etruscan city of the dead — in view of the habitation of the living."

What a strange activity for a child.

"Shall we carve the entrance of a rock-tomb, like the drawing I showed you?" Dark hair falling in his face as he set down the fishing gear. What child wouldn't enjoy feeling singled out, special? What child wouldn't delight in taking turns with his fish knife to carve an elaborate house-front into clay, then being hoisted onto his shoulders so she could cut stick figures on the triangle shape above the columns? But as she'd wriggled down and begun to hollow out a true entrance between the columns, he'd grabbed her back, scolded her. Yes the Etruscans had carved tombs deep into the living rock, but this was only clay. It would be dangerous to burrow in there.

In deeper now, when it turns out she isn't special after all. Burrow deeper still! The hot sun baking the outer clay, the blood roiling through her brain as she carves her way to darkness, hacking out great reckless chunks with the stolen butcher knife.

Eventually she hears him calling. So what? She will live here. In the night she will bring blankets, a camp stove, food.

When she feels the down-rush of dusty earth, it is too late to call out or do anything but curl up like a snail and wonder, almost triumphant, if perhaps she will not be found till centuries later. Will she be fossilized by then, the clay turned to limestone at last, her curled body too?

What she smells next is his fear. Sharp as a knife it cuts a channel ahead of him, the stink of it. She keeps her eyes closed after he gets her free. He collapses to his knees outside, crushing her tightly to him, saying, "Jesus Jesus Jesus." Her hand creeps to his armpit. She breathes his fear from her fingers, and the smell of love and almost-death. There will never be anything, ever, to match that moment.

Adonis Flower

CLARE WOKE; THE BUTCHER of Florence had not battered down her doors in the night.

On chill air from outside flowed the scent of grass and herbs. The woods were loud with birdsong; in her sleep she had pictured a tap suddenly opened, a faucet pouring out melody and birds. A cuckoo started calling. She waited until it reached fifty, then swung her feet out of bed, felt the chill of the terracotta tile, slipped barefoot into her boots, pulled the hunting coat around her shoulders and walked onto the stone balcony beneath the wisteria arbour.

Light rushed across the valley, springing the far hills into view. As she leaned on the railing, she imagined being on the prow of a ship, the house racing towards morning.

She turned to close the glass doors. An envelope fell to the ground from the scrollwork above the handle.

THE PAPER WAS CREAMY and stiff, the up-thrusting script so like her uncle's British boarding-school writing. She retrieved the envelope gingerly.

An invitation.

Someone who described himself as the owner of an adjoining property was hosting a party in her honour, that very night. This had been arranged, he wrote, by the "wealthy chap who took you under his wing in London, Sir Harold Plank." For as Clare was undoubtedly aware, the note went on, "old Harry Plank" had delegated an archaeologist in his employ, a chap who was staying just down the hill, to set up contacts for her.

"Old Harry Plank." Clare couldn't help a flush.

The spiky script went on to explain that "a goodly number of Etruscan glitterati" would also be attending. They were champing at the bit to hear about her fascinating travels, and of course to meet the niece of "the elusive Geoffrey Kane." Sir Harold Plank had even couriered a carton of Clare's recent book about the Amazon. Copies had been delivered to each of the expected guests, including the writer's Italian brother-in-law, a young man who had established a refuge for endangered plants and various other species, "and with whom you will have so much in common, for the lad also knows all about the Amazon."

The writer signed off, "Eagerly awaiting the pleasure of meeting an illustrious fellow writer! Your good neighbour Ralph Farnham." In a postscript, he warned her to be on her guard before she went out sketching. "I'm sure your uncle was a fine chap. But do be wary of those bloody ferocious dogs. I'm told that Sir Harry's archaeology chap barely escaped with his life when he went exploring in your uncle's woods."

Your good neighbour. She could see this man already: the old-school tie, the blue blazer with the crest, the supercilious familiarity with the likes of "old Harry." The prospect of the party filled her with dread. She had not expected to meet a gaggle of glitterati not only familiar with her book, but including one who knew all about the Amazon. No way to get out of this. The man was coming to pick her up at seven, "Because, dear Signora Livingston, though my wife's property adjoins yours, you will never find your way here on your own."

She shoved the invitation into the pocket of the hunting coat. Tonight was a long time away. Maybe her suitcase would fail to turn up. She could hardly be expected to meet all those glitterati in the boots and jeans she'd worn from London.

SHE WALKED DOWN ONTO the grass, then skirted the front of the house, reaching out a hand to touch its stone flank. She came to a fence with a gate and a stile. The path beyond was rank and overgrown, leading into dark woods. What had Ralph Farnham meant about ferocious dogs? For that matter, who had been looking after the place? Who had left the bowl of fruit on the kitchen table, the milk and cheese in the bright yellow fridge? Or made sure these pots of geraniums flourished? There was so much she would have to ask the solicitor, once she'd made an appointment to see him.

Behind the house, orderly olive trees graced terrace after terrace up the hillside as far as she could see. She scrambled around the end of the house and up to the first terrace, still worrying about dogs.

Natural gardens had sprung up in the hollows around the olive trees, golden ox-eye daisies, wood forget-me-nots, chamomile with starry flowers; then, farther out, the soil was disked and rough. She settled on a stone and let her eye travel the patterned landscape, the rows of cypress, the patchwork fields far below, all brooded over by the ruined tower on the hilltop across the way. The tower had been built by the Medici, she'd read. Once, long before, that same hill would have held tile-roofed Etruscan buildings, a temple with brilliant painted god-figures flaring against the sky.

She shook her head, the amazement of actually being here sinking in, remembering how as a lonely little kid, inspired by her uncle's stories, she had wandered on the ridge behind the farmhouse with the fake Italian tower — she and her inseparable friend, the little Etruscan girl — the two of them wily and adventurous, even bolder than Etruscan women were reputed to have been. They changed the fate of the entire Etruscan nation: for it had been foretold that the Etruscan civilization would last but ten generations and then a great trumpet would sound, signalling the collapse; but the two of them, two little rebellious daughters of a priest king, refused to allow their great civilization to turn up its toes. They broke into the temple where the trumpet was kept and threw it crashing and splintering onto the rocks. The course of history was changed.

It was seductive to sink back into that heroic reverie. How much easier imagination was than life. No need to face up to the glitterati, for example. Hadn't the same applied to her adventures in the Amazon? She'd been prepared to go; she'd been desperate to go. But, having been prevented, she had gone there anyway. Mightn't she have achieved something just as strong, or stronger, if not for one egregious bit of imaginative self-indulgence which could invalidate all she'd tried to do? She had to smile, no matter what, thinking what a sneaky self-subverter her imagination really was. In her book about those travels, hadn't she been trying to do exactly what she'd attempted with the little Etruscan girl long ago — to stop the inevitable? Change the face of history?

She pulled herself back into the present. No soaring of imagination was going to get her through the problems that faced her in fighting off her aunt's legal threats. Looking down on the old house, a presence that seemed almost alive, she knew that she would do everything she could to keep it. It was so beautiful. No, more than that. Almost a natural part of the landscape, the ancient stones and the roof that was like a complex puzzle, the many levels of tiles blooming with patches of lichen, the chimneys with their own tile roofs like small pagodas. A gleaming copper gutter ran along the roof edge, connected to bright copper downpipes. This was clearly new. Geoffrey had left everything in good shape. For her. *With forgiveness.*

She would agonize no more.

Nevermore.

She said it aloud, for good measure, and in that instant she caught the movement of a tiny shape, in a stony hollow, a throb of silver splitting into red before her eyes.

HAD SHE TRULY SEEN the bud splitting open? The petals were still trembling, the blossom catching light in its blood-red cup. The shock of seeing this blossom here, as if the web between reality and imagination had dissolved, made her dizzy.

Nevermore.

And it appeared.

How often, as a child, Clare had made her way up to her uncle's room in the tower, secretly, to read the story of Myrrha, the child mother of Adonis. Myrrha exiled to wander the earth as punishment for her unspeakable sin. And this flower, here, was *Anemone coronaria,* the blossom that had sprung from the blood of Adonis when, later, Aphrodite held her young lover dying in her arms. Already in the sun it had split wide to show the stamens springing from the black mound of its female centre in the upturned skirt of petals. Clare knelt bare-kneed on the stony soil. Carefully, without touching it, she cupped the small bloom in the hollow of her hands.

∽

THE QUIET MORNING BLEW apart. A roar, a puff of black smoke. A stooped figure emerged from a shed on a higher terrace, pushing what looked like a giant rototiller. He caught sight of Clare, shut off the sputtering motor, and started down a track at the edge of the trees.

"*Ah signora, benvenuta!*" A smile that showed a scattering of teeth. "*Signora, scusi, scusi,*" wiping his grimed hand on the seat of his pants, "*Sono Niccolo!*" his grasp like the clutch of a gnarled oak.

He began explaining, in a volley of almost unrecognizable Italian, that he worked here, had always worked here, for her uncle, and before that for someone else. She scrabbled for words she'd been practicing in Vancouver, but was no match for this volley of local dialect.

So — she finally managed to ask — these were her uncle's olive trees?

He nodded. Yes, her uncle's trees, and (a rope of words that she half-managed to disentangle) it was his great pleasant happiness to look after them for her. She must not worry. Of everything he was continuing to take care.

Was it safe to walk here then? she asked. Would it be dangerous to come back in a few minutes, to sketch this little bloom?

She was impatient to return and paint the anemone, to capture it, capturing her unruly feelings that way. She would need to hurry. This anemone was known also as the windflower, because in the slightest breeze the petals would release.

Niccolo's face had grown stern. Why would she ask if it was safe here? This was her property.

But the dogs?

Dogs? Had she seen some dogs?

No! But someone had told her ...

He made an explosive noise that blew fingers of both hands wide. This was mischief, she thought he said. This was someone making *superstizione,* spreading that old story.

Old story?

"*Assolutamente malo!*" he said. Evil, worse! For someone to spread this old story of the devil's dogs. He had cultivated these olives for her uncle for twelve years, and before that for the old ones down the hill, and these were the most fertile hectares in the zone. To say anything else was the talk of snakes and worms. No. This was her place and he would keep it safe. No need to worry about dogs. He narrowed his eyes with an expression that made her think of a wall of ancient stones. He and his wife had no other life now but this duty they had accepted, to care for the property that had been passed to the niece of Geoffrey Kane.

"*Allora,*" he said, as if this settled the matter, gesturing towards the main road, "*Marta viene. Subito!*"

"*E Marta parla Inglese!*" he added, in a tone that suggested this clinched everything else he'd said.

Clare heard the wasp-like buzz of a new contraption. A woman in a lilac-printed cotton dress, sitting very upright on an ancient scooter, turned into the lane.

"AH SIGNORA CHIARA, BENVENUTI *in Toscana! Sono Marta, Marta Dottorelli. Scusi scusi, sono tardi. Come va?*" All this was wheezed in a high-pitched voice that carried with the power of a buzzsaw. The woman switched off the motor, jammed the kickstand into place, and pulled two bulging net bags from the carrier. Clare scrambled down steps leading from the lowest terrace, past the washing lines to the kitchen door. She found herself crushed in the arms of the small powerful figure, the net bags swaying somewhere behind.

This contact was so unexpected, so overwhelming, that Clare felt the start of tears. The woman had dropped what she was carrying. Holding Clare out at arm's length by the shoulders, gazing into her face, reaching up to touch her hair, her cheek, as one might outline the face of a beloved daughter, "*Ah bella bella, bellisima!*" she exclaimed. "Yes, you are just as Signor Geoffrey described. An angel, *veramente una Botticelli, si si si.* This hair, eyes like the sea!" In her whirlwind of exclamations, she sucked Clare into the kitchen. She said Clare had not eaten yet, she was sure. She had brought a still-warm cake of chestnut flour. She would make some coffee!

She pulled out a wraparound print apron, and a pair of slip-on plastic shoes to replace the leather pumps she left at the door. The other bag was full of greens and weeds she had cut this morning along the roadside: dandelions for a salad to give "Signora Chiara" strength, and *ramponcioli* and nettles, which would make a fortifying soup. Yes of course she knew where everything was; she had been coming here in the mornings twice a week for twelve years. Oh, no. Signora Chiara was not to worry about the paying. This had all been arranged by Signor Geoffrey!

Signor Geoffrey had promised she and Niccolo would stay on, Marta explained; he had promised they would remain, to give the house and the vineyards care.

After all that, Clare could not possibly dash back to the terrace to paint the anemone. She drank the fierce coffee that had erupted from the tiny stovetop espresso pot. She ate the chestnut cake. When she returned to the sunny hollow beneath the olive tree, the windflower had flown so completely that she could not locate the stony hollow where it had been.

⌒

CLARE WANDERED THE TERRACES. These olives must require so much care. The trees looked ancient, almost sculpturally pruned and carved. Niccolo had tended them most of his life? He would be jobless if she sold? But he was old too, almost ancient, wasn't he? If she did manage to hold on to the place, how would she afford to run it? Not for the first time, she cursed the divorce settlement she'd agreed to, which had been based on her going back to work in the botany lab and her hope that the Amazonia book would bring in real money. Her husband had been happy to foster that; he helped set up contacts for her, leading to publication with a prestigious American university press. He'd also been propelled by a sense of guilt, because she would have been along on his Amazon expedition if he hadn't left her to satisfy his lust with the sharp-toothed student with the ring through her nose.

The leaves ruffled silver. It felt like a memory of a different, parallel life, wandering among these trees. The sun streamed down with the sweet weight of honey. She found a grassy hollow and lay back, studying the quality of the light. Painting here would require a different palette, not the supersaturated tones she'd called up for her jungle scenes. A blue wood forget-me-not nodded, almost out of focus, near her cheek. You are *Myosotis sylvatica,* she told the little blurry flower; you are part of the family of the mints. It made her feel safe, not a fake at all, to know this. *I know the name of everything,* she told herself, *and what I name I conjure into being.* She pictured herself like the goddess Flora wandering the fields, bestowing names, making things real, bringing them to view; and wasn't that what her paintings of Amazonian flora had done, whether she had actually set foot there or not? Had she not brought the endangered and voiceless into view?

As she drifted, she heard a distant whistle that reminded her of the dog whistle her husband used to use. But Niccolo had said there were no dogs. This reminded her of her husband, too. When she'd asked her husband if he was sleeping with the girl whose thesis he'd been supervising, he'd said, Jesus, I can't handle all this suspicion, I can't even look at a student without you getting suspicious. She'd said, The trouble is, I remember how you looked at me. He'd said, *You.*

Circaea Livingston Philippiana

A COURIER VAN WAS backing down the lane when Clare returned to the house. She found Marta in the kitchen with a butcher knife in her hand, in front of a large crate. Marta whirled to face her.

"Ah Signora, I was hoping to find the right tool, for you to open this — look what has arrived."

It was a case of Brunello di Montalcino, Special Reserve. Straight from the winery, courtesy of Sir Harold Plank. "To cheer your palate, inspire your brushes, warm your introduction to the Tuscan sun," read the accompanying note, handwritten on embossed Plank Foundation stationery. He'd added a private phone number, too: his flat in Mayfair. He must have couriered the note to the winery in time for the wine to be couriered from Montalcino.

The envelope had been lying on the kitchen table when Clare came in the door. "*Allora, Signora*" Marta had said. "See how careless the delivery man has been — how this letter just fell off when he set the case down, and not even sealed!" Clare was so surprised by the gift, that only later did she wonder if the kettle boiling on the stove had anything to do with the note not being sealed.

Marta sang praises to the lavish nature of the gift. "It is the most famous of our Tuscan wines. This must be from someone who likes Signora Chiara very much."

"No no," Clare said quickly, remembering the moment over lunch in London. "He's just a business contact. An archaeological contact really."

"*Ah! U' arqueologo!*" Such a stony look, before Marta pulled the vacuum cleaner from a curtained alcove and hauled it up to the next room. Clare heard the clatter of it being dragged down the ladder stairs, then its fearsome howling in the room below. What was that about? She'd never had anyone work for her before. What had she said wrong? *Archaeologist?*

She shrugged, lifted a bottle of Brunello from the case, closed her eyes, ran her fingers up and down the cool, upstanding cylinder.

Someone who likes Signora Chiara very much ... Harold Plank had made that much clear. And she'd liked him, too. Though later she'd wondered if it was only when he learned that she'd inherited the property of Geoffrey Kane that he had decided to help her. ("A fine writer, your uncle," as he plucked an oyster from the shell.)

SHE'D COME ACROSS HIS name back in Vancouver — an eminent figure who had endowed the British Museum's new Etruscan gallery and was said to dispense largesse to select projects around the world, though he never travelled himself. When she got to London, she'd tried to make an appointment to see him, and had been stalled: so she'd barged right into his office and set one of her books on his desk. She signed it with a flourish before he could object. After he'd leafed through, carefully examining the full-page illustrations ("Very nice, very nice") he looked up and carefully looked over the length of her, then invited her to lunch at Simpson's in the Strand. It wasn't till the treacle pudding that he'd offered to set up Tuscan contacts for her. Then he'd offered to move her from her Bloomsbury hotel to a "nice little suite at the Ritz, more fitting for a lass like you."

Such cheerful North Country forthrightness. She'd pictured the enormous grey-satin room, the soft forgiving light from alabaster sconces. How she would remove his plum-and-grey-striped tie, his striped shirt from Savile Row. How she'd solve the little trouble of slipping down his crisp white boxers, with his penis springing through the fly. But there had been no hard feelings when she refused. In fact, his face had taken on an expression of wry delight, as if such a refusal were something rare.

Earlier, he'd been telling her about a cabinet of curiosities he kept, "in a nice little Edwardian inlaid case that fits into a corner of my study in the Yorkshire Dales." She pictured her refusal being placed into that cabinet too, tucked into a vial of cloudy ancient Roman glass, along with select items of Etruscan bronze such as she'd been so intrigued with in the Museum.

In the Etruscan gallery she'd moved along from case to case, pulled by objects that had a strange sense of brightness radiating from them. A bronze hand beckoning, green with age, with little horned men growing out of every finger; a dancing woman wearing pointed shoes, whirling, the movement evident in her whipping sleeves, a seven-tiered incense burner balanced on her head. Every functional object brimming with the energy of a further life that seemed to simmer inside the cast bronze shapes. She could look at those things for hours; she could look at them for a lifetime and still see something new. Did this wealthy man, this philanthropist who had endowed the collection, experience this too? Did he enjoy looking at them so much that some pieces had found their way into that inlaid cabinet in the far Yorkshire Dales? She had no reason to believe this; it was supposition, based on the discomfiting suspicion that the morals of others might be as unruly as her own.

The sound of the vacuum had long since stopped. What on earth did Marta find to do down there, or for that matter in the house at all, day after day? How often did she come? When Clare went downstairs she found Marta leafing through a copy of her Amazon book, though she wasn't sure she'd left the case open earlier in her rush to get out her painting gear.

Marta threw out her arms. *Allora,* who would have known that Signora Chiara did such work? This book was *splendido, molto molto notevole!* And to think that she, Marta, had the honour to have in her house now not just a painter, but an author, *un'autrice famosa!* All this wheezed out in what Clare couldn't help picturing as a verbal smokescreen to cover the embarrassment of being caught.

"I'd like you to have one of these books," Clare said, to make up for her doubting thoughts. "Here, I will sign one right now, for you and Niccolo." They stood together, as Marta proudly turned the pages of her copy.

Marta paused, at the one illustration that Clare always tried not to think about. She studied it intently. "*Che cosa strana!*"

Clare felt her jaw and shoulders tighten. Extraordinary, the things the body decided all on its own: as if it had to gear up for a fight of some sort, when really, who in the world was going to call Clare on this, or even know?

When Marta had tucked the book away, she told Clare that the lawyer's office had called. She said that Clare had an appointment for nine o'clock on Monday morning.

Clare said, "Then I'd better call back to confirm."

Marta said there was no need. "I have already done this for you, Signora Chiara." She urged Clare to come upstairs and have some of the nettle soup. Clare decided to put off setting a few ground rules: and that she'd prefer to make her own arrangements about such things. She praised the soup lavishly instead. She said she would like to sketch the weeds that went into such a healthful soup, if Marta would tell her where they grew.

Marta, shining the copper pans, turned, wiped her hands on her apron. Her glassy stare made Clare think of a fox she'd seen once in the window of an antique shop, stuffed with secret knowledge.

She said, "Signora Chiara should take care. A beautiful woman wandering alone in these hills."

"Take care of what? The house book says there is nothing to fear."

Ah, but there were strangers in the district now, Marta said. Sicilians. Telephone workers, they claimed to be. She resumed scouring, giving fierce attention to her task, even though the pots were brilliant before she started. Clare lifted another spoon of soup, her hand shaking. No doubt she was just tired. Of course she was tired, all the travel, all this so new; but it was starting to feel unreal to have these helpful figures moving implacably into her life: the husband, Niccolo, like a gnarled tree stump come alive, and the glassy-eyed Marta with the red-grey hair. Yes, like the fox-figure in the window.

Then, "Oh Christ!" she heard herself say, as some of the green liquid spilled onto the front of her silk shirt. "That does it. I won't go."

The scowl Marta turned on her was enough, alone, to banish the green stain. A puff of irritation. "Signora, when I have finished this, I will wash your blouse."

Clare protested.

Marta insisted.

She said that if the Signora was going to go to the party in her honour — and if her luggage still did not arrive — then *naturalmente* it would need to be washed!

Clare frowned. Had she told Marta about the invitation? In the tangle of two languages, and her dismay at finding her movements so closely monitored, she wasn't sure, anymore, exactly what information had been passed between them.

"*Allora!*" Marta said, "All the same, the Signora will need to learn who the good neighbours are!"

And the good ones, it seemed, did not include Ralph Farnham and his Italian wife, Federica. Ralph Farnham thought he *ate the cream,* just because he'd married into the family of the Inghirami; and the Inghirami themselves believed they were the cream. In the old days, they had owned all the land in these near hills. But even though the father had lost that land, and lost his money, Signora Federica still behaved as if it all was hers, and had continued to ride her horses all over Clare's uncle's property before Signor Geoffrey had it fenced. Also, the husband of Signora Federica's good friend, the Contessa, was the local archaeological inspector; he had tramped all over Clare's uncle's property too, with his thick eyeglasses peering as if he had any business there. Clare would meet this Contessa and her husband at the home of the bad neighbours too, Marta warned.

Marta threw her rag into the sink. She pulled off her rubber gloves and threw them in the sink as well. "*Allora,* now give me the shirt." Handing Clare the blue-sprigged cotton wraparound apron, she said "You can wear this." Then her face softened. This was such a mercy that, ridiculously again, Clare felt the start of tears as Marta's roughened hand stroked her cheek.

"Beautiful Signora Chiara, you must forgive me if I am sometimes cross. It is not you. It is the life in general. Now go and have a bath in the tub downstairs. Tonight you need to be rested!" She held out her hand for the shirt.

Clare's silk shirt was long — almost a tunic when she wore it outside her jeans. She pulled it up to start unbuttoning. Marta's eyes widened with shock. Clare started to turn her back. "Sorry!"

Marta grabbed her by the shoulder. "What is this?" She reached towards Clare's belt buckle, snapped her hand back as if it might get burned. "Why do you wear this?"

Clare frowned. "I always wear it. I've had it for years."

The big silver buckle was in the form of a goat head, heavy, showy. But Clare wore it for quite other reasons.

"*Maligno!*" Marta said. "*Pericoloso!*"

Clare tried to laugh this off. "I know it's in pretty bad taste."

Marta blew out her cheeks in a puff of disapproval. Then she sighed, spread the hands that *the life in general* had roughened, as if there were just too many things about Clare that needed to be corrected. "*Allora,* go! If I do not wash this now it will not be ready. Afterwards, I will take my *motorino* to the store and buy some things for you to eat, or you will starve. No no no. This I always do. For me it is no trouble." She squeezed lemon on the stain, rubbed in salt, went out the back door.

I'M GOING TO HAVE to get control of this soon, Clare told herself. But in fact it was a relief to slip obediently away in Marta's apron. And really, when had she ever, truly, been in control? Maybe only during the years she'd worked on the Amazon book, absorbed in the twinning of scientific accuracy and make-believe?

She paused on her way to the bath to admire the remaining copy she'd brought with her. Despite the serious qualms its publication had raised in her, she loved that book. She stroked the glossy cover, noting again the sheen she'd achieved on the ribbon-like petals of the *Galeandra devoniana,* the elegant curve of the stems, the intricate pattern of the roots. The painterly quality of the botanical portraits had received some fine reviews. Yet Clare had begun the work for reasons personal, out of profound shock to learn that a fifth of the world's plant life was headed for extinction. In the Amazon this meant that many plants would die that had yet to be discovered, identified. She had not expected the work to get such notice. If she'd foreseen it, she would have been more careful, she later told herself many times, and would not have felt the constant jitter of apprehension ever since.

She flipped the pages, allowing belligerence to ripen towards the entire academic establishment which she pictured, still, as crouching ready to find fault — and towards Dr. Lester Wildman, her ex-husband, in particular.

∾

IT WAS ON THE night she'd learned for certain not only that her husband was sleeping with the doctoral student, but that she, Clare, had been bumped from the Amazon expedition and the student was going in her place, that Clare had created the painting of *Circaea Livingston Philippiana.*

She had already taken a leave of absence from the botany lab to prepare for the trip. Amazonia was hers; she refused to give it up. She'd lived in it, in imagination, for an entire year: canoed rivers teeming with piranha, trekked jungle paths braving all manner of poisonous snakes, waded swamps roiling with crocodiles, fallen asleep to the racket of howler monkeys. Indomitably, through heat and mud and teeming rain, she had crouched on sopping logs or in tippy dugout canoes to capture — to save! — likenesses of its creatures and its plants.

And I married you just *to get there,* she'd almost hurled at Lester Wildman, though this was far from true.

She'd set out to attract him long before she'd known he was hoping to put together such an expedition. He was not only head of the department, but he knew everything, talked beautifully, had travelled widely. A rangy, almost ugly, incredibly compelling man in his forties, old enough to be a father figure, the mentor she'd always longed for. Married, but she'd told herself the appeal was intellectual, not much more. At that point, Clare had still been reeling from the end of her off-and-on affair with her childhood psychiatrist. (To the psychiatrist's credit, he was the one who'd given her the strength to make it as far as grad school.) She had decided to devote the rest of her life to recording and painting all the grasses of the world. Grass was so humble. It got so little respect. "In art I mean," she'd explained to Lester Wildman when she visited his office to put the thesis topic to him. "Think of it, where do you ever see grass in paintings, except to be trodden underfoot, or to provide an anonymous carpet for some woodland scene? Take Manet's *Dejeuner sur l'herbe.* The *herbe* may get top billing, but even the loaf of bread gets more respect. Or Monet's *Field of Poppies,* where the entire field is just a blur."

Dr. Lester Wildman said, "All the grasses of the world! Would that leave you time for lunch?"

She had been with Lester Wildman for seven years, one way and another. Secret girlfriend, open girlfriend, marriage-breaker, wife;

then just another in the string of his betrayed. When she learned
that he had crossed her off the expedition, she threatened to make an
enormous stink, to blacken his name with the university as a serial
philanderer, go to the press, whatever it took. But what good would
it do? If the university cut the funding for the trip, she would still be
sitting there at home. She could see she'd scared him, though.

So she made the deal. She would write the book she'd intended
to write, and she would execute a series of paintings of the endangered flora of the Amazon basin, as she'd dreamed of doing. She
already knew the subject so well that she wouldn't really truly need
to be there, though it broke her heart. Eminent Dr. Wildman would
supply her with the alternate resources she required. She got him
to sign an agreement promising her access to herbarium specimens
from collections across the continent. Beyond that, she would use
photographs as reference, and botanical articles and any other source
she chose.

THE PORTRAIT OF THE *Circæa* began as a doodle that same night,
fuelled by rage. It was a version of deadly nightshade, which she'd
read was a distant relation to the Amazonian plant that provided a
basis for one of the recipes for arrow poison.

The painting took on a life of its own, as she began to combine
implausible elements: giving the flower a rocket-like appearance,
exaggerating the curled-back petals behind the pointed nose cone
of the anthers, drawing in some darkly shaded fruits like tiny pome-
granates with cracks opening to sharp-barbed seeds. Gorgeous, she
dreamed it into life in botanical exactitude: side sketches of the root,
some split-open fruits showing a larger view of the poison seeds. A
mix of Paynes grey with ultramarine and magenta produced a virulent purple for those fruits.

So there it was, her first discovery on the expedition — named
not in her own honour, no, but in that of the supposed revolutionary
ancestor her aunt had often talked about.

When she signed the painting, she added the little stick figure too, half-hidden among the leaves, which she later added to all the paintings for the book. During the rest of the work, which took her two years, she kept *Circaea Livingston Philippiana* near for inspiration. She had not intended to include it in the package she sent off to the publisher; but, somehow, it got in with the rest — perhaps a subconscious desire to bring the whole project to a halt before it was too late? Though to be fair, nowhere in the written text had she stated that she, personally, was the one trekking through the swamp and rainforest. She'd merely phrased things in a careful — if extremely lively and first-hand — sort of way. And, during that two-year imaginary trek, she had become convinced of her ability to convey truths with a clarity and perspective that might have eluded her if she had actually been battling the rigours of remote Amazon travel while experiencing the urgency to record as much as she could of the botanical riches of that endangered part of the world. Terrible, if by this one piece of egregious self-indulgence, the whole work might be smeared with disrepute.

Still, when the art director wrote and asked for details of the imaginary plant's find spot, struck by the weird beauty of it, asking for clarification that this was a new species Clare herself had discovered — at that point she could have made an excuse to withdraw at least that one painting, couldn't she? Instead, stubborn bravado kicked in. She'd written back to say it had been found almost hidden by the spray of the cascade that plunged from the lost world atop Mount Roraima, a waterfall of such height that it was lost in mist before it reached the ground.

❧

AS CLARE STARTED INTO the bathroom alcove in the semi-gloom, her toe struck a solid rock-like thing. It was a large chunk of brain coral, intended as a doorstop she supposed, now bloodied from her wounded toe.

She limped across and started running hot water into the tub. She'd be turning up at this gathering of Etruscan glitterati not only dressed in jeans, but lame as well.

Lame, but very cautious and well behaved, she told herself. She would not let her nervousness propel her to that extra drink, especially with Ralph Farnham's Italian brother-in-law who knew *all about the Amazon* there. She was a serious woman on a serious academic quest. As the bath filled, she stared into the steamy mirror, traced the face there, leaving a cartoon outline: the too-wide-apart eyes, the sharp cheekbones. The off-kilter mouth of a bad angel.

Chiara, my angel girl.

SHE HAD TO CLUTCH her gut. A pain, sharp as fire, ran up from her insides into her throat.

How could she have imagined — here, in his house — that she could keep all that tamped down?

She reached for the brain coral, in an urge to smash that pretend-oblivious face in the mirror. Then she heard Marta start the *motorino*. Marta, who peered and pried. What had she been up to down here when the vacuum was whining? Had she peered into Clare's things? Had she tried to pry into the case that held her uncle's ashes?

That obscene request of his.

The plastic case was where she'd left it, squat and ugly, in the other room on the floor. She'd better find somewhere safe for it, till she came to terms with what to do about its awful contents. How could he have requested this of her? Who was he, anyway, who had he become? That obituary. Had he thought it terrifically clever, that Shakespearean echo, leaving his wife his second-best regrets? Clare thought of the desperate sparked cleverness he'd had, and how her aunt had always cut him down. Did he have to die to get the last word in? Was that why he went back to the States to die? To get the last word in? In all the years since his disappearance, what could he possibly have known about the girl he'd abandoned to the aunt and the grandmother and the ancient doctor on the night the evidence was scraped away?

How could she have acceded to his request about the ashes; refusing to think about it, except as part of an adventure, popping the cremated remains into the plastic makeup case, telling herself she'd been clever when the customs guy in Rome shook the heavy case and she'd given him her best smile and said, "Makeup. I need a lot."

She began tearing books from a shelf to make a hiding place.

So many books.

Did you read all these? she wanted to scream.

And why why why did you bring me here?

In her half-blind state, she dropped a large volume; it landed on her damaged toe. She let out a howl.

The villain this time was *Ancient History,* with *Revised Edition* appearing below the title in gilt letters on the cracked-leather spine. Ancient history, revised. Something appeasing in that thought. When she flipped the book open, the old pages released a soothing smell of knowledge long contained; a sweet druggy feeling stole in, of drifting back to a distant time, beyond her bad time, beyond the good time that had preceded it, to a time where she could disappear or become another person altogether, a priestess casting enigmatic divinations, a warrior queen. She turned the pages, admiring the etchings set into the text. A page came loose in her hand. She tried to work it back so that it rested firmly against the binding, and in doing so caught a glimpse of an etching on the second side.

A face on a coin.

For a moment she was back on the autostrada, catching the profile of that man in her mirror, the grand furrowed brow, the high-bridged nose, the up-thrusting chin. She shook her head, remembering her idiotic reaction: rolling down the window, then zooming off. The startled look on his face — she remembered that clearly, too; how it had said, Come back, come back, you've got it wrong. Our meeting like this was fated.

No, I didn't get that wrong, she thought now; that's exactly why I ran away.

The mouth on this coin-face held a hint of petulance. And so it might. This was Mithridates of Pontus, scourge of the Romans in the East; a man who had been determined to get what he wanted for a long time, even taking a small dose of poison every day of his life in the hopes of holding death at bay.

She slid the page firmly back, then cleared a space on the shelf and hid the case that held the ashes behind *Ancient History* and other books.

TWO

Nightingale Hill

A RED ALFA ROMEO came to a stop at the bottom of the arbour steps. A man in a panama hat got out, tripped, recovered, saluted and clicked his heels together at the door, knocking his hat askew.

"Ms. Livingston, I presume! Ralph Farnham at your service."

He sailed in on a gust of gin, peering at her with eyes wobbly but sly, taking in the shirt, the jeans, the belt with the silver goat's head buckle, even the ring with the fire opals on her wedding finger. She was glad she'd pulled her hair into a stern knot.

She explained that her suitcase had gone missing, and he said that was not a problem. A gap-toothed grin. "But tell me — would I gather from that western-looking belt you are wearing that you are an equestrian type? My good wife will set aside every antipathy if that is so!"

Happy messenger, then; the man explained that his wife, with what he called rather an Italian sort of failing, still regarded a considerable chunk of the land that Clare's uncle had fenced in as being hers, and in fact had been conducting a legal dispute for years. But Clare needn't worry! Now that she was actually here, her lawyer, who as luck would have it was also his wife's lawyer, would set things straight before the matter got to court, where, goodness knew, it could take years. The basis of the problem had to do with family pride, nothing more.

"Never marry an Italian, dear girl!" he added. "Not only will you never be good enough, but you will marry countless generations of ancestors, too."

He began to stride around the room, his old-fashioned jodhpurs flapping over his skinny hips, as he peered at everything high and low, even giving the Romulus and Remus lamp a whistle.

"Mysterious chap, old Kane. Kane the Shadow, I've heard him called. Though I maintain that your good uncle was entirely in his rights to publish articles about his rambles among tombs and ruins, despite never bothering to make contact with the local archaeological pooh-bahs. Hurrah for him I say, for thinking his own thoughts, publishing his own annoying lay conclusions. Quite delicious, really, the way he managed to get up academic noses."

He peered out the window. "Hang on — I don't see the Lamborghini."

Clare was still trying to take in what he'd said before that. *Kane the Shadow.* Was that some clubby British jest, and would it turn out Farnham and her uncle had been best pals? Was the Lamborghini reference part of that? No. It seemed that her uncle had been a sort of local joke, the sight of him cruising the lanes and byways in a vastly expensive yellow car whenever he made it up from Rome.

"Did he sell it before he left for the States?" Farnham asked, giving Clare another of those ferrety looks. "He must have been a very fond uncle, all the same, to leave his Tuscan property to you."

Clare walked to the door. The man was every bit as loathsome as she'd anticipated, but she was damned if she'd show how close that hit had come. "We'd better get going."

"I do hope you're not nervous about meeting some types who are not exactly fans of your uncle's work." His eyes made another trip from head to toe. "I'm sure a girl like you, who's trekked the far reaches of the Amazon and Orinoco, is not likely to be phased by a swarm of waspish academics."

"I married one. I carry anti-venom."

He laughed. "And you'll find an antidote, in any case, in the presence of my botanical brother-in-law. Gianpaulo is a great favourite
with the ladies. Word has it the lad's rogered every pretty girl from
here to Timbuktu."

∾

FARNHAM KEPT UP A stream of talk as the red Alfa raced down the
rutted road, then up a narrow valley at the base of the hill with the
ruined tower. He gestured down a lane.

"That's where your hermit lived. Down there."

"My hermit?"

He explained that a few hundred years earlier an artist had fled the
intrigues of the royal court of France and settled in a cave to devote
himself to studying the native flowers of this area. Clare could save
herself hours of tramping through the woods by going up to the
museum in the town, where several volumes of the hermit's plant
illustrations were kept in the archives, available for study.

"The archaeologist who's out here on behalf of your good friend,
Harold Plank, lives down that lane as well," he said.

Your good friend. She caught the prurient tone. Was that what
people here thought, all those she'd meet tonight, just because Plank
had taken such an interest in helping her? Well if it helped with
her work here, why not? Reluctantly, she noted a familiar slippage,
picturing herself moving through her time in Tuscany half-obscured
by a swarm of glinting little lies, which might at least serve to deflect
attention from the larger untruth about her Amazonia book.

They flashed through a settlement of stone houses, then past
young fields collecting the last of the sun in emerald spikes, then on
up a very twisting road.

"A word about your friend Plank's archaeologist chap," Farnham
added. "I fear you'll find Luke Tindhall to be one of those rougher
sort of Brits, not averse to showing off the chest hair. Probably a secret
Scot at heart." He chuckled and repeated the phrase, as they hurtled

through a set of broken pillars and crunched to a stop in a gravelled courtyard surrounded by stone buildings linked by archways and roofed passages. "So here we are. *Poggio Usignolo.* Nightingale Hill."

TWO MEN IN IDENTICAL Hawaiian shirts were decanting wine from a carboy into pottery jugs, in a breezeway just ahead. "Our two resident archaeology types," Farnham told Clare in a carrying whisper. "We call them the mollusks. They're quite attached. Though I believe recently there's been a little flurry ..." He fanned the spot where his own heart might lurk.

An alarmingly handsome blonde youth turned. This was Anders Piersen, from Denmark. "Out in Tuscany doing his doctoral project," Farnham said as he introduced them, "Though lately I'm told this consists of Anders here zooming off on his Vespa to go field walking in Umbria, following close behind our illustrious Dr. William Sands."

The other man straightened. He was gigantic both in girth and height, with a craggy, much-furrowed face.

"And Carl!" Farnham feigned surprise. Talking over the big man's scowl, he told Clare that Carl was a well-known architect from Berlin, where no blame had been attached regarding the collapse of a new bridge across the Spree. "All the same, Dr. Bernhoff has decided to devote himself to the study of Etruscan dental appliances now — trading one sort of bridge for another, what?"

He sidled off into the kitchen.

"He is a shit," Anders Piersen said.

"Pish tush!" The German turned to Clare, as if consideration of Farnham wasn't worth the bother. He told her how they'd picked up the wine that very afternoon, at a cantina where you pulled up in your car and pumped a carboy full of it, "just as though you were pumping petrol." He filled a glass and held it to the light. "This has travelled well." He handed it to her with a smile.

She took a long sip, then another. "Well-travelled indeed. *Prosit!*"

He nodded in appreciation of the toast; they both drained their glasses. As he was refilling them, a tall man with a white ponytail came out of the kitchen door and shouldered past without speaking, lost in thought. "William!" the Danish youth called after him. Then in a loud voice, "No matter. Soon I will be Doctor Anders Piersen of Aarhus. This will happen despite the reluctance of the illustrious Doctor Sands to read my dissertation." The white ponytail disappeared into a side passage without turning.

"Come," the German said to Anders, "We must finish with this job!"

Clare took her refilled glass and slipped away towards a dusky terrace.

≈

A POOL ON A lower level caught the last rosy light. Clare set her glass on the balustrade. The gas-pump wine seemed to have drained away again; it had not buoyed her as she'd hoped. On the far side of the terrace she heard a woman's brassy American voice, joined by a mellow Italian one. She didn't look around.

The view was so remarkable. How dreadful to be standing with laughing people in the background, an empty glass in front of her, looking out over countryside that her uncle had made seductively real to her. There, directly across a narrow gap, was the city supposedly older than Troy, topped by the ruined tower. There was the Etruscan wall. There, to the south, a glimpse of Lake Trasimeno where Hannibal had won a battle that had turned those waters red. What if I crack apart tonight? Clare thought. What if everything flies out, a black cloud of leather-wing bats and devils, like in some medieval painting?

The moon was rising behind the house. If her uncle's property did adjoin this somewhere in the woods, surely she could bushwhack her way home with the help of that moon. But the young Dane, Anders, came up beside her, proffering a platter of red, oozing bruschetta.

He stared at her with such alarming intensity that she wondered if he was going to ask her to read his thesis. Instead, he started telling her how keenly he had been following the work of Geoffrey Kane, how he looked forward to talking to her about it when they could find a quiet opportunity. She took a slice of bruschetta and held it, trying to control herself enough to speak.

"Here," Anders finally said. "I will give you this." He reached into the pocket of his shirt for a newspaper clipping. "Please remember, I am the one *simpatico* you can trust." He strode into the house.

He had given her an article from the *International Herald Tribune*. By Fufluns. Her uncle really had used the name of the Etruscan Dionysus.

To find herself holding that bit of yellowed newspaper was one thing too much. She shoved the clipping in her pocket, wheeled around, and took a blind step towards escape.

SHE FOUND HERSELF GLUED to a stocky weathered man, with the tomato-garlic thing oozing between them.

"You're supposed to eat it, not wear it," he said as they peeled apart. "Just a little Italy tip. When in doubt, treat anything they hand you as food."

He was very tanned, but shaggy; he made her think of a shaggy lion. His eyes were so blue she wondered if he wore contact lenses.

He would be the archaeologist who worked for Sir Harold Plank. The giveaway? The half-unbuttoned shirt, the chest hair.

"You must be the niece of Kane," he said.

It was marvellous and pathetic how one's mood could turn around. A vain, grizzled man looking at her in a carnivorous way. She found herself laughing.

"The niece of Kane? And this is the mark of Kane?" she said, looking down at her shirt. "What a mess. And yours too!"

"Don't give it a thought. I was wondering how to introduce myself."

"I'm leaving. We'd better pass like mess-ups in the night."

"Terrible idea."

"We'd have to stand with our faces to the wall."

"We'll face them together." He doubled his fists, pummelled the air. "We'll say we were attacked by errant comestibles and had to beat them off with sticks."

"That could work."

He dropped the fists and looked weary, as if the nonsense had taken more out of him than it deserved. He turned to gaze out over the valley in a Lion Rampant sort of way. He might have been a blocky statue, if Clare were to ignore the hot-hide smell pulsing through the lemony aftershave. The silence extended. She studied his big hands braced on the stone wall. Wide fingers. A battered ring twisted to form a snake with a ruby eye. He was consciously letting the silence harden, she thought. She could feel silky currents side-slipping in the dusk

"I've seen your book," he said. "Your friend Sir Harry tells me you're tackling Tuscany now. Where to after that? Karnak, I suppose."

She tried to remember where Karnak was. "I'm not sure that fits my schedule."

"What? Not see that famous wall which records of the spoils of Thutmose the Third, from his campaigns in Syria!" His voice shifted into the singsong. "*And My Majesty saith, all these plants exist in very truth. My majesty hath wrought this, in order for them to be before my father Ammon, in this great hall forever and ever.*"

He turned sideways, one hand above the other, palms down, like a figure in a frieze. "Carved in hieroglyphics, of course."

"THIS GUY TRIES TO sound erudite, but don't be fooled." The brassy-voiced woman who'd come up beside them made Clare think of one of those ballet figures by Degas: a short tulle skirt, platform sandals laced like ballet slippers, black hair skinned back before it fell into a long braid, and clusters of gilded oak leaves on her ears.

She laid her palms on either side of Luke Tindhall's face, kissed him on each cheek, oblivious of the man with the white ponytail now frowning at her side.

"All Luke really does is throw money around," she said to Clare. "We have to keep buttering him up, hoping he throws some in our direction. I'm Nikki Stockton." She shook Clare's hand. Her grip had crunch. "This is my husband William Sands."

The husband gave Clare a grave and attentive nod.

"William is the director of an excavation in the hills in Umbria," the ballet woman said, "A hilltop fortress settlement that spans all the Etruscan centuries."

Her husband was shifting his feet. Luke Tindhall was shifting his too.

"We hope you will come up and see the dig," the woman said, "even if Luke here has such a busy schedule. Right, William?"

But the man with the white ponytail turned and walked away.

Luke Tindhall stood back, sizing the woman up. "So Nikki, what do we have here tonight? In training for the *Giro d'Italia*, are we?" And Clare realized that the ballet costume was actually put together out of lycra bike shorts under cheesecloth-like panels, and a lycra muscle shirt.

"It's a mood piece," Nikki said. "To get you in the mood to pedal up to our dig."

She then turned an almost hungry intensity on Clare, and started to rave about how moved she'd been by Clare's description of the dangers facing the biosphere of the Amazon basin, and how she had felt as if she were actually there with Clare on those travels.

"By the way," she added, "I'm a sort of artist, too."

She pulled at one of her oak-leaf earrings. Bits came to pieces in her hand. She undid the drawstring of a little silk pouch she wore on a cord around her neck and tucked in the gilded fragments, all the while explaining that she worked in the conservation lab associated with her husband's dig, where she did measured drawings of the archaeological finds. As she went on to describe the work, Luke started tapping his foot. "There is this really enlivening tension," Nikki was saying, "between the detailed hours of measuring and recording, and the magic of reconstruction. How from a few recovered fragments it is possible to recreate what an artefact would have been when it was whole." She pulled at her other earring, which also came to pieces in her hand. She stuffed these into the embroidered pouch.

"That's so pretty," Clare said, empathizing with this clearly nervous performance.

"This? It's handy." Nikki gave an elfin grin. "I keep little discarded things in it. Like thoughts." Then she bent and peered at Clare's waist. "I've always wanted a belt with a big silver buckle. Did you pick that up on your travels?" Clare noted the strands of grey in the long black braid as the woman then exclaimed, "Why it's a goat's head! Where did you find it?"

"I won it, in a rodeo."

They all laughed. Clare excused herself to go and sponge her shirt.

∽

NIKKI STOCKTON WAS WAITING in the corridor when Clare came out of the powder room. She led Clare to a spot further along the terrace under a gnarled wisteria vine, where a round table had been set with bright pottery dishes, a clutch of wine bottles in the centre. Ralph Farnham was there. He said the wine had been sent along in Clare's honour from the Sienese estate of Gianpaulo, the botanical brother-in-law, who was a bit delayed. He eased Clare into a chair where all the bottles had their labels turned in her direction: a mini-phalanx of rearing unicorns, symbol of the brother-in-law's sanctuary for endangered species, he explained.

The wine was so dark it was like sipping liquid garnets — garnets from caves where unicorns really might still hide, Clare thought as she sipped. The entire setting was a fantasy, an outdoor Aladdin's cave, and when she looked up into the vine she saw a chandelier made up of hundreds of Venetian glass flowers, each with millefiori petals that threw bouquets of jewelled light. Farnham said the chandelier had been designed by a famous glass master in Murano, as a gift from his spendthrift brother-in-law to his wife Federica. Clare heard a small tinkling sound. One of the glass petals had fallen on her plate. Across the table, Nikki Stockton gave that elf grin and spread her hands as if to say *don't blame me*. Clare cradled the tiny petal in her palm, noting how its curve held a scattering of still-tinier flowers, turquoise and rose and lapis, with ruby centres as well as minute gold stars. She would take it home for inspiration; a good omen surely for a flower artist starting on a new venture.

She felt Luke Tindhall looking at her. She tucked the petal under the rim of her plate. Beside her, washed into indiscretion on a tide of his brother-in-law's wine, Ralph Farnham began telling of a scandal involving his wife's mother. Clare only half-listened, conscious of Luke Tindhall's stare. "A lovely mess!" she heard Farnham say in conclusion, "Only in Italy, old dear. Unless you count our Royals …"

AS MORE GUESTS APPEARED, one or other of them squeezed in beside her whenever the previous one got up, like musical chairs. A bearded Italian with a beaky nose introduced himself as Vittorio Cerotti, and, in a fate-filled tone, said that while he was the local inspector of archaeology, yes, as Signora Livingston may have heard, he was also "the husband of this beautiful apparition," indicating the woman who hovered behind. "The Contessa Dottoressa Professoressa Luisa di Varinieri."

The Contessa! A vision indeed, though hardly as Clare had expected. She was wearing an outfit that might have drifted straight from one of the famous tomb paintings in Tarquinia, a gauzy dress and red boots with curling toes and a headdress that reared from her shoulders like an elegant cobra hood. When the vision settled beside her, Clare found herself confessing about the imaginary adventures she'd engaged in as a child with the little Etruscan girl; how she'd spent hours imagining the clothes they would wear, poring through her uncle's books on tomb painting and a reference book about Etruscan mirrors.

"You must call me Luisa!" The Contessa seemed charmed. "Of course, fashion is so much more important than some bluestockings would have you believe. For as I am sure you know," she sweetly added, "by studying the costumes that are portrayed, particularly as engravings on Etruscan mirrors, we are able to pinpoint quite accurately the era of such discoveries."

She leaned close. In a caffè latte voice, she confided to Clare that it was one of her greatest tragedies that, although thanks to such mirrors there were excellent records of what Etruscans had worn through the ages, still, as things stood, the entire popular literature of the Etruscans had been lost.

"However, your uncle, in one of his last articles, hinted at quite a remarkable discovery. Perhaps soon we will have tea and, as you might say, compare notes?" In the warmth of that almond smile the long-forgotten sugary sensation of a schoolgirl crush settled on Clare. She wanted nothing more than to become a helpful friend to this beautiful older woman.

When Luisa di Varinieri rose, Carl slipped into her place. "We are all fond enemies around this table, *ja?*" he said. "This is the sad case with academics. We are all in hot pursuit of intellectual treasure. I believe every one of my dear friends here is equally intrigued to know what Geoffrey Kane may have discovered, what information he might have left behind in his notes and papers."

Clare nodded. She held out her glass, determined to ignore the truth she'd just glimpsed slithering through the jewelled light. Perhaps none of this — the wine, the friendliness — was really about her. Maybe her entire life had not been about her, if she looked at it that way. "Here's to intellectual treasure, then," she said to Carl. They clinked glasses and refilled. At her request, he taught her toasting phrases from other parts of the world, where his work had taken him: *Na zdrowie* in Warsaw, *Noroc* in Bucharest, and, in Catalonia, *Txin txin*. She told him about drinking manioc liquor among the Yanomami, a wordless experience, she said. When the young Dane took Carl's place, she said *Skaal,* and thought no wonder the big German was in love with him, anyone would be; he smelled as compelling as he looked, just the faintest whiff of well-washed armpits overlaid by tarry soap. Anders was a linguist, he told Clare. She was just about to tell him about the Yanomami, and the night she'd spent among them in a hammock in one of their great circular grass houses, when the man in the white ponytail sat down across the way. Anders began in plangent tones, sure to carry, to talk about his doctoral thesis, in which he proved a positive link between the ancient language of the Etruscans and modern Ukrainian.

A TERRACOTTA TRAY PUSHED through the beaded curtain in the doorway, followed by a figure in a white dress with many descending ruffles. A dangerous coil of ash dangled from the cigarette in the centre of the red pursed mouth.

Federica.

Federica glared around. "Would you believe Gianpaulo was halfway here when Eleanora called to say their girl has croup! So now he is on the way to Bologna, yes! I have had to call Eleanora to say, 'Please do not make me have to tell you that just because you run the family business you do not run all our lives.'"

She caught sight of Clare.

"Ah, of course." She came around, grasped Clare by the shoulders — taking in the sponged shirt, the belt, the boots, the jeans. "You are the niece of my difficult neighbour, who never had the courtesy to call on me." She kissed Clare on both cheeks, then made her way back around the table, flopped into a chair, crossed one brown leg over the other, pushed both hands up into her cap of short black hair. "Oh that woman!" she sighed, through a curl of smoke.

"Meaning the wife of the little brother," Ralph explained. "Please do not imagine otherwise."

IT TURNED OUT THESE people all knew each other well. Some had been students together on an international dig, years ago. There was laughter about how terrible the food had been; how all the men had loved Luisa because she'd shared the salami from her sandwiches. Only her husband didn't laugh. Clare pondered the symbolic possibilities of salami. And, as the talk curved more and more into Italian, she was content to observe, stealthy as a lizard, in the tangled vine of laughter and in-talk.

She saw how Luke Tindhall rolled his eyes whenever Dr. William Sands made a point; she saw how the beautiful Contessa's eyes dwelled on William Sands in an almost proprietary way; she saw that Carl, the German, was indeed sick with love for the Danish boy, and how the boy's sad gaze was drawn to William Sands, and how William seemed oblivious to these looks, or shrugged them off. Indeed how, as the evening wore on, his mind slipped away to the hilltop settlement which his excavation was bringing back to life. Earlier he'd told her his team had come upon an extensive temple complex on that hilltop. Clare pictured it now: on the roof, huge gilded figures had once walked the sky, the gods that had lived before the gods we knew. He is an outsider like me, Clare observed as he absented himself in thought.

Then, in an instant, the table became electric. The beautiful Dane reached across for a bottle of wine, at the very moment that William reached for it too. Their fingers touched. William's hand recoiled. His glance ricocheted across to his wife with such force that Nikki broke off her conversation, looked up, caught the anguished look in the young Dane's eyes. That was how Clare remembered it, seconds later, when Nikki Stockton had already resumed her conversation, smiling brightly, twisting her long braid into a loop, letting it fall.

Clare knew she should avert her stare, but wasn't fast enough.

Nikki looked up again, turned that bright smile on her. "We haven't heard anything about Clare's adventures yet!" she said in that brass-bell voice.

"Oh, I'd much rather go on listening to all of you!"

"*Aiii,* enough archaeology!" Federica said. "I agree. Our guest of honour must tell us of her adventures. I have promised my brother I would tell him everything!"

"It's hard to know where to start."

"How about orchids?" Nikki said. "William likes rare blooms."

Federica banged the table. "So we will hear about orchids please."

"Orchids?"

All eyes were on her. She could hardly back out now. She stood; she felt the belt with the silver buckle straightening her backbone, the goat head grinning.

"The sheer gorgeousness of *orchidae* is their most compelling feature, naturally …"

She felt her hand reach up, to remove one pin and then another from her hair, while at the same time she slipped into a scene that she had imagined for her book, a painting that had taken weeks. She was gliding into it again as she had during those weeks, seeing and recording every detail.

"Imagine rounding a bend on a muddy trail, and coming on tiny *Brassavola* hanging in cascades, like ropes of pearly spiders. Breath-taking! In the columns of green light filtering from high above. And the silence. Sometimes in the rainforest the racket is remarkable. But sometimes the silence is so deep that you feel yourself completely absorbed, invisible, though you know that around you are hundreds of silent, watching eyes. Picture stumbling upon the rare blue orchid, glowing in the humid semi-dark! One can search for weeks and never come on one."

She had them. They were rapt.

"But to a botanist the diversity of *orchidae* is equally interesting." She smiled, to indicate recognition of the edge of pedantry in her tone. "Did you know that some orchids are big as shrubs, others are vines? Or that in Australia there's a variety that even grows underground?"

Her husband had mentioned this. She had never truly understood. He was actually in Australia at this very minute, having invented another expedition of his own, to escape from his new wife's unexpected onslaught of triplets. (At least I didn't do that to him, Clare thought.)

"Orchids have a long history," she moved on quickly. "The ancients valued them for treating sexual disorders, the name deriving from the Greek for testicle, because of the swollen underground stems. I am sure you are familiar with the Doctrine of Signatures put forward by Dioscorides, which holds that if a plant looks like a human organ, it is good for treating that particular part of you."

Luke Tindhall clapped, managing to bring a note of irony to the sound.

She reached for another sip of the garnet wine, then took her audience in a dugout along the flooded waterway linking the Amazon and the Orinoco, then on an expedition hacking its way over the *Serra Tumachumac* through to Roraima and into Venezuela. She paddled them in search of caimans, describing how in the dark you could tell the different species by the colour of their reflected gaze: the little spectacled caiman with his golden eyes popping up like pince-nez above his snout; the dwarf forest one with his orange stare; and the dreaded gigantic black caiman with the ruby red glare. She talked of the fearsome bugs, the gorgeous birds, the silent snakes, the racket of howler monkeys in the night, and the jaguar's terrifying call.

"*Fantastico!* Were you often frightened?" the beautiful Luisa asked.

"Sometimes it was terrifying, yes. Oh, but at the same time, you must imagine the thrill and beauty of those jungle calls echoing through the forest's majestic solitude ..."

All the time she spoke, Luke Tindhall was looking at her. They were all looking at her. Her tongue was silver thanks to the wine from the *terroir* of the unicorn; her tongue was silver and her words were gold, and the evening turned out to be about her after all.

LUKE TINDHALL DROVE HER home. As they got into his chunky antique car, he asked if she would like a tour around the area next day, the tombs at Orvieto perhaps, or the very interesting museum at Murlo, an hour's drive through the hills? Perhaps a little lunch along the way?

She settled into the creaky half-sprung seat, breathed in the leathery smell of the old car, and the smell of Luke. He began humming. She caught him glancing at her out of the corner of his eye as he turned out of Farnham's drive.

"Aren't you going the wrong way?"

"The magical mystery tour."

He turned off onto a narrow track that followed the level of some abandoned terraced land. The headlights caught gnarled ghosts of frost-killed olive trees, then plunged sharply downhill, burrowed through woods, straddled a dried-up stream. When they came to a rusted iron gate, which he wrenched open and failed to close, she thought, At least I know one thing about him now: he wasn't born on a farm.

They emerged onto an open patch. She recognized the black silhouette of the hill with the ruined tower, directly across the way. He stopped the car, came around and opened her door. The grass was silvered by the moon. She felt hazy and insubstantial as he put a hand on her shoulder, which was the best way, in the dark, only flesh, not even words. Things rustled in the woods, maybe foxes. Two bats crossed the air in a looping sweep, one within wing tip of the other.

"Careful," he said, "Better stay close to the car just in case."

Did he mean because of dogs?

A light flared across the rocky patch where they were standing. He was brandishing a torch. "Look," he said. "I have not mentioned this to anyone, for good reason." The glaring circle slid over an area of large oblong stones. "The cut suggests that this was laid down well before the Romans. On your land. This leads directly to your house." He angled the beam to where the stones succumbed to grass and spiny weeds, the barest overgrown path disappearing into farther trees.

Had he brought her here to show her a bit of ancient road?

The light swung full on her face, catching her out, catching the whole humiliating swarm of emotions in her moth eyes, her expectation, her willingness and loneliness and need to be obliterated by another human body.

"Right," he said, "Come on."

Before she could say anything, he was helping her back into the car. They bumped along again, through pools of moonlight, pools of shade. When the track arrived at a second gate leading from the woods to her house, she jumped out of the car without another word.

The Wild

CLARE WOKE TO THE ringing of a phone. She heard a beep on the answering machine. Luke Tindhall's voice. Another beep. Gone.

She pulled the duvet over her head. Bits of the previous night started to rain down. She burrowed under the pillow. She'd not only talked too much, she'd given a lecture — all that was missing was the slide projector. Then the drive home. Was he coming to pick her up this morning?

Oh, absolutely no! She jumped up, pulled on her jeans. She would ignore the death-knell headache. She grabbed a pear, a slab of cheese, her painting gear.

She would expunge the whole of the night before, and especially that moment when he'd turned the light on her and seen right through her.

It was useless to tell herself last night everybody hadn't seen right through her. *He must have been a very fond uncle.* To pretend that the whole dinner had not been pulsing with a creepy frisson of the unspeakable that she had been giving off. But she had her own singular method of escape.

She headed up into the olive grove and then the woods, refusing to think about the devil dogs Niccolo had said did not exist. She climbed along a hillside of myrtle and oak, trying to clear her head of everything but the unfolding of one scene, then the next, like the backgrounds of Renaissance paintings. No wonder all the great art came from here.

She settled on a rock beneath a scraggy oak where a clump of early poppies flickered, truly all silk and flame. Ruskin's phrase. The small flames wavered even in the quiet air.

DURING THE TWO SOLITARY years in her cramped sun porch studio in Vancouver, Clare had imagined herself painting in the wild, with the voice of an amiable, tough and exacting companion whispering in her ear. The voice of the extraordinary Margaret Mee, who had first brought the Brazilian Amazon into bloom for the world to see — who had travelled by leaky boat and dugout to the remotest regions, facing every sort of difficulty and danger. Not just the creatures of the jungle and the water world, but drunken rubber tappers with murderous intent, and tribes rumoured recently to have eaten those who offended them. Clare had read and re-read the diaries. Right into her late seventies, Margaret Mee had made painting trips along the Amazon and its many tributaries, bringing to the world the first awareness of the tragic destruction there.

And now here Clare was, in the wild, plodding through a swamp of emotions, with a headache that would have done a rubber tapper proud. She took a deep breath. As she began sketching the poppy's stems and leaves, as her pencil traced the shape before her and at the same time created a line that had an elegance of its own, a thrill of pure pleasure ran through her, warm as chocolate, addictive as a direct infusion of the essence of the woodland all around, the quiet sounds, the rich scents.

A gust set the leaves of all the trees and bushes rustling. When the poppy ceased trembling, she turned her attention to a single bud, the rough texture of the calyx, the tiny swellings at the base of each hair. Only the buds had these hairs. The hairs themselves she would leave until later, when she brought the finest of her brushes into play. Then how sensuous, to turn to the looping contours of the petals as she sketched in the full flowers; to slip into the depth of satiny red-black where one petal shaded another.

She began to create the shadow mix: a squeeze of ultramarine from the fat crushed tube, then alizarin, then a small dollop of chrome. First the stems, then the leaves, then the blossoms, finally emerging in three dimensions yet still colourless. This was a lovely point, when the work could almost be complete as it stood. The way we could see, if we could see clearly in the silver of the moon. The way she might even have seen last night but for the wine, when she stood with the man on the rocky patch of ancient road and everything was silvered.

The preliminary green coat to bring the plant into vividness, shade by shade. Metal yellow, once again, combined with Prussian blue and a speck of crimson.

The poppy is painted glass, seen among the wild grass far away like a burning coal fallen from heaven's altars. Ruskin again. A tall order to mix that colour. Start with a thrilling spurt of Winsor red, then lemon, drop by drop, gentled onto the petals, skirting the ovaries. A thin liquid glaze, which quickly dried.

Painted glass! She recognized a prickle of loss that had been on the edge of her mind all morning — the petal that had fallen from the chandelier the night before. She'd meant to take it home.

A second glossy coat of red brought up the crinkly surface of the petals, the tiny reflections of one another the petals held. Now for the black markings: black was never truly black. She felt the pull of this thought, tempting her to follow down its twisting path. She pulled back. This moment required as much concentration as grand prix racing, as with the finest of brushes she outlined the stamen filaments, a delight she never ceased to feel at supplying such tiny details. Those stamens with their delicate stems, waving their lolly-pop heads, and the radiating pattern of striations on the ovary at the centre of this cluster, and the almost-invisible hairs on the closed bud and on the poppy stems.

The sun had arced across the sky. The bell from the saint's basilica tolled as Clare applied her final brush strokes. She felt herself becoming small enough to slip into the miniature world she had created. No one would find her here and bring her to account.

೨

CLARE SLOTTED THE PAINTING into the aluminium case in her pack.

She let the flickering of the flower fill her head to stave off the hungers that could settle; nothing to do with food, nothing to do with anything she ever understood.

Red. A country to get lost in, all on its own. Crimson, carmine, cochineal — all those little bugs dying in the cause of flaming colour. Red lead. Red arsenic from Brazil. Vermilion made from cinnabar, and cinnabar itself, more an exotic destination than a colour.

This was not the path she'd come along before. It was chilly now. In the falling light it wasn't hard to imagine nymphs and satyrs wandering these ancient hills. She had the sensation of being watched, though not by human eyes; just an ageless watching. The track disappeared into a slope overgrown with last year's bracken. She realized she had been following some animal path. Through thick brush she caught a glimpse of the hill with the tower, and thought that if she plunged straight down the slope, surely she would find a proper path. But her feet went out from under her. Suddenly, she was scraping down a rocky cliff, her fall broken only as she managed to grab hold of a bush. How far? Twenty feet? Thirty? She came to rest in a nest of brambles.

She was about to untangle herself, when she froze. A flash of movement below. Then a moan. She peered through the tangle of vines.

Four legs. A single back.

Even the sight of the two pairs of dropped pants, of William Sands's white head thrown back, of Anders Piersen with his arms braced against a rock, didn't dim her sense that this was the rutting of a single mythic beast. And like the watchers she'd imagined moments ago, she watched. Only when the double creature reached its double spasm, did she shrink back to be out of sight.

She was not sure if it was gulps of weeping she heard from the Danish boy. But she was weeping; hiding her face in brown leaves and tiny shoots of new bracken, flooding them with salt.

THE WOODS WERE FULL of normal sounds again.

Had she made that up?

She heard the whine of a Vespa somewhere not too far.

When she pushed her way out through the brush, she saw she was on the rocky bit where Luke Tindhall had stopped the night before. How had she ended up inside the fence? Shaken, she sank down on the stretch of close-fitting stones.

A line of ants was making its way along one of the stones, unaware that they were travelling the ancient Etruscan road. Had Tindhall actually said this was part of an Etruscan road? The area was wide enough to take a horse-drawn wagon, like the old one she used to play on behind the barn. She knelt, ran her hand over the stones, let her thoughts escape into the possibility of where this might lead, if it really had been a road. The pavers were much larger than cobblestones, and so closely fitted that barely any grass grew between. The stone she knelt on reached from the tips of her fingers to her shoulder, and was about two thirds of that in width. All were roughly this size, the outer ones worn with deep grooves, as wide apart as a wagon's wheels.

Might this once have led from Cortona? Did this slope connect to the back slope of the city by a ridge farther up the narrow valley? Maybe this was once a major route, right past her uncle's house and on towards Umbria, to the Tiber, then down to Rome? Now she wished she'd paid more attention the night before.

AS SHE WALKED ON, the paving disappeared and the track became so overgrown that she was amazed Luke had taken his car through here.

She caught a glimpse of the tiled roof of her uncle's house through dense trees. Then she saw the stream, angling down the wooded slope above.

Surely this was the scene in the ugly painting in the downstairs room! She sat on a rock, tried to calm her imagination. The water ran in sparse rivulets before it reached this overgrown track, but she could see from the wide jumble of the rocky bed that with rain this might become a torrent. And those rocks, so badly depicted in the painting, were as large as the paving stones she'd just passed, and also worn into deep grooves. What if they were part of that same ancient road? What if they'd been thrown about by an earthquake long ago, but previously had led to some secret votive spot above, not rediscovered until this moment? What if only since the quake had the water followed the line of least resistance down the ancient paving?

She began edging her way uphill along the stream bed, following its gentle curve through a growth of tall alders bearded with moss. She scrabbled from stone to stone, emerging eventually into a high boggy meadow where the late sunlight flickered with blue butterflies and bees. At the far end a limestone cliff, horseshoe-shaped, circled three sides of the grassy space, but debris had slipped down from the slope above. Perhaps that earthquake long ago? Great rocks and bush-dotted scree, with the cliff face showing only here and there. Above, the hillside continued thick with brush and trees, no trace of cultivation.

She scrabbled up a knoll to her right, hoping to gain a view, amazed to find how high she'd climbed in following the gradual looping of the stream. She was on a level with the tower on the opposite hill. When she turned in the direction of her uncle's house, she could look right down on the olive terraces; back the way she'd come, where the stream flowed from the meadow, the tall alders now blocked the low rays of the sun.

So, if not for those trees, it would have been possible to look right up to the ruined fortress from the meadow — and possible for anyone up there to peer down into that sweet secluded spot.

If not for those trees, her meadow (already she thought of it as hers) would be a secret no more, crowded with butterfly catchers and picnic parties.

Then she noticed that what she'd thought was debris that had slid down the cliff was actually a series of separate mounds, covered in rock and brush and trees. They too would have been in view of the city on the hill but for the intervening growth of trees. She heard her uncle's voice: "Here we have the essential element for an Etruscan city of the dead — in view of the living!" Could those be burial mounds, over underground tombs? Maybe painted inside, replicas of real Etruscan houses, beautiful houses for the dead, right here on her property?

A sudden sharp whistle from the direction of the olive grove made her whirl around.

Nothing but the encroaching dark.

She stumbled, and stumbled again, as she scrambled down the slope and across the meadow; she slipped on rocks as she navigated the stream. Bushes whipped and scratched as she forced her way along the overgrown path, scrabbled over the stile. Ahead of her, the house hunkered dark, empty. The scent of wisteria enveloped her, followed her inside when she'd managed to get the door unlocked.

∾

THE LIGHT ON THE phone machine was blinking.

She'd not played Luke Tindhall's message, that was it. The answering machine was ancient, one of those with keys and a playback tape. Then that voice with its mix of upper-class and rough: "So sorry, a bit of a hitch, I've had a sudden call to ... Rome." She noted the hesitation, as if he'd pulled the destination from a hat, before he went on to say that he'd arranged for Dr. William Sands to show her around that morning, instead. "... However, I've managed to root out a collection of your uncle's newspaper pieces. I'll pop them up the hill in half an hour, before I head off to the train. Cheerio."

"Cheerio!" she said back, "Old bean!"

There was no package she could see outside the door.

But there was a second message on the machine. Nikki Stockton had also called that morning, on behalf of her husband William, to say that unfortunately William couldn't show Clare around as arranged by Luke after all. Something had come up.

"So," the brassy voice was saying, "I was wondering if you'd like to go with me, instead." She'd left her number and rung off.

Nikki. The ballet woman. That costume. That bright pixie smile. Clare saw her stuffing the shattered oak-leaf earrings into the little pouch at her neck — then the moment when Nikki looked up and saw her husband's hand recoil from Anders's hand. The scene in the woods flared up, as Clare played the message again, listening for a shadow under the bright tone. She played it twice more, looking for what? Something that might link the two of them? A sinew of pain? When she had erased the message, she realized that there would surely be a recorded answer message on the machine. Whose voice would she hear? She sat for a long time trying to work up the resolve to play it.

In the end it was hard to tell. A man's voice, yes, speaking Italian. "*Pronto. Lasciate un messaggio dopo il segnale acustico, per favore.*" A message put out by the phone company, possibly.

She played it over and over.

THREE

The City on the Hill

IT WAS MORE THAN seven hundred years since the holy Santa Margherita of Cortona had made her way back across the wide Val di Chiana in disgrace, and entered the city to seek absolution, which was not immediately forthcoming. She had sinned in more than one particular.

She'd had an unfortunate start, being born not only beautiful but remarkably intelligent, with doting parents who made the mistake of sending her to be educated.

Then the mother died. The wicked stepmother came on the scene. The girl was ripped from school and made to work on the farm. But the damage was done. She had learned to read. Her head was filled with the ideals of the great romances of the age, *La Chanson de Roland, The Romance of the Rose.* Thus, when the handsome young lord of an estate across the valley chanced to come riding by, Margherita chanced to stray into his line of sight. She repulsed his advances. She knew there could be no proper relationship between a peasant and a noble. Yet, one dark and stormy night, she took a boat out onto the lake below the farm. The storm picked up. The boat flipped over. The young nobleman rescued her. And, now that fate had so conveniently spoken, she gave in and went off to live with him on his estate near Montepulciano.

For nine years she lived openly with him in great wealth and splendour, and she bore him a son. She gained much respect from the people of the town, even though her lover's family refused to let them marry; for, in addition to her beauty, she had a quality that transcended social strata. Sometimes, though, she was stricken with an inexplicable sadness.

Then one day the young mother, now at the fullness of her beauty, was sitting in the tower room of the villa her lover had built for her, working at her tapestry. She glanced up occasionally to look over the fields and woods where he had gone off hunting. Suddenly, his favourite hunting dog came up the stairs and tugged at the mink-edged skirt of her silk gown. She followed the dog into the woods, to a spot beneath a spreading oak where the ground had been disturbed. With her bare hands the young woman joined the faithful dog in scrabbling through the earth, scratching frantically in terror.

To this day no one knows how the young man was murdered, or who did the deed.

And, though beautiful Margherita had been admired in the town, it turned out that she hadn't been that much admired. His family cast her out. She set foot across the valley, which was wild and swampy in those days, carrying her child. When her father refused to take her back, she sought shelter among the Franciscans. But they, too, turned her away. She was too beautiful, they said.

Finally, to rid herself of that fatal beauty, she scarred her lovely face, rubbed ashes in the wounds, knelt on hard stone and wept tears of blood, until at last the figure on the crucifix bent and summoned her to the business of sainthood; she was to restore the sick to health, raise the dead, enter the politics of the town by negotiating a peace between the Guelphs and Ghibellines.

Yet scandal followed her into her final holy days on earth. Malicious gossip spread about the long hours she spent in a cell high on the mountain, communing with her confessor. Not until she breathed her very last breath was her saintliness affirmed. As her soul left her body the air was filled with a cloud of fragrance, a wonderful perfume of flowers.

Now the holy Santa Margherita lies in a glass casket in the church on the hill, on the far side of the ruined tower.

∽

CLARE THOUGHT OF THE saint's story as she started up the road to Cortona for her appointment with the lawyer. It said a lot for the town, she thought, that their favourite saint had been followed all her life by scandal.

When Clare had first read the story, in Vancouver, she'd thought it started out like a classic fairytale. But in truth, what a complex and real woman the holy Margherita must have been. An impatient driver honked behind Clare, then zipped by in the precise three-second interval required to avoid a head-on collision with a tourist bus. Clare resisted an urge to cross herself.

In switchbacks, the road climbed past terraces of olive trees, past a church built where the Virgin had once appeared to workers in a lime pit, up and up towards a cluster of ochre and cream and apricot houses floating surreally on a cloud of pink blossoms — till finally it skirted the massive Etruscan wall, providing vista after vista over the plain that ran northwards towards Siena, Florence, and further fabled destinations.

She found a *parcheggio* shaded by lime trees, where cars had installed themselves with happy disregard for allowing others in and out. She followed two young mothers pushing baby carriages up a long, steep, cobbled street. Steadily they pushed, in their five-inch heels and short black skirts, talking, cooing encouragements to their babies, gesturing with their free hands which held cigarettes. Little shops, like glass-fronted caves, were tucked under brooding stone buildings on either side. When she finally reached the top, and stepped through an archway into the main piazza, *Fantasy* was the word that fluttered down from the tower of the Palazzo

Comunale and settled in her heart.

The entire place seemed so hushed, despite the hum of voices and the steady undercurrent of footsteps echoing against stone buildings that were crenellated, arched, fronted by loggias or balconies, like a stage setting.

She sank into a wicker chair facing the piazza and ordered a cappuccino. Then, thinking of something she'd read in the guide book, she called the waiter back and changed her order to a caffè corretto. She was early for her appointment with the lawyer, and nervous. The waiter smiled gravely, as if it were not at all remarkable to want a doctored coffee first thing in the morning. With an almost pharmaceutical air he asked her which method of correction she would prefer: "Brandy? Grappa?"

"Which do you suggest?"

"This depends on what you wish to correct."

She said she had to visit her lawyer in half an hour.

"*Allora,* grappa." He clicked his heels. "*Subito!*"

As she waited for her drink, she pondered a tricky question she wanted to ask the lawyer. Hadn't she heard that if there were the possibility of archaeological remains being found on a piece of Italian property, not only would the landowner not be allowed to undertake any excavation, but any finds would belong to the State?

But how to raise such a question without tipping off the lawyer (who, it seemed, was also Ralph and Federica's lawyer) to the possibility that there might be such remains on her uncle's property?

The waiter brought the thimbleful of espresso and the correction separately. Clare tackled the grappa first — a burst of firewater with a lingering and not entirely unpleasant aftertaste of gasoline. With a swoosh of iridescent wings, a flock of pigeons settled in the centre of the square. She imagined the morning here had been waiting for this moment to unfold. Metal shutters started rolling up. Shopkeepers appeared in their doorways and stood in the sun. Two girls in dangerous sandals ran to meet one another in the middle of the piazza in a swirl of pretty skirts. A covey of weathered men ambled in, discussing some serious matter in rumbling tones. A policewoman blew her whistle to stop an illegal motorist, and when a man dressed entirely in red walked towards the comely official figure, the police-woman blew her whistle at him too. The clock tower stood against a brilliantly blue sky.

"YES, IT IS A constant pleasure is it not?"

She turned to see Carl, the large German. He was wearing a crisp seersucker suit today, a fine leather bag over his shoulder.

"Many pardons, Miss Livingston, I did not mean to discompose you."

"No, no. Please." She gestured at the empty chair.

"I saw you observing the lively activity of our little city." He lowered himself into the seat across from her. "The buildings surrounding this charming space are of such a human proportion, are they not? Yet also theatrical, the emphasis on the façade, to accommodate a culture where so many of the rituals of life take place in public view."

She smiled. "You put it so well."

Perhaps he was the one she could sound out about the legal rami-fications of finding archaeological remains on private property. "Are you planning to settle here permanently now? Is it tricky owning property here? I read an article describing Italy as one vast under-ground museum, referring to the fact — exaggerated, I'm sure — that there are so many buried antiquities that it's hard to put a shovel in the ground, because if the smallest artefact comes to light the whole building project gets shut down."

But she'd lost him. She followed his gaze across the square. The young Danish man, Anders, was in conversation with William Sands. How beautiful Anders really was, in his tight jeans and his lime green t-shirt, his golden hair combed up this morning into spikes; you'd have to be made of stone to resist if he grasped your shoulder the way he'd just grasped William's. But William pulled away. Anders stood for a moment looking at the hand that had just been shunned. Then he turned on his heel and started up a tiny side street, lost to view.

"I must beg you to excuse me," Carl said. Clare watched as he crossed the expanse of the piazza with remarkable speed for one so large. She pondered the sad fact that his palpable hurt, as he lumbered like a comic figure across the beautiful piazza, almost lightened for a moment her own concerns, as if we are all beads on an abacus of some great summing-up of suffering, she thought. She turned her glass round and round.

"Miss Livingston, I have been remiss."

"Oh!"

For here was William Sands. She felt her face go hot. The raw image of yesterday superimposed itself over the tall straight serious figure standing before her.

She invited him to sit down.

He said he couldn't stay, he had just come from a brief appointment at the Museo Etrusco; however, he wished to say that he was aware that he had lacked in courtesy the other night at Farnham's in failing to express his condolences regarding her uncle.

Such stiff words. She wasn't sure why her initial impression of him, from that night, came back with such force — that she liked him. Because he had held back from talking about her uncle? Or because the scene in the woods had left her with such an archetypal impression, as if she really had seen some mythic beast, which he and Anders both had been overpowered by — and that a man so determined, qualified, serious, could like anyone else be swallowed by that beast?

"Perhaps I should explain that I have serious reservations about the last articles your uncle wrote," he said. "They stir up wrong attitudes. They give the impression — which one hoped had been abandoned years ago — that archaeology is about finding things."

"It's not?"

"These days we like to think it is about finding out about things. There is quite a difference."

Hoping to lead the conversation in a helpful direction, Clare pulled out her notebook and asked him to elaborate. All night she'd been dreaming about those mounds in the meadow, peering into them sometimes the way she'd once peered into an Easter egg she'd been given as a child, which had a little round glass window at one end and a tiny scene inside. Surely there must be some radar that would allow her to peer down through the surface of those mounds. William was the person who would know.

As he eased himself into the chair across from her, though, she felt another pang for Nikki Stockton. This was such an attractive man, his very seriousness making him seem someone you would like to crack — was that the attraction to the younger man? The serious face, with freckles scattered across the pale skin; the very clean white hair, pulled back. She imagined how he would have looked when his wife first met him. He would have been a redhead then, she thought.

He was telling her how his site had been vandalized over the winter. Someone had dug a rough ditch right across the temple area on Poggio Selvaggio, destroying precious evidence, in search of treasure. "So perhaps I am over-sensitive. But the kind of articles your uncle wrote can stir up illicit appetites."

He glanced at his watch. She noted the scratched crystal, the leather strap that was almost worn through. He gave her another of those beautiful grave smiles. His eyes were the colour of gravel in a stream, with that pebbled clarity. And he took his leave.

How could his wife stand it, she wondered. She started towards her appointment with the lawyer. The image came back to her of that pixie woman in her ballet costume put together out of biking gear, teasing Luke Tindhall, making smart remarks. Then Nikki's expression after that electric moment at the dinner table when William and the Danish boy both reached for the wine.

THE LAWYER'S OFFICE WAS on the only level street in the town. One building joined to the next, almost like a cliff face, the little shops tucked in below. Clare paused in front of a window displaying just a single yellow linen dress and a pair of elegant high-heeled sandals like the ones on the young women who'd run to meet in the square. She felt guilty of an offence, in such beautiful surroundings, to be wearing the same silk shirt (washed by herself this time, so that it still retained a blush of tomato stain) and jeans. When she entered the office of lawyer Dottore Alfredo Bandinelli it was obvious that the young woman who looked up briefly (fashionable jacket of military cut, white shirt with flaring cuffs) was someone who would never end up glued to another person by a piece of oozing food.

The woman's dark, heavily outlined eyes turned back to her computer. Clare coughed. The perfect pale fingers continued to fly over the keyboard. A woman in thick spectacles came out from behind a milky glass door and fell into a long conversation with the younger one.

Clare coughed again, then said, "Excuse me. I believe I have an appointment."

"Signora Livingston?"

"Yes ... *Sì sì.*"

"But I have called you," the one with the glasses said with a frown. "Signor Bandinelli has needed to be detained away. I have already left you a message, one hour ago."

"Oh. I guess I'd already started out."

"*Peccato!*" A look implying that the shame was Clare's, for such over-promptness.

"I suppose I should make another appointment."

"No. It is better when Signor Bandinelli returns I will call you."

"But I need to be able to plan."

"Signora Livingston," the woman said firmly, "Dottore Bandinelli has urgent family matters that have detained him. I cannot have any idea, when he might be able to return. *Mi scusi,* as soon as he can know, I will call."

As soon as he can know, I will call. Mi scusi this is so. I will call, you will know!

As she went back out into the street, the words rang in Clare's mind like a childhood skipping rhyme. What exactly did she need to plan? She'd keyed herself up, hoping the lawyer would have some personal word for her from her uncle, or that he had possession of his notes and papers. Now she'd avoided disappointment. Maybe that was the secret of life. She took another look in the window with the yellow dress. Avoid disappointment at all costs. The goat's head buckle caught the light and grinned.

I WON IT, IN *a rodeo,* she'd said the other night, and got a laugh. Almost true. It was a dark amulet of sorts, to keep her conscious of a moment very long ago when she had won something in a split-second decision. A rancher from Oregon had picked her up on Fisherman's Wharf, after she'd run away from the farm with her boyfriend and he'd left her stranded alone in San Francisco. The rancher said he could give her a job. He trained girls for the rodeo circuit; they had to be pretty ones of course, but they also had to know how to ride. Goat-tying was one of those events. "It's quite a skill," he told her. "They let the little sucker out of a chute, and you ride it down and throw yourself off and flip it over and tie up three legs with your piggin' string." It sounded fine, it sounded like exactly what she needed to get a lot of other things out of her mind. On the way over the sierra to his ranch, he stopped at a tack shop and he bought her the belt. "She's going to be a great little rider, this one," he'd told the guy at the counter. She caught the look they exchanged. When they drove off again, his big hairy hand never left her knee. But it had been a snap to shake him when he stopped for gas — a sprint across the highway, and only moments waiting in the hot mean central California light, before a semi pulled over, the first of the blameless rides that eventually landed her safe in Vancouver with the dear old woman who'd helped her turn her life around.

Still, that moment in the tack shop could so easily have spiralled her in the other direction. With his hand on her knee, then moving up casually bit by bit towards her crotch while he hummed along to the radio, she'd been sure it was the other path she would take. Just go the inevitable way, the way she deserved and half-wanted. She still didn't know what had made her run. The belt tied her back to that girl who hadn't decided to run, just did.

"*CIAO, HELLOOO, CLARE LIVINGSTON!*"

The Contessa Luisa di Varinieri was striding towards her from the direction of the piazza. Before Clare turned to meet her she checked her reflection in the shop window, as if she might have visibly smeared herself with those memories just now.

"This is so wonderful!" Luisa exclaimed. "Vittorio and I have been very much disappointed not to have had you a little more to ourselves the other night."

She gave Clare a kiss on both cheeks. She was wearing big gold earrings the size of jar lids, which gave Clare's cheeks two little slaps.

"Vittorio and I have been so hoping that you would come and have some tea," Luisa said.

Even if the invitation was motivated because the Contessa *so hoped* that Clare had come upon those non-existent papers of her uncle, well, why not? Clare, too, wished she'd found them. If anything worthwhile from her uncle did turn up, maybe we could work together, she was thinking now. It was fascinating to postulate the discovery of popular Etruscan literature, not just material to do with religion and ritual. She remembered seeing a photo of an Etruscan funerary bed; it had carved stone replicas of folded linen books beside the stone pillow. What fun to discover what those lusty people, so fond of banqueting and wine and dance, really read in bed.

Also, Luisa and her husband, the archaeology inspector, would be the very people for Clare to sound out regarding her own quest.

"I saw you talking with my dear friend William a few minutes ago in the piazza," Luisa was saying.

Perhaps Clare frowned? She felt a pinch of unease to think that nothing here might go unobserved. Luisa caught that.

"Oh, we know everything about each other in these little towns," she said. "It is the blessing and the bane of Italian life that we live so much in public." She fluttered her beautiful hands. "I was very glad to see him talk to you."

She leaned close, exuding a musky amber scent. "William has these little problems at the moment, and I feel sure you will want to help." She glanced around as if someone might be crowding in to listen. "You see, the funds for his excavation might be in trouble, because of a stupid girl."

"A girl?"

"A student on the dig last summer, who unfortunately is also the daughter of the chancellor of William's college. William had to send her home to Santa Monica because she had such a monstrous attitude. Now she has spread all sorts of lies."

"Oh. But I don't see how I —"

"If someone could pass back a report to London, to the Plank Foundation, of how very important this excavation on Poggio Selvaggio is, it might be very influential for William to find new funds."

"Isn't that Luke Tindhall's job? To assess these things?"

"Ah, Tindhall!" She threw up her hands. "He and William are unfortunately most *antipatico!*"

"Well then, if your husband … if Vittorio is the inspector of archaeology in these parts, wouldn't it be more persuasive if he made the recommendation?"

Luisa spread her hands, an expression half-helpless, half-amused. "In confidence, I must tell you that there is a little long-ago history between William Sands and myself, which makes it complicated to put such a proposal to my husband. I know you will understand."

Whatever the implication of that was, Clare couldn't help feeling a sweet twisty pleasure in being pulled into the confidence of the beautiful Contessa.

"You see, since I met you," Luisa said, "I have not been able to help wondering whether someone who had the direct ear of Sir Harold Plank perhaps could assist?"

Clare flushed. Harold Plank must have quite a reputation among the Etruscan community, a community she was beginning to realize was very small.

The direct ear of Harold Plank.

She had to smile, recalling his ears. She'd spent a good two hours with them inclined towards her across the table at Simpson's in the Strand, over their plates of oysters, rare roast beef, treacle pudding, wine and port — ears unusually large and turned forward (*the better to hear you with, my dear*), shell pink and shiny, as was his bald head. The most seductive memory of that extremely seductive lunch was the way the man listened — a gift surely rarer than anything he kept in that cabinet of curiosities in the Yorkshire Dales.

How much direct-ear time did a case of Brunello imply? Clare had planned to write a polite note of thanks, figuring that was that. Now Luisa was telling her that what Sir Harold Plank must be made to understand was the great importance of William Sands's work. Luisa suspected that such slow and painstaking excavation of a settlement was not the glamorous sort of project that Sir Harold wished his foundation to fund, even though it was revealing a picture of Etruscan life over a period of many hundred years. Plank would be hoping for Tindhall to come upon some more sensational discovery, such as artefact-filled tombs.

"Do you think there are any undiscovered treasure-filled tombs?" Clare interrupted. "Ones that have not been rifled long ago?"

Luisa laughed. "Treasure filled? We serious archaeologists never admit that this is what we hope."

"But?"

"My dear. Here is what it is important for Sir Harold Plank to know. In Italy, the situation is a little unfair. It is not simple for a foreigner to get a permit to work at any Etruscan site. If Sir Harold has these dreams of glamorous exploration, he must put them away. William Sands has managed to get the permit for his work because of an early friendship with my father, who was a keen amateur archaeologist, and well-connected with the Soprintendenza. If the Plank Foundation is looking to help a worthwhile project, they should look no further than William's excavation on Poggio Selvaggio."

She stepped back, a pretty laugh belying a look that was stern.

"It is a sin, truly, that in Italy the strict bureaucratic procedures are not quite as important as personal connections. But it is well to understand."

"All the same," Clare said, "I don't see how I —"

She stopped. She'd been about to explain that she did not have that sort of influence with Plank, but then she caught the grin of the silver goat's head in the shop window. How could it hurt to have that little extra gloss?

"Look, why don't we go and have a coffee," she said. "You can fill me in on the procedures over here."

Luisa glanced towards the clock tower on the city hall. "*Accidenti!* Now I am very late for an appointment with the Director of the American School. How busy they keep one; one hardly has time to breathe."

Clare felt a sting of foolishness at the picture she'd just formed of settling down with Luisa at a little table in the piazza, the two of them leaning close, easing into further intimate chat.

"But we are expecting you for tea." Luisa took a card from her briefcase and pressed it into Clare's hand. It listed degrees from Florence, Oxford and Bryn Mawr.

She blew Clare a kiss. "I will be very cross if you do not come!"

"Oh, absolutely I'll come," Clare said. Then, glossing that fib with a second one, "About Harry Plank," she called, "I will drop a word in his ear."

ROMA 5984W

AS CLARE WALKED BACK towards the piazza, she noticed pots of white daisies set out along the street. The woman in charge of the *profumeria*, who was tending the pot outside her shop, charmingly and fragrantly explained to Clare that the daisies were set out in honour of the seven-hundred-and-tenth anniversary of the return of the holy Santa Margherita to the city.

In the window of an antiquarian bookstore, the saint herself appeared, though not as Clare thought the real saint would have looked. The holy apparition had just raised a local boy from the dead; her face was uplifted in reverence, mouth half-open, eyes rolled back, as if that was all there was to being really holy. Surely the real saint, the woman who had so gloriously erred, would not have worn such a soppy, cow-like expression.

How would a person look, though, if they'd just raised another person from the dead? Lean, determined? Awestruck? Terrified at the responsibility of what it turned out they could accomplish if they set their mind to it? How would an artist show that essential quality? A physical sensation fused up from Clare's toes along the inside of her legs and through her gut. A sudden flare-up of desire: *That's what I want to show, even in a flower, something revealing as all that.*

❧

LATER, IT SEEMED TO Clare that the rest of the day had the inevitability of one of those dreams in which things repeatedly slip sideways, yet some not-quite-understood quest leads you onwards.

She returned to her car with the mission of driving to the top of the town where the basilica stood, where the actual saint lay in her glass casket, the woman so flawed and determined that she had ripped away her beauty in sacrifice to transcendence.

The guidebook said getting there was easy, yet immediately she got lost in the labyrinth of streets. After many wrong turns she found herself on a narrow track outside the city's upper wall, with a teetering view over roofs and towers. An impatient driver right behind forced her through an archway into a tiny piazza with a playground, a bright red phone booth, houses with flowered balconies all around — and seemingly no exit but to drive down a shallow set of steps, then along the narrowest of twisting alleys, until she faced a wall with a barred gate.

The gate held a sign. This was where Santa Margherita had entered the city all those centuries before.

Did Clare get a chance to reflect on this? A Land Rover was right behind her, and behind that yet another car, the driver leaning on the horn.

The man in the Land Rover got out, came forward, bent in her window, controlling his expression with some difficulty as he told her that a footpath marking the Stations of the Cross led up to the basilica from here, certainly something that would be very interesting for her, he was sure. What she should do to clear the traffic, at the moment, however, was to carry on down the steep diagonal track to her right. Yes, it was a proper road, despite the cobbles. She should not worry about the policewoman in the piazza below, just drive slowly into the throng of pedestrians and reverse through them into the area with the statue of Garibaldi. There she would be able to find a parking spot. This was the way it was always done.

Today he was wearing faded jeans, a tan shirt with rolled sleeves. But she had recognized him, immediately, from the first glance in her rear-view mirror.

BY THE TIME SHE managed the tricky turnaround in the Piazza Garibaldi, he'd spun his Land Rover into a position ahead of her, blocking her exit and keeping all other traffic stopped. He sprinted over, still with that marvelling look on his face.

"Someone is pulling out. There, see! You can back into that spot."

The policewoman raised her baton threateningly at him and laughed, while Clare did back into the spot.

THE MAN FROM THE autostrada, yes, though driving a different car. *Italy is dangerous.* Dangerous indeed. Now she knew who he was. She'd spotted an enamelled badge above his licence plate showing a rearing unicorn, exactly like the labels on the dangerous and delicious garnet wine. This was Federica Inghirami's brother, the one who'd rogered every woman from here to Timbuktu.

He didn't need to know who she was, though.

He put some money in her parking meter while she was still in her jeep, then leaned in her window again, saying, "Please, you will wait this time? Please?"

Those eyes. She got the same jolt as on the autostrada. His joyous ridiculous seared expression showed he felt it too.

She tried to collect herself while he reversed the Land Rover into a spot that clearly indicated the illegality of parking in front of a church across the little square. "This is so wonderful!" he said, when he'd sprinted back. "But not amazing, no." He looked embarrassed, clicked his heels together, looked even more embarrassed. "Permit me. I am very forward. My name is Gianpaulo DiGiustini. I will hope to prove my correct intent." With the same determined but self-conscious look, he began pulling out identification: his driver's licence, his identity card, his library card, his membership in the cooperative where he took his olives to be processed, the badge proving he regularly donated blood,

"Oh, stop. Stop it! Please. It is amazing. It's wonderful. I agree."

"And so you will believe the reason I have driven up behind you on the autostrada, the other day? I don't need to prove I am not what you might call a highway masher?"

"I'll believe anything you say."

"You will not try to make another getaway?"

Not a chance. The danger was in walking down the street together without setting the place on fire. All those sparks shooting back and forth, the whole street glowing, maybe even radioactive, her boots turning into ruby shoes. As they walked to a café table on the piazza, Gianni was greeted by one person after another, mainly women all happy to kiss him on both cheeks, and a young giant of a man with a Russian name who came bounding out of the *tabaccheria,* also to kiss this Gianni on both cheeks before he stooped to kiss Clare's hand.

"Whew, I'm dying for a cappuccino," she said as they sat down.

He glanced at his watch. "If you wish. All the same I believe the hour for that has passed."

"Is it so strictly controlled here?"

"Not for North Americans of course. But I would suggest a small Cinzano so close to noon."

"I'll have a glass of prosecco, then. And an espresso on the side."

THE SAME WAITER WHO had earlier brought her the *correzione* came to their table. Maybe she should thank its lingering effect for the buzz she was feeling. She studied this electric Gianni when he took his eyes off her for a moment. The upturned chin had both the noble determination of the coin-face in the book, and a hint of the same childish petulance.

She said, "I noticed you have a unicorn above your licence plate. Is that significant?"

He narrowed his eyes. "Do you believe in the unicorn?"

She said, "Yes and no."

"Ah!" He sat back, smiling. "So you hedge your bets."

When the prosecco came, he lifted his glass. A flush spread across his face.

"*Salute* …" he began, with the expression of someone about to make a speech no matter what. He started again. "*Salute*, ROMA 5984W."

"Hello?"

"This is your licence number, is it not?"

"I have no idea."

"But you must understand that this number has been embroidered on my cerebral cortex for the last three days."

"That sounds sore."

"Sore?" He frowned, assessing this so carefully that Clare could almost see the stitches going in. "No please," he said, "Do not smile too soon. I confess, when I pulled up behind you on the highway, I was just a man doing a good deed for a woman in a very plain, disguising hat who might have been in trouble. Then we saw each other in your mirror. Just your eyes, I saw." He held his hand, bandit-like, to the bridge of his nose. "A dazzling bolt of blue. And then — poof! You drove off and left me only the vision of the golden spinning of your hair! It was at this moment, without even conscious thought on my part, that ROMA 5984W became embroidered on my brain."

He looked ridiculously relieved to have completed the speech. To have achieved the moment at which they sat here with two glasses of sparkling wine in the lively piazza, with the crenellated tower outlined against the sky, was to him a kind of artistry, she told herself; he might have said the *dazzling bolt of blue* line even if she was ninety; it was like the creation of a fine sonata they could play together, and why should the other player in the duo feel demeaned because the performance would be a short one?

Now he was distracted, reaching for the briefcase he'd put under the table. He asked her if she knew the films of the great Marcello Mastroianni.

She frowned, nodded.

There was a scene in one film, he said, where the great Marcello, wearing a white suit, meets a beautiful woman at a spa. They are standing beside a mud bath. She is wearing a wide black hat. The wind blows off her hat. It sails into the midst of the bath of mud, which is the size of a swimming pool. The great Marcello, without a moment's hesitation, wades in and brings it back. What a scene! A man might live his entire life without a chance to live such a scene. Yet there was he, Gianpaulo DiGiustini, standing beside the autostrada when a beautiful woman's hat blew into a muddy field …

He reached into his briefcase, brought out an oblong box, removed the lid.

Her hat.

AGAIN HE LOOKED ENORMOUSLY relieved to have brought that off, not just the retrieval of the hat, but the story, the presentation, his eyes sparkling with a kind of delighted apprehension, as if she still might smash this delicate cardboard castle of a moment he had somehow managed to construct.

She took the box warily in her hands; her good old vintage hat, her serious hat, worn in moments of her life when she needed a prop to disguise whatever else she was, if only from herself. She lifted it out. It released a powdery, dismal scent.

What to say?

"Does this mean I'll be emperor?" she asked, wishing, right away, she hadn't given an opening for more soppy lines.

"*Brava!* So you know this story of the Tarquins!" Then, catching her mixed feelings, he shook his head, looked distressed. "But I have put my own desire to impress you ahead of one iota of good sense. Why should you accept back this hat? You have thrown it out, and with good reason if I may say so. You were right to run away. Perhaps, after all, I am what in your idiom one might call an inadvertent highway masher."

True enough, she didn't want it back. But she put it in her bag. She laughed and said it was an amazing thing he'd done.

He brightened, relieved. And, dangerously, she couldn't help picturing him as a boy, then a growing kid, dreaming up grand performances and repeatedly having them go a little wrong, never able to resist when the next great idea came along.

Now he was asking how it was that she had come to be driving down through the upper sections of the town, not a route many visitors attempted.

"ROMA 5984W, you are obviously an explorer."

Now this Gianni DiGiustini (was he Federica Inghirami's half-brother?) was saying that the basilica was indeed a most important thing to see. Perhaps she would allow him to guide her there? Perhaps they might find a suitable place where the splendid hat could be sacrificed, so it would never find its way back to disguise her again? (That look again of trying too hard to hit the right note.)

Of course she would allow him to guide her to the basilica. She hadn't yet given him her name. In a little while, when the lovely performance had played out a little more, she'd do the smart thing and slip anonymously away, heeding her own sound advice about avoiding disappointment.

∞

AS THEY WALKED BACK along the central street, Gianni called "*Ciao, Petronella!*" to a dark and handsome woman watering a pot of daisies in front of the leather shop. "Allow me to introduce to you my explorer friend ROMA 5984W, who will lead me on a climb to your basilica." They chatted briefly in Italian, drawing Clare in, but talking faster than she could follow. Then he bent in a mock bow, saying that he would see the woman "at the wedding." They parted, with a kiss on both cheeks. He said, "*Allora, a più tarde, Santa Mia!*"

"For every year she does become our veritable saint," he told Clare, steering her over to the window of a camera shop, where a series of photos showed the same woman dressed in a long white medieval robe on the steps of the town hall which had been turned into a stage. "The piazza has been jammed," he told her, "And when she speaks, you could not hear from the crowd the dropping of a needle."

The dropping of a needle. Clare smiled.

"Yes, she does not play the saint. She is the saint. She will tell you how when she spoke the words of the saint, she was filled with such a great joy that it changed her life." A look of perplexity winged across his face. "These moments are so fine, so very small, are they not?" He held up his thumb and forefinger, measuring a hair's breadth; his fingers were long, the nails short, the knuckles scarred. "These moments when the universe inside us tilts a fraction, almost nothing, and yet everything is different after that."

When they got to the Piazza Garibaldi, Gianni made an arrangement with the policewoman to ignore Clare's meter when it expired.

THEY CLIMBED THE STEEP cobble road to the gate where the saint had entered the city. Gianni said it had been locked for years. "Perhaps because we know already that we will never see her like again."

Some little boys were kicking a football in the street. The air was hot and sweet, heavy with the fragrance from a flowering acacia in the garden of a villa across the wall.

He began to tell her about the saint. Clare did not let on that she knew the story. She breathed the Arabian Nights scent of the flowering tree across the wall, and Gianni's became a different story, told in a voice she hoped would never stop, just as the girl in the story knew better, knew that though she wandered into fields where the handsome nobleman would see her there would never be a proper relationship between a man of his rank and a simple peasant girl. And though the girl goes off with him to his estate and lives openly with him in great wealth and splendour, sometimes she is stricken with an unexplainable sadness.

The man at Clare's side broke off, seemed to forget that Clare was there. "*Triste*," he said. "But why?" He looked different, as if the charming nonsense had been a cover-up for attributes he didn't like to show.

Don't, she wanted to say, *Don't turn serious now. Please.*

"Oh, but I have been guilty!" he exclaimed, as if he'd heard that. "You must forgive me for getting lost in my own small thoughts. Especially when I have been so rude as to make a jest, to introduce you to my friend as if you were a licence plate."

"Not a problem. I kind of liked travelling incognito."

"But it was not correct. It is one of the less sterling aspects of the DiGiustini; sometimes we are not very wise."

"Are there a lot of you?"

"In the present tense, very few. But we have the habit of tracing the footprints of our folly back through many generations. An Italian failing. Do you know of the Battle of Fossalta?"

"Not yet."

He clapped his forehead in mock surprise. "But this was so recent, only in 1272! After defeating the Ghibellines, the Bolognese beat the enemy swords into ploughshares, giving a start to our family's business, which has been manufacturing farm equipment ever since."

Clare remembered Ralph Farnham's lament: *Never marry an Italian, dear girl! Not only will you never be good enough, but you will marry countless generations of ancestors too.*

"When you meet my mother," Gianni said, "she will quite possibly begin the conversation by explaining how she is a descendant of the tragic Giovanna Galuzzi, who at the age of eleven hanged herself from a window of the family tower when the boy she loved was murdered by her father, in 1274."

"You say your mother was a descendant of that little girl who hanged herself?"

"I will admit this makes it very remarkable, yes, that my mother is here at all."

He stopped. He shook his head. Then, "Come, are you ready for our hike?"

A Specific Against Terror

INSIDE THE BASILICA, THE air was crisp. Brilliance was the second shock. Clare had read that there were those who disapproved of the recent redecoration, over a hundred years before. Radiance poured through the west-facing rose window. The vaulted ceilings were the deep blue of an evening sky, and sprinkled with small gold stars. The pillars were layered in white and terracotta marble; every surface was patterned in designs like the patterns on Venetian paperweights. There were angels in any larger space. A church built to hold the body of a woman so beautiful that she had to scar her face and rub ashes in the wounds in order to touch the heart of God. But look how she got her own back in the end.

Clare wasn't sure what she was supposed to do. The only other occupant of the church was a black-robed priest who nodded to Gianni as they entered, then swished away behind some arches. Gianni had been silent once they entered the basilica. He walked to the front and knelt. She walked up one of the side aisles, quietly as she could, her steps echoing. The glass casket of the saint gleamed behind the central altar.

She was so slight, yet even in death ferociously determined. Her papery skin clung to her skull, sinking into the huge dark hollows of her eye sockets, emphasizing the magnificent arc of her nose. Her little brown hands were folded on her stomach. Clare tried to picture those fingers digging into the earth on the day when her lover's dog returned without his master. The beautiful Margherita would have been wearing satin slippers. Now her feet were bare, the toes pointing upward, fragile as bird bones, supported by another cushion of gold-embroidered brocade. Under her black cape she wore a dress woven in cream and black checks, the perfect garb for the humble, self-effacing and determined exercise of power. She may have become good, but she had dealt in what was humanly possible.

Clare reached out to touch the glass. This girl, this saint, had healed the sick, had stopped wars, had raised the dead. The glass was cold.

She heard Gianni speaking softly in a chapel to the side — perhaps to the priest? Then she saw he was alone, with a cell phone to his ear.

OUTSIDE, CLOUDS HAD ROLLED in. Clare stood waiting in the entry of the church, aware that she still had the fatal hat. If it started to rain she could put it on. She decided to start down on her own, avoiding further disappointments. Then she noticed a container in the entry, soliciting donations for victims of a recent earthquake. The hat wouldn't do a lot of good, but who knew? Maybe it would bring some other man with a very short attention span into the life of some other woman. She was about to move away, when a further idea pinched her. No. Outrageous. She took a deep breath, drew in her waist. But the belt tightened until she took it off. She weighed the silver buckle in her hands, finally stuffed it deep into the pile of clothes.

When the man who'd spent such a long time on the phone with someone else came out of the church, he took her arm and guided her down. He was solicitous, careful, guiding her over rough spots. By his silence, she supposed it had been his wife on the phone. She supposed he thought it would matter to her that he had a wife, that

Canadian women didn't know how to handle a little lark. She hated how close he was to being right. She'd made a sacrifice up there. Why? She'd rid herself of the thing that for years she'd imagined cinched her into a certain type of being. But here she still was, dreaming herself into more than she could possibly have. They came out onto the cobbled street leading down to Piazza Garibaldi. The mist had thinned to suspended rain.

"But you must be cold!"

She said no.

"And I am again remiss! I have been caught up in some small perplexities, and I have let them bite my tongue."

"I'm sure a journey along the Stations of the Cross is not supposed to be filled with cheesy chatter."

"Cheesy." He was standing in her path, looking down at her. "This would apply to a chatter full of holes?"

No doubt about it, he was very attractive, despite the thrusting chin, the forehead careening into that major nose, the skin a little pitted but no way cheesy.

He said, "*Aiii!* But also I have forgotten about our errand with your hat."

"That's okay. I managed to offload it."

"Offload."

"As in dump."

He looked at her closely. Of course he knew it was a rebuke.

"It was private, then, this offloading? A satisfactory event?"

"Yes, it went just fine."

He glanced away from her, frowning — then sprang up a little rocky bank to a wall overgrown with a riot of rock roses, their papery pink flowers gathering light even in the mist, returning a moment later with just one bloom.

"I have been so foolish, all this time since we met," he said. "I would like to offer this."

She held it in the hollow of her hand. "*Cistus incanus*," she said.

"I read something about it just last night, in a book of folk herbal remedies. It's described as a specific against terror."

"Thank you for telling me that, Clare Livingston."

There. Her name.

She said, "And you are Federica Inghirami's brother."

"I am very much her brother." Again that heel-click, that mock self-presentation — followed by an involuntary flash of distress? He said, "Though as you might have guessed, we have had different fathers." Was that the scandal that Ralph Farnham had gleefully referred to? (*Only in Italy old dear. Unless you count our Royals ...*) The famous mother, Clare thought, the descendant of an eleven-year-old suicide.

"I confess I recognized you right away," he said. "Not on the autostrada, no. I didn't get a chance. But I have, of course, your beautiful book. The moment I looked in your car this morning, I knew who ROMA 5984W was. I beg you forgive me this game. Indeed, I had come over from Siena today with the hope of finding you at home. But then, such coincidence! To find that Clare Livingston was also the one who had left me spellbound on the autostrada. So I put off explaining. I think this was the reason." He shook his head. "Though it is hard to track one's motives in these matters. I confess it was something I do not entirely understand."

"Yes. Me too."

They stood looking at each other then, in the mist, with all the foolishness gone. He took her arm again. They walked on. When they reached her car, he asked, "You will accompany me to the wedding, yes? I will pick you up on that day, at five?"

"I don't understand."

"You have misled me with your excellent Italian. I believed you understood when we discussed this plan with Petronella?" This was such outrageous nonsense that he was laughing as he said it; but then the abashed look again, as if this wasn't really what he wanted to say, or who he was. He looked so absolutely perfect in the setting, with the intricacy of tile-roofed houses and cypress lanes climbing the hills behind him, and fine beaded mist settling on his wild but shining hair. He explained that the wedding was a pageant celebrating the six-hundredth anniversary of a marriage. No, not one of his trouble-prone ancestors, but a lord of this city, to a noble girl from Siena. The whole town in medieval dress. Petronella would be the mistress of ceremonies.

Unfortunately, he had just learned (he tapped his phone as he explained) that in the interim he must return to his estate near Siena on urgent business. Would Clare do him the honour of attending this pageant, as his guest, in ten days' time?

It would be lovely to accept. But she wanted it too much. She was still that person who would never be satisfied with just the small gifts, but would always want what she couldn't have.

She didn't need to let him go just yet, though. "Tell me about your estate," she said. "You're saving endangered species."

His eyes lit up. "Also we bring things back. Do you like this thought of extinction in reverse?"

"Unless you're thinking of Tyrannosaurus."

"No, unicorns will be the biggest"

"They come around a lot, do they?"

"You are mocking me."

"Goodness no."

"Our unicorn has very few believers, yet every day he appears somewhere in the world, on coins or castle walls — often fighting with a lion. I suppose you will tell me you also do not believe in the lion."

He had taken a stance in front of the statue of Garibaldi, echoing the bearing of the great hero himself, hands clasped as if leaning on a sword, looking into the distance.

"You will say the unicorn is a mythical beast. And I will tell you that of all the mythical beasts he is most pervasive and the oldest." Gianni began to pace. "In the valley of the Indus, our unicorn was carved into seals used as a form of passport, an early form of money! So you see he grazes exactly at the root of human industry and commerce. How long ago do you think this fashion for our non-existent creature begins?"

"I don't …"

"Almost five thousand years! But then, let the doubters rejoice!" Gianni threw up his hands, backed into the path of a reversing car, stepped forward without noticing near-death. "A thousand years later Signor Unicorno disappears. Is he gone completely from the earth? No, he is on his migration route. Stage by little stage he moves on to Mesopotamia, up through Anatolia, then eventually over to Europe, where we still see his image every day!"

He was gathering a crowd. The leader of a tour group paused, holding up her triangular flag, beckoning her followers in closer.

He snapped a sprig of lavender from the bed below the statue. "And why can it be that with all this evidence, we still refuse to believe?"

The tour leader shook her head. None of her charges knew either.

He crushed the lavender; the scent mingled with the exhaust of cars. He said, "Think of all the creatures on the earth that have lived, then disappeared. Think of the hole in the universe this makes. An entire species gone, and the earth is silent of their thoughts. So this is what I try to do —" He turned desolate gleaming eyes on Clare. "I try very hard to believe. And I make a place where, at least, rare creatures can come and be safe. And after that … who knows? If there is one thing we can be sure of in this universe, it is that what seems to us irrational can become scientific fact. Who knows what shadows might unfold in our deep woods, if given peace to breathe?"

∽

SHE IS SCRABBLING IN the earth with her beautiful bare hands, tearing her nails, tearing her white skin. All night this dream returns in one guise or another. Sometimes she rises from her glass casket and trudges back across the swampland following the dog, sometimes she is walking beside the boy she raised up from the dead and he complains that he is tired, and she is stern and tells him this is not the time for that. Sometimes with her fingers deep in earth she feels her lover's bones, only his bones, but he is standing to the side and he says the bones are a warning of the danger she led him into. When she turns, he is no longer there. She thinks, *But the ashes are safe behind the wall of books.*

Angel Girl

THERE IS NO WAY to skin off the fur of what you've done and who you have been. There is no excuse, either, for saying she was young, she was an orphan, she needed love so badly, she was led astray. Her body has been ruined. She will never bear another child after the one the ancient doctor with whisky on his breath scraped away. But even more lasting is the verdigris of spoiledness that she carries, will never shed, along with the knowledge that it was inevitable, that no matter how far she goes back into her childhood can she see a point where the story could have changed.

No child is born rotten, the sage authorities will tell her. She knows better.

CLARE WOKE AND STARED up into the rafters of the bedroom at the bat thoughts hanging there.

The point is not that she has agreed to go to a festival, a wedding *festa,* with a man who may be a womanizing scoundrel (after all, she has only heard this from his bitter brother-in-law); the point is that for hours after she came home, she actually imagined herself stepping through the slurred-up canvas into a new land. All the signs were there. Even the ridiculous business of the returning hat. Even the business of "sacrificing" it in front of the basilica of the saint, and then sloughing off the silver belt as well, that eye-catching reminder of who she really was. She tried to tell herself that this had nothing to do with the man whose twisted forgiveness had brought her to this country. With one gesture she would be different in every manner. Free. Maybe she pictured herself as the reincarnation of one of those Etruscan dancing girls in the glass case in the museum, whirling, whirling, with a seven-tiered candelabra on her head and little lions at her pretty toes, rescued to dance again for new eyes. The truth is, the past never lets any one of us go free.

There was perhaps one moment, long ago, that hinged her future.

IT HAPPENED AT THE end of October, the year that Clare started middle school. A tall girl of thirteen, with fine-spun curls. *Chiara. My girl with angel hair.*

But it was leading nowhere, wasn't it?

It had been lovely when she was very small. He would take her hand and together they would climb the stairs to the tower. He would steal an hour, poring over her dead grandfather's ethnographic work. He had imagined coming to the States would be a brief adventure, "but then I met your aunt and fell in love." So sad, his tone. Clare had become his accomplice, listening to things no child would give a hoot about, straining towards understanding. Such power she felt, to see the darkness in his eyes give way when he felt he had a small vessel eager to be filled with his own lost dreams.

It had been thrilling when she was ten, eleven, twelve. To be special. To have a secret land where they went together in imagination, travelling by foot or mule along the pathway of old-fashioned words, to cities and museums and brilliant tombs. Flying on the wing of myth carefully made safe for tender ears.

But she'd long ago discovered the real stuff in his bookshelf in the tower. She went there when he was elsewhere, waited till he was elsewhere, so she could touch his things, close her eyes and breathe the air he breathed, and after she had put his pipe into her mouth —

moved the bitten stem in and out between her lips, wiggled the tip of her tongue into the small bitter-tasting slit at the end — she would then pick up the Ovid and read versions of those same stories that made her hot all over. The things that happened to these girls when they strayed into the countryside to gather flowers. Leda. Europa. Versions of their peculiar adventures were already familiar from his telling, but even then Clare had sniffed the darker incense that coiled behind his beautifully spoken words.

He never spoke of the likes of Myrrha. But surely it was not so dreadful to imagine a version where the bold girl crept into the bed of a lover — no relation, really — just inconveniently the husband of an undeserving aunt. Far less damning, anyway, than the imaginings of Myrrha with her excuse that farm animals did it all the time, bulls mounting their own calves, stallions mounting their fillies. Easy for the bold girl to imagine her hands growing his long fingers, letting them explore, always with results that left her weak with the loss of something she would never have.

Now that she was becoming ripe, sometimes she'd catch a moment of indrawn breath when she came around the corner and their eyes met. Then came the aunt's pronouncement that her uncle had his own work to do upstairs. Clare should not be going up there all the time to get help with her homework. "If you need help with your math, come to me. After all, I'm the one who balances the books."

Clare had been a top student till then, the surest way to lay claim to his attention: to study hard, to come up to his room with her questions, to stay and settle in a deep chair with her homework, breathing the air made dense with his tobacco and his thoughts, his thoughts of her. She was sure they were of her. Of what they would do one day soon, how he would finally have had enough of being husband to a witch who denigrated the success of his writing. How together they would make a break for freedom. This had started as fantasy, an alter-life she led: how they would travel not as uncle and niece, but as lovers. Nothing wrong, as long as she could go inside of it the way she entered a book, feel it pulsing the way the life of a book pulses inside its covers. But as she became twelve, thirteen, the book more and more frequently crept open on its own, till she could no longer close it up. *So Myrrha's mind, weakened by wound on wound, wavered uncertainly this way and that … no respite for her love except in death.* Amazing, to find exactly her own story there, so close to his hand. She was sure he read it. She knew the whole of it by heart. It ended badly, yes, but that was long ago.

THAT GIRL OF THIRTEEN. Books jammed up against her chest as she walked along the highway after she missed the bus.

Eric Klassen, picking her up. Star of the basketball team. Old enough to be in grade eleven though he got held back a grade. He sidetracked down to the canal, and she let him kiss her, and before she knew it he was hard and hot and when she stopped him he made her hold it. And when she started crying, first he was sorry. He'd been watching her for so long, he said. Thinking about her for so long.

When he drove her home he said, "What're you acting like such a virgin for? Everybody in Skagit County knows your uncle does you all the time."

After that, she was very good. She did not go up to her uncle's room. Sometimes her looks got tangled up with his, and she smiled, and if she glanced sideways at the mirror above the old oak buffet, it did not seem out of place to see the face of a bad angel staring back.

MEANWHILE, A PUBLIC CONCERN had blown up. Her uncle had learned of plans to bypass environmental hearings regarding a nuclear plant. He wrote a piece for the local paper that got picked up by the *Seattle Post-Intelligencer* and even *The New York Times.*

Shortly after this, she looked out the window at school and saw him standing by his car. When she sneaked out, he took her for a drive. He said he had come to an important decision. "And you, Chiara, are the one I needed to share it with."

The one I needed. It was like flying in a dream. She knew he was going to leave the aunt. He and Clare would travel to all the places he had always told her they would go.

He said, "We'll find a beach to walk on, and I will tell you my plans."

SO THEY WALK. THE tide creams in. Bleached driftwood, the waves, and the sand beneath the rising water carved into ripples thick as arms and thighs all interlocked. He takes her hand and helps her over.

She frees her hand, willing him to chase her, and skips from rock to rock and around the next point, where she balances along a thin log that has come to rest across two others. Laughing, he comes up and puts his hands around her waist and lifts her down. His face becomes solemn. He draws a finger down her cheek, down the length of her bare arm. She feels herself burn into being, like a falling star.

"I have decided to run for County Commissioner," he says. "I filed my papers this afternoon."

She frowns. She can see he doesn't like her frown. She can see a wash of emotions cross his face as he struggles to remember: *She is just a child. Be patient. Explain.*

He says, "I have been told I have an excellent chance. I will run on a platform opposing the nuclear power plant. Think of it, Chiara. I will be in a position to make a difference." When she still does not react, he says, "Your aunt opposes me. Things will be somewhat difficult at home. But I know I can count on you as my ally. That gives me courage."

Her heart breaks for him, too, even as it floods with disappointment.

Can this be as far as his imagination reaches? To envision posters with his picture along the highway, and then an office with filing cabinets and forms in triplicate? Oh, no. Oh absolutely no, she will not allow this to be his fate.

"You can't," she says. She is so sure, at that moment. A girl-woman at the pinnacle of her power, the apple of her uncle's eye, she's always known that. The angel girl who can do anything. She sees the waves coming in, washing right up to the base of the point they have just rounded. Yes, anything, even turn back the sea if she must.

"You can't be County Commissioner, because everybody is talking about you," she says. "They're talking about you and me. Everybody says we do things. We have to go away. To Europe. Like you always promised."

Into his silence, she repeats, "Like you always promised."

He drops her arm, walks away.

Would he have left her there alone, if the wind had not suddenly risen, if the waves were not now lashing at the point? If they were not cut off by the high tide?

Everybody says we do things. As she watches him go, she catches a pungent whiff of why he's walking away so fast, as if the wishes in him had long been hot coals ready to flare.

"But you love me," she says as she runs after him. "You know that." Her arms are around his neck and she makes him look at her. He does. He looks at her and she kisses him, just as always in her bed at night she has imagined, kisses him first chastely and then opens, a ripe fruit. He shudders, responds, and she is alive, lit with her power and his surprise.

The moment after, punished by what her power has let loose, she is weighted, pierced to her centre by a man whose face is already averted, blind with tears.

IT DIDN'T END THERE.

For a month she thought it had.

They had to scramble up the cliff because of the tide. He helped her. At the top she said she was sorry. "It didn't happen," he said. No further word the whole way home.

When the election signs went up, his were not among them.

The other thing that didn't happen was her period. The medical book in the library suggested that at her age irregularity might be normal. But she knew. What did happen was that she started letting Eric Klassen take her home from school, and after a few days she let him take her down to the canal again, though she felt only the force of it, blotting out every other thing.

One Sunday, when her aunt drove off to a horseshow in Blaine, her uncle called her up to his study in the tower.

He said, "Chiara, I am a lost and ruined man."

He said, "Come here."

They didn't speak. She hardly heard his beautiful voice again. They moved into another land where everything was touch, his fingers alive, warm and sculpting. But the genii of the place had turned her to metal. She denied the shocks that went through her body. She thought if she was careful, he would begin to talk to her again. That beautiful voice. So she was good, very good; she wanted to be very good so he would see that what he was doing was all right. But when she left the tower, she heard him pacing, shouting No!

She went back up and said, "Don't worry. I do all that stuff with Eric Klassen too."

THE AUNT FOUND THEM out. That is the short ending of the tale. The aunt pretended to be going off for the weekend, but parked the truck at the grandmother's cottage and walked back the half mile and tiptoed up to the tower. The aunt had other evidence as well — for one thing, the boxes of Kotex that Clare had left untouched. Clare was almost happy, imagining that now the truth was out her uncle would come to save her, and save their baby. But even before the business with the doctor, he was gone.

It wasn't hard to persuade Eric Klassen to run away with her. She told him about the abortion, but she wasn't honest. It turned out he had a heavy sense of moral responsibility for such a randy kid. He tried his best. He really did. Though after the first week on the road, what he wanted most was to take her back to the farm, and marry her, and somehow at the same time go on playing basketball.

FOUR

The Secret Meadow

CLARE WOKE IN THE dark, rain pounding on the roof, the rush of it down brilliant copper gutters. The sound confirmed the essential understanding she'd pulled from the night of dreams where her past invaded. She could not stay here. The gift, as she'd always really known, was tainted. She'd been handed it as a test. She imagined him picturing exactly how with her greedy nature she would accept, succumb again, never get free of the twisted Möbius strip of guilt and forgiveness. She would confound him, then. When she did manage to see the lawyer, she would sell. She would give the money to her aunt. Split it with her. Resolved, she slid into deep, almost druggy, sleep.

BUT WHEN SHE THREW open the shutters to the wet morning jittering with raindrops and sparks of fire, her interior landscape started to glitter too. The tree by the window had become a jewelled tree, every leaf and twig trembling with diamond points of light, magic, like the thought of Gianni, how she had agreed to see him again.

YESTERDAY SHE'D ARRIVED HOME from Cortona to discover evidence of Marta Dottorelli's organization everywhere. Notebooks neatly stacked on the trestle table, though Clare had left them strewn. Pencils with chew marks segregated from the others. The book about

Etruscan witchcraft she had brought from Vancouver now bundled up inside a linen cloth, wrapped the way a friend in Vancouver kept her tarot cards to prevent the leakage of arcane power. Her suitcase had been delivered, and Marta had unpacked it and organized the contents in the cupboard and dresser drawers, even her awful underwear.

Marta seemed to have discovered the newspaper clippings which Luke Tindhall must indeed have left somewhere in the arbour. Clare found the manila envelope propped against her notebooks, the flap suspiciously wrinkled. Steamed and resealed?

The truth was that Clare had been too narrowly balanced on a high wire of excitement to deal with any of this yesterday. Instead, she'd searched out the giant bar of Tobler chocolate from Duty Free, settled down with the copy of *Anna Karenina* she'd picked up in London, and happily lost herself in the whirl of unhappy families with multiple names, diminutives, patronyms.

AFTER SHE'D SHOWERED YESTERDAY's foolishness away, she unwrapped the book of Etruscan magic. She folded the linen cloth around the envelope holding her uncle's newspaper articles instead, and tucked the bundle out of sight.

The book of magic came from an antiquarian shop in Vancouver, a goodbye gift from a friend. Clare had barely glanced into it, though it had inspired the direction her new book might take. Now, as she looked through it, she shook her head, wondering how much was hocus pocus. It had been written in the eighteen-hundreds by an American folklorist who claimed to have mined deep caverns of Tuscan peasant wisdom. The illustrations purported to be reproduced from Etruscan artefacts, but they held heavy overtones of Victorian faux-serious naughtiness, and the text, telling of the folklorist's meetings with a mysterious *strega* in Florence, gave details of spells, for good or ill, said to have lingered from the time of the Etruscans. Extremely creepy some were, involving the skinning of cats, the killing of spiders, the blinding of lizards; ways for women to rid themselves of love rivals by making comfits of disguised menstrual blood for their rivals to eat. No wonder Marta had covered it up.

When she heard Marta enter through the kitchen door, Clare stifled the urge to hide the book. Marta came and peered over her shoulder. Clare heard that disgusted lip-popping noise.

"*Boh!* These are not things to meddle with, Signora! This book — who is it written by? An American? What does an American know of these things?"

"And what do you know about them, Marta?"

Marta's hand tightened on Clare's shoulder. But then, in another of those unsettling about-faces into kindness, "Come, Signora Chiara," she said. "Let me look at you." Instead, Clare found herself burying her face in her hands, hardly knowing what was wrong — maybe shreds of the night's murky dreams still clinging, but the interior sparkling of the morning was going on, too. "Come," Marta said again, "Come, come, come!" Clare found herself rising, a great lump in her throat, as Marta put a hand on each of her cheeks, then pulled Clare to her thin chest. "The Signora is at the moment somewhat *perplessa,* yes? A little lost? To come here to this strange country, to start on this big work of a new book? And missing your good uncle, too."

She released Clare and with one of her worn hands touched first Clare's forehead, then her chest, then either shoulder, in a blessing. "What you should do is to go down into the valley and visit the great princely tombs," she said. "These will be useful for your research, more than books like this."

"But —"

"Now Signora Chiara. You must listen, please." Marta shot a stern glance at the chimney mantel where Clare had propped the painting of the poppy from the other day. "Yes, this is a fine poppy that you have painted. And perhaps you have found it growing by the roadside. Good. But you must listen when I tell you of dangerous things. It is not good to read such books as this ..." she broke off and crossed herself, "And it is not good just now for a beautiful woman to wander in our hills. If you need to study the wild plants, you will please go to the museum and study the work of our hermit. The paintings are a national treasure, available to study. They have all been copied onto plastic film, the microfiche."

Clare took a breath to protest that she had her own way of working. But Marta turned the subject back to the tombs in the valley. This was where the princes had been buried, many generations and their families, in tombs that were themselves as big as hills. They were the only surviving tombs in the area. Very remarkable. Very rare.

"What happened to all the other people then? The ordinary ones, not princes?"

"Beh!" Marta said. "What happens to us all? We live. Then we are dust."

When Marta had gone downstairs to clean out the bathroom drains, Clare assembled her painting gear and crept out the kitchen door.

THE NIGHT'S RAIN HAD turned the stream into a torrent; even the path along the level was next to impassable. No one casually wandering by would get the idea of trying to follow such a violent flow up into the woods. It was hard and slippery going. Clare had to beat her way through the thicket along the side, clinging to bushes and alder branches for support. But, when she finally emerged from the trees, the meadow was a bowl of steaming light, brilliant with the glitter of millions of little flowers holding drops of water at their centres. Millefiori, she thought, remembering that chandelier.

But I am not thinking of you now, Gianni DiGiustini, she thought as she made her way over the spongy grass. I'm not thinking of the expression on your face when you looked in my car window. Probably it's what makes your type so irresistible, that you actually feel such joy with each new woman, that you can pass along that gorgeous malady, fatal to others but never to you. If you cross my mind today I will simply wave you away, as one is supposed to in meditation when thoughts of any sort come up.

She caught sight of a patch of *Cistus* growing on a nearby rocky slope, picked her way across the soggy meadow, scrambled up. The tissue-delicate flowers were like little rosy gifts that had just come unwrapped; their yolk-yellow centres glowed. She settled on a flattish rock. She breathed in the smell of grass and stones and bushes warmed by the sun. She set to work.

FOR THE NEXT DAYS, Clare was careful to dodge Marta's watchful eye as she made her escape to the upland meadow. She knew it was ridiculous to sneak around, and also to lock away the new paintings in the sideboard, pocketing the key. But Marta's presence was so very present. It seemed impossible to reach a clear understanding about a set routine. Yes, yes, yes, Marta told her, she had come to Signor Geoffrey every second day. Yet these days varied. Clare never knew when Marta would turn up, to begin all over again the sweeping, cleaning, scrubbing that she had done the time before. Niccolo, too, was always somewhere about, working in the olive groves or dropping by the kitchen door with offerings of eggs from his chickens, cheese from his goats, early lettuce from his *orto*. It seemed churlish to chafe under all this hard work and largesse.

One morning, after several days of such hide-and-seek, as Clare again started up to her secret meadow — that was how she thought of it now, her secret, hers — she had not gone a hundred yards when she encountered Niccolo.

Where was the Signora going?

The Signora lied that she was trying to bushwhack her way over to the town; hadn't a trail led around the end of the little valley from here once, connecting this slope to the town? Only for the *cinghiali* he growled. Only for wild boars and porcupines and foxes.

But then his knotted sentences took on a kinder tone. He said he had been on his way to find her, to share some of his concerns:

the need for a new cultivator, the problem of finding help with the harvest when no one in Italy wanted to work anymore except the Albanians and Poles. He guided her back through the gate and up into the terraces of olives, while he explained where rock walls needed repair and new planting needed to be done. The roof of the tool shed needed replacing.

Clare was alarmed, but ashamed too, that she'd been living in a bubble of her own dreaming creativity and had thought of none of this. She admitted that she had no idea what her finances were. She would have to wait until she could see the lawyer.

Ah, but the Signora was not to worry too greatly, he said, his tone switching into one of consolation; he and Marta had given their entire lives to the care of the property so that Signora Chiara could inherit the good fruits of the land that they, Niccolo and Marta, with their four hands — he held out his gnarled ones — had long assumed the responsibility of attending. He continued to steer her uphill, telling her many things. She gave up trying to understand, just walked with him in the sun and let the deep rumble of his voice wash over her. When they reached the tool shed he gestured to a stone bench, invited her to sit, brought out a large green bottle, two·mugs, a round of bread, which he cut with a machete, holding the bread against his chest. Then he turned the implement on a wedge of pecorino cheese, and shared his morning snack with her.

DURING THOSE LONG DAYS (while in the offing the wedding pageant glittered, and Clare's veins still buzzed with sparks), if she was not painting, she wandered among the hillocks at the base of the horse-shoe cliff, examining the mounds that became more and more tomblike under her attention. She poked here and there among the bushes for possible ancient entrances. Sometimes she stretched out in a grassy spot on top of one particular hillock with her ear to the ground, imagining a chamber underneath containing carved funeral beds, the soft whisper of the grass persuading her that she was overhearing ancient dreams rustling among treasures that some long-ago woman had selected to accompany her to the afterlife: a bronze mirror so she could keep her looks, its reverse side engraved with a mildly salacious scene from myth to amuse her on her travels, and at her bedside one of those linen books which Luisa di Varinieri hoped to come upon, the prized possessions of a woman convinced she could take it with her. And who, in fact, for several thousand years, had managed to do just that!

The meadow's botanical abundance was another enigma. Clare came upon plants with variations she could not identify, even in her Italian wildflower book. She began to dream that this upland meadow might be a refugium of sorts, sheltering plants once nurtured by an ancient civilization and then gone wild. Around the tomblike mounds asphodel grew, famous in myth as food for the dead; but these buds presaged uncommon blood-red blooms. Star of Bethlehem clustered around the base of those hillocks too, but with variegated petals, a firmament of little gold-and-white stars shooting from bulbs that might be plump with ancient secrets.

Her painting became unorthodox — sometimes as if she were taking wing, seeing the meadow the way a bird might, or a butterfly, a mosaic of shapes and colours, of grass and diminutive flowers, yet always with the botanical details correct, other times settling very close, making compositions that were more like patterns, massed starry blooms rising out of a mesh of leaves, or white spikes angling in lank disorder, or the fragile tissue-paper glory of pink rock roses linked and overlapping one another, and then the dark tunnels that opened through the tangle of stems, and a crosscut depiction of the layers of soil beneath, through mulch and subsoil and stony ground, where the roots and bulbs lived, and the hair-like filaments that probed and sustained underground life that was electric with the further story she imagined.

Her imagination dwelt on the further story.

When she paused and looked up through the screen of trees towards the town, she no longer acknowledged the ruined Medici fortress at the top. Instead she saw sun flaring on a temple with a gilded roof, towering with ancient gods. She saw a funeral cortège winding down from the city and along a narrow road, then up the route that had long since become a stream. She heard the blast of curved trumpets, then the sweeter music of the flute players as they led the way. Pretty girls strewed the path with flowers. A covered wagon pulled by white oxen carried the dead one. Young men followed in chariots, ready for the funeral games.

∽

IT WAS NEARLY SUNSET when she returned home after another day of such buoyant work and dreams. Marta had left her a pot of soup simmering; amazingly heartening, the iron taste of roadside weeds. No one had ever cared for Clare this way.

Still, as had become habit, Clare locked away the sheaf of her newest drawings. Not that there would be any chance of Marta being deluded as to what she'd been up to. But the work represented something at once so promising and fragile. She felt it could not bear the scrutiny of others.

Clare stood for a long time, looking around the beautiful room, pondering the other enigma: that nothing had lodged here of torment or guilt, which surely her uncle must have felt, guilt and twisted anger, or he would not have framed the bequest that way. The walls sheltered her. The little winds rustled in the chimney of the fireplace and whispered of how the hearth would warm her in the winter. The shutters promised to restrain the summer sun, promised that as the days went by she would feel more and more easy in this house, the excitement of the painting she'd been doing helping her to accept that it was right for her to be here. The house held no vibrations whatsoever of what might have gone on here when he came up from Rome.

Marta didn't know what he'd done in Rome, something for that big American paper, yes, and it must have been important because he had an apartment on the Piazza Navona too.

Did he drive here? Clare had asked yesterday, hoping to lead to the question of the Lamborghini. Marta had shrugged as if to say, What did Clare imagine? That he flew? Several times Clare had tried to ask about the car. Marta always looked blank. She and Niccolo did not have time to think of Signor Kane's cars; he rented them, perhaps. If they were blue, green, yellow, it was all the same to her. But yes, he did come here often. It was noisy in Rome. He liked to come here, where he could think. He liked to tramp the countryside, getting himself far too tired, "… looking for our little treasures. Though *naturalmente* those treasures have been all gone long ago."

YESTERDAY, MARTA TOLD CLARE a story, while she was taking down all the dishes from the kitchen shelves and washing them with baking soda and putting them back, plates and bowls and mugs made by a local pottery she said, with a design of a castle on a hill.

"In the old days," Marta said, throwing her rag into the sink, "before your archaeologists tramped over everything, we who lived on the land did sometimes find things in our fields. My Nonna's fiancé uncovered, once, a beautiful jewel, a scarab, with his plough. He gave it to my Nonna when they became betrothed. And just before Nonna died she promised it to me."

Marta found a tube of glue and began mending a broken cup she'd discovered at the far back of the top shelf, giving Clare a look suggesting that she might have been the one who'd broken it.

"But then the priest came," Marta said. "He saw the scarab lying on the table by the bed, and he made my Nonna give it to him, saying it was important for the archaeologists to study. He would have to give it to the museum. He told poor Nonna this was for the safety of her soul."

Marta set the cup on the windowsill with a warning look that it should be left there.

"So you see what all your archaeologists have done," she said. "Digging everywhere with their little spoons, making us thieves for what we find even on our own land!"

She turned her attention to the sink itself, pouring in baking soda, then vinegar, setting off an eruption.

"Your uncle would not listen. He would tramp the fields in every weather, *Madonna!* If not for that perhaps he would be with us still. From the first I told him after all those years of archaeologists swarming, our poor fields were left with no treasure."

ᗡ

THE ENVELOPE OF NEWSPAPER clippings that Luke Tindhall had brought still rested in a drawer of the sideboard, safely wrapped in the linen cloth. Harold Plank had been the one to tell Clare that under that pen name of Fufluns, Geoffrey Kane had set himself the project of tracing the footsteps of George Dennis, the nineteenth-century author of *Cities and Cemeteries of Etruria.*

Fufluns, she thought, as she stared at the black shape of the Medici fortress against the sunset. As always when she returned from the meadow, her head buzzed with questions about what might lie beneath the maddening hummocks in the field. There was no one she could safely ask.

Fufluns.

Why had he chosen that for a pen name? The Etruscan Dionysus, god of plenty and of too much plenty. The god of madness, drunken revels. The god of possession, whose stare was said both to bind and to release.

A few lights down in the valley winked through the dark, as she returned to the sideboard for the manila envelope. She slit it open.

SPREADING THE CLIPPINGS ON the table, she hardly dared read them. Might his writing give back his voice to her? Might he have written all of this with her in mind over the years, words erasing the memory of girl as specimen on a slab, ugly and inevitable, a thing literally spoiled? Might he have resolved something in her favour when he chose to become that complex god?

But this stuff was dry. The articles were a gloss on George Dennis's work — and not very well done, she decided.

He had woven in his own observations, yes, and brought the reader up to date on new discoveries at the burial sites and changes in the cities, quoting George Dennis often, at the same time tailoring his prose to a sort of stiff approximation of Dennis's style. But where was the heart of the man who had dreamed all his young life of making just such an exploration?

Tindhall had organized the clippings with the most recent on top. Clare fetched the one that Anders Piersen had pressed into her hand, and saw it was the same as the one Tindhall had marked with a star.

"Happy the man who with mind open to the influences of Nature journeys on a bright day from Cortona to Perugia!" my guide George Dennis informed me, as I continued in his footsteps one recent day. "He passes through some of the most beautiful scenery in all-beautiful Italy, by the most lovely of lakes, and over ground hallowed by events among the most memorable in the history of the ancient world. For on the shores of 'the reedy Thrasymene,' the fierce Carthaginian set his foot on the proud neck of Rome …"

Odd, but when he quoted directly from his source, her uncle's own presence came back to Clare with a queer stab of revulsion and joy. The smell of pipe smoke on his Fair Isle sweater, the feel of that sweater on her cheek and those rainbow colours as she half-closed her eyes and let the big words fly over her and breathed in uncle smells of safety and exclusiveness. But Dennis's familiar prose was followed by Fufluns's stilted faux-Victorian style:

> Setting my own foot on a route almost in view of that broad expanse of water, I came upon a stretch of paving, all but overgrown.
>
> Now it is not uncommon to come upon patches of Roman road; however, examples of Etruscan roads are a great deal rarer. Hence my interest on discovering — on this now-untravelled slope — a short stretch of paving unmistakably Etrurian in nature, judging both from the size of the stones and the wide-spaced grooves, characteristic of those marks left by centuries of funereal traffic through the necropolis at Cerveteri ...

Clever though. Clare had to shake her head. The "stretch of paving" must certainly be the stones Luke Tindhall had taken her to see. Her uncle would have known of it for years. It was right on his place after all. Yet he'd saved writing of it until the very end. To stir up exactly the likes of Luke, snooping on behalf of the likes of the Plank Foundation?

> I look forward to describing more fully, in a longer publication, evidence that this discovery indicates a major *polis* in these same hills. If so, one can be certain of burial places nearby. For without exception Etruscan burial places are to be found within sight of the nearby settlements, at a lower level, allowing a strong sense of connection between the cities of the living and the dead.

Yes, but how ironically misleading. For the "major *polis*" was of course not some undiscovered city, but Cortona itself. She imagined the dry pleasure he might have taken in feeding this clue to all those academics who had been condescending about his work, hoping to send them tramping eastward searching the hills directly above "reedy Thrasymene."

Or had it all been intended mainly for her?

Seek and ye shall find.

Maybe he'd imagined her to be far more cosmopolitan than she was, that she actually read the *International Herald Tribune* or *The New York Times*. Was this the way he'd finally hoped to speak to her? A breeze stirred the wisteria vine outside. Who had he been then, the man who wrote these dry pieces, which all the same had got the academics buzzing?

Lamborghini

THE PREVIOUS NIGHT IT had struck her as such a reasonable and straightforward idea; she was amazed not to have thought of it before. She would call the Rome bureau of *The New York Times*.

But it turned out that paddling a backwater of the Orinoco might have been easier than finding a phone number in Italy. In frustration, after half an hour of delays and incomprehensible recorded Italian messages, she was about to pack it in, when Ralph Farnham appeared.

This time it was a tweedy riding cap that emerged from the red car. Tight whipcord britches, knee-high boots. Even a leather switch. At the door he struck a lion-taming pose.

He was on his way to the train station to collect his literary agent, who had flown in to Florence. He'd dropped by en route because of a little problem he believed Clare could help him solve.

Well now, Clare said, she'd run up against a little problem of her own.

When she explained, he said it was a pity she hadn't called him the day before, when he'd been down in Rome. They could have bearded the offices of that august establishment together. But as luck would have it, he had the number of *The Times* right here. He pulled out a scuffed leather agenda, and wrote it down for her.

His problem, then, turned out to have to do with those famous non-existent papers of her uncle. The thing was that, with his agent on the way, it was crucial both to Clare and himself that he get a gander at those papers.

His personal suspicion, he said, was that the book Geoffrey Kane had been working on had nothing to do with archaeology. Yes, Kane had spent nearly twenty years working in Rome. And yes he'd scribbled a bit about the Etruscans. But when one considered what merely floated to the surface of Italy's beguiling ruffled waters, one had to imagine that those years in Rome might have resulted in one hell of a political story.

Farnham wanted that story. Political corruption, Mafia connections, bank scandal, hanky-panky in the Vatican. He could spin it all into a crackerjack novel, into gold.

Gold, he added, that he would be prepared to share.

Gold, furthermore, that he could use as leverage to persuade his good wife Federica to drop the foolish legal dispute about that upland corner of Kane's property.

Then Marta appeared. Without even a *bongiorno* she came bustling up from the kitchen with the vacuum cleaner and began to suck up non-existent dirt, encroaching on Ralph Farnham now here, now there, so that they were moving around the room together in a sort of polka to the rhythm of the ancient machine's helicopter roar, until he edged out the door, Clare following to thank him effusively for the number, so sorry, she said, that she couldn't help, but if anything did come up that related to the sort of work he had in mind she'd be sure to let him know.

∽

IN THE END, WHAT Clare learned would have filled a nutshell, if one hard to crack. The man she spoke to, the current *Times* bureau chief, had run articles by "old Fufluns," yes, but had never in fact met Geoffrey Kane face to face. The office only had five other employees, he said, and none of them were writers. Most of the work came in from freelancers. There had never been an actual Fufluns sighting as far back as anyone around the office could recall. From the tone of his voice, Clare gathered that "old Fufluns" and his dry archaeological articles were a bit of a joke.

Clare finally said, "Maybe you've seen him, and didn't know? A man in his late fifties. Who perhaps drove a yellow Lamborghini." She was immediately conscious of how pathetic that sounded. "There must be hundreds in Rome, yes, I know. But maybe you've seen one parked, somewhere near?"

It turned out that he had indeed noticed a very fine canary yellow vehicle of that make, parked here and there in side streets around the Piazza Navona. He'd been curious, too, because of the fancy licence plate frame. It had a frieze running around the rim — he'd seen something similar in the Etruscan collection in the Villa Giulia — a frieze of peculiar-looking creatures, half animal, half human.

"But you never saw the driver?"

He thought a bit. Clare could hear phones ringing in the background. Sorry, the man said, he'd have to go. But — yes — once or twice he had noted that same car creeping though the Eternal City's eternal traffic jams, driven by a sour-looking man in a Borsalino hat.

A SOUR-LOOKING MAN IN a Borsalino hat could have been anyone. Except for that detail of the frieze, which jogged something in Clare's memory.

She brought out the two volumes of *Cities and Cemeteries of Etruria*. In the second volume, in the section about the ancient stronghold of Chiusi, on a loosened page as if he'd turned to it many times, was a drawing of a vase made of the smoky black ware known as *bucchero*. The vase was studded with grinning masks, and banded with a frieze of fantastic human figures with the heads of animals or birds. Clare remembered how this had fascinated her when she was young, fascinated her because the book said that they were likely taken from some myth that the Etruscans had cherished long before they'd ever heard of the myths of the Greeks. Like the great clay figures that had once towered on the roofs of their temples, the figures on the frieze were gods now lost in the mists of ancient times.

Why would he have had such a frieze on his licence plate unless he, himself, had come upon such ancient pieces?

She hurried to the sideboard, pulled out her meadow paintings and scanned each one carefully, as if she might catch some inkling of what her upland property might hold, as if some synapse in her brain might be jogged to remind her of something she had seen but ignored.

Tightrope Show

WHAT A MISTAKEN EXERCISE. Not only did the paintings hold no clue, but they fell to pieces before her eyes. They were not at all as she remembered. When she'd worked on them she'd felt so inspired. But hadn't the upcoming wedding festival glittered through her veins during all those days? Hadn't dreams involving the Italian fevered her to do this work so unorthodox, so winged and free? Now they struck her as messy, overblown, self-indulgent. "*Boh,*" she said, echoing Marta. *Who does the Signora think she is?* She felt sick with disappointment.

She spread the paintings out again, wondering why they should strike her this way now, why the courage and boldness she'd felt in the meadow should be replaced by a critic sitting on her shoulder. A critic in a Borsalino hat?

But a vehicle was turning into her lane. Nikki Stockton, the ballet woman, jumped out of a large orange van.

TODAY NIKKI STOCKTON WAS wearing earrings put together out of gilded nuts and bolts, a short flared scarlet skirt and long black tights, bare feet in the kind of high cork-soled platform sandals that could do her a lot of harm if she were to fall from them. She had a big leather satchel slung over one shoulder. Wide brass bangles shimmied as she strode forward, arms out to the side as if this simple activity were an unconscious tightrope show.

Clare scooped up her paintings. It was foolish to imagine that Nikki might catch some clue in them about what might lie underground in the meadow — though come to think of it her husband had been prowling in the area of the Etruscan paving, along with Anders. But she didn't want Nikki to see the paintings anyway; she didn't want anyone to see them.

∽

NIKKI HAD DRIVEN OVER to invite Clare on an excursion to the dig at Poggio Selvaggio, in three days' time.

She said she'd come over personally — she dipped in a mock curtsey, as if Clare were royalty — because she'd phoned Clare some days ago, about something else, and left a message on an answering machine. Then later she realized that she must have had the wrong number. A bright grin.

Clare felt herself flush, remembering how she'd played the message over, listening for a hint of pain in the cheery voice, the memory of the scene in the woods flaring up again, Nikki's husband fucking the Danish boy.

"Oh my goodness," she said, "I didn't even realize I had a message machine. Since I got here, I've been out and about so much!"

"No problem," Nikki said. "I've been angling for an excuse to get together. Besides," she patted the satchel, "I've brought your book, which I'm hoping you will sign for me."

Then she asked how Clare's new work was going.

Clare gave a shrug and spread her hands. "I've been so busy with research that I haven't even opened up my art supplies."

She caught Nikki's glance at those hands so deeply smudged with ground-in paint. She rubbed her fingers together, shaking her head. "Italian newsprint! It's even worse than ours at home. Look at these hands." She gestured to where her uncle's newspaper clippings still lay scattered. "I've been poring through my uncle's columns, which I know your husband disapproves of. Serves me right!"

The phone rang. As Clare hesitated, thinking she'd ignore it, the machine kicked in and with perfect timing there was Luke Tindhall saying that he hoped she'd got the phone message he'd left a few days ago. That the newspaper clippings he'd delivered in her absence had proved to be useful.

The voice paused, maybe waiting for her to pick up. "Right," he finished off. "Now that I'm back from Rome, if I can be of any more assistance, do give me a buzz."

NIKKI WAS FIDDLING WITH a strap on her sandal, pretending she hadn't heard.

"What's the deal on this Tindhall character, anyway?" Clare said. "He made that date to show me around the other day, then gave a phony-sounding excuse to back off." (This was getting worse and worse, Clare realized, given how William had backed off from that date too.) "So, should I give him a buzz?" She mimicked Luke's tone.

"Luke Tindhall!" Nikki tossed her long pigtail.

She said that for *two years in a row* she had spent weeks writing up applications to the Plank Foundation. And what came of it? *Nada. Zilch!* And now Tindhall, the Plank Foundation's representative, was actually out here, supposed to be looking for worthwhile projects to fund, and had he even responded to Nikki's repeated invitations to come up to the site? Oh, he was happy to be taken out to lunch on the project's limited funds and eat his way through the entire Tuscan menu, starting out by mispronouncing "bruschetta," which drove William wild, but would he even deign to come over to the lab to look over their finds from previous seasons? No, he was totally evasive.

"Of course my husband doesn't exactly suffer fools gladly."

"And he thinks Luke's a fool?"

Not exactly a fool, Nikki said. Luke was alarmingly knowledge-able, but such a show-off. On that lunch when William corrected his Italian, Luke had started going on about how he'd eaten all around the world and never once been called on his pronunciation, "… and then he started spouting bits of Arabic and Finnish and goodness knows. The type of person that William absolutely cannot stand. Of course there aren't really a lot of people that William can stand."

A little laugh, as if this was the drollest thing.

Nikki began circling the room, arms out and tilting this way and that, as she explained how she, herself, had to be the glue that kept the whole excavation project together — a sticky business, the many things that she, as that glue, had to do. It wasn't that William couldn't be bothered, but that his mind was always several levels higher than every other mind, and someone had to tend to the everyday details like, for example, being nice to people.

"*Ecco!*" She took a bow.

Those people who *had to do everything*. Nikki's performance reminded Clare, uncomfortably, of her aunt — another who'd had to do everything, and so could never keep any employee, because no one else could do it right.

Nikki stopped pacing. She gave her braid a tug, as if to keep herself still. "About Luke Tindhall, though," she said, "Now here is a funny thing."

SHE SAID THAT LUISA had told her that Federica had told *her* that on the day following their dinner party, Ralph Farnham had been meeting someone at the airport in Rome, and he had spied Luke printing out a ticket at the automatic booking kiosk.

And then, *somehow*, as Nikki put it, Ralph had found himself peering over Luke's shoulder. The ticket was for Ankara.

"Would the Plank Foundation be spreading its wings to the Middle East, do you suppose?" Her look implied that Clare was sure to know.

Clare realized that she'd been glad to see Nikki arrive, that all the time Nikki had been striding around her room and ranting she had been imagining how they might actually become friends, do fun things together, maybe even today. Go out somewhere and have lunch, a fine antidote to the disappointment she'd felt when she looked at her work again. She'd been so alone, so self-focused, slogging through a swamp of emotions too. Coming face-to-face with that sour-looking man in the Borsalino hat when what she'd always hoped, she realized, was that he'd made something joyous out of his life.

But pal-ship was not why Nikki was here. Nikki was here to make use of Clare's supposed special relationship with the great Plankish Potentate.

How would Nikki ease into it? How many more circuits of the room would it take?

Nikki pulled out one of the chairs by the oak table and sat down primly, knees together, back very straight. She simply said, "Look, I've been hoping you could help."

What she hoped, Nikki said, was that when Clare came up to the dig — and if indeed she did find the work of value, of course — that she could pass the word along to Sir Harold Plank directly.

"And then we could do an end run around Luke Tindhall altogether."

Clare smiled a smile she hoped befitted her role as the protegé of a British Peer. She ran her hands through her hair. She said, "That would involve doing an end run around Lady Plank, of course." Nikki's eyes widened, so clearly tickled to see where this would lead, that Clare couldn't resist expanding on the just-invented Lady Plank. "I gather she's one of those formidable Nordic types. Aesa her name is. Harry says it means 'Stirs Up War.' But sure," she added, "I'll do what I can."

⁓

THE FINAL PAINTING IN Clare's book of Amazonian travels was the one she considered the most powerful. In it, a decaying tree hosted the rare *Selenicereus wittii,* a plant with uncanny writhing pleated wrinkles and protrusions, the whole merging from green to red. Ghostly trees stood behind, in swampy water. Smoke filtered through. Between the dead trees were glimpses of animals fleeing fire, the terrified face of a spider monkey, the singed wing of a macaw.

When Nikki pulled out her copy of the book for Clare to sign, she asked Clare to sign that particular painting as well. "Ever since the night I met you, I've looked and looked at this. The way you make one smell the terror and feel the pain. I feel like I was there with you, plunged right into that scene of fire and burning flesh."

Fire and burning flesh.

Her voice was that same un-nuanced brass, but illogically Clare felt the temperature dip, the way a sudden chill is said to fill a room as some unseen presence passes through. How foolish to think that a particular need had been loosed here of some all-consuming sort. Did Nikki imagine a hot cord between them? That if Clare could paint a scene that radiated such pain, she would understand how Nikki was peering into the shadows of her marriage? Clare took a deep breath of the suddenly altered air, and breathed in Nikki's almost rawhide smell, which she hadn't noticed before.

They'd been bending together as Nikki turned pages of the book. Clare pulled back and reached for her fountain pen.

"Yes of course, sure, I'll sign this one, if you like."

Each full-page illustration was set into a thick white border. Clare inscribed her name with a flourish, and drew in the little stick figure. She loved the feel of the fine pen, which she'd bought for herself when the book was published. She had intended to use it for drawing, too, because — unusual in fountain pens — it worked well with India ink. But so far she hadn't used it for anything but book signing. It was a talisman, a treasure, one of the few expensive things she'd bought for herself.

Nikki took up the pen, weighed the fine balance of it, admired the sleek black shape, the gold nib.

"Does this accompany you on all your travels?"

"Oh, absolutely," Clare said. "It's had a very adventurous life. It even fell overboard once — a bit scary, diving into piranha-infested waters to get it back. I wrote the entire first draft of the manuscript with it." She laughed. "A word of warning, though. Never try to carry a fountain pen through airport security in Brazil. They're terrified you'll barge up into the cockpit and try to write a sonnet."

Before Nikki drove away, she mentioned the collection of botanical paintings that were kept in the archives of the museum. She said she'd been thinking it might be helpful to Clare if they went there together. She could help Clare wend her way through the archival chain of command. These things weren't always straightforward over here. She said that if Clare was free, they could go up to the museum tomorrow. She began leafing through a notebook, pushing ahead to set up this plan. She tore out a page where it seemed she'd written the museum's number even before coming here.

"How about if I call and make an appointment, right now?"

"Oh, my!" Clare said, "*Accidenti*, as they say here! Tomorrow I've finally got an appointment with that lawyer."

WHY HAD SHE DONE that?

She could perfectly well have gone with Nikki to the museum. There was no appointment with the lawyer, whose important family business was taking a good long time. Clearly Nikki needed someone to talk to. In a society where everyone found out your business even if you went as far as Rome, maybe she had pinned her hopes on Clare as a seasoned outsider, a world traveller who could help her navigate the foreign land she'd surprisingly stumbled into upon discovering her husband was in love with a pretty boy? And God knows, Clare thought, I could do with a friend. But how could she hope to have a friendship with someone she'd lied to so many times in just half an hour? Inventing Lady Plank. Giving Lady Plank the name of the Rottweiler her ex-husband had got rid of when it bit the postman!

She caught a flick of movement on the ceiling. The jewelled lizard beady-eyeing her again. Flick! Gone! How did they manage to come and go before her very eyes? Like the truth of any other thing. She turned and looked into the sideboard's cloudy mirror. She started twirling, as she had that first day, round and round. There and gone, there and gone. She sank, dizzy, onto the couch. When she rose, she saw Nikki had left the page with the number of the museum archives. She decided to go there tomorrow anyway, on her own. She called, and a Dr. Ruccoli, who spoke excellent English, said yes of course, *certamente,* she could see the ancient volumes, though, he emphasized, she must come promptly at ten.

It wasn't until Clare reached for her beloved pen to record the appointment that she realized it too was gone.

Yellow Dress

CLARE GAVE THOUGHT THAT night about how to get her pen back. Nikki must have slipped it into her satchel — accidentally, of course — when she put the book in there. But Clare still felt guilty about Nikki. The better person who now and then attempted to get out decided that before she called about the pen, she should try to do something in response to Nikki's plea for help regarding the Plank Foundation. Having let the fiction of a special relationship with Sir Harold Plank grow even wilder, the paradox was that she really couldn't call him now.

Still, she could at least call dreadful Luke Tindhall and persuade him to go along with her on the expedition to the dig. After all, he'd said she should give him a buzz. She decided she would do that, as soon as she got back from the museum.

UP IN CORTONA THERE were posters for the wedding pageant every-where, and workmen in medieval dress were stringing lights and erecting bleachers in the piazza where the museum palace loomed. It was three days until she would see the famously philandering Italian again. If, in the meantime, some other woman had not caught his attention by throwing away a hat, a shoe, a thong ... She tried to put the event out of her mind as she climbed the four flights of stairs to the museum archives.

Dr. Ruccoli had instructed her to come promptly at ten. But when she got there, "*Sfortunatamente,*" she was told by a man with crumbs on his magnificent moustache, "Dr. Ruccoli will not be able to be in today." This other man had no idea that Clare had been expected — and no knowledge about the hermit's work. He flipped through a card file, but found no listing for this hermit. He disappeared into a back room, and was gone so long that she began to suspect that a caffè corretto had summoned him to the bar across the piazza.

While she waited she studied a family tree that covered one whole wall across the room, a painting of a true leafy tree, with white name-filled little globes attached to every outstretched branch, the generations of some ancient family strung out like Christmas lights, and a helmet and sword and shield at the base of the trunk, emblazoned with the family crest.

Eventually, the man with the moustache did push back through the green baize door. As he set down three large leather-bound volumes, he told her that whoever her informants were, they had been wrong. The paintings in these rare volumes were the work of a wealthy abbot who had lived in the valley below, the Abate Mattia Monetti. Yes, a hermit of the same vicinity had played a part in the endeavour, but had been merely the abbot's helper, his plant-collector.

The man called in an assistant to keep an eye on her, and then she heard him clattering down many stone steps to the street below.

WHAT A RESOURCE WAS here! Even though the drawings were not exceptional — a patient record done in ink, washed with colour — still, as she turned the pages it began to feel like taking hold of a kindly and responsible hand, walking with this long-ago presence through the local woods and hills, every significant plant noted, its find spot recorded. I know this man, she thought; he is someone with the same passion the best part of me has, the need to record these smallest, most fragile fleeting living things. She decided that the patient humble work really had been done by the hermit, but that he'd allowed renown to pass from him, with all else. She imagined him fleeing the royal court, leaving behind the politics, the intrigue, maybe heartbreak too. It was peaceful, wandering with him through the pages, slipping back through centuries.

But then the family tree on the far wall began to distract her. She started hearing an aristocratic gnat-like chorus, all those generations going back to valiant noble ancestors humming that she, Clare, was going to attend a historic re-enactment of a wedding in the company of one of their young ilk, and she had nothing remotely smart enough to wear. The yellow dress from the shop window on the main street drifted in, swishing around the room, skimming over the table, flaring in the dim mullion-windowed light, brushing against her then darting away. She glanced at her watch. Soon the shop would be closing for the long midday break.

SHE RAN DOWN THE narrow street towards the main piazza, shocked at herself for dashing away, for arranging to spend a small fortune, too, to have the contents of those volumes photocopied from the microfiche the museum had made, and all because of a dress that would almost surely be sold.

A voice hailed her. She caught that edge of upper-class and rough. She knew who it was before she turned.

"Clare Livingston! Halloooo!"

Luke Tindhall, standing with his arm raised, the ruby eye of the gold snake ring catching the light. He'd seen her stop. There was no use pretending she hadn't seen him too.

No time now. Too bad.

༜

CLARE LAID HER NEW purchases on the bed.

Imagine spending what amounted to two weeks' salary at the lab for a linen dress so short there was barely room for it to wrinkle, a pair of spike-heeled sandals, a clutch of creamy silk panties that were little more than wisps, and a strapless bra, a marvel of Italian engineering, accented with tasty little butter-coloured flowers.

All that, and she'd blown the opportunity of helping Nikki Stockton as she'd planned, by snubbing Luke Tindhall. She flinched to think of how she'd left him standing in the middle of the piazza, with that foolish raised arm. What had her time in Italy actually been but a wrong step here, a wrong step there.

Clare Livingston, the great explorer, forever lost and scattering such a trail of bad karma that she never would be found.

∾

AFTER A GOOD NUMBER of rings, the phone in Harold Plank's Mayfair apartment was picked up to the rumbling of someone who might have been wakened from a siesta. Clare nearly clicked off, but when she identified herself he sounded pleased. She pulled herself together and thanked him warmly for the Brunello. She'd been meaning to write a note, she explained. She hoped he'd understand that during her first days in Italy she'd been so busy.

Good, he cut in. He certainly hoped that his man Tindhall had been helpful. He chuckled, said that as Tindhall had been *ex communicado* since Clare's arrival, he'd taken that as a sign that his man had been satisfactorily showing Clare around.

The word *Ankara* had been on the tip of Clare's tongue — as in, how helpful it had been for Luke Tindhall to drop off an envelope of her uncle's newspaper articles before he flew off there. But what if Harold Plank didn't know about his man's trip to Ankara?

She went straight to the point instead, about the excavation at Poggio Selvaggio, the important work of Dr. William Sands, how fascinating it sounded, how she'd been invited to go up there.

Oh yes, that settlement site, Sir Harold Plank said, his tone implying, just as the Contessa Luisa di Varinieri had suggested, that this sort of project didn't much spark his interest. But of course, he said, if Clare thought it was something Tindhall should take in, he would call Tindhall, immediately, and insist he go along.

When she'd hung up, Clare ran her finger along the phone cord, as if a clue might have settled among the coils. So what had Luke's trip to Ankara been about? She couldn't help an unfortunate little flip of fellow-feeling for someone who, like her, might have a slippery relationship with the truth.

The Orientalizing Bead

WHEN CLARE THOUGHT OF the trip to Poggio Selvaggio later, what flashed before her was a dreamlike picture of a group gathered round to peer at some small incongruous thing that had assumed mysterious importance. The plan, as it evolved after Clare let Nikki know that Luke was coming, was that Luke would pick Clare up en route, and the whole group would meet at a certain crossroads in Umbria at ten, after William had collected some students at the train station. He would also be picking up two women from the Middle Eastern Institute in London, scholars he'd met at a conference on "The Future of the Past" the year before, who were travelling on to Jordan after a whirl through Tuscany. Carl and Anders Piersen would be coming too, from Chiusi, where they had recently moved into an apartment. Vittorio Cerotti, the inspector, would be along although his wife the Contessa couldn't make it.

Oh, and how dreadful about Clare's pen, Nikki said. "That's a bitch — but hey, it's sure to turn up."

LUKE WAS THREE QUARTERS of an hour late. His antique car looked freshly washed and waxed, and the bulky, lionish totality of him looked intensely washed and waxed as well, contradicting the sullen look he gave her. The scrubbing hadn't dispersed the cloud of pheromones jittering around the inside of his car, as he manhandled it through curve after curve, the ruby snake eye glinting.

When they came to the intersection at the bottom of her hill, he turned west instead of east, saying that Harold Plank wanted her to see the great Orientalizing tombs, just up the valley.

"When exactly did Sir Harold suggest this?"

He shrugged. His resolute blockish silence started to eat up the air. But then a lake of poppies swung into view, blood-red against the surrounding green, and a huge mound rose out of a field, a hill covered in grass and bushes and trees. If the land had not been cleared around its base for ongoing excavation work, this gigantic "melon tomb" really could have been mistaken for a true hill, bigger by far than the hillocks in Clare's meadow. Of course, this had been built for generations of princely families. But the old question nagged her, the one Marta had tossed aside: where had all the less princely people been buried?

What did archaeologists have to say about that? she asked Luke. He too tossed the question aside. The valley had been the bread basket of Tuscany for almost three thousand years. Any smaller tombs down here — and the Etruscans always placed their cemeteries on a lower level than their cities, he told her, in a superior tone — would have been ploughed under centuries ago. Or they would have been victims of the *tombaroli*.

"Do you mean professional tomb robbers? Who exactly would they be?"

He shot her a look. "They don't fill out census forms."

He turned the car, headed back onto the smaller road that would take them to their meeting place.

∽

THEY WERE VERY LATE. But Luke's arrival was greeted with delight by the two women from the Middle Eastern Institute, who turned out to be old Cambridge pals. The reunion sparked laughter and merry bursts of Arabic. William Sands looked grim. Nikki took Clare's arm and thanked her again for getting Luke to come along. Nikki was wearing a black mad-hatter hat and cut-off overalls with a huge enameled poppy pinned to the bib. "Here," she said, "I found this in the market. It's for you." Before Clare could protest, she'd taken the brooch off and was pinning it to Clare's shirt. Clare noticed her fingers were stained black with a pearly gleam that looked like India ink.

They drove off in a convoy to the upland meadow where the excavation's other vehicles were parked and the trail to the dig began. Vittorio Cerotti had fallen asleep waiting in his car. By then it was well past noon. Luke took charge of the tweed-skirted British women as if it were *his* expedition they were on. Clare followed, curious what she might learn from their barky voices ringing through the trees.

She heard them quizzing him about how on earth he had ended up working for "dear old Harry Plank." Whatever was Luke doing diddling around with the Etruscans? "Darling, we know you're a Stone Age man at heart! Last we heard, you'd finagled your way in with that team taking another look at Qal'Jalam, now that Iraq has settled down a bit." Luke said too right, he'd signed on as field supervisor, and in fact he'd come up with one fucking earth-shattering piece of stuff. Unfortunately, the director of that project was such a king-sized prick that the Iraqis had pulled their support and the finds got spirited off to Baghdad, likely never to reappear for another eight thousand years. But anyway, one did have to earn a living, and the Plank Foundation at least gave him a chance to get out of sodding Britain from time to time …

William Sands caught up with Clare. She struggled to keep one ear on the conversation up ahead. The women were trying to tease more information out of Luke about that earth-shattering find that had been spirited away. Had he really come on something dating from the Samarra period? At Qal'Jalam? Surely he was pulling a fast one …! He was teasing them right back: "Say no more, say no more — a nod's as good as a wink to a blind bat …!" William Sands was explaining that when they got to the top Clare would find that only a couple of trenches had been reopened so far, but he'd been sure that she would like to get a glimpse of the operation from the get-go. Further up the trail, Luke Tindhall was clearly revelling in the stream of questions the women were firing at him, egging him on. They wondered if his secret might have anything to do with the way he'd recently been spotted snuffling around in Eastern Turkey? Surely he didn't think word wouldn't get around …? "Let's just say the sands of Qal'Jalam offered up a small epiphany," he finally said. "Meanwhile, in a sacrifice to British archaeology, I have taken on the assignment of minding that considerable stunner you saw getting out of my car, keeping the lollypop warm for Harry."

Laughter. "Good old Tindhall, you never change …!"

The British voices bounded ahead and were lost in the trees. Clare turned her attention to William's fine gravelly stream of words.

WHEN THEY REACHED THE top William led Clare to a spot on the re-excavated ramparts, enormous stones that had been first discovered beneath much over-growth by Luisa di Varinieri's father. The toponym attributed to this hill, "Poggio Selvaggio," had given Count di Varinieri the clue to start looking around.

"*Poggio Selvaggio,*" Clare said. "*Wooded* hill? Or could *selvaggio* also mean 'savage'? As in 'savage hill'? Is that what you think? That it was long ago named by the locals, when there were still a few startling remains of a temple up here, or even a kind of ancient racial memory of all those colossal pagan-seeming buildings before they crumbled into dust?"

William's fine approving smile helped wipe out the ridiculous chatter she'd just overheard. He said her suggestion was right on. The buildings themselves would have been built of timber. Only the foundations remained of this fortress settlement that once loomed formidably over the plain.

Lake Trasimeno gleamed below, a flat green jewel. William went on to describe how the view over the plain would have changed over the centuries: the marshes of the valley drained by the Etruscans, becoming fertile, only to be let go wild again by the Romans, then the swampy flat land battled over again and again in medieval times.

"One of my colleagues describes it as a dance; referring, that is, to the movement of the very landscape over the centuries. So you see," he said, "that we are not entirely lacking in poetic fallacy in my profession."

How attractive this quality of his was, so serious, almost without humour. But deep. She thought again how she might want to crack a man like that, and never succeed, never know that some deep unexpected fire was going on inside. She was conscious, too, of Nikki and Anders and Carl a little farther away. Nikki had hiked ahead with the two of them, and now she was making some joke that had them all laughing. What did it mean that Carl and Anders had moved on to Chiusi? Had she, Clare, allowed her imagination to go wild in the matter of William and Anders? Had she really even seen what she'd thought she'd seen?

William reached into the bag slung on his shoulder and pulled out a small clay pan pipe. Without change of expression he began to play, until the rest of the party had gathered around, the haunting mood broken only by a loud cough from Luke.

For the benefit of the newcomers, William then explained what this settlement would have been like during the Etruscan ages. He walked them through the area where the tile-roofed houses would have been, and the workshop where a weaving industry had been pursued and pot-making too, and the storerooms where ceramic vats had been discovered still containing residue of wine — so it was possible to conclude even what sort of grapes these people had grown. He pointed out the foundations of the great temple, and the temple altar — its location verified by the spring of water in the woods, very near. This would have been essential for washing away the sacrificial blood. Nearby, a year ago, they'd found evidence of a healing sanctuary, hundreds of votive offerings, small terracotta body parts, hands, feet, breasts, even uteri and other internal organs, offered by the sick in the hope of a cure. The significant thing about this excavation, he said, was how it was revealing to their team the story of both elite and humble lives, a story quite different — broader — than could be learned in the excavation of a tomb.

A lovely feeling took hold of Clare; to think that a living sense of the past could be recaptured from such small clues as a scattering of loom weights, or the deepened shade of earth where kilns would have been, or the alignment and shape of foundation stones. She watched Carl step into a newly opened trench and run his hands over a column base carved almost three thousand years before, as if conferring with a colleague. Then Anders spotted a sherd of pottery, which proved to hold a fragment of an inscription. Such writing could have had magical intent, he said. The belief was that if one wrote down a name, one was able to affect it.

He raised his voice. "We have in our national museum in Copenhagen many spear points with words inscribed, to make sure they hit their mark." Then, louder still, "But when I write the name of William Sands, it will have no effect at all." He strode off towards that spring of water in the woods.

Clare glanced around, wondering how on earth Nikki had taken this.

Instead, she found Vittorio Cerotti, the archaeology inspector, looming at her side.

HE TOOK HER ARM, then dropped it as if this might have been an affront. His whole face flushed; Clare even imagined his pointed beard taking on a fiery reflection as she felt the heat of his discomfort. He started telling her about the vandals that had struck this site during the winter, how he believed some precious votive objects might have been carried off, things that could have imparted considerable understanding about the religious life here.

"*Tombaroli?*" Clare asked, trying out the word.

Then, remembering Marta's warnings about Sicilians masquerading as telephone workers, she said, "Would they be gangs of criminals, maybe even Mafia, from the south?"

Vittorio lowered his voice, even though the rest of the group were peering into a trench some distance away. He said that *tombaroli* could be almost anyone. They could be from among the local villagers or farmers, or even from the towns. "These can also be people who puff themselves up with a misplaced sense of honour," he said. "People claiming to be liberating our precious things, rather than letting the bureaucracy seize all the cultural treasures and lock them up in museums.

"The hard truth, however, is that most pieces are smuggled out of the country — all context lost — often broken up to be sold for bigger profit. Bits of the same vase sold to museums or collectors around the world. Even though there are international treaties now to prevent this, the depredation goes on."

He took hold of her arm again, his beard quivering with the urgency of the message. "I hope, Signora Livingston, that when you write you will make clear that this activity is not to be considered part of our quaint Italian ways."

He leaned closer. He said that unfortunately he was also compelled to tell her something he hoped she would not write about.

She promised.

She suspected this was what every writer did.

Very recently, Vittorio Cerotti said, artefacts had been turning up that were clearly from this very inland area. Some had been given over to the police by an honest antiquities dealer, others had been discovered after finding their way to a dealer in Switzerland. These were principally pieces of black *bucchero* with designs distinctive of this region, yes, but slightly different than material from any previously known provenance.

"Therefore we are forced to think there must be current illicit digging going on." He turned morose eyes on her. "I believe that your uncle may have stumbled on the source of this material and intended to write about it. I fear that after his death some other persons have followed his clues, persons unscrupulous but intelligent. If you could do anything to help such further dislocation of precious knowledge, it would be an enormous service —"

He broke off. Clare followed his glance to the trench where now, instead of peering into it, the whole group was down in the trench itself, examining something the diggers had just unearthed.

∾

WILLIAM SANDS WAS HOLDING a single bead.

Yes it was a tiny object, he was explaining, but a rare one in this context. He called the new students to come close. "Such a find is particularly useful, because it is what archaeologists consider a diagnostic," he said. "It tells a story."

As Clare craned forward, she saw it was a brilliant blue. Amazing to think of it lying all those centuries in the earth, then blinking awake to catch the light, like a knowing blue eye.

Indeed it was very old, William was saying, as if catching her thought. The bead would be from the Orientalizing phase, the time when exotic objects began to be imported from far abroad, from Egypt, or the Middle East, a possession indeed exotic in those times, before glassmaking in these parts. To find it here was highly significant, clearly a status symbol among the Etruscan elite, "which tells us much about both the age of this settlement, and who the inhabitants would have been."

He explained to the students how any find, no matter how small, should never be removed from a trench before the exact find spot is marked by survey instruments, photos taken, the colour of the surrounding earth checked against a chart, after which the object should be zipped into a plastic bag — he took one from his satchel and popped the bead inside — ready to be transported to the conservation lab.

"So," William continued, "Here we have added verification of the historical importance of this site —"

"Yes!" Luke Tindhall plucked the bag right out of William's palm.

He unzipped the plastic, removed the bead, then passed it to one of the British women, inviting her to inspect it before passing it around to the others.

"But surely," he said, "Dr. Sands has overlooked the far wider information one could glean if this bit of glass were sent for chemical analysis!"

He turned to the rest of the group, feisty and delighted. He explained how, by flaking away a sliver of glass and subjecting that to an electron microscope, the composition would indicate where the glass had actually been made, which might in fact reveal a local Etruscan glass-making tradition, a valuable clue to the technical skills in this society, telling much to anyone who cared enough about how the society procured its raw materials and organized its labour force, and even what the political ideologies might have been.

Clare could almost hear the shocked zinging up of eyebrows among the students at this performance. But one of the Middle Eastern Institute women looked to be stifling a smile. Insider talk began batting back and forth between Luke and the tweedy woman. There was some story they both knew about a bead that had been stolen at a dig in Turkey during a press conference intended to raise funds. "Poor old Ian," Luke was saying, "The Turkish government was pressed by fundamentalists to shut the dig right down. I believe you were instrumental in helping sort that out, Marianne."

"But who would want to steal something so small?" one of the students cut in. "Something of no monetary value whatsoever!"

I would, Clare thought.

The bead had come to rest in her hand. She looked down at the bright little object, and felt the weight of centuries. It nestled at the intersection of her fate line and her heart line, precious because of the deep well of information it contained. If it were hers, she would keep it just to herself. Need flared through her, leaving a remembered childish taste, and her fist curled tighter. A tiny sphere containing such an odd balm of consolation. She clenched it. Such a tiny thing. She did want it. Surely a very small thing to want.

No one was looking. She could slip it in her pocket. Later, she would wear it on a slim gold chain near her heart, a secret talisman. She glanced around. Still no one was looking; all were listening to Luke — before becoming transfixed by William's white-faced reaction as he stepped up and grabbed Luke by both shoulders, radiating such rigid anger that Clare feared he'd crack right open as he shouted, "Enough of this!"

Clare opened her palm and let the bead wobble there. But — how had it happened — she looked again and the bead was gone. She saw it lying on the ground by her boot. She moved her foot to cover it up.

Everyone remembered passing the bead to someone else. Confusion, consternation. After a moment, Clare said, "Let's search!"

She got down on her knees. Others did too. As she palmed it away from where she had been standing, she had no idea how this would play out.

BUT SHE COULDN'T STAND the look on William's face. Not just the loss. His realization, too, that someone in the group was to blame for carelessness, or worse.

"Oh eureka!" she heard herself shout.

She handed the bead back to William. His look — as if she were the person he would have expected to solve the crisis.

Then he strode off without a word, and headed down the trail.

ﾟﾟ

"WELL YOU CAN STRIKE that one off the list of duty visits," Luke said to the tweedy Marianne. He was driving the two women to the station to catch the train on to Rome. "Imagine dumping you on that hilltop after marching you up there in this heat and then waffling on and on, with so little to show. No wonder the bloke's college is rethinking the funding."

"It is?" The big one in the backseat with Clare leaned forward, releasing a puff of camphorated air as the seat shifted with her weight. Luke bumped from the field. Clare's head hit the ceiling.

"They're about to cut him off," Luke said. "And so they should. I've read the field reports, yards of filler. You saw it today, a huge kerfuffle about what? One bleeding bead."

"Oh but listen —" Clare said.

Marianne interrupted, "I thought for a moment I'd stumbled into that endless battle waged last year in the pages of *The Past Today*. Old Warberton hammering away at his pet theory, based on the evidence of a few carnelian beads, that Troy had been just a small barbarian outpost. And Heimlich fighting back."

"Heimlich out-manoeuvred him all right."

"Tindhall, you are droll as ever!" Further cries of delight. "Whatever are you doing among the humourless fate-bound Etruscans, when the Middle East has need of you?"

"*Inshallah!* The will of my employer."

A burst of Arabic then, out of which popped words that sounded like *jamilla* and *jager* and, alarmingly, *bint* — at which both women flicked a glance at Clare. Marianne said, "*Har Batata?*" The fat one giggled. Luke shrugged.

"OKAY, WHY DID YOU do that?" Clare asked when the two women had been left on the train platform.

"What, pray?"

"Everything you could to ruin William Sands's reputation, just for starters."

"I suppose you think your friend Harry has limitless funds. Listen, there are a dozen worthy projects going on here just now. My job, like it or not, is to separate the wheat from the chaff. Why should any of those scarce resources go to bolster the work of a pedantic pin-sized intellect like Sands?"

"That's pathetic."

"Right. I should amend that. An unbearable pedantic, whose ragtag team is harbouring an architect facing criminal charges in Berlin and an hysterical Danish poofter."

"You're absurd."

She closed her eyes. She would not spare him another thought. All that chatter in Arabic. *Har Batata!* He made her think of those boys who kicked girls in the schoolyard when she was little, just because they were girls. How she and another girl used to keep veering close to the kicking boys. They were the damaged boys; you could see it in their curiously mean faces. It was so easy to get them into trouble, exciting too, to shriek and run away.

Sky Black as Pearl

TONIGHT A MAN WHO believed in unicorns would take Clare Livingston to a wedding that had happened seven hundred years before. Clare repeated that sentence to herself as the small pot of espresso hissed. She would regard the evening with Gianni DiGiustini as just that: unbelievable, a loophole in time. A reprieve from the debacle of the day before, her attempt to do one good deed having backfired, Luke and William surely firm enemies now.

Not to mention the business of the bead.

Tiny artefacts were misplaced all the time on digs, she tried to reassure herself. Surely the theft of such a thing could be judged tiny on the grand scale of personal larceny, or the larceny of nations for that matter: whole continents taken over, pilfered, treasure appropriated by other nations, or melted down. It was ridiculous to keep having flashes of an alternate reality in which she stole it. She had never in her life stolen any inanimate object. Of course she had appropriated a large chunk of a continent, she realized; but still it was ridiculous to keep feeling, right through her gut, the beadness of a bead — to feel how even a tiny act of theft can leave the thief hollowed through the centre the way a bead is. To recall how snugly the bead had nestled between her heart- and fate-lines, to feel weakened by such a near-escape.

In the end there was only one way to put all that out of her mind, and calm her jitters about the coming evening.

AS SHE STARTED UP the creek, preoccupied still, she slipped on a mossy stone. Half in water, half on the verge, with her nose almost buried in the ferny streamside growth, she caught a flash of purple and gold. A tiny plant was unfurling there, something like a woodcock orchid, yet nothing she had ever seen in life or in any illustration. In the excitement of once again coming upon something most unusual, everything else went out of her head. She scrambled to clear herself a nest among the ferns. She imagined herself approaching the orchid's capture with a kind of reverent stealth. As she drew it to her paper in a net of lines, then embarked on a thrilling struggle to achieve the dark purple-brown of the curling petal, the way that it faded into Renaissance gold — to depict the hair's-breadth stripes at the base of the petal — the sense came over her again that was richer than anything she knew. She thought, When I am doing this, I am true. She made a vow.

༺༻

WHEN SHE RETURNED TO the house there was hardly time to bathe and change. Storm clouds were bunching in the west. She shivered in the skimpy yellow dress, with no suitable wrap to cover its spaghetti straps. Then she remembered the shawl on the low table behind the fireplace chair, where the ugly lamp wired to the bronze she-wolf lurked. There was no time to ponder whether the cloth would be stained or ripped. She heaved the chair aside, tipped the heavy statue one way and the other, to inch out the cloth from underneath. The table lid angled dangerously when the statue slid to the edge — then slapped back down onto its squat cubed base.

The cloth was undamaged, beautiful. It wrapped around her shoulders in a shimmering silk cocoon of gold and blue and plum. She put everything back in place, hurried to tidy the room, the beautiful room, feeling a flush of pride. *He will see how I live, in this beautiful room.*

The painting of the orchid rested on the table, still damp, propped on her portable easel.

∽

THE LAND ROVER PURRED so quietly that if Clare had not been hovering by the window she wouldn't have heard him arrive.

There he was.

He closed the door of the vehicle with barely a click, bounded up her stone stairs with such a light step, shining hair floating and settling. He was wearing dark silk cotton pants and a shirt of the same blue, and a white linen jacket loose over his shoulders. When she came to the door his look of gladness was so intense that she could hardly breathe. She backed away. "Oh hello! I'll just go and get my wrap." In the bedroom, in the mirror, she thought her pale un-made-up face did catch the light in a way appropriate for a woman setting out with a man who traced his family history back to some tragic tale of love and suicide in medieval times. She pulled the shawl around her shoulders. The beads on the fringe gave off tiny music and the colours of the antique cloth seemed fitting.

But when she went back into the other room, he was polite, correct, preoccupied.

He took the key from her, closed up the double doors to the arbour, and took her arm so she wouldn't twist her ankle on the stone steps in her teetering shoes. In the car he turned an unsettling look on her, somehow both amused and sad — as if even before they'd started out she'd failed some silent test. The dress? Would his famous dangling ancestor have disapproved? Could this even be why the girl flung herself from the tower? Not out of foiled love, but in a flash of precognition at how the family reputation for *bella figura* would eventually be so shamed? *I must not be at all how he remembered,* she thought. She studied his hands on the wheel as he steered gently around the many turns down the hill — the slim gold wedding band, of course: no other jewellery, just the ring and the watch, and on his right hand a white scar along the middle finger. She recalled Luke Tindhall's rough-handling the wheel, the ruby ring winking.

"So how are your unicorns doing?" she said after a too-long period of silence. "Were they glad to see you?"

Again his quizzical smile. "Clare Livingston! You are very beautiful tonight, if I may say. And even more to me a mystery."

A little late for that.

"I take it the unicorns are okay. And you? You've had an okay few days, too?"

"I have spent some time both very interesting and also very disturbing," he said. He smoothed a hand across his forehead, as if the disturbance was still there.

He said he'd wished she could have been with him to meet his Romanian friend Radu Radescu, the ethnobotanist, who had dropped by on his way back from a trek through the Amazon which had revealed how — even since Clare's extensive travels, it seemed — vast depredations were going on, the forest receding under ever-newer threats.

That was terrible to hear, devastating. Yet she'd so hoped not to get into a discussion about the Amazon tonight. She was silent.

Gianni was saying that Radescu's trek had taken him up the river Jari and over the Serra Tumachumac, then through to Roraima and into Venezuela, where he had climbed into that lost world that Clare had written about so well.

Yes I did, Clare thought.

This had been largely because she already knew Gianni's friend Radescu. She had interviewed him at length by phone, using one of her handy aliases, after Radescu had returned from a previous trip. Radescu had written about the use of *yage* and other hallucinogenic plants among the tribes, of the brilliant whirling spiritual universe the participants of such rituals entered; he'd written as well of the vast unwritten botanical pharmacopeia such threatened tribes had once possessed. When, in turn, she wrote about the loss of botanical knowledge, and the more recent near extinction of the tribes themselves, she'd been disconsolate. It was shaming that here, now, selfishly, she was wasting her sorrow on the way this evening was likely to turn into a perilous game of hide-and-seek.

Gianni gentled the car through the maze of walled lanes at the bottom of her hill, and again she couldn't help thinking of Luke Tindhall's rough driving. At least there had been none of this *you are even more a beautiful mystery* stuff. ·

And yes, she'd written an entire chapter on the wonders of trekking into the lost world atop Mont Roraima, where she'd come upon her remarkable *Circaea Livingston Philippiana* in the spray of Angel Falls. She'd taken particular delight in writing of that area because when her husband returned from his trip through those parts, the article he'd published in *Botany Today* had been full of footnotes and convoluted academic jargon, almost incomprehensible.

GIANNI DROVE THEM STRAIGHT to the Piazza Garibaldi. He pulled into a space that said No Parking. The policewoman put a ticket underneath his windshield wiper and they exchanged a solemn double cheek-kiss, he and this comely agent of the law. He took Clare's arm and guided her along the street towards the main piazza.

Everybody knew him. This, at least, was the same as before. The man from the grocery store doffed a triangular hat with a long feather. The secretary from the lawyer's office, now wearing a high and noble turban trimmed with pearls, sedately grabbed him by both ears. Was he asking himself what he'd got into, walking arm in arm with a woman in an outfit not even an Italian could pull off — the dress that was far too short, the sandals she could hardly walk in, the whole ensemble topped off with a table cloth?

He guided her up the narrow passage leading to the next piazza. After a bit of back-slapping with a man in monk's garb collecting tickets, he led her into the stands, though no ticket came into view. He guided her towards the section where the seats had cushions.

The great medieval stone palazzo loomed across the square, black against a sky that had turned deepest indigo. Beyond a roped-off area, the entire piazza swayed with a crowd so thick that the coloured garments and oval faces had a wavering pointillist effect. Music faded and swelled as bands approached from different directions through the surrounding spaghetti strands of streets. Small white lights flickered on, outlining the name of the Savings Bank of Florence on the crenellated building next to the grand palazzo. Trumpets sounded. The woman from the leather shop, Petronella, walked into the piazza wearing doublet and hose and a long-feathered hat. At her signal, the palazzo doors groaned open. Half a dozen horsemen skittered out on mouthy steeds. Little drummer boys emerged.

GIANNI BEGAN EXPLAINING, IN a careful travelogue sort of way, that seven hundred years ago the occasion would have linked not just two noble families, but two cities — as was the custom in those days, such alliances frequently forged by marriage. Clare was squeezed close to him, now that the seats had all filled. He gave off a crisp woody sort of smell that reminded her of how this morning, at the streamside, she'd slipped and buried her nose in green foliage. She wished she was back there, doing something she understood. She remembered how when she was painting the orchid she had made a vow: how she'd had a flash of the unique self that was her, how everything she looked at, all around, was something only she saw in just that way, and if she could cleave to the quiet business of recording that, she would be true.

She had left the painting on the table imagining that when Gianni came, he might see all those things about her in it. He hadn't even given it a glance.

He was being so careful, courteous, explaining how the town was divided into five sections, represented by the five groups of musicians that had come together in the square, each with costumes of different sets of colours; but his discomfort loomed out of him like a separate gargoyle presence, shadowing her enjoyment in this spectacle completely. How could another person do that to you, how could you let them, why should it be so hard to shake that shadow off?

More trumpets. At last the bride and groom emerged, the bride's horse rearing, circling, threatening to trample the long train of her white dress as it trailed across the stones, until the groom — very like a real groom, young and resolute and confused — sprang from his horse and helped the girl down. The two of them walked forward leading a solemn retinue, including small costumed children looking important and proud.

And no matter what, it was beautiful, serious, believable; not just a pageant put on for tourists, Clare thought, but holding some far deeper meaning for the town. She wished she was here on her own and could enjoy it, without this fine-smelling man glowering beside her.

When the marriage vows had been exchanged, celebrations began: a performance which in the old days would have been a night-long romp, as Gianni dutifully explained. Flag bearers sent shadows swooping over the palazzo walls like giant moths, tumblers rollicked, acrobats swung whirling balls of fire. A chorus of lute-shaped girls sang madrigals. Finally, with the lights still low, a flock of very little girls in white dresses came sweetly down the stairs of a palazzo at the side, playing recorders; a flock of intense little angels.

The battlements were glittery through the rainbow of Clare's lashes when the piazza suddenly flared up with light.

∾

AS THEY MADE THEIR way down from the stands, the claxon of an ambulance sounded across the square. People squeezed between them in the rush to see what was going on. Gianni turned and gestured that he thought he was needed over there.

She went back and sat down. The crowd thinned, the ambulance left, she didn't see him anywhere.

When she finally did catch sight of him, he was deep in conversation with a woman on the far side of the piazza. His sister, Clare realized as her vision cleared after the first flush of pique. Federica seemed to be giving him a piece of her mind. Her cap of short black hair bobbed and glistened in the flood lights like a furious black beetle, while he stood with his hands spread, palms wobbling up and down, as if weighing what she said. He turned to walk away. She caught his sleeve.

Was Federica upset because she had spied Gianni with a woman not his wife? Surely she was used to that by now.

So was it because she'd seen him with Clare?

Suspicions swooped in then, huge and winged, like the shadows the flag bearers had sent swooping over the palazzo walls, suspicions so dramatic they were almost enjoyable. What if this was about the property dispute? What if Federica was so intent on that because she knew about the hillocks in the meadow? Indeed, what if Federica and Gianni were actually involved in the illicit activities that Inspector Cerotti had talked about? Hadn't he said that *tombaroli* could be anyone?

She saw Gianni reach for Federica's cigarette and drop it and grind it out, saw him lean in and tilt her chin, bend to kiss her, then whisper something in her ear.

"OH HELLO," CLARE SAID when Gianni finally joined her. "No one died, I hope."

Silence. Oh God, maybe somebody had died. But he shook his head. He said that an old friend, the local grocer, had suffered an attack, yes, but the medics said he would recover. It had been a reminder, he said, that life was very short. "We must not give it too many complications."

Clare said she'd drink to that.

He gave her a close look, that sad smile.

He sat down beside her. Then stood again.

"I have been guilty," he said. He knocked his forehead with his fist. His wedding band caught the gleam from the string of lights advertising the Savings Bank of Florence, and she thought, So now he's going to confess that he has a wife.

When he sat back down she concentrated on the remarkable shine on his woven leather shoes, though the shoes themselves were not new shoes, in fact they were very well-worn — maybe ancestral shoes, passed down through all the generations since some ancestor had beaten swords into ploughshares in Bologna? One thing she knew: it was not the wife who shined those shoes. The wife would be too busy running the family business, wasn't that what Federica Inghirami had said that night at Farnham's? "I have had to call Eleanora to say, 'Please do not make me have to tell you that just because you run the family business, you do not run all our lives.'" Clare liked that turn of phrase. *Don't make me have to tell you that I don't give a damn about your wife,* she'd say when he confessed.

He cleared his throat. "When I came to collect you, I could not help noticing the watercolour painting on your table. The little orchid."

"Oh that!"

"The painting is very unusual indeed."

Unusual. He'd hated it. She'd wanted him to see it. And he'd hated it.

Something wobbled on the edge of this, though. Maybe the mention of her painting was just to distract her, in case she'd seen him plotting? Could there be any doubt that he and his sister had been plotting? Look at his nervousness as he crossed his legs, uncrossed them, rapped his knuckles against that protruding chin.

"I have never in truth seen one like that," he said. "Not with that particular striped lower petal, the exaggerated twisted tongue, those colours."

"Yes, I was thrilled to come across it," she said, recognizing how important it was not to let him know where she'd come across it.

"Do you think you have discovered, perhaps, another new species?"

She laughed. "New species? No. It was discovered centuries ago." She gestured towards the palazzo across the square. "I found it growing in the museum archives, in the volumes of those wonderful old botanical paintings. The librarian kindly made me photocopies of all three volumes."

He smiled. He said that he too had spent many hours with the remarkable collection, though strangely had missed that particular example. He said that perhaps soon, together, they might track down the true living specimen, where it still grew.

She looked away, embarrassed for him now, for such a transparent attempt to inveigle his way onto her fenced-off property, onto her upland meadow. Surely that was what this was all about.

"But this is terrible," he said, springing up again. "For me to invite you here and then to have left you on your own for so long! Come, we must have some refreshment."

⌒

IN THE CENTRAL PIAZZA all the tables were full. But the waiter in front of the Bar Toscano saw them coming, whipped a tray of crockery from a service table just outside the door, pulled out a chair for Clare. Gianni clapped him on the shoulder. After a few words together the waiter went off smiling, saying, "*Ah, sì! Sì sì sì sì!*"

How, in just the short passage from one piazza to another, had Gianni managed to transform back into the man she'd spent a week having fantasies about? He leaned towards her and, with a kind of gleeful intensity that made her feel she was in an unsafe vehicle at top speed, started telling her a convoluted story she only half got, about a botanist he'd studied under, who had been a student of the famous Cappelletti.

He pretended to be astonished that she didn't know of Cappelletti, the former head of the Botanical Gardens in Padua, the oldest in Europe. He said that he too had worked at those gardens in Padua for a time, when he'd finished his studies. That was before — a pause in the rush of words — before other things drew him away.

Then a look of sadness winged across his face. "Cappelletti's watchword, you must understand, has been 'In nature you must never wear blinkers.' This has been the most important lesson in my life. Though it has been hard."

The waiter returned to set down tall, cone-shaped glasses brimming with a pale liquid that gave off a medicinal smell. Gianni raised his glass. He said, "*Cheenarrrr.*"

Clare said, "Cheenarrrr to you."

He laughed, and wrote the spelling of the drink on a paper napkin, after catching the waiter's eye and ordering two more. *Cynar.* A very healthful liqueur, he insisted; brewed by monks, from artichokes.

She took a sip of the pale liquor. It slid down with such monkish reassurance that she took another.

"You must understand," Gianni said. "Cappelletti was a man of insatiable curiosity! This has led him, for example, to his remarkable discovery regarding the life systems of resin fungi. And then —" Gianni threw up his hands, "By cultivating the species, Cappelletti was able to show that the organism does not utilize the elements of the resin itself to live, but rather its impurities!"

She caught a woman at a nearby table wondering what the handsome Italian could possibly be saying to captivate his companion. Clare wanted to laugh; if she'd had another hat, she'd have thrown it away, too, just to have the incomprehensible dissertation about resin fungi go on and on. The sky against the town hall tower was black as pearl. The piazza was lit up like a stage, groups of people gathering, gesturing, embracing, drifting into new groups or strolling from the scene. An opera. Someone should burst into song. A balcony jutted from the building above, entirely suitable for Juliet. Now the intense young man across from Clare was insisting she must come with him to Perugia. His mentor, the student of Cappelletti, alas, was no longer there; but it was essential that she visit this *Orto Medievale*, this refuge of medicinal plants in the monastery of San Pietro.

"You will like it there much," he said. "When I returned, after some years of living a life where I was not at all engaged, when I sat within the walls of that monastery and breathed the exhalations of the healing plants and listened to the sound of bees, I understood I could no longer pretend to live one life and dream another. This was when I decided I must take all my best energies to save what I could of this earth's things. I know that when you walk through this place, when you follow the intricate philosophical paths that have been laid out, when you breathe the healing air, you also will find yourself in the centre of the truth of your own life."

The truth of her own life. She felt a prick of warning. But he leaned forward with that wind-rushing intensity. "You see, it is essential to believe that we are not bound up in the chains of the past, that our planet does not have to plough like an ocean liner ahead to its own destruction, that we can take the reins again, stop the chariot. That each one of us holds the golden key to our own lives!"

"My goodness."

"Do you think I am extreme?"

She laughed. "Heavens, no."

"Yes of course I am," he said. "I am a fool tonight, hardly know- ing what I am saying, because I have decided I must tell you a thing I have not dared so far."

She bit her lip. Couldn't he just go on talking about resin fungi? But his frown was resolute.

"Ever since I have read your book," he said, "Yes, more than once — for it was sent me by a colleague in the States — I have been fascinated with your paintings which are so proficient, so beautiful. Some much more than that. Some so full of life that it is possible to hear the rush of it bursting through the stems and leaves. I have been intrigued by how work so praiseworthy for its botanical accuracy might also be said to be infused with your dreams."

So it was going to be a night of hide-and-seek after all.

But not a game. Not for her. If he knew Radescu, he knew everyone. He could kill her book and all she'd foolishly hoped it might accomplish.

"And in particular," he persisted, "the remarkable nightshade which bears in part your name, which was growing, you tell us, in the spray of the Angel Falls."

"Right."

"*Allora.*" The long scarred finger reached up to touch his eyelids; first one, then the other, so they closed, as if only in the dark he had the courage to say whatever he was intending. She longed to close her eyes, too; to make this stop, or turn it into something else; the way she had closed her eyes when her uncle touched her, when she had managed to pretend he loved her. In the piazza people were jostling, laughing, joking. A labourer went by with a barrow. The man dressed all in red whom she'd seen on her first morning here was now trying to shove a bundle of hangers into a bucket far too small.

Gianni looked up.

"Ever since then, I have longed to meet the woman who so eloquently has brought attention to one of the planet's most endangered and most essential places." He grabbed a fist of hair, as if to pull free the difficult words. "And now, since I have met her, and since I have come to know what a fine person Clare Livingston truly is — and then, tonight, when I have seen an example of how she may intend to use her extraordinary talents to present the flora of my own country — I have at first been taken aback, I must confess. But now I realize — as I said earlier — how it is foolish to make unnecessary complications ..."

Such a sad, pleading expression; as if she could easily rescue them both from those complications, and free him from this embarrassment, by just admitting that her beguiling nightshade had been a fake. Surely she'd have the good grace to do him that little favour.

She had balanced long on the ledge of pretence. She was so tired from balancing there. Was it possible that there was someone who could see right through her, and not judge and condemn? She picked up the glass of monkish liqueur. It, too, urged confession.

What a fine person, he'd said.

But once confession started, where would it stop? If she opened the tiny door it would all come out, her entire life of lies, lies concocted to cover other lies. Even to the child psychiatrist she'd lied; inventing more and more to keep him happy and intrigued. But this man, she saw, with his sad, beautiful amber eyes, was the one who might really trick her into true confession. And then what would be left of her? She glimpsed a splayed faceless flattened figure, like those outlines drawn on sidewalks after a shooting.

She took another sip of the liqueur, which seemed prepared to argue on her side now. *Who could ever prove your illustration was false,* it whispered through the grill of the confession box. For yes, the terrible big truth was that even species that no one had yet seen were dying out. It was entirely possible that her *Circaea Livingston* was the very last of its kind. She felt tears spring to her eyes at the thought that no one would ever come upon another!

Yet Gianni was pressing on, this relentless man who insisted that she confess her sins — no doubt because it would make him feel better about his own?

"So now I must ask you," he was saying, "What drew you to the Amazon? What moved you to make your extraordinary paintings of that region, to discover a new species? I had meant never to explore this. But tonight, I realize that I must understand." He leaned closer. The tilt of his chin reminded her of the moment when he'd bent to kiss his sister and whisper in Federica's ear.

"Understand what?" she heard herself demanding. "What?" she said again. "My account of the Amazon wasn't personal enough for you? I left out a few of the ten thousand insect bites, the chiggers, the worm that burrowed in my scalp?"

She heard her voice rise.

"Some reviewers thought it praiseworthy that mine was not just another macho adventure by some guy setting out to prove how tough he could be. Now you're saying it was like I wasn't really there? That's a little problem I have. The more deeply I feel about things, the less I am really there."

He shook his head, distressed. But she couldn't stop. "Believe me, my ex-husband used to complain about that, too."

She caught him glancing at the opal ring on her wedding finger.

"Yes, very ex," she said, now utterly fed up. "I exed him. Crossed him off. I keep this as a kind of amulet. I believe opals stand for tears. So are we finished with the third degree?"

She tried to push back her chair. He took hold of her wrist.

A FATHER PASSED BETWEEN the tables with a little boy who was hopping up and down, calling out to someone ahead in his little foghorn voice. The father bent, so gentle, *"Piano, piano."* He rested one hand on the top of the boy's head; they walked on, joined in this way, the boy bouncing beneath his father's hand.

Clare watched them as they crossed the piazza. Gianni watched them, too, his hand still on her wrist. When they turned to face one another, it seemed they had also crossed an expanse that arched over so many essential things.

He lifted her hand so the three small opals flashed their rainbow light. She loved the ring; not a wedding ring, but an heirloom given her by her dear great aunt Calliope, who'd given her shelter as a runaway teen.

Now it was his wedding band that gleamed. He caught her glance and might have started to explain. She ran a finger across his palm, up into the space where his shirt buttoned at the wrist. He drew in his breath. "Shhh," she said.

✑

DOWN THE MOUNTAIN IN the dark, purring around corners, following a string of drivers; along the faded pink and yellow street at the base, where a light above the door of a bar illuminated a stand of melons, a few old men on plastic chairs; through an intersection onto a still smaller road across the plain. They were going to a *ristorante* at Passignano, on the lake. Gianni said Clare would like it very much. Across the flat land between fields and then up through Ossaia on the toe of the next ridge. A song on the radio, a lullaby he said had been popular a few years ago. "*E per te ogni cosa c'e ... ninna-na, ninna-ne ...*" The leather smell of his car.

THE HEADLIGHTS CAUGHT WAVERING fringes of palms. Gianni parked the car on the curb. A pier led out to where the *traghetti* docked, the little boats plying to and from the islands. There was a castle on one of the islands, he said. He said they would go there one day soon. He looked at his watch. It was not nine o'clock; if Clare wanted, before they went to the restaurant they could take a walk out on the pier.

The moon was sailing with fat silver clouds. He said that on the island with the castle she would feel like she was on the Aegean. "The water with the same green brilliance. When you walk through the dark of this ruined castle you come to a room that opens onto a balcony above the lake. There you have a flash of blue and green and purple water, and the hills of Umbria."

We will go there. Her hand next to his, on the rail. His profile against the brilliant light-filled clouds.

He said the castle had been a monastery long ago. Then a wealthy family bought it. Now there was an old caretaker who would guide them through the ruins. When the caretaker took them to the chapel and swung a flashlight over the peeling gold-starred ceiling, those stars would shower at Clare's feet.

"Oh please," she laughed. "You don't actually look like someone who says such goofy things."

"No? How then do I look?"

"When I first saw you — when you got out of your Mercedes — you made me think of a face on a coin. Later, when I was going through a book in the house, about ancient history, there you were."

"Who was this, pretending to be me?"

"He wasn't very nice."

"No one with a face on a coin is very nice. It comes from being too close to the money. Not a problem I have."

"This one was Mithridates of Pontus."

"He was not so bad. It is true he had every Italian in his kingdom put to death, the little children too, but perhaps they had misbehaved. We have learned from this, it is not good to over-discipline."

For a moment more his face remained in silhouette, the noble puzzled profile of a king with weighty problems. When he turned, when they looked at one another, it was delicious to decide to let expectation spin out a little longer, then join hands and run down the pier, across the park, across the street, up the steps of the *ristorante* where their table waited by the open window.

LATER SHE WILL NOT recall quite what they said. It was easy, buoyant — the way you can sometimes speak a foreign language in a dream. What she will recall is how they foraged through the menu, like famished children. She will remember *tagliatelle* with seafood bathed in saffron, and a noble white wine from Montepulciano fetched from the private cellar of the restaurant's owner. Above the table a lamp of tasselled silk held them in an island of mellow light, and beyond this, the ebb and flow of many conversations. The fine attention Italian diners gave to their food. The large party of Germans at a central table, where a beautiful blonde child raised laughter by loudly calling "*Ciao!*" over and over, and, at the instigation of a party of elderly Italians nearby, "*Ciao bella!*" She will remember that they both ate prawns rolled into zucchini flowers, and that they finished with a *sorbetto* of passion fruit.

THE STORM DID NOT start until they were back outside. A flash that split the clouds and sent the moon to cover, and then another and another. Fat drops of water exploding on the sidewalk. By the time they reached the shelter of his car they were soaked. The rain banged on the roof, "*E per te ogni cosa c'e ...*" At Ossia, the street through the town was like a river. "*... Ninna-na, ninna-ne ...*" Lightning seared the sky, exposing the city on the hill, the Medici fortress, and the buildings huddled on the slope bleached to bone.

A crash of thunder directly overhead. "Does this happen often? I'm sorry. I hate storms."

"I think only very strange people like them. Like me. You should not be sorry."

Maybe he would understand if she explained. But what each flash made clear was how she would never do that, yet how she was tied completely to the past, and how desperate she really was. She saw the triumvirate leaning in, giving a belligerent thirteen-year-old girl the third degree — her aunt, her grandmother, and her ancient doctor — her aunt's face slicked by vengeance into a pale determined slate. She heard the leaded panes of the windows of the farmhouse rattling the way they had that night. The trees soughing and snapping on the ridge. She smelled the old living room's damp and musty smell. She remembered how in a great crack of lightning all the lights went out. It was not until years later, not till she was married, that she understood how badly the doctor had botched the procedure. She would never have a child.

The rutted road was a torrent as Gianni bucked the car up her hill.

Before she could say anything, he was opening her door, a small penlight in his hand. The rain had stopped, but water poured from the gutters and the stone steps were slick. His light played around the terrace. They stopped by her door. Behind him, the Medici fortress loomed against the inky sky, a warning of all she had no right to expect.

She rose on tiptoe and kissed him lightly on the cheek. "Good night, Gianni. It was lovely."

She couldn't see his face, his shape merging with the formidable outline of the broken fortress. "… Then I should call you?"

She said, "Oh, yes. Please call."

The Gardens of King Herod

ALL NIGHT SHE TOSSED and turned. Had it been a mad thing to let him go? Or the proper Italian thing, which someone of Gianni's background would appreciate and understand?

She thought she'd only slept for a minute. She heard the ringing of the phone. She heard Marta's voice, explaining that Signora Livingston was still in bed.

"No." She rushed out, bundled in a sheet.

It was Luke Tindhall. He was calling, he said, because his employer had called him and wakened him from a perfectly good sleep, merely to get his impressions of the dig at Poggio Selvaggio.

"And?"

"And?" Mimicking her voice. "And were you a good boy, Tindhall? Did you lie through your pearly whites?"

"You are a reeking idiot, you know."

"Beg pardon, Ms. Livingston. I must say that you, on the other hand, were looking very fetching last night, wrapped in that splendid bit of cloth." She pictured him making a gleeful sardonic bow. "And so you've come to know the famous Gianpaulo. Ah, well. All the pretty ladies get to know Gianpaulo DiGiustini sooner or later, though I'd imagined you were made of sterner stuff. Don't worry. I won't pass it on to Harry Plank."

ALL THE PRETTY LADIES.

She'd known that, hadn't she?

How unreasonable to trail into the kitchen and tell Marta she was ill, she was going back to bed. Marta should go home. How unreasonable to curl under the covers in a ball, until she heard the sound of a car pulling in. Then how unreasonable to leap up, start wildly brushing her hair, pull on shirt and jeans.

It was Ralph Farnham. This time she did manage to stop him at the door.

He, too, said she'd looked fetching last night. "Late, were we?" eyeing her rumpled state.

He'd dropped by, he said, because Federica had told him that their joint lawyer was back in town, and he'd been thinking that the lawyer must have those papers of her uncle's that she hadn't been able to locate, and so he'd thought he'd let her know the chap was back, because his agent was dead keen.

"Hang on," Clare said. "Don't get too close. I think I might be coming down with another bout of dengue fever. It's catching as hell. I'd rush right home and take some *Echinacea,* if I were you."

༼༽

TIME TICKED BY. CLARE didn't dare go far from the phone. She got out the photocopies of the hermit's botanical books, and forced herself to select some suitable local plant to work into a composition. She settled on *Erythronium bifolium maculosum,* liking its spiky little upright blooms which looked hopeful, though ugly.

As she sketched it in, she felt the plant resist. She tore the sketch in half, started again. When she looked up she saw the painting of the orchid, still propped against a vase. She heard Gianni's comment. *Very unusual indeed.* She rose to hide it in the drawer of the sideboard, with the collection of her meadow paintings.

Instead, she took the rest of the paintings out, spread them, and reassessed them.

They, too, were unusual — certainly for work purporting to be purely botanical. But even with their flaws they were alive, she thought now, and they reflected true moments in her life, the best of her. Important to remember that when she'd painted these, just as with the little orchid, she had been true. There was one place in her life where she could go, where she was true.

All the same, when she set back to work, not just the *Erythronium* resisted, everything resisted. Some great immoveable ice block had settled over her, encompassing her. Blocked. She'd never felt this before. She closed her eyes and tried to look at the situation objectively, say from across the room. What to do about the woman frozen inside a mammoth ice cube?

The phone rang. It was Gianni.

He had to confess regret, he said, that their evening together had so abruptly ended.

She said, "Me too."

Even though she could see all those pretty ladies dancing round him, maybe even in her meadow, dancing round and round in a ring, she knew by the sick relief flooding her that of course, no matter what, she would join in.

HE MUST HAVE BEEN calling from the bottom of the hill. When she stepped from the bedroom shower, he was bounding up the stone stairs. She could have called out for him to hang on. Instead she went through, wrapped in a big lavender-smelling towel, and beckoned him in. The next thing was obvious. She would let the towel fall. Or he would come and remove it.

But that ice block had moved to the centre of the room, and they were peering at each other through it. He said, "Oh I am sorry to have —" She said, "Oh, no. I didn't know you'd get here so soon —" He said, "Unfortunately I was —"

She said, "I'd better go and dress. Just make yourself at home," dipping in a mock curtsey, holding the hem of the towel.

He was carrying a thick manila envelope. He put it on the table, looked around the room. "Could I perhaps look at that little orchid again?"

She said sure, she would get it out when she came back.

Like hell, she thought, glancing at the sideboard where she'd stowed it along with all the other paintings.

Could I perhaps look at that little orchid?

Imagine coming into a room where a woman was half-naked, and asking that. The face in the mirror when she dressed was the ugliest face she'd ever seen. She pulled her hair into a knot.

⌒

CLARE MADE COFFEE. THE ice block followed, and hunkered between them in the centre of the kitchen table. She began to wonder how she could have thought he was attractive. Look at him sipping from the mug with the castle painted on it, centuries of seigneurial correctness behind that sip. In every generation, the rustle of pretty ladies off to the side. Look at him examining the design, God only knew what was going on inside his noble forehead. Look at that ridiculous big nose and tilted-up chin.

It was a relief when Niccolo tapped on the kitchen door, hunched and gnarled, the shadowy branches of the old quince tree gnarling cave-like behind him, so that for a moment she thought, *rescued by a gnome.* Niccolo was holding a green plastic thermos. He said Marta had sent him with soup, because the Signora was not well. He eyed Gianni suspiciously before he started back up the hill. Clare found herself wondering if Marta had really sent the soup, or if Niccolo had brought his lunch soup as an excuse to check on her visitor. Gianni had broken off his contemplation of the mug. She offered him soup. He said no, he did not think at the moment he could eat.

Then he clapped his forehead, as if rescued. "But I have forgotten!" He ran up the steps into the living room, came back with the manila envelope. He pulled out a fat academic-looking publication with a creamy white cover, grey-blue printing. *The American Journal of Archaeology.* He handed it to Clare. She found herself smoothing her hand over the ivory-feeling surface of the cover, wondering what sort of a reclusive dolt she really was that it should make her feel happy just to hold the journal, then to flip the pages, see black-and-white photos set into text about excavations around the world, footnotes, book reviews, a hefty index, graphs and maps. Gianni had brought it because it contained a long article on the excavation of ancient gardens, written by a friend.

"Gardens? I had no idea there was such a specialty!"

His face lit up — and then the whole room lit up. He said the very earth itself was the artefact some archaeologists studied. He said his very dear friend was now an expert in this field, as Clare would learn when she read of his friend's excavations of the gardens of King Herod the Great, in Jericho.

"Herod! Who made Salome dance?"

"No, that was I think the uncle. Still, even with him, we must not be too quick to believe the stories that we hear from these many centuries away. This is, in part, my point."

He turned to photographs and diagrams, which detailed the process involved in the excavation of the gardens of that biblical king. He seemed relieved by her interest. He explained that through his friend's work, gardens once so marvellous and lush that Cleopatra had forced Caesar to obtain them for her from Herod — these gardens had been able to come alive once more, at least in our minds and understanding, in the way such archaeological projects could bring things back to life.

"The palm groves where the balsam grew," he said, "the famous Balm of Gilead! See here what would have been the luxuriant plantings in Herod's courtyards — all revealed in this plan, discovered by the changes in the earth, the variations in the stratigraphy …"

Clare leaned close to the folded-out plan showing the many phases of the excavation. It was fascinating to think of recapturing something as ephemeral as a garden. To think that the earth itself could hold subliminal memories.

"And from these excavations of Herod's gardens," Gianni was saying, "we learn that he was not such a terrible king as his enemies have told us, but a man who loved flowers."

"That seems a bit of a leap. I'm sure that lots of really bad people loved flowers."

He admitted that, yes, this king had done some bad things, and also he went a little mad; however, Gianni's friend had assured him that the story of the slaughter of the innocents was "… what you might call perhaps, in your idiom, somewhat dicey historically. We must think, too, about the general ethos of the times."

"Oh sure," Clare said.

IT WAS BEAUTIFUL TO watch Gianni now, in his excitement. To find herself caught up again, as with his riff about the unicorns, the resin fungi thing — to be whirled along, not knowing where he aimed to take her.

He was walking back and forth in her kitchen, which had been designed for people much shorter. He dodged clusters of lavender and dried herbs hanging from the beam between the table and the stove. He plucked a spray of tarragon, crumbled it, buried his face in his palms, looked up, widening his eyes in pleasure at the scent, as his words tumbled on.

From clues in the earth itself, he said, it was also possible to gain a new understanding of ancient minds. He said his friend had also been privileged to work with the great Wilhemina Jashemski at Pompeii, where even in their smallest, most humble shops and tiny homes the inhabitants had devoted space to flowers. Thus it became clear that the Romans, too, were nicer people than previously had been supposed.

He paused, fixed her intently. "On their streets of tombs as well," he said, "they planted the most lovely and fragrant plants to nourish the spirits of the living and to feed the dead. My friend helped to excavate these gardens on their streets of tombs."

He'd said it twice. *Their streets of tombs.* So this was where it all had been leading!

He closed the journal, as if the preamble was over and the real subject about to begin. He would make up some excuse now, she thought, to inveigle his way up to her own street of tombs.

She tried to remain detached, yet interested. What would he say, exactly? What would she say? Did she really have a member of the *tombaroli* in her house? Would she soon have one in her bed? The suspicion of being used, manipulated, was queasily exciting, though her gut clenched too. Breathlessly she watched him spread his hands, his surprisingly scarred hands.

"I also have made the earth my choice," he said. "I have changed my life to do this. For this reason, truth and accuracy of botanical depiction have become of prime importance to me."

Truth and accuracy. She'd been ready to take a tomb robber to her bed, and he'd turned into the chartered accountant of botanical correctness?

"Oh yes," she said, "absolutely. Accuracy is important in my work. But as to truth," she gave her head a little knock with her fist, "I'm afraid you've caught me out in a fib."

His dark eyes flared over her.

She said, "I promised to show you the orchid. But I decided it didn't cut the mustard. This morning I ripped it up."

HERE WAS NICCOLO AGAIN, at the door. This time, she went right out and closed it behind her, took a breath of morning air, remembering how fine it had been sitting in the sun outside Niccolo's shed, sharing his morning snack, understanding almost nothing that he said.

Niccolo had hurried back to warn her that once again he'd loosed the dogs in the fenced woods. There was evidence of strangers tampering with the wire.

"I thought you said there were no dogs."

No, she had been mistaken, he said; he'd told her that she was in no danger from the dogs, because since her uncle died he kept them penned. This was followed by a thick wordy tangle.

She thanked him for letting her know.

Because, even if she'd understood, she would not have believed a word, not from Niccolo, not from the man in the kitchen. Who knew what Gianni was really after, or what he saw in her? He'd got her right in so many ways. Yet he'd misjudged her in ways that she'd never bring herself to explain. It was like being stuffed inside a bag to think of trying to explain. What did people want? A diagram of the north and south of her? Warnings of false lodestones and the places where the map ended and she had more than once slipped off? As she turned to go back inside, she saw that the sky had sealed over with the white of a blinded eye.

∽

"LISTEN, GIANNI —!"

In the space before she stepped back into the kitchen, resolve had settled on her.

But he wasn't there.

She heard the scrape of wood on wood. In the living room she caught him turning from the sideboard, with one of her meadow paintings in either hand. Others were spread on the table.

"What the hell?"

He laid the paintings down with extreme care, his face growing very pale, all of him paling, the arms in the white t-shirt falling to his side and becoming whiter than the shirt, or so she imagined. She imagined all of him fading away, a shape held up only by his clothes, pale with shame. When he looked up he was frowning, though.

He said, "I could not believe that you had truly torn up that fine work." He was looking straight at her, through her. He said, "Of course I should not have done this, but now I am taken by these compositions." He lifted another from the drawer. "Such feeling, such imagination! Ah, if only —"

She couldn't help gratification flooding through her (*such feeling, such imagination*). "But what?" she demanded. "If only what?"

He looked so stern. "If you were illustrating a fairytale," he said, "this would be one thing. But here I see you again, as with the orchid, inventing variations for our native plants — making these fantasies for a publication which, I had supposed, was to be a serious study of our native flora."

He still had the nerve to lecture her? A married man famous for exponential feats of womanizing and a meddling snoop as well, taking the moral high ground?

Almost anything would be okay but this — okay if he'd bounded across and said what a sweet little faker she was (though she wasn't, not with these), still it would be okay, and she would trust him the way she'd decided moments ago that she would as she'd stepped in the door, and she would take him to see her hidden meadow. But this agonized inner wrenching of his — it filled her mouth with the sour taste of childhood upchuck.

He took a visible breath. He said, "Very well, I will plainly ask why you do this counterfeit work, which does not go at all with the truth of you."

"Why should anything about me disturb you so much?"

"You know!" he said. "You do."

SHE DID.

She'd been holding it off, but right from the first instant on the autostrada, in that first glance, there had been the flash of fate. Rescue was what she'd felt when he came up behind her on the highway. The flare that could burn away the dross of both their lives. Alchemy — however unreasonable and unscientific.

If only he would complete the rescue. The room had begun jittering in the glare of an oncoming migraine from her past.

But he pressed on, saying how fine she was, how talented, saying how devastated he would be if she came to his country with such talent and used this in creating an imaginary place, filled with clever fabrications ...

"I have no idea what you mean!"

Again he said, "You do! You must!" He said she of all people must understand how the beauty of the world was often a responsibility too much to bear, for he had seen this in her paintings.

"Oh, Clare! What I would do to have your ability to capture the world as it truly is, and turn it into an image transcendent. But to have this gift and use it falsely —"

"Falsely!"

He glared, his hair springing wild as he picked up the painting of the orchid. "Then can you show me the place where this grows?"

The room was closing in. "I told you, it grows in there." She pointed to the pile of photocopies.

"Where? In what page?"

Now the faces of the long-ago inquisition were pressing. *Bad. Wicked. Obscene. Ruined.*

"This is sick," she managed to say, bile rising in her throat. "I absolutely don't get how you can come here and make these accusations."

"Because I fear for you!" But he looked lost now, too. "Because I need you." He took a step towards her. "Because I am so lonely. Clare!"

SO LONELY. SHE HAD the impression of his face shearing into pieces at this confession. Oh and how well she knew the way loneliness could leave her feeling branded, shameful.

She thought of the little boy she'd imagined, always overreaching with some grand idea, now grownup and wanting to save not just the endangered world but her too. Tripping up again, mismanaging the whole thing, aware now not only of botching that, but of giving away some disgraceful emptiness in himself.

She wanted to hold the moment while she found the words to set this right. But her body was already spinning out of control, the room spinning too, and sickness burning up into her throat. Her face twisted as she tried to stem this, and she could see him misreading her expression, assuming it was disgust at the shameful part of himself he'd just blurted out. She struggled for control. It was no use. She had to dash out onto the back terrace where her stomach heaved and heaved.

Whatever she was trying to get rid of, she would not. When her breathing settled, she heard him starting his car.

FIVE

The Shades that Absence Has

CLARE HAD EXPECTED THE long-absent Dottore Alfredo Bandinelli to be careworn, pale, and distracted, surrounded by tipping heaps of untended paperwork. Instead, behind a vast polished desk, which held just a single piece of sculpture in deep blue glass, Alfredo Bandinelli was tanned and alarmingly good looking. His eyes held a hooded alertness that sent her own scurrying back to the sculpture. This turned out to be a male torso with a glassy penis butting up against the plinth.

When she came out of his office a half hour later, she felt as if she were emerging from a murky funfair tunnel where strange objects had flown at her in the dark, maybe bats. She tried to figure out exactly what she had learned.

She had clung to the hope that he might have had custody of her uncle's notes and papers, and perhaps — no matter how wrenching — some personal communication her uncle had intended her to have. But there was nothing. Further, not only would there be "some small delay" before the legal complexities regarding the boundaries of her uncle's property could be solved, and consequently a delay in transferring the title, but — alarmingly — there also turned out to be what he called "the small matter of your inhabitants."

She was still trying to get her head around the implications as she started back down the level street. She passed the store where she had bought the yellow dress. A single pair of silk pyjamas graced the window now, the sort that one might slip into late on a night when the yellow dress had been removed by someone else's long, scarred fingers; pyjamas to sip prosecco in, play footsie in, before the whole business started up again; pyjamas intended for an Italian woman who knew what was going on. As it turned out, the yellow dress had been, too — and certainly not for the likes of Clare, who could not spend half an hour with a lawyer without becoming more confused than before. She'd nodded as Alfredo Bandinelli leaned back in his sleek leather chair, made a steeple of his fingers, and talked about those "inhabitants" of hers, "who inform me that your esteemed uncle promised to make provision for them, in perpetuity, to go on living and working on this piece of land which they have only with greatest reluctance been forced to sell to him ten years ago …"

She paused at the window of a *pasticceria,* an Aladdin's cave of piled-up meringues and jewel-like sugared fruit and slabs of nougat, and stacks of the famous *panforte* of the region, in a dozen varieties, pale, dark, peppered, fruited, chocolate-covered, or dusted with a snow of powdered sugar.

A chocolate mousse cake was front and centre.

"In other words," she'd said to Alfredo Bandinelli, "I am the legal owner of Marta and Niccolo Dottorelli's home?"

He'd said yes, that this would with "seeming assurance indeed appear to be so." Therefore should she, "in times of the future," become free, herself, to sell the land, she would be dispossessing the Dottorelli family, contrary to what had been "her esteemed uncle's wishes." Though, true, there was nothing in writing to this effect, there was, all the same, "the burden of their believability in such matters, which has proved to weigh heavily should such disputes be unfortunate enough to proceed to court."

Clare went into the pastry shop and bought the chocolate cake.

She carried it along to the public gardens where she settled on a bench that looked out over the valley.

It was a day of thick-grained coppery light. The far hills had disappeared. Gone, too, was the hill town where the saint had run off with her noble lover. Clare sliced into the cake with the plastic knife she had asked for in the shop. A knife and a plastic coffee spoon. It was surely sinful to compare the saintly woman's predicament with her own. But there was this. Ever since those peculiar, painful moments which ended with Gianni driving away, something had happened in Clare's bones. Not that they had become fragile, leached of love, but that her bones felt crystallized, prey to rays of baleful energy from the great god-awful light years of empty sky. How to explain the need to feed those leached bones? Looking across the valley into the dense coppery mist, she found herself wondering what might happen to another sort of woman who really did hold saintly potential. Santa Margherita's lover died, love died. But, afterwards, what if her transformation truly had been cosmic; what if her bones started picking up holy vibrations like an old-fashioned radio crystal set? For the saintly, of course, that would be food enough. Clare cut another slice of the oozing cake.

Something else had happened. Clare's easy facility with brush and paints had left her. Her work now was stiff and prissy and ultra-correct, and she tore up sketch after sketch.

The chocolate mousse cake was doing its good work. As she dipped spoonfuls straight from the box, the world around looked even more beautiful for being inaccessible behind this thick pane of downright worthlessness.

∽

LATER, AS CLARE DROVE up her lane, she sighted Nikki Stockton's orange van. She didn't see Nikki, until something hit her on the head. The woman was stretched out on a high branch of the old oak tree, that grin of hers hovering up there too. Less than anything just now did Clare, covered in chocolate, want to find Nikki Stockton waiting in a tree. Had she dropped by to relive the awful day at the dig? To make Clare feel worse by trying to make her feel better?

Nikki swung herself down from branch to branch, her wide gypsy-looking skirt poofing out around her like a parachute as she jumped.

On the drive home, Clare had wondered seriously, for the first time really, what on earth she was doing here. Her aunt was after her, demanding that she sell the house, and threatening legal action if she didn't hurry. But even aside from that, how could she, Clare, have imagined succeeding in the project of living here? She was not one of those people who came to foreign places and bought houses and had brilliant insights and wrote amusingly of all the loveable local characters. She'd met two local characters, and they bullied her. She'd fallen in love with a man who tried to bully. Since then she'd been waiting for him to call.

"I hope you'll forgive me for just dropping in," Nikki said, picking herself up from the ground. "That woman who works for you was just leaving on her *motorino*; she said you'd probably be home soon, from your lawyer."

Nothing for it but to ask Nikki in. "And look!" Clare said, "I seem to have this cake. Chocolate turned out to be essential, after meeting with the lawyer."

"I can relate to that. In our experience the whole country is covered in legal documents two miles thick."

She followed Clare down to the kitchen, but luckily refused a slice of cake. Clare would have hated her to see the mess inside the box. She made tea, and poured it into the castle-pattern cups, noticing too late that she'd given Nikki the mended one. Nikki didn't say why she'd come. She sipped her tea and looked around the kitchen with bright pecking eyes.

"How's the work going?" she finally said.

Clare had noticed ink stains on Nikki's hands again. She pictured her in the archaeology lab making drawings of shards and fragments, then engaging in the *magic of reconstruction* that she'd described. She felt sick with envy at the thought that at least Nikki's work must be going fine.

A loud knocking at the arbour door excused Clare from having to say anything about her own work.

THE DRIVER OF A florist's van was holding a long white box a little smaller than a coffin, which he insisted would be too heavy for the Signora, and carried down to the kitchen. When she lifted the lid, the room flared with the light of three dozen yellow roses, emitting a scent of lemon and paradise.

She read the card. Forced a smile. Turned to Nikki with a helpless shrug. "Sir Harold Plank must have got the impression that his Man in Italy didn't behave well the other day. But he should have sent these to you."

Nikki volunteered to cut the stems while Clare fetched the copper ewer from the mantel in the other room. Clare could hear her going at it, while she stood by the fireplace and took deep breaths. Roses. From the wrong person. And there'd been that moment when her heart had ballooned into the stratosphere. She glared around the room to force back stupid tears, then caught the eye of the bronze she-wolf behind the chair, still saddled with that ridiculous lamp. She should throw the thing out.

She joined Nikki in arranging the flowers. No matter what, they were beautiful, though several seemed to have lost their heads. She found herself cheered at the thought that even a rose could lose its head.

᪥

CLARE FOLLOWED NIKKI'S VAN around curve after curve, oak forests on one side, a narrow valley on the other, then down through a little town in the next valley.

"These days I've started painting shadows," Nikki had said to Clare, when they'd finished their tea.

"Shadows?"

"Yeah, I take away the objects and paint just the shadows that they cast. It's fun. Why don't you come and see?"

Nikki and William had purchased their old farmhouse from the Contessa's family ten years before. The land all around the area had once all belonged to Luisa's family too, Nikki said, as they walked up a narrow cobbled path. She pointed out the roof of a much larger villa, just visible through the treetops, where Luisa had grown up. Now Luisa owned just a small stone cottage, even further up the hill, which she used as a retreat for work and study.

They passed under a great fig tree shading the flagged entrance yard. The adjacent tall narrow building was a tobacco drying shed, Nikki said. She and William were renovating it into a guest house for visiting friends.

Inside, waiting at the table, was Luisa di Varinieri herself, drinking a cup of chamomile tea. She scolded Nikki for buying herbal teas when there was chamomile growing just outside, between the stones, and mint as well. She told Clare that her own little cottage was redolent with the sweet curative scent of drying herbs. She said that when Clare finally came to visit their apartment in Cortona, Clare would be most interested to learn more about all such local lore, which she, Luisa, had absorbed while growing up, "as naturally, you understand, as one breathes in the country air."

Luisa launched, then, into the reason for her visit — which was to tell Nikki that she must teach William to behave, at last!

"What do you imagine my father would think, if he knew that the work he had begun — on what was then, of course, his property — should be in peril now because William refuses to concede one iota of his pride. Yes, yes, yes, Vittorio told me about the debacle the other day on Poggio Selvaggio. How idiotic to be rude to Tindhall, then stalk off."

Clare tried to interject on William's behalf. Luisa waved that away. Oh certainly, everyone knew that Tindhall was impossible, she said. But this was not the point. The point was that Nikki would have to teach William better manners in general, because his refusal to suffer fools greatly compounded his troubles.

"And if I may say so," she added, "William should also be a little careful, in future, about his association with young acolytes."

Clare was glad that she'd been standing by the open back door just then, and that she was wearing her camera. She turned away and snapped shots of the view over the fields. A scene came back to her that she'd witnessed earlier, up in the public gardens in Cortona. A young woman and a child had been sitting on a bench across from the playground, the child scuffing pebbles, the woman with her chin towards her chest, the two of them quite separate from all the other mothers and grandmothers who were knitting, talking, giggling on the benches just beside. The branches of the lime trees swayed above, just coming into full heart-shaped leaf. But the bronzed sunlight seemed to cast no shadows, and Clare had a sense of how in this small, supremely beautiful place there would be no secrets, either; this would be the price people who lived here would pay.

Now Luisa was telling Nikki that she would just pop back up to her own cottage and bring down some proper herb teas. She had one made from artichoke leaves, which William should be drinking. She said she insisted that Vittorio drink it. An excellent anti-choleric. She would be back in half an hour.

When she'd driven off in her Cinquecento, Nikki said, "So — are you ready? I'm dying to see what a real artist thinks of my first efforts." She stood with her hands on her hips for a moment, head to the side, sizing Clare up, then pulled down a ladder in the kitchen ceiling, which led to her upper sanctum, she said.

"After you," she said, with a mock bow.

Then, "No. Wait. It's such a mess up there. Give me a minute."

It was considerably more than a minute that Clare waited, listening to Nikki rustling around, opening cupboards, bundling things away.

IN THE ATTIC, FOUR low windows gave onto four different views of the Umbrian countryside — or would have, if the attic had not been crowded with pieces of lumpy furniture stored there ever since various of the houses on the di Varinieri estate had been sold off.

"Luisa still feels she has ancestral rights to the attic," Nikki said. "But these are kind of like company." She opened the lid on an upright piano, played some bars of "Chopsticks," took another of those theatrical bows, then flopped into a high-backed chair. "So anyway ..." gesturing across the room. "What do you say?

In a space cleared by a low west window, vegetables and various types of fruit were arranged on a plank set on bricks: onions with papery skins, artichokes, some ruby plums, an eggplant, golden pears. On an adjoining table, a sheaf of watercolours was loosely spread. The shadow paintings. Not a bit as Clare had tried to imagine as she drove here — not sharp outlines of negative space. Instead these were compositions of deep pooling shades, *all the shades that absence has,* Clare thought — with, between them, just the faintest mottling of shapes that might have been. Evocative and lovely. They caught Clare's heart; then a pinch of envy followed. Nikki was watching her closely. But before Clare could find words for the stirring melancholy effect of these pieces, a downstairs door slammed, and the Contessa was back, calling "Nikki, Nikki!"

"They're so remarkable!" Clare said quickly, "They take my breath away." Nikki brushed past to go back down. Clare leafed through the shadow paintings again, while the voices of the Contessa and Nikki rose and fell just out of range. She heard the two women go out the front door. She looked around the attic, wondering what other work Nikki had stashed away, presumably unfinished pieces she didn't want Clare to see. The door of a cupboard across the room had a corner of something sticking out the bottom.

In Vancouver, Clare had a friend who claimed that when she had people over, first she would fill the mirrored cupboard in her bathroom chock full of marbles, which made a loud betraying clatter when a curious guest opened up the cupboard to have a peek.

Clare stood with her fingers poised above the handle of this cupboard door. It was a corner of wallpaper that protruded underneath, a pale blue background and some sort of trellised pattern; it had been drawn on, Clare could just partly see, with dark inky lines.

Her face.

When she pulled open the door, nothing clattered out except the image of her own face, repeated again and again on wallpaper draped loosely from one of the cupboard shelves, her face worked into the pattern of a climbing rose with fat horny stems, five fleshy leaves, against a grey lattice that also held a nasty-looking bird with an evil eye. She could see all this clearly because of a candle — a burning candle — on a higher shelf inside, which had guttered and then flared as she opened the door.

It was very old wallpaper — probably an end left over from some room in the villa where the Contessa had grown up. As Clare absorbed the shock of what she saw, she had to smile at the thought of what Luisa would say if she knew what Nikki had done to this roll of antique paper which, almost surely, she would still think of as hers. It took just a second more to grasp that the shelf with the candle held an arrangement of other things all associated with herself — not just associated, but hers. Her pen, angled atop another ink drawing of her own face. Really well done, she had to admit, just a few swift lines. But also something that gave her a further start — a blue plastic bead glued to the centre of her forehead like a jewel in the forehead of an Eastern bride. For an instant, she thought it was the bead she'd almost stolen. Could Nikki have caught the moment when she'd held it longingly in her hand, read her expression? Her castle-patterned mug was in there, too. The one Marta had glued together, holding five yellow rosebuds. So that was how those roses lost their heads. And, right below the candle, where it fully caught the light, was the Venetian glass petal that had fallen on Clare's plate that night at Farnham's. She remembered Nikki grinning at her across the table after it had fallen, *Don't blame me!* In the candlelight, the tiny flowers in the glass flared jewel tones and the gold stars cast elongated shadows like figures with stretching arms, seven of them, like a flock of dark angels unexpectedly set free.

CLARE HEARD THE CONTESSA'S car drive away, heard Nikki come back in the door. She blew out the candle. What was Nikki thinking to have a candle in that flammable space; was she mad? She kicked the end of the wallpaper inside and closed the cupboard.

When Nikki got back up the stairs, Clare was examining the watercolours again. She and Nikki looked through the sheaf of them together and discussed the challenges of working in this medium. Nikki said that until she'd been inspired by Clare, she had not attempted any artwork at all, beyond archaeological drawing. Clare asked Nikki how she got those poignant colours, what paints she used?

Terra rosa, Nikki said. Moon glow, raw umber.

HOW COULD CLARE HAVE driven off and said nothing? Nikki would know she'd looked into the cupboard. Had that been the point of asking her over? For her to look?

Or would she know? The candle could easily have gone out on its own. Clare had not taken the pen.

She had hesitated, yes, before she closed the cupboard door, unwilling to leave the pen. What had stopped her?

Certainly there was something very creepy about all this; but marvellous, too. In the way a completely unexpected glimpse into another person could be marvellous, filled with wonders, monsters, the uncanny. What had Nikki intended her to see inside that cupboard? An installation piece? A shrine? Her face — beautifully done, yes — but making of Clare something that she was not. No hint of the struggles and ugliness her face had succumbed to, lived through. Her image, gridded again with that fleshy flower, that ugly bird, but looking supercilious, sublime. She thought of Nikki staring at the painting in her Amazonia book where the writhing *Selenicereus* fastened onto the tree trunk, pulling out its essence. Artists did that. She did that. She hoped she'd left the pen because she had not wanted to take away the instrument vital to Nikki's new work, creepy as that was. But more likely, she'd left it because it had just seemed plain unlucky to be the one who did anything to break off someone else's moment of creative flight.

Much later — all night — the colours of Nikki's shadow paintings pooled in Clare's dreams, and those words ran through the channels of her sleep as if they were the lines of a poem she had forgotten. *Terra rosa, moon glow, raw umber.*

Pizza al Diavolo

THE WORD *TOMBAROLI* WAS in Clare's head when she heard Marta's
morning clatter in the kitchen. *Tombaroli.* As if the word had crept in
under cover of Nikki's shadow paintings or had been lurking in Nikki's
cupboard along with the pen, and this was how the pen had gotten
into Nikki's cupboard. It was not Nikki's fault at all; the *tombaroli*
did it. Clare burrowed further back to sleep, ignoring Marta's clatter
designed to get her up, snuggling as long as she could into numbing
sloth. Since that morning with Gianni, everything she'd done had
been worthless. The idea about an Etruscan magic book was worthless, too cheesy for words. Gone was her ability to paint. She felt
like one of those early flying dinosaurs that might, for a moment,
have managed to lumber into flight, showing off, swooping over its
companions who were getting more and more earthbound as they
munched up the giant ferns, until suddenly it was sidelined by some
abstruse Darwinian imperative and came crashing to the ground. It
did feel like a kind of genuine extinction, a part of her that had been
extinguished — not Gianni's fault, she knew that, but something
in her that for inexplicable reasons had just gone missing, a part of
her psyche.

And now, on top of her other problems — deciding if she was
going to fight to stay on here, fight her aunt, fight Federica Inghirami

if she had to, fight to find herself a new lawyer — she would have to talk to Marta about the information Alfredo Bandinelli imparted to her yesterday. She would have to do so carefully, to ensure that Marta and Niccolo would not think she was planning to dislodge them from their self-imposed duties or their home. This was such a daunting prospect that if Marta had not come into the bedroom with a letter the postman had just brought up the hill on his *motorino*, Clare might have stayed in bed all day.

It was a letter from a New York editor whom she had queried right before she'd left for Italy. She seemed to have persuaded this editor that the lavishly illustrated book exploring ancient magic and herbal lore was a most promising idea. The editor just needed sketches and a detailed outline right away, in order to convince the money people.

Remembering how she'd woken with the word *tombaroli* in her head, Clare decided that perhaps the editor would go for a different, but maybe even more intriguing, slant; this thought stirred her own curiosity. It propelled her out of bed.

MARTA WAS SCRUBBING THE terracotta tiles with borax. Clare asked her to sit down at the kitchen table. "I want to interview you," she said. She made a show of getting out her notebook. "You will be my anonymous source. If you can give me any information, or any suggestions of people I might talk to, I will handle all that with great discretion of course."

She didn't mention anything about the illicit artefacts that Vittorio Cerotti had told her of. She said she had read an article about *tombaroli* back in North America.

Marta stared.

"What I read made a lot of sense to me," Clare said quickly, giving a spin to what Vittorio had told her, as if it might truly be honourable for Italy's artefacts to remain among those Italians who appreciated them, rather than being locked away in the basements of museums.

She'd barely started when Marta began to sneeze. It was the borax, she said. She opened the door to the rear patio and began swinging it back and forth. Then she got down on her knees and continued scrubbing. She knew nothing about what Signora Chiara was asking, she said. Signora Chiara must excuse her because she had still much to do, and tomorrow it was her niece's wedding. "How can I put on my good silk dress with these hands?" She held them out, raw and red, as if their condition were Clare's fault, as if it were Clare who had asked her to start rooting out the baking pan and cake tins from under the stove and now, too, to start piling them beside the sink, as if there was no end of tasks Clare was asking her to do and yet Clare came and bothered with questions about tomb robbers, *Madonna!*

∽

SINCE THAT AWFUL SCENE with Gianni, Clare had not ventured near the meadow.

Once or twice, remembering Vittorio Cerotti's concerns, she'd thought she should double-check if illicit digging had been going on somewhere up there. But that seemed so far-fetched, and the place was tinged now, spoiled by Gianni's accusations, the shipwreck of that scene. It made her queasy still. But with this new idea — and after Marta's strange reaction — she decided she must check back again.

Overnight a sharp wind had cleared the metallic atmosphere. How peaceful the place was. Star of Bethlehem still blossomed, un-trampled, among the hillocks she'd imagined would be tombs; and, as she'd anticipated, the asphodel had produced a blood-red bloom, like a signal, a marker of the nourishing roots that lay below. But then it was the voice of Gianni that she was hearing, *On their streets of tombs as well, the Romans planted the most lovely and fragrant plants to nourish the spirits of the living and to feed the dead.* She saw him spread his hands. She reached out to touch his wrist. He told her that he had made the earth his choice.

As she hiked here, she'd actually told herself that she had rid him from her system, that a new project, a new involvement, would serve to put the final kibosh on the episode. But here he was again, racing through her bloodstream like a dire infection. The thought of seeing him again was hopeless. She was not going to search him out. He was never going to call.

As for the rest, as she explored the field again and all the humps and hollows, she had to admit that there was no secret in this meadow. The lawyer's words came back to her about the *burden of believability*. So believe this, she told herself, seeing the shimmering wealth of meadow life which, if she approached with her sketchbook, she knew would stiffen, rise against her, do everything to repel her advances; believe this: any distracting fantasy about what might lie buried here is exactly that, a distracting fantasy; these bushy mounds are just bushy mounds. Illogically but incontrovertibly, the very lack of illicit digging made that clear. If her uncle had had anything to say to her, if he had left any clue, she would have come upon it by now. It was pathetic that she had allowed herself to get excited about a dreadful oil painting and a message stamped on a plastic mirror.

She sought out the shade of a small umbrella pine on one of those bushy mounds. She felt ancient, older than the stones below her, as she closed her eyes.

∽

A WHISTLING SOUND WOKE her. The one she'd heard before, sometimes at dusk, sometimes in dreams. She sat up so fast that she scraped her cheek on a thorn. *He did have something to say to me. Marta and Niccolo are the ones who know.*

How arrogant she had been; so self-preoccupied.

Marta and Niccolo knew everything about her uncle. If he'd left papers around, Marta would have read them; if messages had come in on his machine, Marta would have played them back; if he'd discovered anything, Niccolo would have spied out his movements and Marta would have read his notes. There would be very little of her uncle's life that those two would not know. They would have seen this as their right. Caretakers, taking care.

Perhaps they had things of his still in their care. Perhaps they had been withholding them until they found out Clare's intentions with the place. Perhaps that was what Marta's crustiness had been about.

WHEN SHE EMERGED FROM the wooded path leading from the topmost olive grove, Clare found herself looking down into a wide flat-bottomed basin where crumbling outbuildings sprawled at the base of a further hill, windows gaping or shuttered, arched and half-barricaded doorways big enough for machines to drive through. The house itself sat higher on the slope, patches of pinky-red stucco flaring in the evening light. Barn fowl were settling for the night. Some dogs barked out of sight. Then Marta came out onto the steps. She was wearing a deep blue smock sprigged with little flowers, as if she'd been cooking. She waved and called Clare into a single large room lit just by the strobes of a television at one end, a blazing fire at the other. Gone was any sense of hostility. Perhaps all that had been needed was the courtesy of a visit from Clare?

Niccolo rose from a deep chair in front of the TV, where he'd been watching a clip of a former prime minister singing. Marta ordered them both to sit, gesturing Clare to the big kitchen table. She took a ball of dough from a blue-striped bowl, flattened it with a yard-long rolling pin, set it on a flat stone among the flames, put an aluminium lid on top and covered that with ashes. "*Pizza al Diavolo!*" Niccolo rumbled from his velvet chair. When Marta took the lid off the bread, he heaved himself up, performed a bent soft-shoe shuffle on his way to get a sausage from the larder, then started cutting it up at the table. He poured out rough, heartening red wine. Marta sliced the hot loaf into eighths, opened each piece and slipped in some sausage, urged them both to eat. The TV was showing a beach scene with palm trees.

"I'VE NEVER TASTED ANYTHING this good!" Clare said.

The fire crackled. Outside the evening now threatened rain, but the room felt safe and cave-like, despite the blare of light and sound coming from the screen, where a handsome man in a silver tailcoat was stepping from level to level of moving platforms, belting out romantic decibels.

"I have been wondering," Clare finally said, after summoning some clear Italian words, "whether my uncle left you anything to keep for me."

Their two blank faces were all attention to the television now.

"Whether he left you any of his things here," she said in a louder, slower voice. "Perhaps asking you to wait until you thought I was ready?"

Marta jumped up, brought a bottle of deep green oil from the sideboard. Niccolo poured some into a saucer, pushed it across to Clare, cut her another wedge of bread.

"Here," he said. "Taste! He has left you this, from the trees that are now yours."

He said she should regard the greenness of the oil. Her terraces were very rare for the quality of soil. This was what her uncle had left, and he, Niccolo, had only hoped ...

He stopped talking, mid-sentence.

THE SINGER HAD BEEN interrupted by a news flash. Two tweedy men were holding up a two-handled vase. The TV lights brought out its smoky black lustre and the fantastic shapes carved into the handles and around the belly in a frieze. The vase had been discovered as it was about to be shipped across the border to Switzerland, the news-reader said. Clare didn't get how or where, because, "*Boh!*" Niccolo went across and turned the television off.

Marta was standing and giving Clare a bony hug. Niccolo was saying he would with pleasure drive the Signora home, because — there was the thunder! Quick! Look! Already the first drops of the storm. No good for Clare to protest that it might be better for her to wait till it was over. He bundled her out into his three-wheeled truck and bucked it down the winding road, which was indeed suddenly awash, the headlights battering against a wall of water, worse than when Gianni had driven her home. Niccolo dropped her at the end of her own short drive. She was soaked by the time she got in.

⁓

NEXT MORNING, THOUGH MARTA came to work, she was quiet, watchful. There must be some great underground warren of unspoken local information, Clare supposed. Someone they knew — or someone in their family, or someone at the wedding they were going to attend today — must be suspected by Marta and Niccolo of being in the business of liberating the country's treasures, as Vittorio Cerotti had said was their excuse.

Marta's silence was so uncomfortable that Clare protested, as nicely as she could, that Marta should not be here today; she should be home getting ready for the wedding. Marta just shook her head and went on sweeping.

"Here, let me give you a hand with that, at least," she said as Marta started shifting the kitchen table.

"No, Signora, there is no need."

"But I don't know where else to go," Clare said, in a mock-wistful voice. "I am temporarily *perplessa.*"

Marta turned on her. She took both Clare's thin white hands in her strong red ones and held them tight. She said that if Clare had lost her way, she should walk down the hill to the church of San Angelo and sit there for a while. Did Clare know that church, by the field where a week ago was the fair? This church had stood there for a thousand years. The stone walls had heard a thousand years of big and little human sin. Even those who did not believe could bow their heads and learn to find their way.

She dropped Clare's hands and crossed herself. "Your uncle, before he left from here the last time, was angry when I told him he must do that. But he was in his last months more lost of heart than ever, always with a temper. I know he did what I suggested. For when he returned that day, he was changed. He came in and sat for a long time at the table." She nodded back towards the other room. "He wrote some things. When I saw his face again, it was calm."

"Do you know what happened to the things he wrote?"

"Beh!" Marta cut her off. "Why do you come and make the questions about his things. I have had Niccolo all night with the migraine because you come into his house and suggest we have something that we should not. What did Signor Kane have in any case that we would want? His furniture? We have the furniture more suited to our likes. His dishes? We have the cups and saucers of our parents! We have all our own things that we like!"

"Oh, no — please! I mean just his papers, his letters, the things he wrote. I was hoping that he had left you those, to keep for me. Because I've discovered nothing here, not one scrap."

"Ah." She softened. Yes, she said, she herself had thought it strange. The night before Signor Kane had left for America, his long table had been cluttered. He had already given Marta his old portable typewriter for her to take to her grandchildren. He had never been modern. That old typewriter was all he'd used, and she had wept when he gave it to her, but he had told her to cheer up; he'd said he was going to buy himself a laptop in the States to use at home when he returned. When she left the house that night all his papers were all over the table, as if he'd been sorting things. When she returned next day, there was nothing. Just some ashes in the fire.

HER UNCLE HAD BEEN angry? *But when he returned from San Angelo that day he was changed?*

Clare did find herself hiking down, thinking she would visit the church. It was unlikely she'd find stray thoughts of her uncle's lingering there; but if the building dated from the time of Charlemagne, maybe some sort of ancient wisdom would seep from its walls.

The roadside was brilliant with the riot of flowers calling attention to themselves, a carpet of purple vetch, plum red snapdragons, clustered spike of *aconitum,* the red-stemmed towers bumbled over by huge black bees. Her fingers itched to take a pencil, a chalk, a brush, even a pen. She thought of Nikki Stockton's fluid lines in ink. What was that pen getting up to this morning?

When she reached the bottom of the hill, she found she couldn't enter the church in her agitated state. Instead, she found her steps turning in a different direction, towards the cell of the hermit whose work she'd come to have a kinship with. So what if the cell was somewhere near the old mill where Luke Tindhall lived. He'd be off on some other jaunt, maybe pursuing that "intriguing little possibility" he'd mentioned to the British women, sneaking around behind the back of his employer.

She started off through the little village. She passed a small run-over snake, its body flattened in the shape of a question mark, its tongue a splash of red. The road climbed through vineyards. In the angle of a terrace wall ahead, she saw a niche with a shrine, and a weathered sign, *Molino di Metelliano,* at the entrance of the lane.

The Temples of Eridu

IT WOULD HAVE BEEN so easy to keep on walking. But he was dressed in rumpled khaki. He looked tumbled by cares. Ahead of him walked two cats on long red leashes, as he came out onto the road. Who couldn't help but laugh at the sight of a man walking cats?

"Luke," she said.

He said, "Clare."

"Nice cats," she said. "Do you take them with you everywhere?"

"Oh for heaven's sake, they're not mine. I'm just minding them for my hosts while they're off in the States. One of my few duties is to take them for walks now and then, so I got it in my head to train them to the leash."

"Good practice. Maybe you can work up to ocelots."

She could have walked right by and skipped all that; instead she stood and watched as he bent down and undid the leashes. The cats trotted back down the lane.

A Vespa buzzed up the road, rattling the silence with its wasp-like shift of gears. In its wake the air hung heavy and super-charged.

He said, "Come on, I'll show you my waterfall."

"I've come to visit the hermit, actually."

"Right this way."

When they came to a sign indicating the path to the hermit's grotto, she didn't point it out. The cats were waiting for him by a little wooden bridge over a stream. The bridge led into a lane where alders and rangy chestnuts arched above. Beyond, on a rise, was a fine old tile-roofed house, with pots of lavender and geraniums and strawberries flanking stone steps. He said this had once been the miller's house. The building behind, by the stream, had been the mill. Two millstones leaned against the wall, wider in diameter than he was tall.

He led her along a narrow path between the old mill and the water, then across a bridge made of a single plank. An amber pool brimmed behind a dam of tumbled rock. The pool was shaded, but one flat rock lay in the sun, and on the far side a lacy fall of water slid from the woods above.

She pulled off boots, t-shirt, jeans. She shed underpants and bra, and dove.

He followed. From the centre of the pool, she turned and treaded water to observe. The water was brown and gold and rippled around her. She didn't care about the nature of his stare, whether or not it was amused, admiring or dismissive, whether it was struggling to reduce her to the triteness of a white swimming insect trapped in the amber of the pool.

He was having troubles with the buttons of his shirt. He was not as cool about this as he would have liked. Maybe that explained the meanness of his stare. He looked great against the backdrop of the rocks and trees, a primitive figure, a centaur: shaggy head and powerful haunches and much black curling body hair, his squat effective-looking penis flopping as he hopped to remove one red sock and then the other. The gorgeous curve of his white bum as it slipped beneath the water, before he pulled her under.

∽

IT IS MUCH LATER, late afternoon, when she wakes in panic, unable for a moment to figure out where she is.

She is staring at a framed drawing, a masculine figure making forceful love to a life-size swan, a tangle of powerful limbs and drooping, submissive wings and feathers. She decides she is still asleep, for this image has filled her dreams, the picture and the question it raises, which seemed in sleep to trouble her above all others. In the myth, wasn't it the other way around? Wasn't it the god who took the form of a swan? That phrase, that question, has circled through scenes not of two figures coupling, but of the ordinary anxieties that often plague her nights, the misplaced handbags, wallets, keys, the cars that refuse to start, the conviction that if she could grasp the conundrum of the drawing, the taxi would arrive. Dressed in a sheet she was waiting for a taxi, and plucking feathers from the woman in the drawing.

The shutters are closed. The upturned slats let in the sound of the stream. On the other side of the bed, Luke stirs, heaves himself up, pads into the bathroom. She recognizes the shape of him with a shock of loss, of further panic, as if in all those misplaced objects jangling through her sleep she saw herself. When she hears him flush the toilet she closes her eyes. He pauses at the end of the bed. She feels his stare.

He stands there for such a long time before he bends, runs one finger up the inside of her leg, twirls her pubic hair, traces the line of her hip, circles first one breast then the other, draws a long slow ticklish line down to the hot bruised part between her legs again.

Without opening her eyes, she says, "So now I understand."

"What baby, what?" These words muffled for now he is kneeling on the end of the bed and setting to work again with his impertinent tongue.

"Why the artist gave Leda the feathers."

He does not want to know, of course; though he was pleased when he first led her in here, when she paused to admire the reproduction on the opposite wall, which he explained was a fresco from the town hall in San Gimignano: a medieval couple in a bath, the woman up to her lovely white-globed breasts in hot water. They'd walked back naked from the pool. He'd worn her underpants on his head, a trophy, a celebration of how he'd held her to the hot rock in the sun, how he'd gone at it and would not let her go until she satisfied him with her scream of pleasure.

What baby, what? Now I understand the artist put the woman in feathers to reveal the situation's true psychology, her submission, ambiguous and cloaked, though maybe the mute swan screamed. She almost has to laugh as she imagines his reaction if she tried explaining all of this. Instead, as the slatted light grows dim they carry on, replaying several other myths she remembers from her peculiar classical education: first pinioned beneath him and wondering if that was the origin of the word; then emulating that poor girl, Io, who for her pains got changed into a cow; and then she tries for Semele, who ended up burned to a crisp.

OH, HOW SHE WISHED. For she gave everything, and the room reeked of promise, just as the whole of the outdoors had earlier. Yet time and again, at the crucial point, the flame in her receded. Even on the rock the first time, the scene slammed shut behind a kind of glass partition; Clare was an observer. This was her old story. But from her first meeting with Luke she'd sniffed the promise of something harsh enough to break her through into the actual moment. In some subliminal layer of her mind she'd imagined all of this perhaps exactly as it happened: rough, wordless, and exhausting. If that was not enough, nothing would ever be enough.

Later when they were sitting in the tub, not unlike those figures in the fresco — when she was up to her neck in the hot water of her lies and excited cries — unexpectedly, *Because I am so lonely* she heard. She felt a sick pang. How could she be where she was? She saw Gianni's hair springing up, wild, as he urged her to be something different, better; his face, oddly broken the way it had looked just before she ran out her kitchen door.

I am so lonely.

"Scram!" she said out loud.

Luke said, "Hey. I haven't washed my willy yet."

She turned back to the other one, the real one — the one who peered no further than her slippery surface — and tried to push him under. They wrestled, covered in bubbles, and ended up slipping around on the bathroom tiles in a new sort of embrace, both of them laughing, overwhelmed, delighted.

LUKE COOKED SPAGHETTI TOSSED in garlic and oil. She grated a mountain of parmesan. They drank much of a two litre cardboard box of wine and ate the pasta and then a carton of lemon *sorbetto* he found at the back of the freezer. He poured them both a fine large brandy, which they carried back to bed. They lay in the dark and sipped their drinks by the pale light of the moon sifting through the slats of the shutters. "So tell me my proud beauty ..." he began.

The next thing she knew, it was morning.

∾

CLARE WOKE TO THE sound of Luke splashing in the shower. Her head ached. Her limbs ached. What remained of her brain was mush. She forced herself back into the web of sleep till the smell of coffee filtered through.

The hot water was used up. Her clothes were out by the pool. She trailed into the kitchen wearing the shirt he'd lent her the night before, her head throbbing. Luke was padding around barefoot, wearing an unbuttoned shirt and thick yellowy-white underpants.

"Aren't you a pretty bird," he said. He took a blue-striped bowl and poured it half full of espresso, half full of steaming milk. "Here, get this inside of you." He pulled on a blue-striped butcher apron. "I'm going to make you a first-rate fry-up, girl."

She took one caffeine-laden sip, followed by another. She realized she was starving. And remembered something. The moment came back to her, from just before she'd crashed into sleep, *So tell me my proud beauty* ...

It had been about her uncle. She remembered bits of it now, his pretend-joshing and only half-coherent attempts to steer towards the matter that was all anyone cared about, before he'd collapsed into snores.

Luke was holding the egg carton, demanding, "One or two?"

She said, "I don't suppose you've got any chocolate ice cream stuck away in the back of that freezer?" It turned out that chocolate ice cream, on toast with bacon and syrup, was the precise fuel she needed.

"SO TELL ME MY proud beauty," she said when breakfast was over, "Where exactly were you when you said you were in Rome?"

It was almost sweet to see him squirm.

"Come on," she persisted. "My spies are everywhere, you turkey. I happen to know you were in Turkey. And it had something to do with your discovery at that dig in Iraq, didn't it? Something you'd found that dated back thousands of years, that you were telling those tweedy British women about."

He tried to pretend he didn't know what she meant.

She sat quietly and stared, the memory flashing back as she waited, of how her uncle had taught her to be very quiet just like this as they flicked their fishing lines into the pool where the big cutthroat swam. She waited. She could glimpse Luke's secret swimming when he met her gaze. He half wanted her to see.

The project Luke had joined involved a Neolithic village site north of Baghdad, where the earliest level of habitation dated back roughly to 7000 BC. The team's mandate was to assess and record damage from the recent war, and take some protective measures. But the director had covertly nobbled a U.S. military squad to do a bit of heavy digging, before that group got shipped home. A shocking business, Luke said, and heaven only knew what damage might have ensued if the Heritage Bureau had not got wind of what was going on.

Luckily before that, one afternoon, Luke — he fisted his chest to emphasize the Lukeness of the matter — braved the perishing temperature during siesta time (three in the morning was the start of a normal work day) to explore on his own.

He followed the remains of a mud brick wall at the bottom of the pit the backhoe had hacked down to the lowest village level, and then he, Luke, accidentally struck a corner brick with his trowel in a way that produced a hollow sound.

It would have been unconscionable, of course, to strike it further, to break it open. Yet somehow, as he tried gently to pry the brick loose, it fell to pieces anyway. What he was looking at among the crumbled clay was a rough circle of obsidian, with a polished surface so undamaged that even in the deep shade of the pit he could clearly see his face in the black volcanic glass.

A mirror of an advanced craftsmanship that could only have come from somewhere other than this modest village culture. The obsidian surely from the volcanic mountainous area of eastern Turkey, and the making of it too. An almost identical one had been found at Çatalhöyük, with a similar convex and exceptionally polished planar surface.

A mirror from Anatolia, found at a level at least two thousand years earlier than any other obsidian item had been found in Mesopotamia.

When he lifted the mirror, he found more evidence that in the earliest of times, trade had seeped down the Tigris from a far more advanced culture to the north. He found a clutch of tiny stoppered jars and a nest of copper beads.

CLARE SHOOK HER HEAD, imagining the moment: Luke crouching at the bottom of that hole, oblivious to the murderous heat.

"But then all those finds got commandeered by the Iraqi authorities?" she said. "I'm sure that's fair. But still, I hope you got pictures."

No such luck. Just as he was gathering the pieces, a shadow fell across the pit, and next thing the director was scrambling down and stuffing them into various pockets of his khaki shirt. That was the last Luke saw of that little hoard.

A funny look crossed his face. He reached into one of his shirt's many pockets. "Though I do keep just this with me, for luck — and inspiration."

It was a tiny black jar, acorn-size.

He twisted out the stone stopper, waved the jar under Clare's nose.

For a moment, sharp and poignant, the Gardens of King Herod, with their precious balsam, floated through the bacon-smelling kitchen.

The vial contained a still-potent residue of perfume made from the fabled terebinth tree, he was telling her, a tree native to those same Anatolian uplands, whose resin had been coveted from earliest times as a base for perfume, for its healing properties, and for more mundane uses as well, such as a caulking for boats. "The same ruddy boats that brought that little bundle of exotic goods down the Tigris in the first place from what were then the forested copper-bearing Anatolian uplands," he said.

What this meant — he'd had the spark of insight right there, in that sweltering hole, though he had not told a single other soul to this very day — what this meant was that he, Luke, had likely stumbled upon not just evidence of trade in luxury goods coming down from the north at a far earlier date than anyone had so far postulated, but evidence of a thriving, trading, manufacturing, and very ancient city somewhere up in Anatolia, so far undiscovered.

HE'D HAD NO CHANCE to follow up this hunch. After Qal'Jalam, the business of earning a living raised its head again, and the opportunity with the Plank Foundation was too good to pass up.

He'd spent months, though, poring over maps, archaeological records, topographical information. Most interestingly, reports from the fairly recent discoveries at Cayönü and Göbekli Tepe. There'd been some hoo-ha about the latter — sensational carved stones and T-shaped megaliths had been discovered, indicating perhaps the world's earliest temple — and theories that the area might have been the location of the original Garden of Eden. Still, it was a site that had drawn together the scattered upland population of hunter-gatherers and early farmers for ceremonies, going back some twelve or thirteen thousand years. Think of it, he said — seven thousand years earlier than Stonehenge!

THINK OF IT, INDEED!

"So that's what took you to Turkey the other week," she said. "You finally grabbed a chance?"

He waved that away. It was all much more complicated.

A few months before his Tuscany assignment, on a stroke of luck, he had been sent out from London to Ankara on a small mission for Harry Plank. Then he'd rented a jeep and driven east into Diyarbakir Province, and on towards Lake Van. By then, after considerable correspondence with the local director of antiquities who was an old Cambridge chum, he knew exactly where he wanted to go.

"Which was?"

He put a finger to his lips. "The walls have ears."

So somewhere out there he had, that very first afternoon, spotted a large dry grass-covered hill that was somehow different from all the other dry grass-covered hills between the dirt road he'd taken and the blue-green rise of the Anti-Taurus Mountains. He'd bumped off across barren fields which in Neolithic and Chalcolithic times would have been green and lush, he said, and the hills densely timbered.

They'd had it all, he said. The inhabitants of his unknown city — evidence of which he almost immediately discovered, though once again he put off detailing what that was — had cornered the market not just in copper from those mountains, and obsidian, and perfumed resins, but in timber. The forests had been exploited there from at least 10,000 BC, he said, and there was ample burned evidence in smaller settlements of timbers used for foundations, roof beams, ladders, furniture.

They'd had it all. "But getting and spending we lay waste our powers."

They'd cut it down. They'd traded it away. The climate changed.

Perhaps for that very reason, the worshippers at Göbekli Tepe had buried their shrines and moved away, and Luke's city too had sunk back to be buried in brush and grass and sand blown by the winds of ten thousand years.

AS HE TOLD CLARE this — and then as he got really going, broadening the topic, taking her on a whirl though ancient Mesopotamia — it was almost as if he were addressing an entire lecture hall. Clare found herself whisked past glimmerings of ancient civilizations that still throbbed beneath the ravished sands of poor benighted modern Iraq. His word, "throbbed." Ruins pulsing with messages from thousands of years ago, where so much still remained to be discovered as excavation pushed the threshold of civilization further and further back. He gestured as he talked, and she saw the White Temple of Uruk, its high platform where the peoples of the Tigris had been able to climb closer to their gods, and the temples of Eridu, built one upon the other, where in the debris of one of those temples excavators quite recently had come upon the very roots of the language which would allow the many civilizations of the region to communicate over the next three thousand years. "The roots of cuneiform. Do you get the importance of that? My point is how the centuries recede before us as we dig, and how much remains for us to learn.

"So," he said, turning his alarmingly blue eyes on her. "Now, far north in Anatolia, there is evidence of a major urban centre with the essential markers of true civilization: a priesthood, commerce and trade, highly skilled craftsmanship, dating even from before Hamoukar in Syria, further proving that Mesopotamia was not the cradle of civilization after all. And that is going to knock the smile off a lot of smug academic faces!"

He'd been writing back and forth to his Turkish Antiquities contact ever since, hoping that no one else would get the official okay to excavate in that area until he got the chance to firm things up. Then just after Clare arrived in Tuscany, indeed the night he drove her home after the party at Ralph Farnham's, he'd found an email waiting for him from his friend in Diyarbakir, saying that the former director of the debacle at Qal'Jalam had been snooping around the area. His Turkish friend said that if the Plank Foundation was serious about exploration in the area, Luke had better hurry out and get started on the formalities for getting a permit. So Luke hopped a plane for Ankara next day.

"And?"

Once again he put a finger to his lips, glanced half-seriously around as if the walls really might have ears, then refused to say more.

LATER, WHILE HE WASHED up, he made her sit back and take it easy. She studied his feet on the tiles. The way his toes were crumpled in, as if he'd had to wear outgrown shoes when he was a child. His sturdy legs were a little bowed. Early rickets? What was his background? There had been Cambridge, she knew; he'd told her that his focus had been on the Middle East even then, pursuing the question of urban origins. But for some reason he'd cut his ties with "sodding academe." Then for a time the only way to get out to the Middle East had been to work at excavating "sodding sodden Roman forts" in the British winters, to earn enough to enable him to hitch out on proper expeditions in the summer. At some point there had been a spell when he'd worked as curator in a museum of Stone Age objects in Paris. But the prospect in Anatolia was something he'd been hoping for all his life.

"So what's stopping you?" she asked. "The place you've investigated sounds like something that would be a natural for the Foundation. So what happened when you popped over there? Come on!"

Little by little it came out. It wasn't the walls that might have ears, it was Sir Harold Plank. Plank had no idea that Luke had been putting forward the Foundation's interest in a dig in Turkey. Plank was completely focused on the Etruscans. It was going to be a long and delicate process to get him to broaden his interests and his resources to take on the Middle East. Luke's trip had been to try to keep things gently simmering along till Plank got the Etruscan bee out of his bonnet. But now the Antiquities Bureau in Ankara was pressing to get things firmed up.

"Harry will never go for it. Not until —"

A glass slipped from his hand and hit the tiles. He waved her to stay sitting as he went to get the broom. He kept his face turned away from her as he swept up the glass.

"Listen. I have to be honest with you about something," he finally said.

She got up and took away the broom. "Let's not do the confession thing," she said. "I've got something to show you, instead."

ᴄᴈ

"WHAT THE FUCK?" LUKE said, when Clare led him to the gate into the woods. "Christ! You're not getting me to go back out there. I barely made it out of there once, chased by some goddamn dog."

"Don't worry. I'll keep you safe."

The stream was still rampaging. She tried to point out the grooved rocks. He sniffed. Was that a sceptical sniff? She was nervous now. It had seemed obvious earlier to bring him here; he was the only knowledgeable person she could safely share this with, who had a reason, a need to investigate her theory, and a need to keep it quiet. But it was all starting to look foolish, even to her.

The terrain was rough and slick; halfway up he fell in up to his knees. When they got to the meadow they squelched their way to the far end. She pointed out the mounds, faltering as she told him her entire speculation.

He walked around, saying nothing. It started to rain. He poked the ground here and there, still sniffing.

She said, "So? But?"

He said, "So your idea is that for two-and-a-half thousand years, no one else has had the light bulb go off that maybe these bumps were worthy of digging into?"

"Well —"

"Never mind," he said. "We'll give you an A for aiming high. Christ, I think I'm catching a cold."

BY THE TIME THEY'D clambered back down, it was late afternoon. Clare made hot lemon and grappa. Without speaking, Luke took his drink and crawled under the duvet in the big bed. What a bust the whole thing had been. He'd made her feel foolish. Why?

We'll give you an A for aiming high.

She realized how important to her it had been, her secret, which had kept glinting underneath all the other things that had been going on, glinting even more brightly as her ability to paint posed such frustration. The secret of my meadow. She wished she had kept it a secret. At least she'd still have it.

She lay down on the couch in front of the empty fireplace. When she woke, Luke's clothes were gone and so was Luke. The knobby walking stick was missing from the bucket by the kitchen door.

HE'D LEFT THE GATE ajar. No, he certainly hadn't been born on a farm. Where had he grown up, with that mix of upper-class and rough in his voice? She pictured a boy raised in the impoverished smugness of a vicarage somewhere, learning to toughen up fast in the local school. She squelched along the path. She saw his footprints in the mud. He'd been quick. Maybe he hadn't slept. Maybe he'd pretended he was sick. He had torn and scattered the vegetation along the stream in his rough ascent. When she spotted him he was poking at one of the mounds with that stick. She watched him poke here, poke there, then clamber from one mound to another, peering towards the spot from which the fortress could have been seen on the opposite hill if the trees weren't there.

She felt sick, and at the same time sick with excitement. So he did think there might be something worth exploring here. But he hadn't wanted to let on. Two could play that game.

"Hello!" was all she said when she went over. "You've been having second thoughts?"

"No no. Just another little poke around."

What a rat.

SHE DECIDED TO FIND out more about this person, this "simple Stone Age man" as he'd called himself at one point yesterday. When they got back to her place, she heated a pot of Marta's soup — how had she ever lived without it? — and served it with a bottle of Harold Plank's Brunello. Over the meal, she asked him to tell her more about himself.

He loved that. His apparent apprehension that she was going to accuse him dissolved. He told her about growing up as what he called "a suspect brainy type" in his rough Midlands school; he was the lad who'd read all of Homer in Greek before he got to Cambridge. Her heart softened, and she grew tense for him as he launched into a mixed, bitter and nostalgic reverie about his Cambridge days. How when he arrived he'd found himself in a college that took mainly those from tony boarding schools, the type who had their own packs of hounds; how on his first night of candlelight dining in college he'd been the only one who had not known what a dinner jacket was. Later, he transferred to another college where he'd come to cut a rather posh figure on his own terms. Posh was fine if you did it on your own terms — wearing a dinner jacket and bare feet to garden parties; or becoming known as someone who always had their beer "on silver." But the best had been the fizz of ideas, the ferment of brilliant minds, the hours spent with the best and brightest, tossing around theories and brilliant insights. She got whiffs of beery evenings at a favourite pub; spicy blasts from an Indian place he called "the dear old Taj"; the jangle of bouzouki from someplace else; and the dense murk of late night college rooms where the talk went on and on.

He loved the chance to relive it all again, as their own night wore on, while she stalked through the forest of his recollections.

So why had he left the academic atmosphere that clearly meant so much to him? Something in his life gone wrong? Perhaps not one thing? Maybe all along he'd dug his own pitfalls. But the lost city in Anatolia was supposed to make up for all of that?

Now he snored in the big bed. Clare stared into the empty hearth.

∽

CLARE WOKE BEFORE DAWN, on the sofa. She tiptoed past the closed bedroom door and was about to start downstairs to warm up in a bath, when she heard Luke talking on his cell phone. Even in Italian, even half-whispered, the words came through with British clarity and resonance. He was arranging to meet someone down at the coast. At Tarquinia. To pick up high-tech equipment for archaeological exploration. A job that must be done very quickly but discretely, to keep the authorities unaware.

Clare crouched, listening through the crack beneath the door.

He planned to set off within the hour. And yes, *allora, grazie grazie,* he was very glad his *good friend* understood the complexities of this situation, how it was essential to keep this matter *secret in the extreme*, because *the vultures were out there.*

"I have told no one," he concluded. "No, not even Harold Plank. I will assuredly come alone."

She heard a little under-the-breath satisfied whistling as he hung up.

It was excellent to barge in while he still sat there, naked, cross-legged on the bed; to see his eyes widen, to see him wondering how much she might have heard. To gather up all his scattered clothes and throw them out the patio door.

"What the hell?"

"Bastard!"

"Hang on!"

"Get out of here. Go and feed your goddamn cats."

Excellent, to see him attempting dignity, even ferocity. "For fuck's sake, I don't have to listen to this."

"Right. You don't. And if you ever try to set foot on this place again I will sick the Carabinieri on you, *and* the devil's dogs!"

Under the Earth They Began to Sing

TARQUINIA! THE CITY OF the painted tombs. The place that had shimmered on the edge of Clare's imagination all her life, and doubly so since she'd begun imagining what might lie under her own meadow's hilly mounds. Tarquinia, where the little tombs had brilliant frescoed walls showing scenes of banquets, music, dance and sport, of love and death and the afterlife, scenes portraying the Etruscans — the wealthy ones at least — as they had lived through their predestined generations, in opulence and splendour, under the shadow of the knowledge of their numbered days.

Luke had thought he could persuade her not to go along with him?

When they both cooled down, he tried to convince her that of course he'd been going to tell her of his plan. The reason he didn't want her along was that the world of Etruscology was such a small one. Everyone would know she was Kane's niece. The eyes of the *clandestini* were everywhere.

"Think about what happened with old Lerici," he said.

"Who?"

Carlo Lerici, he said. "A retired industrialist back in the 1950s, who invented a way to discover which humps and hillocks actually contained unrifled tombs. Before long, everywhere Lerici's little

scientific entourage went the hills were alive with wandering shepherds, and bingo — a rash of looted tombs."

"I don't think I'd exactly attract that much attention."

"Don't kid yourself that you're indistinct."

The purpose of his subterfuge, he insisted, was to provide her, as
owner of the land, an opportunity to assess whether her property did
harbour anything worth exploring, without at present disturbing either
the land or the authorities. Because she should understand that when
it came to digging ruins, everything belonged to the State. Naturally,
if anything significant came to light, he would make sure they called
in the proper authorities right away — and the police too, he said, to
provide protection. But it was smart to get a look at how the land lay,
"before we get buggered up in the great Italian bureaucratic mire!"

He talked, as he gathered up his clothes, still imagining he'd be
going on his own.

She went into the kitchen and cut eyeholes out of a plastic shop-
ping bag, pulled it over her head, tied it round her neck with a string.
He was bending over a map when she came back.

"Time for me to get moving," he said, without looking up.

"Great. I'm ready. If I'm travelling incognito, I figure this should
work."

∽

DRIVING TOO FAST AND in silence, Luke threaded the tiny lanes at the
bottom of the hill, took the road towards Ossaia, turned on the radio.
The song she'd heard that night with Gianni began to play. She
reached over and turned it off. They branched across the plain towards Montepulciano, took a long diagonal under that city's walls,
then around many further curves; past woods and upland meadows
dotted with fluffy sheep; past Pienza, designed by a Renaissance
pope; past San Quirico, careening through countryside that offered
such heart-lifting vistas that finally Clare couldn't keep up her side of
the huff any longer.

"What exactly is this equipment we're going after?" she asked. "How does it work?"

In that superior tone of his, he said that his contact was rounding up instruments that "utilized several different modalities."

"Like what?"

Magnetic survey, he said. Perhaps some old-fashioned resistivity. Maybe a spot of GPR. It was technical.

"I'm pretty technical, too."

"Hmmm." The big hand lifting from the wheel. The snake ring glinting. The hand hesitating, then settling hopefully on her thigh. "I noticed."

"You don't know anything about me."

"I know what I like."

The sky was blue. Another castled town popped up on the horizon. They were going to the sea.

They raced through a landscape that kept changing every few miles, scenes now tidy and ordered, now wild. They crested a ridge. Lake Bolsena lay below, a lapis oval set in a ring of hills and woods and golden cliffs. Luke said he knew a small hotel there where they would spend the night. She pictured a room with a balcony, bougainvillea, dinner under the stars. Finally they swung off onto a much quieter road, a straight white country road where ripening wheat glittered under rows of olive trees, the land sloping down to the distant sea, hazy, purple-blue. Tarquinia appeared ahead on a rise: massed buildings, a spire. In a field on the outskirts were many narrow tile-roofed huts, like rows of garden sheds. This was the famous necropolis, Luke said; those were the tombs. The huts were to protect the stairways leading down.

"Ah, and there's Cerotti. Bang on time."

"You don't mean *Vittorio* Cerotti! Luisa di Varinieri's husband?"

"Who else?"

So the august inspector of archaeology himself was Luke's mysterious contact — now waiting to put Luke in touch with some unnamed person who was supplying the exploration equipment?

Cerotti did not look in the least perturbed to have Clare turn up. Perhaps the need for secrecy was all in Luke's mind, the prying eyes of the *clandestini* too.

VITTORIO OFFERED TO SHOW her around the necropolis until it was time to go along and meet the anonymous supplier.

"First I will introduce you to a *tomba* that reflects a period late in the history," he said, leading them down steep stone steps. "This will illustrate the sense of fatalism and despair that was felt at the time of imminent collapse of the culture."

The air became clammy, warmer. He paused, turned back.

"But you will imagine the surprise that greeted the rediscovery of these paintings. Our Etruscans for centuries so silent, their cities vanished, their cemeteries the haunt of wandering shepherds. Yet suddenly, these long-dead people from underneath the earth began to sing!" He flung out his arms, as if about to conduct a choir.

At the bottom of the steps, they were brought up short by a heavy pane of glass; it was necessary protection, for just the breath of observers could cause damage to the painted walls. Vittorio pressed a switch. He pointed out a figure with a bearded profile not unlike his own.

"Here we see Charun with his large hammer persuading the dead man to go through the door to the underworld, helped by his friend the blue demon with the snakes. The snakes also have beards."

He added that he had recently, in *Studii Etruschi,* published an article about those bearded snakes.

On the frescoed walls much of the paint had peeled away, yet the effect was eerily brilliant, the rotting green of the hook-nosed Charun, the virulent blue of the demon in a toga that was the rusty red of clotting blood, the spotted serpents coiled around his arms. Easy to imagine the awe this would have caused by torchlight as a procession entered to lay out another family member on one of the stone beds already holding the remains of others, those uncanny brilliant figures flickering in the torchlight. Clare peered in fascination, but Luke glanced at his watch, worried about the appointment with the still-mysterious supplier. Vittorio was happy to answer Clare's questions though, and to expound at length about the pigments the painters would have used: the dark tones derived from oxides, by-products of mining activities in the Tolfa hills, and blues in part from copper (a recipe lost since Roman times), the greens from malachite. The paints, he emphasized, would have been very expensive, very rare.

When they emerged, he turned on Clare fiercely. "When you write of our Etruscan use of colour," he said, "you must understand it was linked with prestige and status in the eyes of the people. It is important to state how the colours themselves have been used politically, as symbols to express power."

"What was that all about?" Clare whispered, as Vittorio strode ahead along the gravel path. Luke said that Vittorio was an old Marxist, still stuck in the school determined to politicize archaeology, which made his position in the Soprintendenza difficult, perhaps even shaky these days, given a change of wind.

"Which makes things good for us," he said.

Next, Cerotti led them down into the Tomb of the Bulls, where he expounded on the political implications of the scenes of buggery in the pediment. Clare couldn't help egging him on as she took notes, though Luke tugged at his hair in impatience. When they emerged, he pulled her aside. "I don't suppose you'd care to stay here in the necropolis like a good little researcher, rather than coming along any further and for sure fucking the whole thing up?"

"How much time will we have to come back here, after?"

"None."

In truth, Clare was glad to stay back alone. She peered into as many tombs as were accessible to the public, fascinated. They had been cut out of solid rock, yet mimicked real houses of the living, stone ceilings cut and painted to resemble wooden beams — even one sprigged with tiny flowers like a wallpapered bedroom ceiling — another that gave the impression of a tented pavilion, showing trees beyond the tent openings, and a chorus of revellers dancing through, women in see-through floating garments, men in wrap-around skirts held by belts of shells and flowers. She wandered and dreamed that something of such remarkable delight might lie beneath the surface of her own meadow, waiting to burst from the earth to sing.

Cat Among the Pigeons

BY THE TIME LUKE returned to pick Clare up, he no longer felt comfortable stopping for a night, not with all the equipment in the car. The backseat was crammed full of cartons and odd-looking carry cases and bundles wrapped in lumpy plastic, which he'd been unable to squeeze into the trunk.

"That's an awful lot of gear," she said, as they drove away from Tarquinia. "How are we going to pack it all up to the meadow?"

He said they'd only be taking selected items, once he'd got it sorted.

"Like what?"

A long silence.

"Like what?" she said again.

He said for goodness sake he'd have to take another look at the terrain first. His tone was so grudging that Clare started wondering if he was not as familiar with that equipment as he'd like. After another silence he said that electrical resistivity would be one method they would use. The Etruscans tended to pile loose earth around the entrance after a tomb was sealed. Loose earth was more likely to retain water. Ergo, lower electrical resistance.

"Ergo a light bulb goes off in the prospector's head suggesting that's the place to dig."

He started drumming his fingers on the wheel.

"Listen," he finally said, "I've been thinking." He broke off, ran his hands through his hair. "I've been giving thought to how we should manage things."

"The exploration?"

"Well of course that," he said. "But also ..." His voice trailed off. The drumming started up again. They were on a small country back road. Abruptly, he pulled to the side. He turned and looked at her, a long unnerving look. Finally, "Christ!" he said, "Tindhall, get a grip." He shook his head, hit his fist on the wheel, pulled back onto the road. Some miles passed.

The fact was, he finally said, that Harry Plank had been onto him from the beginning about finding a toehold in Tuscany. Now Plank was interested in purchasing her property.

"I thought Harold Plank hated travel."

"He does, but if it turns out that we were on to something, Plank will want to be in on the kill."

"The kill."

"You know, like with the opening of King Tut's tomb at Luxor. Lord Carnarvon arriving just in time to be photographed." He frowned, considering this. "Of course, Carter delayed opening the tomb didn't he? He waited for Carnarvon's arrival."

Clare had figured out, of course, that the roses, the Brunello, all of that, hadn't really come her way because of her. Like everyone else — more than everyone — Plank did want in on the kill. From the moment she'd turned up in London, probably, Plank had seen her as his lead to whatever it was her uncle had discovered, and had set *his man Tindhall* to the task of getting her lined up, little knowing that Luke had an agenda of his own. And, in a sacrifice to British archaeology, as Luke had merrily put it to those loathsome tweedy types, Luke had undertaken the task.

But he'd kept buggering it up. That night when he drove her home, shining his flashlight in her face, then yanking her out of there, *Right, come on!* That day at the dig, making sure the whole thing went wrong. Why? Was that the way so many things in his life went wrong, starting with his time in *sodding academe*?

And I'm as much of a mess-up as he is, Clare thought; maybe that's the sad but undeniably sizzling truth that gets us going.

A few minutes ago, when he'd pulled off the road back there, so nervous before putting Harold Plank's plan to her, she'd imagined she picked up something else in his stare. She'd been shying away from thinking what might come of it if she did not take care. But now she couldn't help asking. "You know that night when you drove me home from Ralph and Federica's? What was that about?"

"What do you mean?"

"You know what I mean."

"Too much to drink." He shrugged.

"Don't give me that."

"Not my finest hour."

"So?"

So in a nutshell, she'd called it right.

He confessed that when Harold Plank assigned him the project of buttering up the botanical lass, he'd obediently read her bio, leafed through her book, brushed up on the history of botanical art, culled a useful phrase or two. He'd studied the black-and-white author photo. The woman was a considerable stunner, which surely meant that in London Harry Plank would have exercised his *droit de seigneur.* But Luke figured he was owed a bit of payback for the way he'd been damn near killed by Kane's dogs.

Then he'd watched Clare during dinner, a young woman having the insouciance to turn up wearing a flashy western belt and boots and jeans among the self-referential Inghirami, implying they were no more fearsome than any other tribe she'd met on her travels! *Well now Tindhall, lucky dog,* he'd started to think. *This one's worthy of a little tussle in the name of British archaeology.*

"That's all pretty sick," Clare said. "But it doesn't exactly explain why you dumped me, more or less, once you'd got me alone in the woods."

It was hard to explain. When he'd switched on the torch to take a small preprandial peek, there were those eyes of hers, wide and troubling as the sodding Sargasso, eyes that could sink a man if he wasn't careful.

"We don't have to worry about you sinking though," she said, hoping she was right.

AT THE NEXT INTERSECTION, a tractor turned out of a farm gate right in front of them. Luke banged his hand on the wheel. "Oh sod it! Bloody hell."

"Come on. It can't be going all the way to Cortona."

They would never know. Luke pulled out into the smallest gap in the oncoming traffic, squeaked past in a blare of horns.

"Anyway, don't imagine for a moment," he said, "that Harry Plank won't set aside his fear of flying to be on hand when the moment of discovery comes. It would all reflect more brilliantly on Harry if the dig took place on property he owned."

"And all this would reflect brilliantly on you. Re: Project The Anatolian Gig."

Luke shrugged.

"I thought you said that if there did turn out to be any remains on my place, I wouldn't be able to sell — at least not for years and years — till a whole archaeological bureaucratic jumble got sorted out."

"Harry's the sort of bloke who can usually find a way."

A FEW MINUTES LATER, when they were twisting through low green hills, Luke said, "Take a look in your side mirror, will you?"

"The Audi? Why not pull over and let him pass?"

"Not a bad idea."

The car swept past. A red Fiat was right behind, which slowed as Luke slowed, until he pulled over onto the verge and let it pass. "That should set the cat among the pigeons," he said, with satisfaction. Round the next bend, the Fiat turned off onto a side road heading east, skirted a rise and disappeared. He tapped the map. "How does that road link up with ours? When will we see him next, do you suppose? We don't want to lose him altogether."

"What's all this about?"

So much had been odd. His vagueness about the equipment he was after, the techniques for its use, even the meeting he'd gone off to with Vittorio Cerotti. What if they'd just gone for a beer? What if he was in the grip of grand delusion? What if she tore open those bags back there and they were full of plastic egg cartons or table legs, not archaeometric equipment?

Just as she was seriously weighing this, she saw the same red Fiat preparing to nose out of an oncoming junction ahead. After they passed, it allowed another couple of cars to go by and then rejoined the line behind them.

"Good for them," Luke said. "Once we get to the autostrada of course the fun will begin. There should be two or three more, changing guard."

HE HAD SET THIS up, he said, because, even without her along, he had no way of getting hold of the equipment without word seeping out. It was better to let the word get out, allow themselves to be followed. After that, he would set up a decoy in the low hills behind Lake Trasimeno, not far from Sanguinetto, a spot that was one of the few remaining pieces of land that Luisa di Varinieri's family had not sold. That was where they would unload all the equipment they themselves did not intend to use, and store it in an old shed there.

"But what about Vittorio Cerotti? He's bound to tell his wife. Is Luisa in on this too?"

"You underestimate me."

He explained that Vittorio Cerotti was one of those contrarians who maintained that the hilltop of Cortona had not been a major Etruscan settlement, at least not until very late, almost into Roman times. According to Vittorio, early Etruscan settlement had been limited to the lower slopes, with a few princely villas controlling the rich trade routes around the base of the mountain and leading into what was now Umbria, towards the Tiber.

"Your uncle's newspaper column about the Etruscan paving seems to have confirmed this for Vittorio, and nicely bolstered his theory that the early elite settlement extended into the low hills above Trasimeno — right into his wife's family property, as luck would have it. But he's never had the funds or backing to explore this. Which is why he's selflessly agreed to aid the Plank Foundation in purchasing equipment for a preliminary snoop around, on the understanding that when anything does officially turn up, he'll get a good chunk of the credit."

"But you don't think there's anything there at all?"

Luke gave one of those shrugs, this time with both hands off the wheel.

Once they'd turned onto the autostrada, the red car did not reappear; but Luke began to justify his suspicions by telling her tomb robber tales. How destructive these people really were, how they searched for any promising hump or hollow, even certain types of flowers, probing the earth with iron rods, breaking through into tombs with rough blows, the ancient stonework caving in, the contents looted and torn out of context. The need for secrecy was not paranoia on his part.

"Who said anything about paranoia?"

"I know what you've been thinking."

"What I'm thinking is that you're much more interested in the archaeology of this region than you let on," she said. "And here you told me that you're a totally Stone Age man at heart."

He gave a noncommittal snort.

"What does a Stone Age man exactly do?" she said. "Officially, I mean."

"Don't tempt me." His hand returned to her knee.

AS THEY HURLED ON up the autostrada, he began telling her about the work he really loved — using, as an example, a period when he'd worked at a private museum in Paris that housed a collection of Stone Age implements owned by Baron Lowenthall. Some of the happiest moments of his life had been spent, he confessed, in the musty basement of the Lowenthall Museum. A specialty he had developed was a technique known as retrofitting. This involved fitting back together stone chips that had been discarded, chipped away, in the process of the carving of spear points by cave dwellers some fifty thousand years ago. When the gathered-up chips were fitted back together, you could tell exactly what sort of tool had been carved out of the larger block, and this told you what animals those particular cave dwellers had hunted, and therefore what they ate and wore. The geological makeup of the reassembled stone indicated how far afield that tribe had ranged and traded, and even whether the ancient tool-smith had been left- or right-handed.

Clare shook her head, half-ashamed, half-alarmed. He was the real thing. She realized she'd regarded him with an edge of suspicion, never taken him seriously, not as this sort of serious and knowledgeable person.

They careened off the autostrada at the Chiusi exit, threaded a network of secondary roads, swung up a rise, crested a hill. Suddenly the lake was there, a flat green shimmer. Luke pulled off onto the verge.

He turned off the motor. He took her chin in his large hand. She smelled leather on it from the wheel, and the hot salt of his skin. His other hand traced her cheek bones, her nose, her ears. She caught a glint of the gold snake's ruby eye.

He said, "Do you think you could love me, Clare?" Then, as he saw her involuntary shock, a quick recoil. "I said could you, not do you."

He started the car and jammed it into gear. They crunched down to the valley.

∽

DO YOU THINK YOU *could love me?*

And then that moment when he'd seen his mistake. Appalling that she was responsible for him showing himself like that, his face so naked, vulnerable, hopeful, then slammed tight. They passed through the narrow streets of a small village. He banged on the horn. An elderly woman wobbled on her bike and nearly lost her loaf of bread.

Clare glanced at his chin-up, scruffy-lion profile. What had her face looked like in the instant after? She remembered the shock on her uncle's face when she'd declared her lust for him — shock and horror at her, at himself — which had lived with her ever after. And now she, grown Clare — wounded, hardened, lying Clare — had been tossed a chance to put just a pinch of ease back into a universe of monstrous and clashing forces. The moment had opened, then shut, in a blink.

They drove around the lake. They passed the palm trees of Passignano. She closed her eyes. Was it possible that if she could just let go of whether or not she did love — just said, *Yes, Yes I could —* might this not turn out to be true? If she could do that, just make that leap, might it not jolt her from aching to hear another voice telling her about resin fungi and the life history of the unicorn. *I am so lonely, Clare.*

They drove up a rutted track that ended at a small stone shed. They carted in bundles of stakes, electric wire, survey tape, a metal detector, and cartons of unknown contents.

By then it was dusk. He secured the shed with a padlock and pushed past her.

She said, "Luke!"

He stopped, but didn't turn.

She said, "The answer is yes."

He didn't move. She was going to have to spell it out. If her next words felt like pity, or the jabs of an inoculation — all to the good. She imagined she could smell the feral, wounded struggle he was having before he turned back to her.

THEY DROVE UP THE hill to her uncle's place, her place, then drove slowly on along the path into the woods. In the dark they managed to heft two great duffle bags and an oblong padded case up the stream bed. They hid these as best they could.

They sat for a while on one of the mounds. Fireflies sparked, small silent fireworks. Then a rustling movement on the sidehill made Luke call out, "Who the fuck's there?" It turned out he'd brought along a revolver. He fired it into the air. The silence that settled held just that single whistle that might have been a bird.

The Contessa Calls

A HOT WIND BLEW in from Africa. Overnight the seasons changed. When Clare stood under the wisteria arbour in the morning, she saw the grass along the drive was brittle, and she felt sere and brittle, too. The phone rang as she stood wondering at the harsh quality of the wind.

It was Luisa di Varinieri on the line, saying how delightful it had been the other day to see Clare "at our old Factor's house, which now of course belongs to William Sands."

Luisa was calling to invite Clare to a little gathering later in the week, the *Festa della Lumache,* the yearly festival of snails, to be held in a small piazza near Cortona's top gate. "This will be excellent for you to write about," Luisa said.

Clare said a snail festival sounded intriguing. "I've always liked the concept of slow food."

Luisa laughed. "And I will insist that William comes!" she said. "But you, my dear, will have to do your part and ensure that Luke Tindhall makes up the ground with William, now you have established — if I may say — this warm contact not just with Sir Harold Plank but with Luke Tindhall as well."

Her tone took on the well-burnished ring of orders tossed for generations down ancestral halls.

"We will see you in the Piazza de Pescadori in three nights' time."

∽

WHEN CLARE DROVE DOWN to the Molino, the cats were draped on Luke's shoulders, limp with feline love. Luke was marching from room to room, muttering, "Total cock-up, total cock-up."

Harold Plank had got wind of his trip to the Middle East, and read everything wrong. Luke had been summoned back to London. There was no time to lose. They would have to get up to her field now and find out what it had to offer, which better be something to make Plank's eyes light up or Luke was sodding toast.

They climbed straight up from the Molino along the path by the waterfall. The stream had all but dried up over those few days. Wind raked through the trees. When they located the spot where they'd hidden the equipment, Luke discovered that only the most rudimentary instructions had been included with the instrument in the black padded box, a gradiometer, which he said might be the only one they would need.

It was hard to watch Luke's struggle to put the instrument toge-ther. *Haste makes waste, little Chiara,* echoed through Clare's mind. When she was little, her uncle had given her a wooden puzzle, an inlaid box with a hidden lock. While she'd tackled the challenge of it he had held himself back, allowing her to learn almost Zen-like patience in the process of sliding this panel, that one — which then revealed further hidden ones — and remembering the sequence, so that eventually, with persistence and patience, she did indeed manage to turn the tumblers of the lock.

She could have helped Luke now. Gone was the patience that must have sustained him in the museum basement in France. He snapped at her when she made suggestions. He crammed this bit into that bit, cursing. He snapped again when she pointed out which was the diurnal sensor on the long white tube, and which sensor needed to face downwards to read the earth's magnetic field.

When he finally got the device assembled and tested, now almost two o'clock, he told her to take out metal pegs, a hammer and yellow rope, and lay out grids in the areas between the hillocks so that later, if necessary, he'd be able to bring the resistivity meter into play.

HE CLIMBED THE SLOPE of the nearest hillock. Let out a whoop. An exceptional reading! He clambered from one hill to another, as the heat of the afternoon intensified. Exceptional readings, yes. But they began to look exceptionally level. Even when he moved down and across the field, the data all came up looking much the same. At five o'clock he laid the gradiometer down. He'd already made sure he was wearing nothing metal, even checking that his jeans had no rivets. He felt through his clothing again, pulled a tiny one cent Euro coin out of a pocket seam. The coin had thrown the whole day's work out of whack.

The following morning was worse. The gradiometer ran out of battery power and they had no charger. They set up an alternate electromagnetic system according to instructions that Luke had managed to get the previous night on the phone, but found nothing that would indicate buried entrances to tombs. Clare began to understand that it would take weeks for them to explore this area properly, even if they did know what they were doing. Finally, despite all he'd said regarding the ruinous methods of the *tombaroli,* he hiked home for a crowbar and began banging it in now here, now there.

"Luke, for heaven's sake!"

He turned on her. "Isn't it about time you handed over the information that you are holding back?"

"What?"

"Don't think I'm not aware that you've got a case full of your uncle's papers. I found that plastic case you hid away behind those books downstairs, with a metal box inside."

"What?" She felt sick, picturing his big hands getting in there — maybe fingering the ashes too?

"I was able to pry the plastic thing open far enough to see the locked box where you cleverly hid what everyone is looking for. I looked around when you were in your bath. Like a fool, I thought I'd wait till you trusted me enough to show me."

"You are absolutely not making sense."

"What's in there then? Let's go down and get it!"

"What's in there is private."

"Private? I turn over my entire life to you, but you're keeping the essentials private?"

He stopped. He looked wild. She thought she could see his thoughts clawing around wildly, too.

"Fuck it. Why are we wasting each other's time?" he shouted. He turned and started off down the field. "You can forget your damn snail festival, too!" he called over his shoulder. He looked almost gleeful. "I know it's intended to get me to make up with Sands. Well fine. But you can say *buon viaggio* to Poggio Selvaggio as far as Tindhall is concerned!"

HE HIKED AWAY. SHE sat in the shade of a pine until the sun fell behind the trees above the stream. She packed up the gear, but stayed on. A new moon dropped slowly. Fireflies blinked on and off.

৽৹

WHEN LUKE FOUND HER, it was barely dawn. She told him to go away. He said he had something to show her. She said she didn't care.

"You will. Hold out your hand."

"So?"

She stared at three terracotta fragments.

He said, "Look! Here! And here! And here!"

She didn't want him to be back. It had been fine alone under the wheeling stars, the black heat wrapping around her as if she were another bush or stone belonging there, nothing to fear, waking all pearled with dew, solitary, free.

Look here! And here! And here! A language she'd grown out of. She slipped back into it with a sense of loss.

"I found these up there," he said, pointing in the direction of the fortress above the town. "Clare, they are convincing evidence that there once was an Etruscan temple on that hill, just as you imagined."

Despite herself, interest flickered as she squinted at the small terracotta fragments. The crevices held hints of crimson and deep blue and small flecks of gold.

"I can have them tested in London," he said, "Which will prove that they must be remnants of rooftop statues on a temple whose foundations are lost beneath centuries of building and rebuilding! A temple looking down into this meadow. You were right all along!"

HE SAID THAT HE'D been completely disgusted at himself for making such a balls-up of their exploration and then saying such unforgivable things to her. When he'd cooled down, he'd hiked up to the Medici tower and spent hours scouring around, just because he was so disgusted at blaming her for his ineptitude. Then, just before dark, he'd found these three tiny fragments.

"When I get back from London, I will set things up for a proper exploration here," he said. "Meanwhile," he was buttoning the fragments back into his shirt pocket, "these little devils are the secret weapon I'll use to pacify old Harry. He'll be eating out of my hand when I tell him the good news."

When she was silent, he said, "Clare, listen. I *know* I've been a total bastard. Don't look away from me. Say something."

Three tiny bits of clay. The secret weapon. The mad hopefulness. When she still kept silent, he said, "Sod it, what's the use?" and launched into a riff of self-flagellation. "Clearly the woman will never forgive you! She will always be thinking, *God what a donkey Tindhall is.* And who can blame her? Tindhall, you will wear that black mark all your life like Cain."

He almost hoped for that, she figured; he was half waiting for her to affirm a lifelong expectation of the worst. But he was a good man in truth, concerned with large important things, though squished into a less admirable shape by the impossible business of being human. She felt a rush of concern for him, which really might be close to love — a kind of thawing, like the slightly ill degeneration she used to feel when snow melted in the spring.

"Oh, stop it!" she said. She thought it might be harder to be him than to be her. Maybe the secret of being with someone was to share the worst parts of yourself. Of course she couldn't share the really worst. But she remembered how she'd felt up at the dig when she'd held the blue bead, the compulsion to possess one small talismanic thing that she'd felt might, paradoxically, protect her in the future, even from herself.

"Listen," she said. "Remember that blue bead up at Poggio Selvaggio?"

He frowned, clearly reluctant to give up such triumphant self-abasement. "Oh Christ. The bead, that bead!"

"Remember when it got lost?"

"Of course. What a sodding kerfuffle!"

"I was the one who did that."

"What do you mean?"

"I dropped it. Then I covered it with my boot, so I could steal it when it was safe to pick it up again."

She saw his eyes widen — maybe even in admiration? Not quite what she'd intended.

"I couldn't bring myself to do it, though. But the thing is, when I had the bead in my hand, I had the feeling that I was holding an entire world of information ... or that it was a small blue eye of truth that I could keep from the world. A tiny cache of knowledge that could secretly be mine. I planned to wear it on a gold chain, here, where no one else could see."

"Crikey," he said.

Bad Dog on a Leash

WHEN THEY ARRIVED AT the snail festival, Clare realized she could have found her way to the little piazza at the top of the town blind-folded. She'd retraced the route so many times in her head, first her failed search for the saint's basilica, then the looping loony descent through tangled streets after driving down that set of stairs on the far side of the square. The details were transfixed, familiar, despite the lanterns in the trees, the crowded banquet tables. She was right back in that day, and straining like a bad dog on a leash to sniff out the trail again to where it had led that day.

Luke kept a tight hold of her hand. They made their way to a table where a familiar group was assembling. Federica kissed Clare absently. The Contessa swished up, wearing a wide-winged hat over a wig with a fat braid that hung to her ankles and a very low-necked tunic.

Applause from Carl.

He stood.

"But Anders and I have decided to enter into the costume contest too."

He pulled Anders to his feet to show off their Etruscan warrior outfits, chainmail vests made of linked-together key rings, pleated battle skirts, plastic wine bottles strapped to their shins as greaves.

"We are armed to the teeth, and ready to take on a whole battalion of snails!"

"This is very clever my darlings," Luisa said. Even her husband smiled. He gave no hint that he'd seen Clare in Tarquinia.

When Nikki and William arrived, Clare overheard Luisa whispering that she expected William to behave. Nikki smiled brightly at Luisa, and Luisa smiled back, their two smiles arching over William like ceremonial swords.

Nikki was wearing a sarong made out of a paisley shawl, and what Clare at first glance thought were wrist-length black gloves. "Are we beyond the fringe or what?" Nikki said, fingering the crystals on Clare's shawl. "Ooops!" They both looked down at the little handful of sparkly beads in Nikki's hand. "I don't know how that happened. You'll have to come over, and I'll thread them back!"

She tucked the beads into the embroidered pouch that hung around her neck. That was when Clare saw that Nikki's hands were completely gloved in black ink, with a little scroll added at the wrist.

Nikki laughed, self-consciously. "I've been getting into my work. I had a little accident, but decided to turn it to good account."

When the Contessa came to stand beside Luke, Clare thought he was rising in a gesture of politeness, but he increased his grip on Clare's hand and propelled her over to a gravelly spot in front of a band, oblivious to the fact that no one was dancing. With a stance very stiff, hair afloat and whipping, he spun her through a sort of tango, then marched her back, resumed his seat.

The lanterns, the starlight, the romantic music, the rustling leaves; it was going to be terrible. But she would do her best. She would.

Carl and Anders were making helmets out of their paper napkins. Anders set his at a fetching angle and turned to see if William Sands was taking note. Nikki's smile flashed like a scimitar.

Platters of crostini arrived. "But these are made with chicken livers!" Anders cried in mock distress. "I thought every course was snail."

"*Liebling,* they are snail livers," Carl rumbled. "You are merely taken in by the fact that every food that creeps upon the ground has the taste of fowl."

This led to welcome laughter and a discussion of the eating of reptiles and insects around the world. "In Brazil, I discovered that fried worms can be delicious," Clare said. "But eating spaghetti among the Yanomami?" She held her fork up, miming a wriggling load. "A bit of a surprise!" When the pasta came, it also lacked snails. Clare caught Anders's eye and together, almost as if on signal, they turned to Carl and said, "*Vass is dass?*" But when snails finally did arrive — shells glistening in a red and spicy sauce, along with tooth-picks, napkins, bread for sopping — the little creatures hunched on Clare's plate like the thoughts she was clenching.

She got up, walked among the tables to the far side of the square, towards the phone booth, the playground, a stone bench. She sat down and let the *festa* flow around her: the talk, the laughter, the cavorting children, the babies held aloft or passed around to be admired. All these good people gathered in this starlit piazza in their little town to celebrate the goodness of a lovely night in June, these people who knew innately how to celebrate. It flowed by on the far side of a thick pane of glass.

"Hello, Clare."

HOW HE LOOKED. AND everything ripping open in front of her, lights, sounds, smells, all coming at her, not painted on the far side of glass. It swam around him. He looked so good. Ridiculous and patently untrue, but he looked uncomplicated, simple, good.

Dusky perfume drifted from the lime trees rustling overhead, a canopy of heart-shaped leaves, silvery on one side, glossy on the other. The clusters of small white blossoms.

She said, "I was in a tomb that had a ceiling like this. It had a painted canopy all sprigged with little flowers."

"You were in Tarquinia."

"Yes."

"I came by to see you."

"Oh!"

When? she wondered. What if she'd hadn't been so stubborn, hadn't insisted on going to Tarquinia with Luke!

He said, "I hope you have been all right?"

"Have you?"

"No." He shook his head. "I have been eaten by my own stupidity and pride — and then realizing that when I left you, you were not well."

She kicked a pebble at her feet. There would be grass in a park like this back home, not gravel. She said, "I felt badly, too. That was kind of a mess-up, that morning."

He knocked a fist to his forehead, "Shamefully, it was not until several days later that the dogs of my pride let go."

She couldn't help smiling. "Are they very fierce, these dogs of your pride?"

"I did not think so. But with you, yes it seems."

She saw Luke across the piazza glancing around for her with a haughty, desperate look. Luke doesn't deserve this, she thought. The lanterns made the shadows lengthen, shorten, sway.

She started to get up. "There have been some changes since then."

He caught her hand. She sat down, and ducked her head, as if Luke's glance would wing above her.

He said, "Clare Livingston, I have been a fool."

Oh, me too, she realized.

Another long pause, while she contemplated her folly and kept her head down so she didn't have to meet Luke's stare. She imagined reaching up, kissing Gianni just on the cheek to say goodbye, how instead they would rise up together through the trees, up through the powdering of stars, leaving behind the tables strewn with snails and bread and wine, and all the gaping people.

She said, "I am involved with someone else, now."

"The one you are with tonight is important?"

"I have to say ..."

"You have to."

"No, damn it. I don't have to. He is."

Gianni rose to his feet. "Come. Walk with me. Please."

He was looking down at her with the same expression as when he'd lectured her about her painting, as if her hesitation was a disappointment not just to him, but to the entire universe. His face so jagged with intensity, the ridiculous imperial profile, the hint of weakness in the turned-up chin. How did he dare?

"Cut it out." She stood up, too. "You've already messed up my ability to work, with all your peering and prying!"

"What? To do your art?"

It was monstrous to pin that on him, a weasel of an excuse, but someone had to pay for the way she still wanted him so much it hurt.

She said, "So stop trying to ruin my life. We had a tiny fun thing going, but you can hardly pretend it was unique. You know what they say in this town: all the pretty ladies get to know Gianpaulo sooner or later. If you laid them end to end they'd reach to Timbuktu."

She saw his look of shock. She heard the echo of her ugly words.

He said, "Then I will walk you back to your table."

"Don't bother. That is a truly bad idea."

"Regrettably, I must go there anyway. I have a message for my sister, from our mother."

"Of course. Forgive me. Do come over. Come and sit down and have a snail. Shall I lend you my toothpick? I'd forgotten. It's all in the family, after all."

"Ah." He made a mock bow. "I am sorry to have troubled you so much."

He turned and walked off in the other direction, away from the table, through the crowd.

Puzzle Box

LUKE LEFT HIS GUN with Clare when he came to say goodbye next day. She agreed to look after herself. She agreed to keep an eye on what he now called *their* excavation site. She agreed to keep on searching for any further clues her uncle might have left, though she knew she wouldn't look any further. Let him hold onto the dream a little longer, convinced that the key to his ambitions was buttoned in his pocket, the secret weapon that might also save his job.

The night before, she'd only just managed to catch up with him as he was heading for the car park. He would have dropped her off at her place without a further word, but she couldn't let him go away to London like that. All the way back, she'd been telling herself that she should be honest, break this off. But there was this other huge thing about him, the crushing complex bulk of him, essential though it took her nowhere, a negating satisfaction beyond the physical.

When he'd gone, she picked up the shawl she'd thrown off the night before. She found the place where the crystal beads had come away in Nikki's hand, a ragged tear which had pulled away a piece of the fabric. Would the beads end up on the shelf in Nikki's attic cupboard? She pictured those black, ink-gloved hands placing the scrap of cloth near the candle, by the millefiori petal, then heaping the beads on top. Nikki, artist of the "magic of reconstruction," as she'd put it. What did she imagine she might reconstruct out of these torn-away bits and pieces of Clare's life?

Clare draped the shawl around herself, drawn to the mirror to stare at this woman who had seen one good man off to London carrying a pocketful of hope, when all she wanted was a chance to slip back into the moment when she'd first put on this beautiful thing for the other one — the one she had irrevocably sent from her life, last night, with her ugly words.

She fingered the gap where the beads had been torn away, picturing the arrangement in Nikki's cupboard, a shrine. Then she imagined the black hands detaching themselves. They were lying there as well, votive objects, like the little reproductions of hands and feet and sex parts found in the healing sanctuary on Poggio Selvaggio. The silk of the shawl whispered around her shoulders. She heard Nikki's voice: "Are we beyond the fringe or what?" For a moment she imagined herself kneeling and telling that pair of black disembodied hands, *Here is what I need to reconstruct ...* She closed her eyes, willing herself back to the day of the wedding pageant when she'd come in late from painting and seen that the sky foretold rain, how in a moment of inspiration she'd crossed the room to free the shawl, pushed back the big chair, shifted the bronze she-wolf to the side.

And something happened. What?

What had happened that she'd overlooked before?

No.

She opened her eyes and stared into the mirror. No. Life wasn't like that. Things didn't fall into place like that.

Okay, so the top of the table had tipped, and then slapped back on its box-shaped base. But if she went now and looked, it would still be just a table top. If the box opened she would find a scorpion or a nest of spiders.

Better not to know.

∽

IT WAS LIKE THE wooden puzzle from her childhood, a box-joint box, though much enlarged. Its corners were intricately mortised so that the entire cube seemed solid and impenetrable, top, bottom and sides.

Had she secretly understood this since the night she'd first glimpsed it, but been determined to concentrate on distractions, good or bad, that might keep her from her life's true core?

Eight moves.

The remembered instruction. *Force is never needed. If a piece does not move with gentle persuasion, it is not its time to be moved.*

Like so much else. Like the clues that had led her to this moment when she was finally able to lift the mortised lid. A course that now seemed obvious and foretold.

THE SUITCASE WAS SHOVED in diagonally, upended. The case he'd carried when he left the farm. He'd taken almost nothing, a few clothes, a few books. Now this same case held reams of pages scribbled, typed, underlined, crumpled and then re-smoothed. Photos. Black and white, taken with his old Zeiss Ikon.

Little Clare. In the haymow, on the swing, riding the saddle blanket on the porch rail, little Clare and bigger Clare. The smile is rapturous and greedy for attention in the centre of squares of uneven exposure, face radiant with the conscious illicit-feeling joy of being the centre, observed, the light of someone's life. *Chiara.*

There were newspaper clippings. He must have started collecting almost immediately after leaving.

SKAGIT TEEN FEARED MISSING …

BOYFRIEND OF MISSING TEEN REPORTED MISSING

"He was a home boy," the mother of a seventeen-year-old basketball star Eric Klassen told this reporter. *"He never would have been the one to get this idea."*

TRAIL GOES COLD ON MISSING TEENS

MISSING PAIR SPOTTED CAMPING ON OREGON COAST

CELEBRATION IN SKAGIT HOUSEHOLD: MISSING SON RETURNS

All this Clare herself had never read. Even more surprising were notices of little exhibitions where her early work had been included, when she was living in Vancouver. Then one mentioning the inclusion of her *Dicentra Formosa* in a volume published by the university. How did he do it? By this time, he'd have been working in Rome. Then the catalogue of a show at the Smithsonian, which had included two of her pencil drawings.

And then — three reviews of her Amazonia book, including the one in *The New York Times*. Could that have been the moment when he decided to leave the property to her?

Didn't all this speak clearly enough? Why leaf through it all again?

THE ENVELOPE, WHEN SHE finally spotted it, was taped inside the lid. Obviously the first thing she had been expected to see, though in her haste to pull out the suitcase she had missed it altogether.

Inside were two hand-drawn maps. The first was clearly of the property here in Tuscany, showing the house, the gate, the stream winding up into the meadow, then cross-hatching to indicate the meadow itself and, more firmly drawn, the horseshoe ring of the cliff behind. No writing.

The other map was puzzling at first, until she realized she was looking at a portion of the Skagit farm, showing the house and the Italian tower and the field below, which she and her uncle had crossed so many times, the field with the bull, with its semicircle of chalky cliffs where once long ago she had dug, and been buried.

She heard his voice. *We'll pretend the cliff is limestone, shall we? Its location would have been ideal for our Etruscan friends — a city of the dead, in view of the habitation of the living! Shall we carve the entrance of a rock-tomb?* Clare on his shoulder taking turns with his knife to carve an elaborate house-front into clay. *The columen, the pediment, the architrave, Chiara …!*

So there it was. She and Luke could have dragged any amount of fancy equipment over the grass, over the mounds, for days, for weeks, for years; they would never have found a thing. If there were tombs, they were carved right into the cliff behind rubble fallen centuries ago.

SIX

Poltergeist

TWO PIECES OF PAPER. What a taunt. What a hugely successful trick.

For the past week, Clare had strained and dug and scrambled, first with wild excitement, then stubbornly, until the truth sank in. Those hand-drawn maps were merely two more misdirections on the trail of tantalizing scraps her uncle had left her, a puzzle pitched exactly to the clever-little-girl mind he used to love to feed, but leading to a final bitter payback.

Nothing. Not an inkling. Day after day she'd scrabbled, shovelled, pried.

"That's it," she'd said late yesterday as she limped down along the dried-up stream, her arms aching from trying to pry boulders, her back bent out of shape. If there was anything to find along that horseshoe rim of cliffs, it had been buried by whatever had caused rocks, boulders, earth to slide from the slope above centuries ago.

The contents of the inlaid box were still spread over the table, the sofa, the floor, as it had been for the whole week. Clothes she'd pulled off in exhaustion, the sink full of dirty dishes, the crowbar dumped by the door.

Luckily Marta had been off all week helping a granddaughter have a baby. This morning she'd be back. Clare was surveying the disaster she had to clean up first, when she glanced out and saw Nikki Stockton driving up the lane. Perfect trickster timing.

CLARE STOOD VERY STILL in her smelly long black shirt — all she was wearing. Maybe she could pass as a shadow if Nikki peered through the glass.

When she finally went to answer the door, Nikki was aiming a camera up into the wisteria vine, bending backwards, one foot stretched in front, an extreme arch to her back, the theatrical effect heightened by her black-and-red harlequin pants, the red blouse with wing-like sleeves that fell and fluttered as she turned this way and that, clicking away with hands that looked to have been bleached though were still somewhat grey, and were patterned now with vines and scrolls that ran past her wrists and up her arms; fine black-ink twining lines, coloured with what looked like henna in several red and marigold shades.

Nikki said, "Oops!" as if she'd been caught doing what she shouldn't. "I hope you'll forgive me for just dropping by so early, but something a bit unsettling has happened."

IT WAS BECAUSE OF Luke Tindhall's name turning up on one of the cartons, she said; so she'd decided she'd better let Clare know.

The day before, a student with their dig had been out hiking in the hills above Trasimeno and had come upon an old shed that had been broken into. There were bits of exploration equipment scattered around, and that torn-open carton which bore Luke's name. So Nikki herself, earlier this morning, had driven over and checked. She'd been too creeped out to go inside the shed, she said, but she'd thought she'd better let Clare know so she could get in touch with Luke, in case the equipment was to do with the Foundation.

Clare said, My goodness and how strange; she didn't know anything about this. But probably, yes, she should let Luke know.

"I was thinking," Nikki said, "maybe you would like to come

along with me, now; because I went home and got a honking big padlock to replace the broken one. But I'd rather have company when I went back there."

Nikki was still outside the door. Clare waved her over to a wicker arbour chair, while she went in and jammed all the papers back into the box, under the bronze she-wolf.

The idea of leaving everything and driving off with this harlequin figure with the hennaed hands sounded like a Houdini-type escape.

She showered, then made a fake call to London in a voice that would carry to the arbour, leaving a fake message for Luke.

∾

NIKKI'S IDEA WAS TO take a back road to a viewpoint over the lake, then sneak down to the shed. She said if the "bad guys" had come back they could catch them red-handed. "Like this …" She raised her own decorated hands from the wheel in a strangling gesture.

No one was lurking near the shed. But Nikki insisted they stick to the plan of sneaking down. The climb involved scrambling over a steep ledge. Nikki went first and braced herself to ease Clare down, and when Clare's foot slipped she was caught in a tight wiry embrace, so that their cheeks rubbed together. Clare caught a whiff of Nikki's foxy smell.

They found a metal detector in the bushes near the shed, wires and gizmos strewn around. This would surely mean that someone really had followed Luke's car from Tarquinia. It was only when she and Nikki had gathered all the equipment up that Clare began to wonder.

Nikki hung back when Clare pushed open the battered door. As it creaked open, she caught a tiny glitter on the floor just inside. A pink crystal. Like one from her shawl. And another, further in. And several more. Maybe the beads had dropped from Nikki's bag when she was here before? But Nikki had only surveyed the shed from outside, she'd claimed.

Nikki was right behind her. "So? Can we carry this stuff in? Is it safe?" She was holding the end of her pigtail across her upper lip, feigning an evil moustache, a devilish kid.

A word flashed up. *Poltergeist.*

Clare said, "All clear. No bad guys. Just you and me. So let's do it, let's get this place locked up."

WHEN THEY'D FINISHED LOCKING up the shed, Nikki climbed onto a large flat boulder. After a moment, Clare joined her there.

Was it really possible that Nikki herself had been the one to break into the shed? If so, the dropped crystals would be a message, wouldn't they?

Clare looked out at the aquamarine jewel of the lake, the far-off towns, the peaceful shore where once a battle had raged that turned the water red. She had said yes, once, right here.

Nikki stretched her red-wing arms. "Anders Piersen is moving into our tobacco shed. I guess you knew that."

"No."

"It turns out that he and William have a surprising amount in common."

Anders was going be William's personal assistant now, she said, the idea being that he could also assume those day-to-day details that had kept Nikki away from her work at the lab, where there was a backlog because the conservator from London was late arriving.

"Talk about the law of unintended consequences, eh? Here's one William didn't foresee when he came up with that very practical idea! Two goofing-off women, just a-sittin' in the sun. So come on — sit — so we can goof off properly." She took Clare's arm and pulled her down.

The morning was full of the scent of herbs and sun-warmed grass. High above a hawk was circling. The sky was that endless blue.

Nikki held out her hennaed hands. "So what do you think? Would I make a lovely Eastern bride? Like Thais?"

"What's that from again? Remind me."

It was from a poem by Dryden, Nikki said. "Alexander's Feast." About a beautiful courtesan urging on Alexander the Great, so that in a drunken revel he burned down the city of Persepolis. She had been listening to a recording of it, which a friend from college had sent her, while she applied the henna. She and her friend used to recite it when they got dressed up to go out on dates; they'd goof around about how they were going to set the town on fire.

She reached for Clare's hand before Clare thought to shift away. She traced a stem of grass up a finger, traced a curlicue at the wrist. Why didn't they go back to her place? she asked. She could do Clare's hands too. Then even if they didn't exactly burn up the town, they'd at least light up the countryside.

The ticklish blade was moving up Clare's arm. "Yes, I remember that now," Clare said. "We learned it in school. It has a chorus that goes 'None but the brave ... None but the brave deserves the fair.'"

She slid off the rock.

Would her life take a turn in that direction, now? She remembered how Nikki had caught her tight when she slipped on the cliff. She looked up. The moment seemed burned there, fiery orange, like a petroglyph. And beyond was the lake where Clare had said yes when she didn't mean it.

She could say yes again.

She could say yes, and yes could bloom.

None but the brave deserves the fair.

"Look, there's a hawk," she said.

∞

THEY WERE ON A FAST road driving east along the lake, towards Perugia.

Clare had fibbed and told Nikki she needed to get home; she had a pressing deadline, a publisher who was hounding her. But Nikki had insisted that there was one place that Clare really ought to see while they were out. Clare's publisher would never forgive her if she, a famous flower artist, missed this chance to visit the remarkable monastery garden in Perugia when she was so near. This was a medieval garden in a cloister, a *hortus sanctus* where medicinal plants were still cultivated, some of which were only otherwise available to see in very old Italian herbals. But the place had been planned, too, as a sort of refuge for the spirit, laid out in a philosophical manner.

A monastery garden in Perugia.

When you follow the intricate philosophical paths that have been laid out, when you breathe the healing air, you will also find yourself in the centre of the truth of your own life.

How many monastery gardens could there be in a place the size of Perugia? She couldn't go there. She would see nothing. She would hear nothing but that voice. But she caught such stark disappointment when she insisted that she didn't have the time that in the end she'd agreed to go along.

It wasn't until Nikki had Clare safely captive in her van that she'd said, raising her moustache pigtail over her lip again, that now that she had Clare in her power she was going to take her, after they'd been to the garden, to a trattoria in the hills where they served a chocolate mousse cake that double-soothed the soul.

NIKKI WAS HAPPY NOW; Nikki was chattering with the determination of someone who would not allow her vision of the day to go off course. She had brought watercolours and extra brushes and she intended that she and Clare would paint together in the cloister garden. Her words tumbled through Clare's thoughts as they drove.

The sky clouded. Everything Clare had sought to leave behind earlier had trailed her. A new worry assailed her. What if in her rush to get away she hadn't properly locked the box? What if Marta pried into it? Or what if the maps actually meant that she should have been searching further up the slope, and Marta had already given the maps to Niccolo who was busy digging up there right now? But worst was the way her past had come fuming out of that box, the musty awfulness that she could still smell clinging to her skin, her clothes.

THEY PARKED BELOW PERUGIA'S city walls. A moving staircase carried them up through a former tyrant's dungeons and underground realms. When they emerged, the day had turned brilliant again, breezy.

Nikki strode ahead, her red sleeves fluttering, leading Clare off the main street and down many sets of pink marble steps. A circular tower topped with a roof like a Pierrot hat reared above a wall; the monastery tower, Nikki paused to say before she darted ahead again like one of those birds in a folk tale, leading Clare on to some predetermined end, through the gates, across a cloistered courtyard, out into a sunny area where the air smelled dizzyingly of herbs. This was certainly the place that Gianni had spoken of. The air was pungent with loss.

"*Giardino dello Spiritio.*"

Nikki picked up a pamphlet and was reading aloud from it in Italian. It explained the metaphorical concept of the garden, how it had indeed been laid out to an elaborate philosophical plan, how every plant had cosmic significance, how at the very centre of the area where they now stood was the Cosmic Tree. A meandering philosophically significant pathway led from here towards a further cloister sheltering the *hortus sanctus,* the garden of native blooms and healing plants.

Nikki folded the pamphlet into her satchel and grasped Clare's arm to lead her onto that path. But Clare could not follow.

"Go on ahead. I'll join you in a minute. I need …"

Nikki frowned, tugged at her long braid, as if this might hurry Clare along. Clare seized the first excuse that came to her. "I need to find something about this in English. I'll go back to the entrance to see if they have one."

"Nonsense!" Nikki said. *"Ridicolo! Che sciocchezze!* The *Signora* wishes a brochure, when she has me as her humble guide and translator?" She fished out the pamphlet again, struck a pose. "*Ecco Signori,* esteemed ladies and gentlemen, in this direction we come to the Grove of Meditation, then pass the Tree of Good and Evil, into the Sacred Wood."

"Please," Clare said. "Don't wait. I'll just dash out and see if I can get some literature to take back with me."

Nikki looked around. A young man was plunging a fork into the grass, on the slope leading to the Cosmic Tree. She hailed him. Clare protested. Nikki waved that aside and explained to the young man, who was coming over, that her friend needed a book about the garden, but in English.

"Ah!" He turned to Clare, with an enchanting smile. "If you will wait just one minute."

Clare tried to stop him, but he'd already dropped the fork; he was sprinting towards an official-looking building by the cloister wall. This was ridiculous; more so, in this place of healing and healthy air, that she could hardly breathe. "Go," she finally told Nikki, not caring anymore if she was rude or not, "Please just go!" Finally, with the mock bow of an offended courtier, Nikki spun away along the main path and on into the Grove of Meditation, the harlequin pattern of her pants merging with the dappled shade.

It was very hot. The young man returned. "One minute more," he said, "and my friend will come. Until then, it is better you wait in the shade of our *Albero Cosmico.*" He walked her to the Cosmic Tree.

The bells in the monastery tower began to ring. A scattering of hard oval leaves drifted down. The young man seemed determined to keep her company. More cosmically aligned minutes ticked by. He gestured to a circular plaque laid into the nearby grass, painted with heraldic figures. "Do you like this? It is my *opera.*"

His *opera*. In other words, he meant it was his "work."

"Are you a painter?"

"A little."

"Do you do other work like this? Do you sell it?"

He laughed. "I do it for joy!"

He picked up the fork again. Probably the whole episode of helpfulness had run its course in a charming, inconclusive, Italian sort of way. How he went at his work in the garden though, the filigree of tattoos on his brown arms rippling as he plunged the fork into the dirt again and again. She couldn't help musing how in Italian *opera* was the word for a job of creative work. One of those simplistic thoughts that strangers had, who knew nothing of this country, never would ...

"*Allora! Finalmente!*" The fork hit the ground. The young man bounded across the lawn. He grasped an approaching figure by the shoulder. Clare closed her eyes.

She did not deserve this.

Gianni crossing the lawn towards her.

Clare standing beneath the Cosmic Tree.

∽

"BUT THIS IS IN Italian."

"Sadly, yes."

He slipped the book into his jacket pocket, where it spoiled the line of his fine wool suit.

He took a deep breath.

"I will presume to say that you do not need a book at all, if you will allow me to point out that this design, laid out by my friend the director, Dr. Menghini, will lead us initially, with good fortune, to the Garden of Eden, where all things can begin again."

She stopped him. "Listen —"

"Oh, no. Please. I am the one who needs —!"

They stood facing one another. An iridescent flash sailed by, a dragonfly. All sound dropped away, not a bird, not a workman's voice. An opera in reverse?

"How did this happen?" she finally said. "How did you turn up? Gianni, why are you here?"

"I came to talk with my friend, Director Menghini," he said, "regarding the symbolism of the haven he has created."

"The symbolism."

"Since a week ago, I have been in need of reassuring structure for my thoughts. Yes, this I must allow myself to say."

He spread his hands as if to balance this against a safer observation.

"I have long wanted, in my own garden, to make a design not just rational and practical — for one must understand that symbolism is not logic, nor is it, as the critic de Campeaux tells us, geometry." She pictured his words clambering up some elaborate trellis, while his thoughts, like hers, were much closer to the ground. "But rather," he forged on, "an experience of the totality which gives birth to the drama of the self."

"Are there resin fungi in this theory, too?"

"If you like, I can put them in." His smile flared, wobbled. Now words deserted them both. A trio of elderly German women crowded by, clucking at the obstruction in the centre of the path. Gianni cleared his throat. His Adam's apple bobbled above his pristine collar. Clare scuffled a pebble. A British family stepped carefully around them as if they were signposts spelling danger. A small child ran smack into Clare.

"I have an idea," Gianni said. He took her arm. "Down there is the shop of the alchemist."

He guided her off the path and down rocky steps to a sheltered hollow at the base of the tower, where they were out of sight. A tiny window looked into a mock-up of an alchemist's shop: a stuffed owl perched beside a skull, evil liquid bubbling over artificial coals, coloured bottles on a dusty table, dry weeds overhead.

"It is for children," he said. "But today, by a special prescription, they are almost all in school."

∽

"I WILL HAVE TO go and find my friend," Clare finally said, when words became a reasonable proposition once again.

"The one with the long braid?"

"How did you know?"

He said he had seen Clare talking with this woman at the dinner of the snails.

"Were you lurking in the background at the *festa?*"

"I did not think of it as lurking. I was meditating deeply on life, like the Baron in the Trees."

"Who?"

He shook his head. Could it be that she did not know this novel by Calvino? Well then, they would have a lovely time, on some winter's night, when he read it to her.

On some winter's night.

As they moved back to the path to the Garden of Healing, he told her how the monastery had stood in wild countryside when it was first constructed; how it had been a refuge during episodes of plague; how its records had been burned by Napoleon; how it had been a passion of his friend Menghini to restore the garden to what it would have been in the time before Columbus, to recreate what a monastery garden would have stood for, a corner of earthly paradise.

They went through an archway into a walled inner cloister. Nikki was sitting cross-legged on a path between the raised beds of plants, sketching with furious concentration, one page, over to the next. As they came up behind her, Clare caught a glimpse of sketch after sketch of long-stemmed flowers with up-thrust bursting petals, all with faces — no, not faces, just hers. Nikki snapped the book shut when she heard their footsteps on the gravel.

Gianni said quietly to Clare that he would like to propose that together they all go to a fine place he knew for lunch. "If you will promise, afterwards, not to escape this time. If you will not give me the hand-off when I drive you home."

She watched the petals of a large blue poppy waver on the shifting air. "The hand-off?" she said, laughing. "Maybe not."

Then, over-loud, she called, "Nikki — I'd like you to meet Gianni DiGiustini."

Nikki said "Hi." Avoiding Clare's eye. "Yes, I remember seeing you at the snail *festa.*"

"Gianni has invited us to lunch," Clare said.

"Oh, Gianni has invited us to lunch?" The same intonation as Clare's. She coiled her braid into a loop on top of her head, and pushed her pencil through to hold it. "Beautiful thought. But you know what? I shouldn't be here at all. While I was waiting for Clare, I remembered that I'd already promised to collect our field director's parents on the train from Florence. And, in fact, now I am late. Oh, dear."

Did Gianni notice how every word vibrated with disappointment? He said, "Well then, if it makes it more convenient, I will be pleased to run Signora Livingston home."

Nikki stood up, brushed herself off, then pushed past Clare. "But tell me," she said to Gianni, "when our field director's parents go to Florence, his mom always heads to the DiGiustini boutique, to pick up what she calls little gifts to take home. Gold jewellery with a horse-harness motif. Is there a connection?"

Yes, Gianni said, that was his stepfather's business. "Tomasso was once a manufacturer of farm machinery, but my mother persuaded him to make harnesses for the more expensive mares."

Nikki said the field director's parents would be impressed to hear that she'd nearly had the real goods for lunch!

Together they walked back to the Corso Cavour, Nikki chatting brightly to Gianni. At the top of the escalator, she broke away and with her arms extended, red sleeves fluttering, led them down through the underground regions of the ruined castle, past traces of ancient roads, piazzas, arched dungeon walls, and out into a late afternoon thick as gold with all that simmered in the air.

The Baron in the Trees

SO THIS WAS WHAT it was all about, the excruciating sweetness of this business that took up such an inordinate portion of the human brain, sweeter than hard rock candy. None of the sorrow of love-making with him, the expectation and the drop. He made her think of the boy in the garden: *it is my opera.* His joy spread marvellous contagion.

"But you are looking at me again," she said, many hours later.

"You don't like that I look at you? Or I should wear a mask?" He brought the rumpled sheet to the level of his eyes. "A blindfold?" He pulled a pillow case over his head. "I should grope?"

"No, I like it too much."

The foolery fell away, replaced for a moment with a look so serious it was scary. "I feel the same."

ON THE DRIVE FROM Perugia, he had been silent for such a long spell that she'd started feeling the same confusion as when they'd started for the wedding. Then he'd stopped the car, fixed her with the first of his scary looks.

"What?" she'd said. "Don't just look at me like that."

After a long silence, he said, "I will have to tell you. They do not stretch to Timbuktu."

"Oh …"

"It is not such a geographical catastrophe as that. The few, the very few women in my life I have been involved with since my marriage —"

"Gianni! I never …!"

"No, this is important. Before we begin together, I need to tell you about my marriage and my life."

"I don't want to hear this."

But he persisted. He said that he should have informed her, immediately at the start, that he had no business to claim anything of her. Nor to lecture her either, on her very small deficiencies.

"You've got that right at least. Though they are not so small."

He said that she had the most beautiful and intriguing deficiencies he had ever seen. "But we are talking now of mine."

She touched his lips to hold them closed. He removed her finger, held it, and studied it as he explained that beyond the fact that he was married, he must tell her that his wife was a woman honourable and beautiful and upstanding, the mother of his two children.

"But she doesn't understand you. It's okay. I get it."

"You have every right to be cynical," he said.

The fact was that Eleanora understood him very well; they understood each other, which in no way made the pain less that they did not jibe, "as you might say in your idiom," in any way other than in the serious commitment to their children's welfare. "Also in our agreement that since I have abandoned involvement in the family consortium, Eleanora will run it absolutely."

He was still talking to her index finger, which was not at all the well-manicured finger of the wife who ran the consortium. A dismal start, Clare thought, that such a small part of her could not stand up to comparative scrutiny.

He said, "Already my mother has broken this consortium once, by taking away the husband of the wife of my dead father's brother. This was before I was born, after both my father and Federica's father died in a tragic accident on the same day."

He shook his head. "It is a little complicated."

His mother was very beautiful, he added. (He was looking at Clare now. Everything she had heard about Italian mothers flashed before her.)

"Gianni, I do not want you to go through this!"

But he had to. He had to explain that though he and Eleanora did not jibe, it was a union he would never dissolve. Never would he submit his children to the shadow of such shame as he, Gianni, had grown up in.

"So my exceptional Clare, for whom I have waited all my life, I beg you to understand that though there have been other women, yes, there has been not one who has filled me with this confusion of delight I feel each time I think of you."

He broke off, as if the great storm of emotions under that noble brow had finally blown away all his words.

She said, "So now can I have my finger back?"

"You must not joke."

THEN, SO MUCH LATER, in the tumult of the sheets, with that same look, almost dire, he reared above her. "'He knew her, and so he knew himself,'" he said. "This is from the story I will read to you of the Baron in the Trees. 'He knew her, and she knew him, and so also knew herself. For although she had always known herself, she had never been able to recognize this until now.'"

He pulled her close, so close. "But the story ended badly," he said. "For in spite of what they learned, those lovers were too wary. The man went mad. The woman spent a long life wandering chilly foreign cities in regret. Please — let you and I take care, that we never will be wary!"

I could die now and I wouldn't care, she thought. He could have women stretching to the moon. He could be an axe murderer and I wouldn't care.

"I am here to protect you," he told her.

"From what?" She wanted to laugh, but he was holding her too tight.

"From everything," he said. "This is my life's calling as you will remember. To protect all things rare."

❧

CLARE LAY BESIDE GIANNI later, in the dark, and pondered how the truth of her that was linked to any former chain of events had dipped to another level altogether. Even in sleep he was irresistible; he let out just the occasional murmur, as if he was slipping through his dreams as gently as a stream; she longed for him to carry her along. But he already has, she thought. She curled into him and allowed herself to drift on that little current, marvelling at how from the first moment this had been fated, a tale where many perils had to be surmounted before the beautiful reward. True, there were dangers still. But as long as she kept a clear understanding of where she stood in this, that she was at the centre not of his total life but at the centre of this lovely dream they were making together, as long as she asked no more — and what more could she ask? — she was blessed.

"CLARE, WHAT IS IT? What?" He was gripping both her hands. "You were sobbing, you were touching all over your face."

He had turned on the bedside light. "You were rubbing your fingers on your cheeks, your forehead, so hard. What a dream. You must tell me. Come." He held her close.

"I don't know," she said. "It's gone. You chased it off. You were here."

"Yes, I am always here."

THE NEXT MORNING SHE woke in a state of happiness so extreme that she thought she should ground herself, for safety's sake. She should call Luke — at least to alert him to the dismal outcome of her searches in the upper field, so he could adjust his plans or schemes.

But what if?

That little thought surfaced, again, about something during her searches that she might have overlooked. She flicked it to the side. She pictured taking Gianni to the meadow to show him what was there, making him the gift of the fascinating botanical questions the place raised.

Again, at that, something clenched. Not just the inevitability, then, of revisiting the matter of her paintings, painful to her on several levels now that her gift had so strangely packed up and left; but the feeling that to go there with Gianni, to the field of frantic hopes she and Luke had shared, would be the true act of betrayal.

But I have already betrayed Luke, she thought, remembering how that first night, in the bath, Gianni had drifted into her mind, and how after that, at unexpected moments, she'd feel an inner little tipsy surge when the thought of Gianni occurred. At these moments everything developed a fevered glow. Surely that was love, which had been incubating in her all along, while the odd barbed thing that had hooked her to Luke was twisted mainly to a fear for him, for the way that he'd torn down his own defences and shown himself to her — seemed to have done that, she told herself now, because wasn't it likely she'd been just a necessary step towards his dream of exploration in Anatolia?

CLARE AND GIANNI HAD just stumbled up from the big bath downstairs, wrapped in towels, when Marta came in. She thumped a warm loaf of chestnut cake on the table — freshly baked for Signora Chiara's breakfast, she said, giving Gianni a look. She thumped down cups and plates, and a pot of espresso so strong the tiny cups jittered with disapproval.

Later, she took Clare aside and told her in a harsh whisper, as if this was something the Italian visitor should not hear, that Niccolo had brought in yet another dog, one who was particularly cross, to patrol her land, because he had developed some further concerns.

Oh good! *Bene, bene, eccellente!* Clare said; the more dogs the better! She played it up. The dogs were part of a drama the two of them were acting out to demonstrate their importance to the place, she decided. She said she hoped Marta would thank Niccolo for taking care of these concerns.

Today she had enough concerns of her own. She was off to visit Gianni's estate near Siena. Gianni had assured her that his wife lived in Bologna, as did his children, too, most of the time. He had such a desolate expression as he told her this. And though his mother did live on the estate, with "ninety percent certainty" she and his stepfather would be at the sea, at their place at Lerici. But Clare had overheard Gianni talking on the phone to that beautiful Mammà; she had heard him mention her name, describing Clare as "*una donna con molti grandi talenti!*", and Clare figured that with ninety-nine percent certainty Mammà would be waiting at some mullioned window to spy on her.

Through the Looking Glass

AS THEY TURNED NORTH off the familiar winding road past Montepulciano and Pienza, a tractor pulled onto the highway just ahead, slowing Gianni's Land Rover to a crawl. This was almost a mirror image of a similar moment with Luke on the road from Tarquinia. Gianni slipped quietly along, almost nudging the tractor's rear, until the farmer pulled aside. The Land Rover sailed past, *and on through the looking glass,* Clare thought: the countryside was transformed as well, everything that had been green and new was now tawny and bristling, the fields dotted with fat jelly-rolls of hay, cloud shadows carving deep purple canyons into the stubby gold.

The road wound past small villages and ruined castles and bosky groves, then further fields — such variation and repetition, like some lovely musical arrangement. She decided to let her concerns about meeting Gianni's family drop behind. She would take Gianni's word that the beautiful mother — and the stepfather stolen from a previous long-established marriage — would be at the sea.

They wound down into a farther valley, where tender shoots of rice were poking up and the morning light was steamy, then patchwork fields replaced the paddies and red-tiled roofs dotted the hills.

"What amazes me about this country is that there is so much country," she said, aware that she'd been silent for too long.

"From my ancestral tower," he said, "I will present you with a most beautiful panorama."

"That's the first I've heard of any tower."

"Oh we have very good defences at La Celta."

She asked what exactly they defended. He turned another of those fond, unsettling looks on her. "Mainly we are involved in bringing back what has been lost. You will see."

Then he slammed on the brakes. "*Aiii,* I have allowed myself to be distracted."

A leather portfolio slid against the back of her seat. Another of those fine, cared-for possessions of his, she thought as she reached back to secure its location; like his shoes, the aged leather of the case was polished to a buttery lustre, revealing an innate sense of the worth of well-worn things. All very well, if there was someone around to do the buffing up. All very well, if you could suddenly spring on someone else the fact of an ancestral tower.

He reversed, pulled in through a gate where stone pillars held urns of geraniums, started up a drive between a double row of cypresses, took a hairpin turn, and then another and another. When the drive levelled she saw, through a leafy screen on the downhill side, a jumble of buildings with a battlemented tower. He turned off the cypress-lined drive onto one that twisted downward. Some minutes later, they drove through an archway into a flagged court-yard with a well at its centre and a stone animal rearing on a plinth, its features so worn away it could be a rodent of some sort.

Our ancestral mouse?

He parked in a farther courtyard. Two big whitish dogs burst from metal-studded doors. Gianni sprang out to embrace them, introduce them. "This is Rudolfo, and here we have Charles, because we thought he had an English temperament." The dog stuck his nose in Clare's crotch, then looked up with mild eyes of the same deep amber as his master's.

His own apartment, Gianni said, was at the top of that tower. He was vague about what lay behind the many doors as they climbed up, fifty-two steps, light filtering through occasional arrow slits.

When they stepped into a darkened hallway at the top, Clare had an impression of terracotta floors, ceiling beams as thick as barrels. A pinkish glow filtered from a room where there must have been an open shutter; she caught a glimpse of a rosy quilt, a doll.

He led her up one more set of stairs to a landing, then through studded doors into a space almost completely dark. With a con-jurer's flourish, he went around opening the shutters on low square windows with stone sills as wide as sidewalks. She barely had time to form an impression — thick rugs, a fireplace, a trestle table with perhaps a kitchen alcove behind — before he steered her through arched doors onto a narrow balcony hovering over a vertical drop. Far below, a slim river wound silvery through patterned fields. A train that looked like a toy was pulling into a tiny tile-roofed train station at the river's edge. Beyond were many layers of hills, each one paler than the last, then beyond those were the deep blue moun-tain ridges.

"Wow."

"When I return here, I think always 'wow' as well."

She asked what those towers were, clustered in the near distance. That was Siena, he said. In the evening, when the sunset caught it, she would see that the whole town gave off a rosy glow from the light it had absorbed all day in its stones.

"You never told me your ancestral acres lorded it over Siena."

"So you like it, then? My kingdom?" He looked almost apprehen-sive. "Now here is something we must perform." He swooped her up like a bride. "I regret I did not carry you up the stairs. But now I formally welcome you, Clare Livingston, to my kingdom where all is yours to command!"

SHE PULLED AWAY so that she was standing again, stung by how foolish she was, after everything he'd explained about his marriage.

There were rules to this sort of thing, lines she had to walk. She must be careful not to step over.

"So tell me, what's the story of this place?" she said quickly, to cover the awkwardness of not letting him carry her over the threshold. "How come it's called *La Celta*?"

He would come up with something foolish, she knew, to ease them over that awkwardness, which of course he had caught.

She was right. His eyes flashed mischief. He asked if she knew the famous medieval English soldier of fortune, Sir John Hawkwood. There had been many other such companies of mercenary soldiers, he said, who had come here to spread much terror, "but the most dreaded was our Celt, who came with a band that played terrible instruments and all wore skirts, and occupied our castle before moving on to Verona. There he took the family name of the Montecchi, just to blend in. You have surely heard of the feud between the clans of the Montecchi and the Capuleti, and the tragedy your Shakespeare later stole?"

"You're absurd!"

"You do not believe? Very well, I will show you to your quarters," — much fake Scottish rolling of the *r*'s — "and then prevail upon you to take a spot of lunch."

But that would mean a trek back down to his car, while in one of those apartments bordering the courtyard, she'd decided for certain now, the Senior DiGiustinis lurked and spied.

"I'm not at all hungry, actually."

"In Italy we always must eat our midday meal, or we will not have the verve afterwards for making love."

"It's un-Canadian, though. We think it's like swimming. You could sink."

"Very well. As you are my guest, we must do everything in the manner your countrymen would approve."

So when she woke up much later, in a bed almost the size of Nova Scotia, she was starved.

SHE HEARD HIM TALKING in the other room. She recognized the already familiar rhythms of a phone conversation with his Mammà. A few times even on the drive here there'd been a small twitter hardly louder than a bat squeak from his pocket, and he'd pulled out the phone and checked the number. She'd come to recognize the mother-conversation tone: humorous, indulgent. These chats were never short.

Clare stretched out in the vast bed, which Gianni claimed had once been the playing field of a Spanish prince. The bed had remained in the tower bedroom since the days when Charles the Fifth had occupied Siena; as he explained this, Gianni had climbed three steps on the far side of the footboard and stood on a little carved-wood ledge there, saying that this was where the Spanish prince had delivered bedtime sermons to his spouse.

"And I suppose Juliet slept here with her Scottish lad as well?" she'd laughed, from the acreage of silk-covered feathers below.

"You do not believe in my Scottish heritage? Permit me to show you, then, my Highland fling." He'd pulled off the white silk shorts, popped the final button on his shirt, done a swan dive that landed him beside her on the cloud-like layers.

Now, in the last light filtering through closed shutters, Clare saw that the bedroom held much more dark carved wood. She couldn't help wondering what scenes those brooding chests and cupboards had witnessed. At the far end of the room, a set of steps led to a trap door in the ceiling. Gianni had said they would go up onto the parapet later to see the stars; he said that here, in his kingdom, there were different constellations altogether.

She found a bathroom through a set of studded doors, a vast marble sarcophagus with polished brass taps that gave out lots of hot water. He found her there and brought a long red flannel robe and wrapped her up. "You smell so good."

"You too. What have you been up to out there? You smell of bacon."

"I have been starting a little spaghetti carbonara; I hope this will be fine. I do not have a lot of supplies."

The kitchen table held a basket with tomatoes and a clutch of basil, and a round of Tuscan bread. Someone called Manfredo had brought the tomatoes from a vegetable garden out beyond the battlemented walls.

"Does Manfredo bring your fireplace wood up all those fifty-two steps as well?"

"Sometimes, *sì*." A vague twist of the hands, as if refusing to limit the possibilities — sometimes carried by Manfredo, and sometimes by himself, and perhaps sometimes by flocks of doves?

The window looked down into the dark courtyard where a wrought-iron lamp threw a faint gleam on the cobbles. She wondered which of the shuttered sets of windows might hold the senior DiGiustini.

She asked what had happened to his Land Rover. He said that Manfredo had taken it to wash, then to the stable.

Of course, she thought.

As they ate, he told her how the place had fallen almost to ruin when his stepfather, Tomasso, bought it.

"You mean these are not actually your ancestral acres?"

He laughed, spreading his hands, letting that particular ancestry escape. "But I am the one who is bringing everything back into shape." He was very proud of what he had accomplished; for example, to have all the apartments around the *castello* brought into modern comfort for his workers.

"Your workers live in the buildings around the courtyard?"

"Yes, many of them," he said. "Around here is generally much life, though this evening I think you have put an enchantment on."

He said that next day he would show her all that he had done to reclaim the heritage of the place. "For imagine! Tomasso even wanted to turn the *castello* into apartments for Americans to rent! What does he care, when he can still have his fine private life up at the villa."

"At the villa?"

"Yes, yes, you will see." He waved his hands, in that vague airy way, in the direction of the hill behind.

Always One Forbidden Room

BEFORE THEY WENT TO bed again, Gianni showed Clare a hand-drawn, tinted map of the whole estate, which hung at the top of the tower stairs. It was really more like an illustration of a kingdom in a fairytale, with the villa as the focal point, situated at the end of the cypress drive, within acres of box hedges, herbaceous plant-ings, landscaped groves with hidden grottoes, and vast slopes of lawn. The villa was large and white, with a double baroque stair-case folding back on itself to a regal arched entrance on the second floor. A fountain with dolphins spouted high plumes of water in the gravelled entrance court.

Very early the next morning, Gianni slipped out silently to meet his manager. Later, a phone rang somewhere in the apartment.

Mammà? Ever present. Never seen.

Perhaps never seen, in fact, by the likes of Clare. For it had all been a ruse, she decided, this story that the parents were off at the sea. They had their fine life up at the villa, and whatever the son and heir got up to in the *castello* they conveniently ignored.

That had been fine with Clare last night. But now, lying in the silky bed, sated, pampered, loved, she started hearing snaky whispers suggesting that having all this — having it and at the same time not having it — made her some kind of laughingstock. Then she was out of bed, wrapped in that long red robe, going through pockets, pulling open drawers, trying the doors to all the lower rooms, now locked, even the one where she'd seen the rosy bedspread and the doll. Eventually, she went to sit in one of the tower windows, cross-legged on the broad stone sill. She watched the sun come up over the far hills, a great ball of light that exploded across the sky, magnified by mist. She pictured the map of the estate, the fairytale kingdom. She thought how in fairytales there was always one room that the visitor was forbidden to enter, a kind of test.

When Gianni returned, he urged her to dress quickly.

"Come, we will find some little unicorn perhaps, for you who do not believe." He led her to his garden, situated between the first defensive wall and a second one, in an area that had once served to shelter residents of the surrounding hamlets from marauding armies.

"Look!" he said. "Something even more remarkable." He gestured towards a mass of scented bergamot among the crumbling stones of the garden wall. "We have some members of royalty who have lingered in their life cycle just for you. Our little Spanish Queens!"

A flash of saffron crystallized the light. A butterfly settled among the blooms, followed by another, a ripple of silver from its under-wing, a pattern of black lace over the velvet wing-top. "She is one of our very rare ones," he whispered. "In many countries she does not anymore exist. Do you know how many in Europe have become extinct?"

It was too terrible to think of. "No!"

"In Holland, this wealthy nation with its tulips and its diamonds, eleven species no longer come. In little Belgium, despite its chocolate and its fearsome civil service, there are thirty-two species which are extinct. Extinct. Is this not a dread word? Shall I tell you their names? Shall we make a poem?"

He walked back and forth in front of the crumbled wall.

"Redwing Skipper, Mazarine Blue, Purple-Edged Copper, Silver-Washed Fritillary ..."

On he went, and on; the litany of empty names the earth was becoming layered with, smothered by the silence of those wingless names. Clare saw herself creeping around in the long red robe, opening drawers, prying at locked doors, a larva of suspicion.

LATER, GIANNI TOOK CLARE around to meet some of his employees. He introduced her to Bastiano Gentili, his manager, telling Bastiano that she was "a most talented and famous artist who has come to grace us with her presence."

When they walked away, Clare asked him, please, not to introduce her that way to others.

He broke a twig from a tree and snapped it, then turned to her with such a look. "Clare, I have been stricken," he said, "Stricken, yes! — to think that words from me might have kept you from continuing the paintings for your new work."

Stricken. Hair, eyebrows, not-yet-shaven chin hairs springing electrically. *Oh I love you.* How else to explain the welling-up need to do anything, anything, to prevent that sad ridiculous hair-springing stricken look.

She took his hands. She said it had been terrible of her to make him the scapegoat for the fact that, well, she was just feeling a little painted-out at the moment.

He looked relieved. He had so much hoped, he said, that this was all behind her now. "But I will make it up to you. I will." His wind-blowing intensity again. "Here at La Celta, where you have time and freedom, I know you will find your muse returns."

Then he took her to see the new lambs. "Tosti!" he called out to the shepherd, "Come! You must meet Clare Livingston, a great and famous artist who has come to us to recuperate her powers." And by the time she met Manfredo of the many duties, "a most renowned botanical artist!" was what she had become.

"Please," she said when they were out of earshot, "Don't do that." She stamped her foot. He stamped his too. He said, "Then I will not."

They walked on. "But look!" He pointed to a creamy flower beside the byre where he kept rare white heifers. "See how this little one, which I believe in English is known as 'common cow wheat' —" He gave it a nudge with his toe. "See how it trembles with anticipation for the moment when you will deign to make its portrait."

So finally she confessed that there was something more than being painted-out going on. "I've lost it." She tried to explain.

He turned her to him, ran his fingers down the sides of her face, as if there were tiny disfigurements in its composition that he could smooth away. "This is why I have brought you here, to my refuge," he said. "To find it again."

"Only for that?"

He smiled. No, he admitted, there were a few other reasons. "Come!" He led her to a haymow above the byre.

AND SO THE DAY passed; Clare was glad to hold at bay thoughts of the villa up the hill.

In the late afternoon, they returned to the walled garden. Gianni said he wanted her to see the hummingbird moths that came skimming in at that hour. But then — from behind a bush — he produced a gift, a most beautiful folding stool, the legs carved, with a seat of tooled Florentine leather. It had been made especially for her, by a craftsman in Florence, to use while sketching in his garden. Gianni had taken the liberty of smuggling along the pack with her art materials, he confessed, which she would find in the drawer beneath the bed.

When he caught her expression, his own face took on a childish, heartbreaking pout of disappointment. Then sternness clamped down.

"You do not wish me to push you," he said. "I understand. Of course this cure will require rest, the breathing of this healthful air.

But then, it will require that you try. Such talent as yours does not leave. You have left it. Here in my garden you will get it back."

She saw him for a moment as a figure on a playing card, two opposite halves, and it was the sweet childish pouting upside-down half that she wanted to walk around the garden with. But he was saying, "For you see, my darling rare one, I have imagined the beautiful work we will accomplish here together. How we will aid and uplift one another."

Aid and uplift? Those snaky whispers slithered in again. *And you, Clare, are supposed to take part in all this aiding and uplifting without being good enough to be invited up to the villa?*

"Gianni. Cut it out!" she snapped. "I'm a really flawed person. You don't know the half of it. And why is it so important that I paint? I think that's all you care about. It's weird. You've got some fetish about my painting."

He turned pale. He put a finger to her lips. Then he took her arm and led her to a bench beside a bush whose flowers filled the air with a citrus perfume.

Did she know, he asked, that this was the famous burning bush? If they should light a match here, on this hot evening, the vapour from the attractive flower would make the air catch fire!

But, he added, he had also learned another thing about this burning bush. It could heal wounds. There was a fresco of this in the museum in Naples, rescued from the wall of a villa like the one that they would soon build.

"Yes," he rushed on, to sweep off her astounded look. "When you and I build our villa, I will make sure to have this little bush by the door, so that when we disagree we can quickly heal."

"Hang on — have I missed something here?"

He sprang up. From behind the same wound-healing bush, he pulled a satchel containing a bundle of books and scholarly journals, including the journal she'd seen before with the article about the gardens of King Herod. He spread a thick glossy book on her knee, then squatted beside her to turn the pages. It was the book he'd told her of, about the gardens of Pompeii, the excavations carried on by a revered garden archaeologist.

Clare did not get a chance to examine that properly, either, because he was too impatient to reveal his main surprise. He also planned to make Clare a gift of a Roman garden.

"First, yes, we will make for ourselves that little villa, something closer to the ground; because when we grow old, it will be too hard to climb the tower. And in the centre of our villa I will make a court-yard with a peristyle garden for my beautiful rare one to sit in and to do her exceptional paintings!"

ᘛ

THAT NIGHT, AS CLARE floated, rare and cherished in the great silk bed, she was caught in filaments where his dreams twined with hers. When she began to emerge from sleep, he was gone. She wondered at the silence. She tried to follow a thread out of her dreams, remember-ing what he'd said the first day: *You have laid an enchantment here.* She lay staring at the great beamed ceiling as first light crept in, at the carved staircase leading to the parapet roof. They had not yet climbed through that trap door, to see the new set of stars.

But there was one door in this castle, truly, that she would have to confront. Not a door forbidding her to enter, but one she must push through. He wanted her to go back to her painting. Why imagine there was something uncanny about his wanting that? He had been thrilled by her ability, intrigued — possessive, yes, but at the same time possessed by guilt, because he blamed himself for damaging her confidence, and also for damaging what he must know had been the great pleasure and refuge of her work.

So she would have to master this. It was the key to the enchanted kingdom, that work of hers. She saw this as she lay staring at the stair-case leading to the parapet, where in this light the carved flowers had become little grinning faces. Gianni himself might not completely know that what he cherished in her, needed most, perhaps the only thing he truly needed, was what he'd seen as her ability to transmute the painful beauty of the world. A responsibility almost too much to bear he'd called it, on that awful day in her kitchen.

Well then. If she was to remain here as his prize endangered love, she would have to put on the brilliant deceptive feathers of her so-called talent again, do it well enough to fool him anyway. As for herself, she thought now that maybe the work had always only been an excuse for not wholly living; that when he'd come along, she'd finally found what living was all about. She had to laugh as she got up, pulled on her clothes. Fine joke that the one thing she needed to keep this life alive was the one thing she could no longer do.

But she would.

Before she started down the tower stairs to the courtyard, she noticed a different door open this morning, on the lower floor of Gianni's apartment. She tiptoed close. Gianni's office. She hesitated on the sill, already feeling a sickish thrill of diminishment before she pushed across the room to the desk at the window, to pick up the photo in the silver frame.

The wife, two children, and Gianni. All standing together in a high-ceilinged room. The children were beautiful. A boy of perhaps thirteen, with dark hair like his father's and the same severe expression that Gianni sometimes wore. A girl who had disobeyed the photographer's instructions and was looking up at her father instead, with a sweet wicked grin, which he was returning. And the wife. Eleanora.

What had Clare expected? A perfectly groomed and haughty blonde perhaps, cashmere twin set, pearls — not the tired-looking woman in a sport vest with the logo of some junior team, the pretty mouth turned down with an expression sad but enduring, the brown hair not much thought about.

Clare held the photo, trying out a pleasing smile that the wife in the photo lacked. She felt the rest of herself disappear, while the smile remained. This was what it would be like, on and on, the fixed smile of the fifth person who both was and wasn't there.

But I can do it, she thought. The wife never comes here. This can be mine. She turned, still holding the photo, and looked around the room that held Gianni's personal things, his books and papers, his telescope, her Amazonia book, yes, on a gilt-edged table, and beside it the big leather portfolio he'd brought from the car. She was tempted to take a look in there. Then, from the sliver-framed photo she caught a flash of light as the sun came in, turning the glass into a mirror. She saw herself reflected and all the figures in the photo gone. Just herself, a woman with hair spun to gold, and behind her, through the reflected stone arches of the window, Siena's distant towers, the whole scene like a medieval fresco: the woman held in love's enchantment, beautiful and feckless, maybe even bad, who slips sideways into a life that isn't hers, slips there, stays there, doesn't care.

She continued down the fifty-two stairs of the tower, crossed the silent courtyard, found her way to the walled garden. Her task this morning was simple: by a simple effort of will and skill to start in on her new life here. The burning bush would be a perfect pick for her new true book, one that would make Gianni proud. It would be a book celebrating his garden and his life. *The Garden of the Unicorn*, she'd call it. She reached behind the bush for the stool.

WHEN GIANNI FOUND HER, she was surrounded by sheets of heavy expensive paper, all torn, scraps holding partial sketches, scraps daubed with colour: the creamy blossoms of the burning bush had curdled as she added cadmium; the ruffled leaves of bryony had transformed under her brush into green sponges; the blue poppy had kept whispering that, try as she might, she would never capture its thrilling shade, never have the energy to make a proper composition of it either: "Why not succumb to being kept and beautiful like me, enjoy your season in the sun? Why all this effort to be something more …?"

"Clare! Darling! I can't stand to see you weep."

He held her, and it was the best of comfort; it was what primordial sea creatures might have felt when they gave up their struggle with the waves and let themselves get washed up onto the hot sand.

◦~◦

LATER, GIANNI TOOK CLARE riding into the woods. They rode past the turnoff to the villa, but she didn't mention it. He wanted to show her his rare pigs, he said, an endangered breed that lived best by foraging for herbs and nuts in the wild. She said, "Oh sure, absolutely I want to see your rare pigs." In truth she still felt so ashamed, so desolate, so lost, literally lost. The woman who had lost what most intrigued him, soon to be supplanted, even if he didn't exactly know that yet; for certainly, as soon as you allowed something to become essential, as she'd allowed Gianni to be, you had already lost all power.

He was mounted on a tall black gelding. He looked splendid on a horse. She watched his hands on the reins, the delicate touch that controlled the spirited creature. She was riding a little bay mare that was his daughter's. The stable boy had let that slip.

She kept waiting for him to glance sideways at her in disappointment as her morning's failure settled on him: then to start finding little other things at fault, which would make it obvious that they were not on the same idyllic wavelength after all. In an upland area, they came upon workmen fencing meadowland where he hoped to raise the almost-lost Pomarancio sheep. She tried to say the right, enthusiastic things. He told her of plans to start a little herd of donkeys too, of a type almost extinct. "A few of these still roam the slopes of Mount Amiata," he said. "Do you know that cone-shaped hill across the Val di Chiana from your lovely property?"

Her lovely property. Where it would soon be clear to both of them that she should return.

"But what my sister is undertaking is the best!" he said.

"Your sister? Sorry, I lost the thread there for a moment."

He apologized, saying that perhaps he had not previously explained his sister's great experiment at her stables, which was to recreate the blood lines of the *Nobilissimo Nappolitain,* the famous Neapolitan courser, a steed which by the beginning of the last century had faded to memory. Federica was involved with the professor of genetics in Naples on this project.

"But how can this be done?"

He said that beyond the money he supplied for this research, it was a matter of "untangling," to put it briefly.

"*You* fund this?"

He hit his forehead. "You see what a small person I am at heart, wanting in a weak moment to let you believe that I am big! I should have allowed you to believe that her husband Ralph is the one, as I know he loves to pretend."

He added that in truth he did not fund it completely. His mother managed to squeeze a little from Tomasso their stepfather; but unfortunately Federica and Tomasso did not much like one another.

"So because I have my own inheritance, and because Federica's father was penniless when he died, I am glad to help."

"I didn't mean —"

"No of course you didn't mean!" Still miraculously so fond, that smile of his. "But there is no reason why you should not ask. It is just —" He shook his head. "All families are complicated, but each Italian family is complicated in a different way. As Tolstoy would have written, if he had not had the great good fortune to be Russian."

SHE LONGED TO URGE him to go on with this account. Sneaky curiosity plagued her now, greedy even. He had his own inheritance? He was not completely dependent, then, on either the stepfather or the business controlled by his discouraged-looking wife?

But it would be so easy to take the wrong step now.

"Tell me about this untangling," she said instead. "Is it really possible, to bring back a breed of horses that has disappeared?"

"Ah!" He looked so happy to explain. "It is of course a research in its beginning stages. Briefly, here is the approach. The Neapolitan has contributed in a significant way to the creation of the Austrian Lipizzaner, among others. And so if we undo this," he spread his fingers as if allowing the complexity to escape, "it will be possible to separate out again the strain."

If we undo this.

Luke.

For the first time since she'd come here, she consciously thought of Luke, pictured him undoing the work of a Stone Age carver by putting the chipped-off fragments back together, the happiest he'd ever been in his whole life. Where was he? She hadn't called him. Had he managed to persuade Sir Harold Plank? What if he was back in Tuscany? What if …?

"So you see," Gianni added, "if such genetic research is possible, why I refuse to despair of the unicorn."

∽

THEY EMERGED FROM THE woodland trail. A wide stretch of meadow lay before them. Gianni said, "Shall we let our horses gallop?" Clare turned her mare on a long diagonal towards a hedged dry stream. The mare sailed across. She galloped on, conscious of the thud of his horse's hoofs just behind, until together they pulled up at the start of farther woods.

He dismounted, took the mare's bridle.

"I think we can have our siesta here," he said. "Tonight we will dine late. This is the habit of Mammà, who is of course expecting us."

He pulled it out of a hat, just like that. The meeting he knew she had been fearing.

Did she know him at all?

Who was he, in fact? What did he actually do with himself all day, all month, all year, when he claimed to be running this estate where everybody did his bidding, even his firewood carried up by doves?

What actually went on in that beautiful brain, along with all the glittering ideas? Had he shrewdly planned the exact moment when he would present the dinner with Mammà as a *fait accompli?*

He put an unnecessary hand to her elbow, as she sprang off the mare. She pulled away to scramble up to a little knoll of deeper grass beneath an oak.

"*Attenzione!* Not up there! There might be snakes."

"Do you know how many hours I've spent tramping in the grass never giving a thought to your deadly vipers?"

"Protected by innocence," he said. "But now that you remember, you must come to know where they hang out."

Oh absolutely, the voices started slithering again, *Get to know where we hang out, and then grab a forked stick and read our forked tongues that have been whispering how you do belong here, Clare — really truly, and not just camped off to the side — how you must connive to make it legal, tie him down, and fast, before he tires of you altogether.*

He was undoing a blanket rolled behind his saddle. He spread it on the grass.

"Darling," Clare heard herself say. "Dearest," feeling her face change, as wrinkles of subterfuge started setting in. "Sweet Gianni, if I am to meet Mammà tonight, and Tomasso, too, you must tell me more about them."

She had just bitten into a delicious, tainted thought. Wasn't it possible that his mother might turn out to be an ally? That Mammà might recognize in Clare a fellow homewrecker who ought to be encouraged; that perhaps she was fed up to the teeth with the hard-working little Bolognese in her vest with the sporting logo?

"*Carissimo,* you must tell me the complicated story about your father and Federica's," she said. "How they both died, as you once told me — am I not right, such a tragedy my darling — that they died on the same day? And how it is that you are the one with the inheritance? Only of course so I do not make the wrong remark and make a hash of things."

"'Make a hash'?" A smile that could break her heart. How easy for this new conniving woman to make him smile. He said, "This is, in your idiom, for to 'spoil' things? Like a greasy American breakfast with too many potatoes? Darling, you will never make this hash."

But he would tell her, yes, he said. Above all he wanted her to know him, completely. This was perhaps the one thing we could do upon this earth, he said: we could give to the one we loved the gift of our true self.

He took a deep breath, raised his hands to his temples, closed his eyes. Almost, she wished she hadn't tempted this poison to race through her blood.

He began to tell her of the shame that he had been born to wear. That was how he phrased it, *born to wear*. She tried to listen from a distance. She watched the start of a great grey gap widening between them. If she was clever, he would never know how far she'd sailed.

When Gianni finished telling the story, Clare could see how the scandal would have been enough to make a little boy determine never to subject his own children to the shame of such a thing. She recalled Ralph Farnham's gleeful comment: *Only in Italy, old dear. Unless you count our Royals,* and she thought that, yes, it might be a peculiarly Italian sort of shame that Gianni had to "wear," as he put it. Nothing he had done himself, and nothing that would later prevent some elderly aunt from settling her personal fortune on him — the kind of shame, in fact, that all who knew of it would quite love: like seeing a little boy dressed in a clown suit whenever he was taken anywhere. Easy to make a farce of it: the beautiful young wife; the feckless older husband who loved nothing more than tramping the fields with dog and gun; the agriculture student, a family friend who came to stay. The inevitable affair. The day of the double tragedy, the husband falling on his gun, the lover falling from his horse. And the lover's wealthy older married brother rescuing the penniless young widow who'd been left with a daughter and an unborn child.

"And when I was born, my dear mother — twice bereaved, and with perhaps misguided romantic stubbornness — linked the name of her lover Giano, the father I never knew, with that of Federica's father, Paulo, in naming me Gianpaulo, making my bastard heritage clear for all to see who had a mind to laugh behind their hands. My stepfather Tomasso allowed this. He has always allowed Mammà everything. But me, he looked right through from the very start. I was the child invisible. Though he made sure, all the years I was growing up, that I knew I was the one responsible for the fact that there was no speaking between the family in Bologna and ours in Siena, that I was tarred with this, you see."

He held out his hands as if the tar were still there, as if it might stick to everything he touched. Clare thought that in the world of shame as she knew it, this might be in the minor leagues. No matter. Tar was tar. Even if no one else saw it, you could never wash it off.

"Only when the family business fell into further trouble," he was saying, "did I become visible. Eleanora's father came with financial rescue. Then it was ordained that the sole remaining marriageable DiGiustini should seal that partnership in marriage."

"Oh my love," Clare said. "Dear love." She kissed his eyelids. She cradled him.

Mammà

CLARE'S COURAGE EVAPORATED THE moment Gianni's cream Mercedes, freshly washed and smelling of new wax, rounded the final upper bend of the cypress drive. High and almost musically ornate iron gates came into view, and then the grounds themselves; they so far outreached anything she'd ever experienced of a higher realm of living that she was almost relieved to see the red Alfa parked by the dolphin fountain, to see Ralph and Federica getting out — Ralph tripping on the gravel, recovering, Federica in the long red dress like a red tree trunk striding impatiently ahead. As the four of them converged at the bottom of the stairs, Ralph pulled Clare into an embrace, whispered in her ear that he'd always admired that yellow frock. "And now my dear, you will meet the fatal trout, you lucky thing."

"Who?"

"I thought you were quicker. I refer to the dear old trout, our former *femme fatale*. You will have to get past Cerberus up there first, though, I fear."

He rushed her up the baroque staircase to introduce her to the austere brown-tweeded figure waiting on the landing at the top. The stepfather, Tomasso. A tall man with very upright carriage and a restrained hound-like face blotched by age, who produced a grimace that might have passed as a smile. When he greeted his stepdaughter, his expression was even more removed. When his wife appeared, Clare thought the look he trained on her was infinitely weary.

"Gianpaulo!" Gianni's mother called out. "How clever of you to bring this lovely girl again."

She took Clare's hand, leaned forward with a conspiratorial purr loud enough for everyone to hear. "I always tell Gianpaulo that you are my favourite of all the girls he brings."

In the moment before, Clare had been thinking that this might indeed go well. Mammà had been making her way across the portico with a cane, looking frail but very game, and much older than Clare had imagined, despite the blonde hair spun into a meringue around the glossy face.

My favourite of all the girls he brings.

Even now, meeting blue eyes vague with charm, Clare found herself reluctant to credit the malice of that remark. Ever since the afternoon, she'd felt ashamed of her spurt of ruthless ambition, if that really was what it had been — all of it washed away in the great flood of sweetness and concern she'd felt for Gianni, pure loving concern, when he'd told his story. She'd thought that if she wore that tonight, it would protect her when she met his family. They'd see she wanted nothing for herself except his happiness.

Gianni was at her elbow, his tone to his mother warm and half-teasing, as if this were the most delightful small folly, to make such mistakes. "But I have told you, Clare is a visitor from Canada, Mammà."

Mammà smiled indulgently at her son. "*Why* did you never divulge that this lovely girl was from America?" She tightened her grip so that Clare felt the slippage of diamonds on several fingers. "Come, we are all sitting through here in the San Gimignano room. I want you to meet some people we have invited just for you. Did you know I was almost born an American myself?"

"Mammà!"

"When my grandfather was ambassador, we sailed out to America you know." Gazing up at Clare, eyes rimmed in pale blue mascara. "Papa had gone ahead on business. He intended to meet the boat and take my mother straight to the embassy, so that when I arrived in the world it would be on Italian soil. But I was too quick for them. I was born aboard the *Franconia,* which meant that I came into the world a citizen of France. Do you know Papa's first words when he saw me?"

She glanced merrily around at them all, as they might want to join in on the family story, then tightened her grip on Clare's hand.

"I was the first grandchild of this generation, you understand, and Papa had promised his father a boy. He was so disappointed that he cried out, 'She is yellow — and she is a girl — and now they tell me she is French!' He never let me forget that. 'She is yellow, and she is a girl, and now they tell me she is French.'"

"Not ambassador, Mammà! Grandpapa was the consul general." Federica Inghirami managed to shift her cigarette far enough to perform her greeting kisses without setting her mother's hair on fire.

"Yes Fifi, of course." Mammà turned back to Clare. "So you can imagine what a confusion this has caused all my life! The Bolognese are very proud of their history, you know, and when you update your papers and they learn that you are a Galluzzi-Carbonesi, yet you were born in the territory of France, they do not know what to make of you."

She took a hobbling step back, still holding Clare's hand, almost a dance step. "My dear, how lovely to see you again, and to think Gianpaulo has hidden that we have this in common. I was born on the way to America, you know. I remember my father recounting to me that on the day I was born one of his workmen said, 'It is a good day, isn't it, *Marchese?*' and he replied, 'No, it is a terrible day. She is yellow, and she is a girl, and now it seems that she is French.' We laughed at that many times, until he died."

"Mammà, we are dying of thirst and Ralph has driven like a fool." Federica handed Ralph the smouldering butt of her cigarette. He dropped it into a planter at the top of the baroque stairs.

Gianni's mother turned to her husband. "Toto, yes come! Why are we standing on the stairs?" Tomasso's expression, as he took her arm, was bleak.

THE CAVERNOUS ROOM THEY moved into had *trompe l'oeil* frescoes on either side. On the left was the town of San Gimignano as seen from a distance, with all its tall slim towers; on the right, a view down onto tiled roofs and countryside, as from the top of one of those towers. In each the artist had included an easel in the foreground, which held an almost completed version of that same scene, and an empty camp stool.

"He wished to be there, you see — so he painted the town instead, but left himself out of it," Gianni's mother was explaining. "I have always thought that was clever. He was a prisoner here, in this house, during the war — or perhaps he was allowed to spend the duration hiding here. I have never quite learned the story."

The domed ceiling swirled with figures rising heavenward on beams of radiance. Little angels peered over the rim. At the far end of the room, through arches of a loggia, was the actual distant presence of Siena, silhouetted against the blue-black evening sky, jewelled in lights. Gianni's mother was saying that the villa had been designed by a famous seventeenth-century architect to take advantage of that view.

Clare had heard somewhere that one did not admire the possessions of the rich, but she couldn't help exclaiming, "This is a breathtaking room."

"Yes, we think it is quite amusing," Gianni's mother said.

AT FIRST CLARE DID not see those guests *invited just for her.* They sat so still, and they were so very small.

"Carolina, Egidio — here we have the little friend of Gianni," Mammà said.

There was a stir among the cushions in a far island of chairs and sofas. A tiny elderly couple turned their faces from a book they had been studying together. Carolina was all in grey silk, with white braids around her ears; Egidio wore a tiny barrel-chested velvet suit, a red stone the size of a quail's egg pinning his cravat. When Clare came close she saw it was her book they had been studying.

But they were not merely Carolina and Egidio. A pause, like a silent drum roll, preceded the introduction of the *Marchese di Barbareschi* and the *Marchesa.*

They sat beaming up at Clare. She felt all the objects in the room coming to discrete attention. Still, their joint smiles were mild, and very kind. They spoke more or less together in a verbal braid, one finishing or starting the sentences of the other, and occasionally both at once.

"So my dear," they said. "We have looked with interest at your work in this volume, and it strikes us as quite adequate indeed, though understandably derivative of Margaret Mee. But most promising. You are clearly young. We speak, it must be fairly claimed without beating around the bush, as the most extensive collectors of such material perhaps in Europe, possessing not only the best of recent practitioners but many rare folios and florilegia." They paused, expectantly.

Clare glanced towards Gianni. Where was this going?

He was studying his shoes.

"And we have been promised," the duet continued, "Indeed, we have been thrilled to come up from Rome for this: we have been assured that we will see new work where the most skilled techniques of botanical art are combined with the portrayal of cleverly imagined species, which might be precisely what we had hoped to find for an exhibition we are planning — a most daring one, we must proclaim — of material along such lines."

"Oh!"

Gianni did not meet her eye, instead crossed the room, pulled a bell rope by the marble fireplace.

"Gianni?"

He raised a hand to ward off her inquiry, smiled a guilty smile, "*Aspetta!* Just one moment."

In less than a moment, a butler-looking person entered carrying the leather portfolio last seen in Gianni's study in the tower. The servant handed the case to Gianni, who set it on the sofa, flipped it open, pulled out Clare's meadow paintings one by one and laid them out on the broad low table in front of Egidio and Carolina.

CLARE COULDN'T LOOK AT Gianni now. She tried to get her feelings straight. It was theft — secretly taking her work, bringing it for these strangers to peer at, setting her up to be publicly judged! But she couldn't snatch the work away. That would be too embarrassing for him. She did glance up. He looked very pale but determined, that tense determined windswept look.

The *Marchese* and his wife leaned close. Clare couldn't help holding her breath as they picked up this painting and that one, glancing occasionally at each other. Despite her shock, she felt a tingle of excitement. She hadn't looked at these paintings herself for so long. Now she saw that they were so — yes — really beautiful. At least to her. They spoke to her. Some with intricate, interlocked, massed compositions, yet paying homage to each individual specimen; others eloquent with secrets shimmering both above and below the soil, delicacy and boldness combined. How they took her back to those hours working in the meadow, when she'd felt she could fly. And now these aristocratic people, these experts, these renowned collectors, were giving them such close attention; surely they would know that these were far more than just cleverly imagined species, that something of far greater worth was going on in these compositions; and then Gianni, too, would accept that these had not been fairytale inventions. The sickening sense of having to prove the truth of her work would vanish, like magic, without her ever having to burst the bubble of enchantment they shared.

Silence in the room. Then the whisper of displaced air from the puffy sofa cushions as Carolina and Egidio at last settled back, looked up at Clare with kindly smiles.

"How sweet," Carolina said. "Have you thought of doing designs for decorator cloth? Or wallpapers perhaps!"

"Absolutely!" Edigio said. "This, for example, is very like the paper in the cabana of the Browns we stayed in, near Galveston, only more meticulously observed."

"We have a very good friend in Como," Carolina said, "who manufactures and exports all around the world! Will we put you in touch?"

Clare caught a covert fluttering of glances among the others, all still standing around as if in the presence of royalty, as perhaps they were. Even Mammà was still upright, leaning on her cane, perhaps not exactly following the contretemps but delighted that something amusing was going on.

Wallpaper.

Clare tried to look as if she had not picked up the devastating slight. Ashamed, at first, not just for herself but for these people, too; for how truly barbarically cutting those sweet smiling remarks had been. But perhaps they didn't understand, she told herself. Perhaps they moved in a higher realm where you could drop these small indictments on the needy, for their own good. Drop them lightly and move on. And maybe they were right.

"But come!" the Marchese di Barbareschi said. "You must tell us about yourself." His wife reached out a hand, drew Clare down between them. "You are from America we understand."

As if on cue, they began to sing in harmony, "*Oh the sage in bloom, is like perfume, boom boom boom boom …*" They reached across Clare to clap one another's hands. "*Deep in the heart of Texas! Reminds me of the one I love, deep in the heart of Texaaaaas!*"

The *Marchese* blew Carolina a kiss. She giggled like a girl. "We had such a romantic holiday in Texas, that time we stayed near Galveston!" Then, seized with a fit of coughing, she rustled for a lozenge in her tiny grey woven-leather reticule.

"Alfredo, water!" Gianni's mother ordered the butler who still hovered near.

Carolina leaned close to Clare. "It has been just a little difficult, as you can see, for us to come all this way from Rome, Egidio with his *reumatismo,* and me with my fatigues."

Another guest came in just then — white-haired, cold-eyed, long-fingered, dressed in pale blue denim. He was introduced as Aldo. He said, "*Santa Maria* I am parched, where in heaven's name are the drinks?"

Gianni's mother said she had forgotten the drinks, because Gianni had been showing the paintings of his little friend.

"Toto!" she called to her husband. "What are you thinking of?"

CLARE GOT UP AND went out to the loggia, trying to collect her emotions and her thoughts. The setting was extraordinary. This was almost the worst, to be here, in this setting, suffering this tangle of confusions. A full moon had risen, presenting a scene of black and silver, everything of an extreme unreal perfection which at the same time felt as if it had been simmering all her life just below her skin. Whose eye could this have been designed for, if not for hers? The succession of descending terraces and clipped boxwood hedges that had been arranged with such intelligence, leading down to a lit-up fountain spraying a basket of water that exactly held the view of Siena, its lights quivering and shifting as if set on this liquid crown, an effect conceived centuries ago by that same famous architect, no doubt, who'd conceived the domed ceiling in the room where little angels had peered at her while the noble couple judged her paintings.

Gianni came and joined her. She should be angry, but how could she be as angry as was called for? It must have been humiliating for him to put her work forward, then to have its worth so saccharinely scorned. The best thing would be for her to plead a headache, ask him to take her back to his place right now.

He said, "Clare you must not take this too much to heart."

So he wasn't even going to pretend it had not been a disaster?

She said, "Why on earth did you do that, hold me out like that?"

He tried to take her hand. She pulled it away. She said, "You did not like those paintings!"

He said no, no, that was completely untrue! He had always known those paintings were remarkable. He had told her they were remarkable. He had felt sure that when the Barbareschi saw them they would recognize such singular talent, despite the slightly fantastical nature of the work.

"I believed their approval would be the drug you needed to bring you back to painting again, and then turn your ability to what so badly needs to be recorded on this earth: what is real and true and often threatened."

"Truth! From the man who believes in unicorns."

He took a breath. "I am so devastated by this, on your behalf. But you see, Clare, as I said before once, I have some fear for you. Please, don't move away. What I must say now is so very hard for me to say."

He said it, though.

At last.

He said that he knew, for one thing, that she had never been to the Amazon; he had many contacts, as she would undoubtedly understand. He confessed that at first he had thought that he would play along.

"But then I fell — bang!" He hit his forehead against a pillar to demonstrate the power of that bang. "And after this, I have wanted to bring you here and keep you safe and nurture you, for I have perceived that somewhere you have been badly damaged by the world. Yet what you have retained is so rare, and you can be so much more!"

Wasn't that what she wanted? Rescue. Wasn't that what she had wanted before, when they stood in her kitchen? Giving in. Being known, sheltered, understood?

Why was she holding back, saying, "Listen! I'm sorry my paintings didn't stand up to those noble people's noble scrutiny, and that the whole thing has been such an embarrassment for you, but —"

"For me? For me I do not care one fig! But I will never again have you exposed to such denigration, and then such foolishness with their damn song! I could have strangled the neck of that little man and pushed his ruby into his gullet."

"Please! I've got to get out of here right now. Just drive me back. Tomorrow you can take me home. It was a mistake to come to La Celta. It gets me confused, if you really want the truth. It gives me uncomfortable ideas that I can't afford. I have to go back to my real life now."

He looked shocked. "This is our real life. We have made all these plans!"

"You made them, Gianni. But you have a few other serious entanglements, don't forget."

"No." He pulled himself straight. He glared. "I have already crossed the Rubicon." He straightened further, into a heroic stance, and she couldn't help smiling.

"You have?"

"I have written to Eleanora this morning, when we came back from the garden, when I saw you so upset. I have told her she does not need me, and I have been blessed beyond all measure to find someone who does. I have told her that you and I will marry."

"Wait …"

For one moonstruck moment, everything did wait. The glittering drops of the fountain paused mid-air. The silvered scene hardened. Even the shadows gleamed metal, reflecting an overreaching wish come true.

Then a throat-clearing just behind. Aldo, of the thousand-dollar jeans.

"I have been delegated to tell the young people we are about to move to the dining room for dinner."

Ring for Champagne

GIANNI'S MOTHER HAD REDONE the dining room to celebrate the estate's mythic roots, the walls papered in a design of Celtic knots set around Scottish scenes: a piper on a hill, a moon dancing on a rill, a stag at bay. She was explaining to the Barbareschi that the silk tartan table covering had been especially woven at Como. The napkin rings were amethyst and silver, each set with a rabbit foot.

Ralph Farnham put a hand on Clare's elbow as he pulled out her chair, murmuring ,"Welcome to the higher echelons, old dear. Didn't I once tell you that nothing could ever be good enough?" He looked pleased to have a fellow traveller on that road. "Just thank your glitzy little American stars that you're the girlfriend," he added, "and not locked in like some of us." Federica shot a scowl mirroring the stag's head on the wall.

Gianni was seated across from Clare, but not directly opposite. A new arrival, Nunziata, had been put beside him, a woman of a certain age, making every effort to fend it off. Succeeding, too. Mulberry hair in wild curls. Green eyes. All the lines and wrinkles falling gracefully into place, under a toffee glaze of sun. How was it possible, also, to wear so few inches of very bright green silk and still signal elegance and class?

Nunziata's husband was in Zurich. There was laughter around this. With Nunziata's arrival, the tide of language swept into fast Italian.

"You must forgive us," Nunziata said, leaning in Clare's direction after another burst of laughter, offering cleavage down which Tomasso was sadly staring. "This is all my fault. I do not to speak your language very well."

But Clare was glad to be left out. Since Gianni's declaration, her ribcage had turned metallic too, like a true cage, so much racketing around inside.

Gianni's bold pronouncement was sure to evaporate — that much came clear, as the nonsense in her chest settled down. Maybe he had written to his wife, but hadn't posted the letter — or if an email, he'd neglected to press "Send." He was making stiff conversation with Nunziata now, glancing Clare's way from time to time, and she tried to telegraph him the message *Don't worry. I know it was just another lovely dream.* She smiled. He looked more worried still, perhaps mistaking her smile for excitement at his supposed decision, imagining she'd taken him seriously, believed?

Carolina and Egidio were in fine form, tackling their antipasto with rapid tiny bites, and more than once bursting into snatches of song. Was this their concept of noblesse oblige, an attempt to keep the party lively and at the same time to cover up what they might now be thinking had been their insensitivity?

Gianni looked increasingly pale and tense, and Clare wondered if she hadn't wished those overreaching wishes earlier today, would he have spoken as he had, and landed himself in such a pickle now?

Look what I've brought on him, she thought. She remembered him listing all the butterflies gone from the world, how he'd made those names into a poem. He'd battled the terrible sadness of extinction by saving what he could — even to the point of a defiant faith in things that never could be what he thought. Like the unicorn. Or her.

The consommé arrived. Carolina and Egidio turned to Clare. "In America, you have such soups!" they said. "We heard the jingle everywhere." Egidio raised his spoon. "*Mmmm good!*" Carolina chimed in with the tune. The others laughed and clapped.

"Signora Livingston," Carolina said. "In truth, you must be just a little homesick for your great country. Eager perhaps to return?"

Gianni pushed back his chair.

"Signora Livingston has no intention to leave. This evening I have asked my dear Clare to be my wife."

The stag's head bobbled on the wall, the rabbit feet skipped across the cloth; Clare had no idea how long it was before it all rearranged itself. If she had been prepared for this, she would have expected argument, outrage. But Gianni's mother was looking at her, for the first time, with piercing interest. Even Tomasso had emerged from his protective detachment to nod across the table at his stepson, wearily, as if to say *Welcome to the club.* Everyone indeed seemed to quicken at the coming scandal, which would in a manner absolve them all by being even more notorious.

But little was said.

"Tomasso. Ring for some champagne," Gianni's mother ordered. "We must acknowledge this interesting news." Gianni was beaming, as if all his earlier tension had been about finding the right moment to make his announcement. Tall crystal glasses were raised, though no one proposed a toast. Even the *Marchese* and his little grey mate seemed unable to rise to the correct ebullient protocol. The meal continued. Talk became general again. Carpaccio followed. Then quail. Clare found herself studying Mammà, *the fatal trout,* trying to calibrate Tomasso's feelings for the woman who had cost him so much, and who was telling the story once again of her origins as a citizen of France, tossing her thin ringed hands, batting her blue-rimmed eyes at Aldo now. Clare decided that Tomasso didn't feel indifference to the once-fatal beauty after all, no. What his restrained expression revealed was pure and intensely loyal hate.

The air in the room began to solidify. Clare imagined herself in distant years, at this table, repeating for the fifth time some story of her own past, and Gianni looking at her in that same way, everything long ago hardened between the two of them, the way the silver scene had earlier. He is the endangered one, she thought; but how skittery the truth was. She watched it dart round the table, thinking that for once she had to catch it, make it talk. Instead, she saw the Roman garden Gianni had promised he would build for her inside their dream villa, the garden where she would sit and paint, and he would watch: the beautiful place, walled up brick by brick, by that watchful love.

Gianni was giving minute attention to the many tiny bones of his quail, looking ravenous, relieved, subsumed by happiness. Clare got up from the table, intending just to find the powder room, but as she passed under the gaze of the little angels on the ceiling of the San Gimignano room, her meadow paintings called out in the semi-gloom. She gathered them together, slid them into Gianni's portfolio, carried this with her to the arched front door as she went out to breathe the air.

Across the gravel court the musical iron gates were singing. It was like a dance, as she took one step down the marble staircase, and another and another, one flight to the right, doubling back to the left. She passed the fountain with the spouting dolphin, and kept going.

To Hell with the Devil's Dogs

BUT SHE COULDN'T GET there from here.

"*No no Signora, non è possibile!*" the station agent insisted. A midnight train ran from the coast to Siena, yes, in one hour. And from Siena she might take a train to Chiusi later in the day, and from there …

Ah, but his brother had a car. His brother would drive her, if indeed she was in such a hurry. "Do not worry, I will wake him, no, my brother will be glad!"

And yes, the station agent said, he would keep the keys of the Land Rover for young Signor DiGiustini, for when young Signor DiGiustini came for them. He was so unquestioning that for a moment Clare let herself wonder if it happened often, young women fleeing from La Celta in the middle of the night. She let herself wonder this to pacify her guilt for the terse note she'd left, after tearing up so many others. And she'd already been so cruel, hiding from the lights of his car as he drove up and down the cypress road in search of her, keeping silent even when she heard his desperate calls. Eventually, when he must have returned to the villa to search the gardens again, she had taken the chance to collect her things, grab his spare set of keys. Write the note.

Gianni, it was lovely. But we let it go too far. I told you from the start

that I was involved with someone else. I will leave the Land Rover at the
train station. Forgive me. Clare.

She told the station agent's brother that she had to hurry, that she
was expecting a guest to arrive from America.

But if Gianni overtook them, it would be fate.

The station agent's brother took her at her word and raced
through the intervening hills and valleys and little villages at an
alarming speed, scattering chickens, wobbling early riders on their
bikes. Clare's awful words coiled through her head: *I told you from*
the start that I was involved with someone else. Of course she never
could be, now. If you were very lucky you got one crack at what
she'd had, the amazing thing she'd had, and if you weren't brave
enough or bad enough or heaven knew what else enough, then that
was that. If I'd been different, she thought. How odd this barrier
was, that separated her from what she could be if she were different:
the she who knew exactly what it was that was happening in her
life, could figure it out. The sky over the Val di Chiana was thick
and grey with smoke. The station agent's brother said there were
wildfires in the hills. In Gianni's refuge she had not realized how
drought had settled. The sun came up red behind the city said to
be older than Troy. The station agent's brother skirted the base of
the hill, just as Clare had the day she'd arrived, which seemed centuries ago, then up the rutted road, then pulled up on her grassy terrace.
No one waited there. The house looked forbidding: hollowed of
love. As she was too, for a purpose she could no longer keep straight.
She threw her pack into the jeep, and crawled in after it. It was
blazing midday when she woke.

Inside, the house was angrily clean, expressing Marta's disgust,
she supposed, at her going off with Gianni. When she and Gianni
were leaving for La Celta, Marta had pulled her aside. "The married
brother of your neighbour, Signora," she'd hissed. "In the *zona* everyone will make poison of this now."

"How will they know?"

The level, hard-scrubbed gaze. "In our hills here, Signora Livingston, when God sees, everybody sees."

That day, Clare had smiled at the sweeping terribleness. Was Marta her rock now? The one she could cleave to, maybe find a scrap of motherly consolation for the awful right thing that she had done at last?

It was late afternoon when she hiked up to Marta and Niccolo's to let them know she'd returned.

No one was there.

As she started back from the old house, across the wide gravelled yard, she caught a bright yellow gleam from inside one of the ram- shackle sheds, a hue so bright, so unnatural, a glimpse so unlikely, that she caught her breath and crept closer.

Not a tractor. The half-gaping door suggested a longer, sleeker shape. She creaked the door wider. The place smelled feral. She heard a rustling she hoped was only rats. In the dim cobwebbed light, she met the slit-eyed complacency of a long, fast-looking car, yes surely a very expensive car, its tires removed, its body propped on olive crates. The Lamborghini.

But could it be here legitimately? She remembered Marta bristling when she'd asked if they had been storing any of her uncle's things, taking her question the wrong way: *What did Signor Kane have in any case that we would want? We have all our own things that we like!*

The lawyer had told Clare clearly that all her uncle's property had been left to her.

Clues rattled through her mind. Things she hadn't picked up, or hadn't wanted to. Marta's indignation when she'd asked about *tombaroli,* Niccolo's constant warnings that she should not walk in the hills. The way they'd bundled her out of their house after the announcement on TV about the looted *bucchero.*

A rush of adrenaline, as she pried open the locked compartment on the dash to take a look at the registration. The courage, then, of someone who'd already cut her losses.

But the dogs? The devil's dogs and now the third one who is not so nice?

To hell with the devil's dogs.

Luke left his gun.

～

THE REVOLVER WAS SURPRISINGLY heavy. How to carry it concealed? How to shoot it, for that matter?

She pictured three dogs coming at her, fangs bared, and shooting herself in the foot. She grabbed the old coat of her uncle's that hung by the kitchen door — how appropriate, a shooting coat — and shoved the gun into one of the big cargo pockets.

When she was halfway up the meadow, it was exactly as she had pictured. Three huge brown-black mastiffs came bursting across the field with gaping jaws. She fumbled in the pocket of her jacket, got her thumb caught on one of the cartridge loops, finally got the gun out, cocked it, aimed at the centre dog and fired. The valley reverberated with a shocking sound, and when she looked, all three of the dogs were on the ground.

The dogs were shivering. It was Niccolo who growled, as he strode forward. Why would Signora Chiara do this, he demanded. His dogs were good dogs but *molto sensitivo*, why would Signora Chiara come with a gun and give them such a nervous shock? Why so frighten him and Marta, too? Marta by now also had appeared. They had come here every day, just as Signora Chiara would have wished, for there had been foreigners prowling again. They both crossed themselves to indicate the menace. *Allora!* With much peril to themselves, they'd made a point to come here — to be seen here — to defend her property.

Two of the dogs stirred, lifted their noses in the air — sprang up — ears forward, noses visibly searching the air currents now. Together, their hindquarters shimmying as they tried to wag their stumpy tails, they came straight to Clare, sniffed her jacket voluminously, licked her jacket, threw their great selves against her as they rose on their hind legs and began to lick her face. Oh God, her uncle's dogs! They recognized, if not her, at least the jacket that she wore. All the tears burst out of her that she'd held back all day, or maybe ever since she'd come to Italy. As she wept the dogs began to howl.

"Nero!" Niccolo called. "Ducé!" He tried to call them off.

"That's okay," Clare said. She fondled the ears of the darker one, then the other with the brindled coat. "Nero, Ducé — *viene!*" she called. "Come!"

The dogs crowded close as she pushed past Niccolo, who hurried after her, protesting it was not safe to go up there, this was where the foreigners had been seen. Clare burst into a run, the dogs still at her heel.

AHEAD, BUT IN AN area she hadn't earlier explored, on the eastern flank of the cliff where she recalled sheer rock with just some over-hanging branches, now she thought she saw ... what? An opening in the cliff face?

Niccolo tried to pull her back, "*Signora! Pericoloso!*"

"*Sì molto molto danger!*" Marta puffed.

Clare shook them off. Yes, an opening, the darkness in behind half-obscured by a tall straight slab of stone. The section of a door?

In front of this gaping space was a fall of rock, but not huge rock. Even as she hurried she was picturing, like a film run backwards, those rocks reassembling themselves into a cliff-like puzzle, with the bushes pulled down to hide it once again. She pictured how a box-joint box master might spy the cracks in a concealing wall that had been so cleverly erected millennia ago. How with loyal helpers, the rocks could be taken down. Then later put back. Then those loyal helpers might dare to take the rocks apart again, when the shameless new mistress of the place had gone off with the married brother of her neighbour.

"Ah, poor Signora!" Marta was saying as she caught up, "We had hoped to spare you this!"

For it was with the greatest surprise, Marta said, that, while Clare had been gone, one of the dogs had chased a rabbit to the cliff edge and Niccolo had noticed some stones that looked as if they had been moved and then hurriedly replaced. That was when Niccolo had gone to get Marta, just earlier today, and they had moved the stones more, and peered in and seen — *Santa Maria!* — an empty chamber carved into the rock. Yes, empty. *Sì sì sì, totalmente vide!* They were sure. For of course they had a flashlight — this was habit, from how often the power failed in Italy. What else could Signora Chiara think? Inside was all exactly as Signora Chiara would now see it! If this had once been a tomb — she crossed herself again — it contained nothing now.

"But we have also thought," Marta added, "Now perhaps we know how Signor Kane has been able on his not-big salary to rent an expensive apartment in the best part of Rome, and then buy the yellow car which, at our place, we have been with much honour guarding in your absence!"

Clare took Niccolo's flashlight, gripped the gun, and scrambled over the pile of rocks, with the two dogs right behind. Niccolo tried to follow. She waved the gun and said no.

She swept the beam of light around the space she'd clambered into. Dank rock on all sides: a carved-out chamber maybe twelve feet by twelve, the ceiling rising in step-carved bands that had once been painted deep blue, deep red, though chunks had broken away leaving a rough gravelly surface on the floor. Benches had been carved into the living rock of the walls on three sides. No — stone beds where bodies would have lain! The walls had crumbled over the years, too, sloughing onto these mortuary beds. On the fourth side of the chamber, bigger rock had crashed down to pile up against a wall that had some sort of niche cut into it.

On the mortuary beds debris was heaped thick in places, yet

in other places the beds were almost bare, as if objects had quite recently been removed. (*Now we know how Signor Kane has been able on his not-big salary ...*) So many things crowded her mind. Anger. Suspicion. Above all, disappointment. She sank down on the gravelly floor against one of the mortuary slabs. The dogs settled beside her, their hot breathy bodies welcome in the eerie chill. What had she expected when she saw the looming entrance? *You weren't supposed to think of treasure for its own sake,* she'd heard that repeated often enough. *You were supposed to think of what it could teach.*

She fondled the ears of the darker dog, whose head was heavy on her knee. "Was he in it together with them, Nero? Was your master a tomb robber, too?" A bad voice added, *And left nothing for me?* Everything she had found out about her uncle left a greater gap. Would he have felt entitled to what was in here? Maybe not just because he owned the land, but because long ago he'd convinced himself he was the victim of a beloved girl who'd turned evil before his eyes, turned rotten, and then led him down the labyrinth of his own desires. Had he never lost the victim's sense of being owed? Or, less dramatically, he'd simply excused his plundering because he needed something wondrous to make up for all he'd lost? *The way I feel now,* she thought. *Yes, needing some tangible reward for saving Gianni from himself.*

Then, in panic: but what if Gianni had followed her home? What if he was down there waiting, right this minute?

She sprang up. The beam of her flashlight made an arc, swung past the rubble wall — then darted back to where another much smaller cavity gaped through the rock, swallowing the light. She'd thought this was a niche. Now she saw that behind the fallen rock was a low stone entrance with walls some five feet thick, blocked almost to the top by the rubble.

HER HEART PUMPING WITH excitement, she managed to tug and push one of the rocks into a position to stand on. She shone her torch through the opening, flinched. The shadow of a horned figure sprang onto the far wall, along with others that might be cockerels, beasts, gods.

The gods before the gods we knew?

As her eyes adjusted, she understood she was seeing a great jumbled collection of smoky *bucchero*, urns, pitchers and vases. These were made fantastic by the bizarre appendages they sported: calf-headed spouts, wide-winged eyes, human figures springing from jug handles, faces peering over rims, the pieces made more extraordinary by friezes in relief around their curving bellies, processions of other gods or animals or birds, or creatures, both man and beast. Many pieces were still standing — others had toppled — but what a crowd. What a treasure trove was here!

Then, as Clare craned into the chamber farther, waved the torch to the side, she caught a mass of rich gleams of what was surely gold.

Gold, lying amid bones.

There were stories about bones in tombs. She'd heard a tale of someone bursting through into a just-discovered tomb and seeing a warrior in complete bronze armour. Then the figure vanished. Nothing remained but the bronze armour, the rest gone, disintegrated, just like that in the rush of new air. Perhaps that story was apocryphal. But Clare knew that finding intact skeletons was rare. In London she'd seen a display of a female skeleton, which had provided amazing details of the woman's life: her age, her diet, her health — she'd had a tendency to a runny nose, facial abscesses, an arthritic hip. Her medical problems would have made her difficult to live with, according to a modern doctor who examined her bones. She'd had children. She'd been a horsewoman in her younger years, a fact unknown about Etruscan women up to then; that like men they'd ridden horses, and astride.

Clare stepped back and down.

Had Marta and Niccolo been interrupted here just at the point of forcing their way into this second chamber? Could she blame them? Wouldn't she love to do that, too?

This was not a time to start balancing one side of the equation against the other.

"Dogs!" she said. "Move out of my way."

Gingerly, she piled back one rock, then another, wedging, bracing, making sure that none would tumble until she had blocked off the opening. Then she pulled a sheet of notepaper from her pocket and tore tiny strips, which she secreted here and there so she would know later, just as a spy would, if the arrangement had been tampered with.

"I will believe everything that you tell me," she said to Marta and Niccolo when she emerged. "So I will mention nothing to my lawyer for example about the car, nor to the police about what you have just this moment discovered here, in my field — if you will arrange to keep watch, night and day until *il Signor Luke* arrives from London!"

"Luke Tindhall is already at the Molino," Marta said. "This morning I had to tell him that you went off with your Italian. I think he will not want to speak to you."

"*Boh!*" Clare said. She asked Niccolo for his phone. He said the battery was dead.

It worked just fine.

SEVEN

The Great Philanthropist

SIR HAROLD PLANK WAS flying to Tuscany to view a demonstration of archaeological exploration techniques. Luke Tindhall, the Plank Foundation's representative in Tuscany, had invited archaeologists working in the area to help with the demonstration, which would employ equipment that the Plank Foundation had assembled to donate to worthy excavation projects afterwards. The event was to take place on property the Foundation was in the process of purchasing from the heir of the American writer Geoffrey Kane.

Would it work? Did Clare care?

She made her way up the dry stream bed, wincing at the trampled vegetation alongside. It was lunatic for this to be taking place in the middle of the day, in the middle of a heat wave — a time when sensible people closed themselves off behind shutters and tried to ignore the shrilling of cicadas and the dry scraping of insects of every other sort, echoed by the slither of snakes and lizards as they ate them up. Luke had a reason for the timing, of course.

The meadow was crackling with the intense dry heat. In the shimmering light that bounced off everything, her first sight was Luisa di Varinieri drifting from behind one of the little hills in another tomb-figure-from-Tarquinia outfit, grape-cluster earrings sending out wobbly bolts of gold as she made a slow tour among the hillocks with both arms stretched out in front of her, holding a willow rod. Then more people began to materialize, like those hidden animals in children's puzzles. William Sands and Vittorio Cerotti, pulling a flat metal box. Anders trailing behind, with long wires. Carl Berhnoff on top of one of the hillocks, literally with his ear to the ground.

Clare sought out the shade of a little umbrella pine on the hillock closest to the eastern flank of the horseshoe cliff. Now, adding to the surreal scene, a figure in a yard-wide straw hat with a black curtain fluttering around the rim was emerging from the shade of the stream bed trail. Clare recognized the red-and-black harlequin pants as the figure approached with preoccupied springy little hop-steps, as if concentrating on a game she was making up, as if she didn't care a fig about the rest but just on a whim had decided to come along.

When Nikki spied Clare, she clambered up to join her. She parted the ruffled curtain of her hat and peered out. It was a Hakka hat, she said. An old boyfriend had once sent it from Kowloon. A boyfriend her parents had not approved of, she said. She'd been young and listened to them. He'd gone off to the Orient. She had married William on the rebound. Years later the boyfriend, who was manager of an export company out there now, had sent her the hat. She said the Hakka people, famously, carried the bones of their dead around with them, and so she'd never been sure what to make of the gift.

"But it's good for moments when I want to travel in disguise."

Nikki hadn't intended to come today at all, she said. It was ridiculous how Plank, the so-called Great Philanthropist, had all these people jumping to his will. But she'd decided it would be a good opportunity to give Clare back her pen, which — *ta-da!* — she'd discovered, after all, in the bottom of her satchel.

The nib was bent and the end was chewed. Clare pushed it into her pants pocket. Whatever she might have said was flattened by the heat. They both watched the peculiar scene in the field. Now on horseback, out of the heat haze, came Ralph Farnham and Federica Inghirami.

"But where is the Great Philanthropist?" Nikki said. "What's with all the secrecy? I wasn't to breathe a word to anyone."

"You know about as much as I do," Clare said. "It's Luke's show. He just told me that if word got out about Plank's visit, a man who has so famously refused to travel, there might be a stampede of reporters thinking he was on to some remarkable find."

"Is he?"

A GREAT ROAR RIPPED away any chance of reply. A helicopter tore in over the trees, blasting wind in all directions, flattening the grasses, spraying petals from the flowers, making the horses rear and snort.

Luke stepped from the machine and held out a hand to portly Sir Harold Plank, who was trying to hold onto what was left of his hair. The rotors slowly stopped turning. The pilot leaned out and flicked away his cigarette. The butt landed in a patch of crispy weed, sent up a spiral of smoke, then flared into a coronet of flame. No one seemed to have the wits to do anything about it, until Clare sprinted past the rest of them. The flames caught on so fast that they danced around her legs as she tried to stamp them out. She tore off her shirt, threw it down, threw herself on top of it and rolled around. She struggled up, sooty, bra-less, idiotic tears streaming down her face, shouting at Luke that this was the dimmest idea she'd ever heard of. To come here with a helicopter and do this damage to the plant life, when everyone with the smallest brain knew that the whole of Italy was tinder-dry.

She caught herself up, shook her head, then couldn't restrain herself from dipping a knee in a mock curtsey.

"Sir Harold, welcome to my humble property."

He smiled. He undid his tie, removed his crisp, striped shirt, exposing many folds of rosy flesh, and put it round her shoulders. He meekly begged her pardon. He hoped she would understand that the true culprit was the gout. He said that when Luke had explained the path they would have to climb, there was nothing for it but to telephone an outfit in Ravenna to send over a copter.

The awkward moment was broken by a different sort of racket, far down the field. Luke's eyes widened. "Well well," Clare said. "Someone must have let it slip." A collection of journalists and TV crews was straggling from the trees.

Luke ran forward, demanding to know what this invasion was about, saying this was merely a small exploration on private land. Vittorio Cerotti moved his shoulders in a heating-up sort of way, as if to keep simmering the great minestrone of rules and regulations he encompassed. But after much talking back and forth, waving of hands, pounding of fists into palms, Luke finally allowed the press to stay; "That is, if Sir Harold agrees." Then he began explaining, in a resonant TV archaeologist's voice, how Sir Harold Plank, "the eminent British philanthropist," had long suspected this area had the potential to reveal a collection of undiscovered Etruscan tombs. He walked the group over and around the hillocks, as he told the unseen television audience that there had been initial excitement at the thought that these might be *tumuli*, the so-called melon tombs of the Etruscan Orientalizing phase. But various tests had produced no such evidence. A major disappointment.

"So here you've caught us resorting to what one might, at first glance, think of as an example of Etruscan archaeology's lighter moments, harking back even to the use of dowsing with a willow wand. Allow me to introduce my good friend, the Contessa Luisa di Varinieri," he said with a flourish.

Luisa smiled an enchanting smile, before wandering off with her wand.

"However," Luke continued, "The wand has refused to confirm our hopes that the mounds might be *tumuli*. Just before we were interrupted, the willow drew us back towards the hillside there …" Now Luke was striding between the mounds, propelling the Great Philanthropist forward. All the press followed. When he got to the cliff, he grabbed one of the overhanging branches and began to scrabble his way up, still half-turned to the TV crew, at the same time pulling the branch aside so he could get a purchase on the rocks. Then a rock gave way. He gave a cry of pain as he landed, his legs buried by rubble.

But no one rushed to help him. The cameras continued to whirr. All the Pentaxes and Nikons clicked repeatedly. Everyone was staring at the suddenly exposed opening in the cliff face.

There would have been a stampede, if not for Vittorio. He grabbed one of the Italians from RAI by the arm, muttered, and the reporter put down his mike and gestured to the cameraman to do the same. Luke struggled up, clamped an arm around Clare's shoulder and hobbled towards the cliff.

Harold Plank, though, in the few moments when attention was focused elsewhere, had managed to scuttle up and over the remaining rocks and disappear into the dark beyond. Vittorio was trying to hold the rest of them at bay, while at the same time both he and William were walking backwards as if drawn by a giant magnet.

It had worked.

This had been Clare's gift to Luke: that he could "present" the tomb discovery in any way he thought best, making sure Sir Harold was front and centre. Luke had expected her to be part of the package, despite her having gone off with Gianni. She thought he'd relished the thought of her boomeranging back, so he could revel in his own humiliation, revel in the way they'd hate and need each other. Of course she couldn't possibly be with him anymore. But at least she could do this.

As for what would happen as this "discovery" proceeded — Clare had insisted that the inner chamber stay untouched, just as she had left it, and that Vittorio Cerotti be present today, to make sure protocol was followed and none of the inner contents came to harm. She still had only the merest hint of what this would lead to. But she felt really queasy that she had allowed the whole thing to become a circus.

Once Luke scrabbled in, he pulled a flashlight from one of the pockets of his khaki vest and swept it around the first, empty chamber, expressing amazement. For the benefit of the press group — still held back at the entrance — he described the funeral benches, the coffered ceiling, adding with resignation that the place had been looted centuries before.

Then he said, "Holy Jesus! What's this?"

His flashlight broadened its arc, and the gloom disappeared in the glare made by television crews from RAI and CNN. Everyone stared at the pile of rock against the back wall, where the farther cavity barely showed. Harold Plank was in the lead again. Shirtless, but not caring about the rough stone, he got himself wedged into the opening like a cork, his flailing legs stopping anyone else from coming close.

When he finally eased himself back out, he held his pen light between his teeth. Gingerly, reverently, its weight distributed between two hands, he carried what might have been mistaken for a greenish, heavily encrusted ping pong paddle.

"Doctor Cerotti," he said, "I turn this over to you with profound apologies for my injudicious haste."

Before he relinquished it, his eyes under the grey bushy brows did a slow sweep of the place, meeting each camera in turn. "We must all step back, now, and allow the proper authorities to do their proper work."

∽

A SECOND HELICOPTER HAD roared in carrying the Carabinieri, as summoned by Vittorio. Two of the splendid fellows in their towering hats were now posted to prevent the press from further peering. To loud complaints, Federica and Ralph had been excluded by the time they had attended to the horses.

According to official regulations, no one should be inside the tomb, and certainly nothing in the tomb should be touched until an emergency team of excavators and conservators arrived from

Florence. Clare was beginning to wish she had not been quite so fastidious when she'd had a chance to explore the inner chamber. Nikki whispered that any minute Vittorio was sure to get a call from his superiors officially kicking everyone out.

Vittorio declared in a sombre inspectorial voice that he, Vittorio Cerotti, in these unique circumstances, would dislike to deny himself the benefit of the wise opinions of his colleagues regarding, at least, this remarkable bronze mirror that Sir Harold Plank had discovered.

Luisa pulled a white cashmere sweater from her tiny gold backpack, enabling the mirror to be laid down without damage.

Then she exclaimed, "But look!"

She pointed out that when the mirror had originally been deposited, it had been wrapped in cloth, leaving what she called "a perfect pseudomorph" of what that fabric had once been. As the mirror had corroded over centuries, the process slowly replaced the cloth fibres with metal, leaving an exact replica of the weave.

Clare leaned close. Yes, it was clear that metal had replaced a swatch of woven fabric, making even the warp and woof of it distinct. But then she began to wonder if an even more remarkable transformation might be taking place, right before her eyes. Was the stern archaeological process being replaced by the metallic heft of Sir Harold Plank? She saw him move close to the inspector. After a quiet rumbling in Vittorio's ear, Vittorio allowed that once his esteemed colleagues had had a chance to inspect the mirror, it might be possible to take a small look into the second chamber.

"So then let's get on with it!" Nikki called out in her brassy voice. "Luisa, you'll never see who's fairest in the land in that mirror!"

But when Luisa turned the mirror over and directed the beam of light at a raking angle, a woman did spring into view. Incised on the ancient greenish bronze, a woman wearing a floating dress and elegant pointed shoes was holding in her arms the naked body of a most beautiful young man.

This brought on a flurry of conflicting opinions. Luisa said the female figure would be Thesan, goddess of the dawn, mourning the death of her son slain by Achilles. Anders declared it was Thesan, but she was abducting her human lover, who was very much alive, as they would see if they took note of the mirror's border of round leaves and up-thrusting spikes, which charged the iconography with the erotic.

Clare moved closer, caught her breath. "No. This is the death of Adonis. The goddess is Aphrodite."

Anders sniffed. There was no record of such a scene in the entire *Corpus Speculorum Etruscorum,* which recorded some three thousand mirrors so far discovered.

But Clare pointed out the pattern of droplets on the front of the goddess's filmy dress. They were not tears but drops of blood. There, at Aphrodite's feet, were flowers, delicate as moth wings, one central flower drooping to show the mound of pistils and stamens. "That is *Anemone coronaria.* The flower Aphrodite caused to spring up from her lover's blood."

Anders said, "Then can our expert tell us about the vine that surrounds the scene with phallic clusters?"

"Aye!" A surprising rumble from Sir Harold. "But that's no ruddy vine. There's something odd in the space just above the mirror's handle. A tree trunk? With some poor lass walled up inside?" He pulled out an army knife with a tiny magnifier, passed it around.

"Myrrha!" Luisa breathed. "Yes. Here we see her arms already turned into branches, which reach up to make the border! *Straordinario!* This is by a master! To encircle the coming fate of the son Adonis within the crime of the mother in this way!"

Harold Plank shut his knife with a snap. "What was her crime?"

"She seduced her daddy, and got grounded for her pains." That came from Luke.

Clare heard her own voice:

"… and for nine months Myrrha roamed,
till at last, 'Oh gods, in case I should contaminate
the living with my presence, or the dead if I die,
banish me from both.'
And roots broke out through her toenails,
and her arms became branches,
and her skin hardened into bark flowing sap instead of blood …"

And then, just as Nikki had predicted, Vittorio's cell phone went off. A grand eminence from Florence was halfway down the autostrada, furious at having had to learn about the sensational discovery from the media. Vittorio said that everybody would need to leave, with the exception of the noted philanthropist Sir Harold Plank, seeing as with great financial sacrifice he had arranged to purchase this land to save it from development. Also, the Foundation's esteemed research director, Signor Tindhall, could scarcely be denied a brief glance into the adjoining room.

Shaken and embarrassed after her outburst, and above all needing to get away from them all, Clare turned and insisted — over Luke's warning glare — that William Sands must be allowed to stay as well.

Perhaps she looked spooky, covered in ashes, face streaked with tears. Perhaps it looked as if she was going to lose control completely. And perhaps she was. At any rate, Vittorio nodded gravely, and William also stayed behind.

Treasure Trove

CLARE WAS STILL SHAKING as she stumbled out into the sunlight and pushed her way past the crowd of journalists and past Ralph and Federica too, catching Federica's malign glance and looking away; that whole story so distant now, so muffled by the surprise the tomb had sprung, the image on the mirror — the scouring personal associations of that — to find such an echo of her own story here.

A woman in a Madras shirt came after her, a reporter from *Newsweek* (Luke really had done his work) wanting a personal angle on this story. She asked, "Excuse me but are you the niece of that man Kane who wrote about the Etruscans and owned this place? Are you the artist who did a book about the Amazon, too?" Clare pretended she was Italian and didn't understand, mumbling that she was only *la ragazza, sì,* of the rich *Inglese,* "I know nothing, *niente.* Bugger off!" The woman shrugged and let Clare alone.

Clare made her way to a shady spot behind the nearest hillock and crouched on a stone; she closed her eyes and saw the mirror, thinking of how it had been wrapped in cloth when it was buried, and its powerful image. Could it really be that today — for the first time in thousands of years — that mirror image had again sprung free?

She crouched until the TV crews and journalists were let back into the tomb. She heard the grumbling of Ralph and Federica as they remounted their horses and rode away. The coincidence of that particular mirror turning up in that particular tomb was too extreme. But was she connecting random dots, making up a pattern, because randomness was so hard for the primitive human mind to grasp? The meadow filled again with the hot snapping sounds of summer silence; silence like the gaps between the tiny fragments of what we know for certain in life, she thought, black gaps, black holes with huge gravitational pull, that could suck you under ...

Oh for God's sake get a grip.

SHE CAUGHT UP WITH Nikki Stockton halfway down the meadow. Nikki pretended she didn't hear, then finally stopped, turned, her straw hat surrounding her in a circle of shade.

"I'm heading off to find one of those chocolate mousse cakes," Clare said to the curtained face. "I wish you'd come."

Nikki parted the curtain. She gave Clare a long agate stare. Clare realized she had never taken proper note of the colour of Nikki's eyes: they were almost gold, with stony flecks. Nikki came up so close that the rim of the hat bumped Clare's forehead. She pulled Clare under, into that woven shade. "Clare Livingston," she said. "I was never going to speak to you again." She backed off. The midday sun struck a hammer blow. "But sure. Let's see if we can rustle up some just desserts."

She turned and ran down the dried stream bed, calling over her shoulder, "Catch me if you can!" jumping from grooved rock to rock, the black curtain of her hat flapping, and the wings of her red blouse. Clare thought it was like following a giant harlequin moth. When Nikki stopped abruptly at the bottom, Clare ran right into her. The two of them tumbled to the ground. They lay there laughing and panting. Nikki's arms found their way tightly around Clare.

"I thought I was in love with you," Nikki said. She kissed Clare. Her lips tasted of straw. She pulled away a fraction, and said, "But in fact it was just another rebound. Or at least I'm way beyond that now."

Clare kissed her back. "But I do love you," she said. "I won't even say 'not this way.'"

Nikki burrowed two hands in Clare's hair. "Yeah, but still it's not this way — right? I still can't lure you back to my studio and paint you with henna."

"Henna maybe," Clare said. "Fucking … no." She traced the line of Nikki's lips with a finger. "My life is screwed up enough already. I'm sad to say."

Nikki sat up and pulled the hat back on. "Mine too." Her voice came, sepulchral, from behind the black curtain. "I've been taken." She stretched her red-wing arms. "'World was in the face of my beloved.' Do you know that poem by Rilke?"

Clare said she didn't. But as she parted the curtain and kissed Nikki once more on the mouth, she let herself imagine that Nikki meant she'd been both captured and set free because of Clare — because of Clare growing out of her fingers, just as the branches grew from the limbs of girl in the mirror.

⌒

UP IN THE TOWN, Clare led Nikki to the *pasticceria,* where they found a tiny booth at the back. They set to eating slices of the ambrosial confection, melting bite by melting bite, the sweetness filling all the places where awkward conversation might have strayed. When they finished, Nikki took her paper napkin and folded it into an origami bird and perched it on Clare's head.

"That tomb was a totally remarkable discovery!" she said.

Clare said yes, she was so right.

"So what's the backstory?"

"Well," Clare began, "What happened was that I … went off, you know."

"I heard."

"And when I came back," she felt her face twist, "I found I had acquired a couple of … beautiful dogs." She buried her face in her hands.

"Dogs?" Nikki had no idea what the dog thing was about. But when Clare looked up there seemed to be a wordless acknowledgment between them of the sweet devastating surprises that the world might hold.

Clare segued from that into the fib that she'd told others. She said that Harold Plank had been at her to sell, and when she decided to explore the property before she made up her mind, she'd found that Niccolo had been doing some suspicious-looking digging in that upland meadow.

"When I started to question him, he got in a huff. And then his wife Marta got in a bigger huff." Clare threw up her hands. "I haven't seen either of them since." She laughed and cut another piece of cake. "So clearly I have to sell. No one to sweep the floor."

She said the disappearance had made her suspicious, though, so she'd called Luke in London to get some advice. "You saw the rest."

"But it was so unfair that you had to leave the tomb," Nikki said, "without seeing what was inside that other chamber."

Clare said, yes, she was regretting that now. But she figured she wouldn't have any trouble getting back in.

"Don't count on it. Once the Gnomes of Florence get hold of things, mere mortals don't have much power."

"I figure I can swing it."

Nikki said she hoped so. She looked doubtful.

"It was amazing, wasn't it," Nikki added. "When those rocks fell, and I saw that door into the cliff face, I had a feeling I was in the middle of a fairytale. The door opening into the mountain. The magic land within …"

Clare winced when Nikki said "fairytale." Nikki caught that. Those trickster eyes, Clare thought, which have sneakily stolen every one of my features, so that now I really am growing out of her fingers.

It was a strange thought, but not really a bad thought, as if a separate life force was at play, using her …

Nikki reached for her hand. "I'm going to give you something," she said, as if she'd been reading Clare's thoughts.

Clare tried to protest.

"No, no," Nikki said. "I don't even know what it is yet. But don't worry. You'll never know it came from me."

Nikki's cell phone rang. Clare could hear Ralph Farnham's hearty bark. Nikki rolled her eyes. She said "Thanks," and "Sure thing," before she clicked off.

"So?" Clare said.

"I'm not supposed to tell you. It seems Federica will rip you to shreds if you turn up."

"But?"

"They're assembling a *Salon des Refusés* of the Etruscan tomb world at her place, to watch the program on RAI that was shot this afternoon, about the discovery. I bet it will be on over at Bar Sport, too."

She was right. When they got to the bar, regular programming had been pre-empted and the soccer fans were kicking up a fuss.

THE PROGRAM STARTED WITH a shot of the four men making their way through the shadowy doorway from the inner chamber, which by then was roughly cleared of rubble, and Luke announcing in a dramatic voice that in there nothing had been touched for some two-and-a-half-thousand years. Imagine, he said, what this discovery might bode! Sir Harold Plank, "brilliant Etruscan expert and head of the Plank Foundation," now believed that more tombs were waiting to be discovered along this cliff, within a stone's throw of Cortona, solving at last the mystery of where the inhabitants of that once-great Etruscan city had been buried.

Even the football fans were paying close attention now, though the Italian voice-over garbled the effect of Luke's words.

Then Vittorio Cerotti crowded forward and began to describe two funeral beds carved in the manner of the Tomb of the Monkey in Chiusi … But William Sands's voice was heard over him, talking about the hoard of *bucchero*. Then Vittorio reclaimed centre stage by mentioning gold. In there lay a stunning collection, he said, pieces of brilliant workmanship: earrings shaped like little barrels, which set the time of burial to around 500 BC; a wide choker necklace of granulated beads; several chest-length chains holding amber amulets of human figures; and a number of decorative pins that were possibly heirloom pieces of the deceased, dating from a considerably earlier period. The gold would be transported to Florence this very night for safekeeping, he added. The remainder of the tomb contents would await the arrival of a team of skilled specialists.

He paused. He pulled at his beard, removed his spectacles, then replaced them. He announced that the tomb chamber held something even more remarkable. He invited the camera close. In a confidential whisper, he said that the chamber held two intact skeletons, a mature woman and a much younger man.

He began to tell a ghoulish, if highly technical story. When he had examined the skeletons, right away he'd seen that the breast bones on each had been removed. Also, there was no evidence of staining on the funeral beds, as would have been left when the corpses decomposed. This, then, could throw an entirely new light on Etruscan funerary practices. Perhaps the bodies were not deposited right after death and left to putrefy! Perhaps they were de-fleshed elsewhere, by an extended grisly process, which he detailed, the ultimate point being that if only clean bones were brought to rest in Etruscan tombs, this could explain the practice of tombs being reopened for new burials, again and again over many generations, and the whole air of celebration around those burials, too.

By the time William Sands regained the spotlight to describe, in greater detail, the hoard of *bucchero*, the patrons of the Bar Sport had had enough. The owner switched the channel.

WATCHING ALL OF THIS, Clare had begun to feel sick at her earlier weakness in leaving when she'd been asked. But surely, she insisted to Nikki, the Gnomes of Florence wouldn't deny her.

"Don't count on it," Nikki said again. "You're up against the red-taped arm of the Soprintendenza now."

Clare said she did not care how many shining Carabinieri in their flak jackets were posted, they couldn't keep her out of there. She didn't tell Nikki the rest. Ever since she'd first glimpsed the *bucchero* pieces a week ago — the friezes, the half-animal gods, the staring wide-winged eyes — she had started getting a sense of her sleeping fingers waking, itching to draw again. She could make something of this. She didn't know what. But she would.

Neverland

NICCOLO AND MARTA HAD disappeared. But they had been honourable in a way. Perhaps they'd always been honest farmers — shrewd, yes, but honest — until Clare's uncle came along with his knowledge, and pried the secret of the tomb from the cliff. Then maybe they'd just spied and observed, perhaps not deciding to "rescue" some of the booty to benefit themselves until after he'd left? She would never know; but the point was that they had not in fact disappeared, along with the Lamborghini, until the day the police helicopter came roaring in.

During the past week the uproar had continued, police whirling in and out, tearing up the grasses, flattening the flowers. The tomb itself crawled with scientific and forensic specialists. Every day when she'd hiked up there, Clare had been met with some stern official stone-face who spoke, she thought, neither English nor Italian but a kind of bureaucratic doublespeak about forms she would need to fill out, numbers in Florence she should call — before disappearing rabbit-like into the dark burrow, leaving her to face once again the implacable tall-hatted presence of the police.

Luke was off in Florence on Harold Plank's behalf; Vittorio Cerotti, too. Both, it seemed, were trying to sort out the bureaucratic tangle of who would, ultimately, acquire a permit to further excavate the cliff face. Clare repeatedly asked Luke to help persuade the authorities to allow her access to the tomb, but he refused to rock the boat. It felt almost dangerous to be near him now. There was something infectious in his powerful, wounded determination to wrench a way forward out of all of this for himself.

Harold Plank was the one who'd promised to see what he could do for her. Alarming, forceful, charming man; Clare didn't like thinking how much she already owed him. With just the lightest tap from his great battery of resources — and a commitment of funding for Federica Inghirami's horse-breeding project— he'd managed to arrange for clear title on the property to be delivered to Clare. This of course freed the property up for him to purchase. She knew he would be prepared to administer some similar "tap" to her aunt's lawyers in Seattle, too. She'd decided not to think of that just yet.

Plank had also, at her persuading, agreed to make a trip to Poggio Selvaggio while he still had the helicopter at his disposal. She believed he'd been up there yesterday. Until she was sure he'd done this, she didn't want to push him to use his influence further in the matter of the tomb.

So finally, a week after the chamber tomb's official discovery, she decided she would just damn well bully her way in on her own.

ᵔᕂ

AS CLARE APPROACHED, WITH the dogs at her heel, the heavy boom of a radio had the meadow grasses cowering. Two policemen were sitting on lawn chairs near the tomb entrance, with a small table between them holding pots of yogurt, a bag of fruit, a round Tuscan loaf, two small roasted birds. They invited her to join them. They were handsome, charming, sweet — and absolutely determined that the entrance to the tomb remain barred to her. It was the regulation. It was out of their hands.

She asked if much had actually been determined inside — were the artefacts still all there?

They shrugged. This was their first shift. They didn't know.

Then how soon would someone turn up who actually did know? She was the landlord here, after all.

Shrugs and smiles.

When she finally decided to ignore them, when she began to clamber over the rocks to damn well go in anyway, they rose together, clasping the submachine-gun-looking pistols that they wore. Their smiles disappeared.

"Are you going to shoot me? Are you going to kill me, because I'm trying to get into my own tomb?"

If they caught the irony, they didn't show it. Before she stamped away, she took a good kick at the booming radio and sent it croaking across the field.

She stormed up the hillside, taking a steep shortcut over to the olive grove, determined to rush home and call the head of the Soprintendenza in Florence, or some higher-up in Rome, or the Pope.

Puffed out at the top, she paused and turned to look down at her lovely meadow; hers for a short time more, silent again at least.

No.

Was that singing down there now?

"*I love to go a-wandering, along the mountain track; and as I go, I love to sing, my knapsack on my back …*"

I must have knocked that boom box cuckoo, she thought.

"*Falderie …! Falderaaaaa!*"

But weren't those familiar voices?

"*Falder ha-ha-ha-ha-ha! My knapsack on my back …!*"

A pair of diminutive figures carrying alpenstocks, wearing straw hats, were trudging out of the woods. What had happened to the *reumatismo,* the fatigue? The two of them were making their way relentlessly up the field, until they came to a stop in front of the Carabinieri. The policemen sprang to their feet, doffed their tall hats. Within seconds they were actually ushering the Barbareschi in through the entrance of the tomb.

And why am I surprised? Clare thought, as she stumbled back down. Why am I even bothering to be shaking mad, to discover that in the rock-paper-scissors hierarchy of Italian law and order, a Marquis tops a uniformed policeman and the owner of the land?

"Do not even think of waving that Kalashnikov at me, you bozo!" she snapped, as she tried to barge past the men now standing at attention outside her tomb. She struggled in their grip. Egidio popped his head out. Carolina followed. After some rapidly twinned phrases in Italian, Clare was released.

The noble couple were all smiles. "Signora Livingston, *avanti!* What a great pleasure to welcome you. We have been on our way to visit you, indeed, but first thought we would come to see this remarkable discovery which we have been seeing on the television."

They drew her in, then whispered, "Please, you must understand that the vigilance of the good men outside the door will have much intensified, of course, since the contretemps yesterday at the American excavation on Poggio Selvaggio — with the disappearance of an artefact."

"What?"

"Quite a little scandal," they said. "Indeed, this little!" Egidio held up thumb and forefinger, a half-inch apart. "What has gone missing has been just one small bead. We saw this also on television, it is all over the news! A matter small, yet very serious, especially when we have allowed the Americans to come and excavate our sites, and then they become lax."

"Oh!" Clare said, "But surely ... There could not possibly be any ..."

Her words tumbled over themselves as she tried to explain that the American, Dr. William Sands, was an academic of the highest reputation, and furthermore ...

"Do not discompose yourself, Signora Livingston." The twin expressions now were strict. "Our time is limited, and we have much bigger things to discuss!"

Bigger things? What could be bigger than such a contretemps? She remembered Luke saying that a missing bead had almost shut down some prestigious Middle Eastern excavation. But surely Harold Plank would use his great influence to help sort this out, now that he and William had established cordial relations. Surely he would.

Clare pulled away from the double hand laid on her shoulders.

What nerve, welcoming her. But at least she was in. She lit her flashlight, ducked through the low doorway into the dank inner chamber.

Everything was gone. Just the funerary beds remained, with their carved stone headrests, and no staining.

There would be much to be learned even from this emptiness, she supposed; there always was: clues in the carving of the ceiling, the beds, the rock shelf where all that dark pottery had stood. She'd have to go somewhere else to see the *bucchero*, the fantastic shapes, the carved friezes that had so fired her imagination. She'd have to inch her way through further tortuous bureaucratic channels.

Carolina and Egidio poked their heads in.

"Signora Livingston, please, we must talk."

Then graciously, sweetly, horribly — crowding into the inner chamber with her, cloying the small space with a powerful miasma of violets — they began an elaborate apology. They had realized, they said, how wrong they had been, how utterly mistaken, and how — yes — stodgy, too.

"Which is unforgivable in us, is it not dear Carolina?"

"Oh yes Egidio, 'stodgy' will not do!"

They came bearing not just apologies, they said, but gifts that would warm the tender tendrils they feared she had subdued within her shy, mistaken breast. On and on went the floral rhetoric, which Clare could hardly follow.

They had come, she finally understood, to purchase her meadow paintings. Ever since seeing them, they had been unable to forget them. Consequently, they must have them. "Or we will be unable to rest, dear Carolina, will we not?"

"And when Egidio is unable to rest, Signora Livingston, I must confess that he quite wears me out!" A girlish giggle. "And so, I beg you to take pity on a woman not quite so young as she once was!"

Clare tried to cut in, terrified that they would start singing again.

"Stop!" Carolina demanded. "We must tell you, also, that we come as self-appointed emissaries from the broken-hearted. We have, yesterday, taken it upon ourselves to pay a visit to Bologna, to speak at length to Signora Eleanora Gasperini DiGiustini on your behalf."

"You didn't!"

They had.

How often, since leaving La Celta, had Clare thought of the photo in Gianni's study. The little girl looking up wickedly at her father; the boy with the level eyes. Eleanora, with her enduring expression. A face pretty, but worn with the demands of keeping so many things together, even strays like her husband, keeping the cord from completely fraying.

Clare had not thought with kindness of that woman, because remembering the sight made her sad; yet, at the same time, she'd recognized the woman's morose implacable strength.

"A lovely woman, and so perceptive!" Egidio and Carolina were saying. "She agreed almost immediately, when we had fully explained, that to stand as an impediment to a love such as yours with her husband would be a crime against love itself. You see …" they joined hands, "Love is to us the thing most important in this universe."

Clare said, "But it's not."

Pitying smiles. "You are mistaken, dear."

"Does Gianni know you did this?"

"We did not have to ask. We knew when we saw a broken man."

"Do his children also understand?"

They looked at one another. The children were blown off in a shrug.

As to the arrangements with Signora DiGiustini, those could be quite straightforward, they were sure. Certainly there would be no problem. The Barbareschi had connections both in the highest legal circles and in the Vatican. However, more pressingly, in the interim, they intended that Clare should paint for them just a few more pieces of her imaginative floral fantasies, so that they could arrange a show entirely of her work, which they were now convinced had no peer.

Clare's flashlight was burning dim. The carved-out rock walls inside the cliff were closing in. She remembered Nikki talking about the door opening into a mountain, the magic land within. The two expectant faces were smiling up at her. Such a fine line separated her now from stepping right through into neverland, with these troll-like figures offering her the poisoned jewel. The ceiling shuddered as a replacement police helicopter roared overhead. She could hardly breathe in the violet-laden air.

"No," she said.

They looked up with disbelieving double blinks.

She said, "You must go back to Signora Eleanora Gasperini DiGiustini and tell her that you were wrong. You must say that her husband was suffering a momentary delusion, and that he needs her help. You must say that the woman he thought he was in love with has done things in the past that even he would not be able to redeem. Tell her not to be a fool. Tell her to set aside her discouraged strength for once, and help him. Tell her to go and join him in his garden. He is lonely. She can help him. Please."

She couldn't see the gnome-like couple now. They had dissolved in the salt of her tears. She pushed out into the flat hot sun, ran down through the meadow, the dogs lolloping ahead. She found them waiting by the jeep. When she opened the door, they jumped into the back. She kept driving until she reached the sea.

Appointment in Ankara

FANTASY! FANTASY.

Clare had thought that, hadn't she, when she first sat in Cortona's beautiful piazza? She was an outsider, a stranger, stepping into an elaborate setting for an opera. Would it help to think of the past weeks as an opera?

She pictured the soprano dipping her pen into her inkwell — not here, at the table where she once listened to absurd talk of resin fungi, but up in the corner room with the balcony, wearing silk just lightly stained by tears, "*Oh caro Signore mio, one last adieu ...*"

Two elderly women started across the square, arms linked, dressed in venerable clothes, attractive shoes with heels no higher than their elderly feet could handle, their bulky bodies leaning together as they smiled and talked of local gossip, of children and grandchildren and great-grandchildren. It was their faces that caught her, faces as beautifully worn as the stones of the buildings around them; these were the faces of those who fitted here, understood exactly who they were.

Yes, adieu. For I have an appointment in Ankara as soon as the property deal is completed, in a few minutes, at the lawyer's. I am going off with the man I "have to say is important." Because he is. And in Turkey I too will do important work at last, making drawings of his sherds, his broken pots; we will make a whole new world out of things that have been smashed.

The thimbleful of coffee jittered in her cup as a noisy group settled at the next table, a man waving for a waiter, a woman spreading a map of the town, another woman opening up the book of a poet who had made the town famous. They were hoping to find the poet's house.

Any moment, Luke and Sir Harold would arrive.

HAROLD PLANK HAD BEEN busy during the seven days that Clare was away. Last night, Luke had brought her up to date on all that had gone on; how Plank had made a fast trip to London, then to Florence, then back to London once again, getting everything in place for next year's excavation; how he had managed to work out an agreement allowing him to become the recognized eminence behind the exploration to take place on her place (his place as it was about to become), though the actual work would be under Italian direction.

But what had happened at Poggio Selvaggio, Clare had quizzed Luke; did that all get sorted out? The disappearance of the bead?

Luke had said she shouldn't worry.

What did that mean? she persisted. Had Harold Plank gone up there? Was he impressed with the work? Did Luke think Plank would be able to help solve whatever the problem was?

Luke said yes, Plank had gone up there. "Crikey, Clare, I've had a few other things to think about." But yes, Luke was sure it had all been sorted out.

Earlier today, on her way to meet Luke here, Clare had learned that this was not the case at all.

She and Nikki had been driving in opposite directions. They both pulled to the side of the road. A grey, humid morning, though now the mist had burned off; the air thick with water and doubts; the Medici fortress casting an indistinct damp shadow. Nikki crossed the road, opened the passenger door of the jeep, and got in beside Clare. How different she looked. Old jean jacket, cotton bandana twisted round her forehead, hands furrowed with ground-in earthy pigments.

"You've been busy," Clare said.

"I hardly leave my studio." She seemed older, carved and dry, but more beautiful. With a flash of the old Nikki, the sliver of a grin, she said, "I'm glad you're back."

"But not for long."

She told Nikki the sudden plan.

"Are you sure this is the right thing for you?"

"Am I sure?"

Nikki gave her a squinty look. Clare said of course she was sure; it had just taken her a while to figure out, that was all.

"Well … good."

"Yes, good."

Clare thought that the look that passed between them, then, encompassed everything that wasn't said — how "good" could mean that, at some point, you had to make a decision, even if that decision rested on the median point between better or worse. How, always, some freewheeling part of each of them would link up, to comprehend the predicament of the other. She recalled what Nikki had said once about wanting to give her something. *Was this it?*

Then she asked Nikki what had transpired at Poggio Selvaggio — what was this thing she'd heard about a theft?

It was ridiculous and terrible, Nikki said. "And I think it was my fault."

When Nikki explained, Clare could see that it might have been.

After Harold Plank had helicoptered up to the dig, Nikki had shown the delegation from his Foundation around the lab. Surprisingly, Plank had spent a long time among the small finds, admiring objects one wouldn't have thought he'd care about: the fragments of black-glaze ware, the terracotta loom weights, the stamped *rocchetti*.

Then — because someone had told him the little drama of how a bead had gone astray on the day that Clare had visited the dig — and how Clare had saved the situation — he'd insisted on seeing that particular bead, too.

"He talked a lot about you, actually," Nikki said. "How does he feel about you hooking up with Luke, by the way?"

"I have no idea what you mean." Clare heard her own tone, still keeping up the fiction of her involvement with Plank; it seemed she would drag her deceits across oceans, they would come humping behind her across deserts to keep her company. *At least I'll never be alone.* "So the bead, though, the bead," she said. "It went astray again? But then surely it did turn up again?"

Nikki said no. She thought what had happened was that when the group from the Foundation departed, she had accidentally left the door of the lab unlocked. Nor had she been entirely sure, later, that she'd remembered to replace the bead in its proper file box."

"You're not that absent-minded."

"No, I'm not. Maybe it was something subconscious, do you think?"

What happened next, she explained, was that when Anders came in the following morning, he reported the bead missing.

"Anders," Clare said.

Nikki shrugged. Of course he had to report it to William, she said.

But somehow the news got out more widely. William was summoned to Perugia to explain to the Umbrian authorities why his operation should not be shut down altogether if this was an indication of the care that was being taken.

"But couldn't Vittorio Cerotti speak for him?" Clare interrupted, "Or Luisa, who surely has pull in those parts?"

Nikki's face pinched up. "Hell no. They have been too occupied these days with the goings-on up in Florence."

So then, Harold Plank, far from setting things right, had issued a press release stating that though the Foundation had been interested in the project at Poggio Selvaggio, he was now forced to disassociate himself altogether.

"And he was never associated with us in the first place. Why should he go to all the trouble to make that statement? And how did the word about its disappearance get out? William hoped to exhaust every avenue before bringing it to wider attention, and that was bad enough, questioning the students and staff, the searches!"

Nikki turned and frowned at Clare, almost as if she expected Clare to help with this conundrum. "And why did I let all that happen, do you suppose? So careless! But Clare, all this fuss for such a tiny object! And really, no one would have wanted to steal it!"

Clare remembered, though, how she had felt when she'd held the blue bead: the flutter of possessiveness just because it was so small, yet told so much. She remembered saying something about that to Luke. Of course Luke had laughed. No, pretended to laugh, she told herself now, as she waited for him in the square. She reminded herself of the worth of the person underneath the complicated crust, some-one struggling to connect himself to matters of lasting importance to the world, despite his faults — despite even what she'd found out about him during the week when she'd run away, which, in an odd sense, was the thing that had brought her back. Yes, worthwhile; the person who held the key to her becoming of some worth herself, finally, as she helped him with his work.

She had driven off feeling guilty after talking to Nikki. If Vittorio Cerotti had been too preoccupied in Florence to speak up for William, it must have been because he'd thrown whatever influence he had behind helping Harold Plank. And if Harold Plank's public statement had anything to do with his ambitions regarding Clare's place, she should do something, right this morning, while she still had the power, while the place was still hers.

She knew she wouldn't stand up to him, not when a smooth tran-sition meant everything to Luke. She saw this truth about herself as constant: how every good decision got fogged up that way. Even the vow she'd made while she was down at the sea.

❧

AFTER RUNNING FROM THE Barbareschi, Clare had bypassed many seaside towns with no idea where she was headed. She finally turned off at the Ligurian city named for the saint who lay in the basilica in the town she'd fled.

She'd sat at a red-topped table in a floating bar, drinking a cold glass of crisp Ligurian wine, still unable to get the encounter with the Barbareschi out of her head. Those awful, unlikely people. How had they arrived at her place? There'd been no indication, when she went down, of another car. Sometimes, as she drove, she'd thought she'd made them up — made the whole incident up — just to propel herself out of there. Their report of the conversation with Gianni's wife was too terrible. Would they go back, carrying Clare's message? Would they set aside their goofy saccharine idea of what love was and persuade the hard-working Eleanora to go to Gianni in his garden, maybe just sit with him beside the burning bush, the bush that could set the air on fire, but also heal?

Across the harbour, the seafront buildings were all painted with *trompe l'oeil*, brilliant cornices, arches, elaborate fake doors leading to fake rooms.

There's always one room that you are not allowed to enter.

If she'd never crossed the threshold of Gianni's private room, never picked up that photo, would she be in his unicorn garden right this minute, flourishing there, even painting once again, under his vigilant eye, his patient care?

She'd ordered another glass of wine and watched the frescoed buildings across the harbour bobbing in the evening sun. She'd eaten a dish of clams, taken a room with a harbour view in a hotel that welcomed dogs. It was through the use of her credit card that Harold Plank had traced her. He'd decided to give her a week to settle down, but she didn't find that out until much later.

Early morning traffic woke her as it veered around the corner just below, on the road to Portofino.

Five o'clock. No cafes would be open. There was no coffee machine in the room. No mini-bar with a pack of nuts. Nor was there any reading matter, except the hotel folder. What had been going through her head when she landed herself here in this room, with two dogs and nothing to eat and nothing to read? Not even a Bible in the drawer, surely an oversight in a room that looked across the harbour to the statue of a saint.

She delved into her backpack, which had been knocking around in the jeep ever since La Celta. Nothing as useful as a toothbrush. Though, for some reason, there was an eyeliner wedged at the bottom.

What the pack did hold was the collection of scholarly articles Gianni had given her. She'd forgotten about them. And the beautiful glossy book about the gardens of Pompeii, which brought his voice back to skewer her with the memory of a little villa, *closer to the ground, with a peristyle garden for you to sit in and paint*. What a cruel trick, to have accidentally dragged along a book invoking that.

The cover showed the reproduction of a mural from the wall of a Roman courtyard garden, with an archway leading in. *There's always one room that you are not allowed to enter*, yes; but you go there anyway. In imagination, if nothing more.

As she began to turn the pages, the same dreamy feeling of adventure stole over her that she'd had when she'd set off up the Amazon river in a small steamer boat from the once famous rubber city of Manaus, in the company of the talented and beautiful Margaret Mee …

She pulled the hotel counterpane around her and she was there, in a garden courtyard in Pompeii, peering over the shoulder of that artist all those centuries ago. She followed him as he moved around the garden selecting an appropriate wall surface for his work; then, as he applied such enchanting detail: a warbler on a branch, a spray of rose leaves behind, such lyric colours, the whole scene so alive. As she began to read the text, the compelling words of the famous garden archaeologist pulled her further into intelligent escape, led her into tiny flower-filled courtyards on humble Roman streets, grand ones in villas that had since been given names impossible to resist: the Villa of the Mysteries; the Villa of the Papyri, whose charred scrolls might still become readable one day; the Villa of the Scandalous Elagabulus, whose dining room had a retractable ceiling that allowed him to smother his dinner guests in cloudbursts of flowers …

Eventually she took the dogs out for a very fast walk, so she could get back to reading more. When she returned, she came on photographs of pollen grains which had been discovered in a loft holding a great store of carbonized plants. Shown as through a microscope, the minute specks of pollen became otherworldly shapes, folding into themselves like shells, unfurling as if winged, each one a composition, she realized, with a blow of something close to lust.

She tore through all this greedily, sitting on the floor by the bed, the dogs curled near, the periodicals spread around her. When she came again to the article describing the garden of the oasis palace of King Herod at Jericho, she found herself going back to it again and again, studying the layered sections of the excavation, the dotted lines showing the surface of the topmost layer of earth built up over ensuing centuries, a broken column bulging through the layers underneath, one sort of earth and below that another, and small stones pebbling the hollows that had once held the priceless balsam plants …

This had some use for her, beyond what the diagram represented. She didn't know what she meant. She took the eyeliner and made a blow-up of one of the illustrations on the tiled wall of the bathroom. She then studied it for a long time, before taking a shower. After the shower, and with some difficulty, she washed it off again.

Five days of reading. At the table by the window, breathing sea air and fumes; at sidewalk cafes; in one floating bar or another, with the frescoed ochre and gold and mint-green buildings across the water flashing in the reflected wave-scattered glare.

On the sixth morning, she became aware of a man at a nearby table watching her.

She had been poring through the article about the excavation of Herod's garden. During the past days, a resolution had been forming. But she'd noticed the man when he came in because he'd made a fuss about ordering a latte; then a bigger fuss when the waiter brought him a glass of milk, protesting first in loud American, then in bursts of French. Finally he gave up, drank the milk, and stared at her.

He had a bowl haircut and white puckered skin, as if it rarely saw the light. *A museum piece,* she thought, smiling, as she raised the American Journal of Archaeology between them. Then it turned out the man was a museum piece indeed. "I'm in there," he said, when she unwisely lowered the magazine to take a sip of her own caffè latte.

She said, "Oh? Where?"

Big mistake, though would it have been better if she'd never known?

He came, sat beside her, and flipped the journal to an article about the Baron Lowenthall's Museum of Stone Age Artefacts in Paris. This was where Luke had worked, she remembered. The article concerned the exact specialty that Luke had told her about, retrofitting stone chips that had been flaked away by Stone Age flintknappers. When Clare mentioned Luke's name, the man's white face curdled with disgust. Oh he knew Tindhall all right. Tindhall had been a minor curator at the Lowenthall, when this man — Morton, his name was — had been brought in as an expert, to retrofit some stone chips recently discovered in a cave in the Dordogne. Tindhall had been fascinated with the process, had kept hanging around the basement where Morton was busy pursuing the delicate task, day after day. Then it turned out that the actual spear point, carved eons from the stone Morton had so laboriously put back together, was already in the museum collection. But when Tindhall displayed the two pieces together, as part of an exhibition that was widely touted throughout Paris, he failed to give Morton a word of credit in the catalogue, though Tindhall's own name, as curator, was all over the thing, front and centre.

As luck would have it, soon after this, Morton discovered Tindhall and the Baroness Lowenthall performing the horizontal waltz, as he put it, in a store room, heedless, in their lust, of the Neanderthal grave goods they'd pushed aside. Morton had moved quickly; Tindhall had been fired.

Of the many thoughts that went through Clare's head, as she left Morton reminiscing on this triumph, it did her little credit, she knew, that the first one was utterly self-serving.

During her days of reading, she had convinced herself more and more that there must have been gardens associated with the tomb in her meadow. But Harold Plank, in his determination to explore farther along the cliff face, had talked of bringing in a backhoe and other heavy equipment to move the rubble. And Luke — even when, earlier, she'd mentioned the possibility of gardens there — had brushed her theory aside.

But the property was still hers. Somehow she would manage to get in contact with archaeologists of the other sort, the garden sort.

Of course, such exploration would need funding.

And now Plank's right-hand man turned out to be not entirely what he cracked himself up to be. This did not mean that in the big things he was a fraud. But surely she could use Morton's information to get Luke to push her case with his employer.

Schemes — dreams — a new road ahead. Fired up with this, she headed back to Tuscany.

CLARE HAD WONDERED, SOMETIMES, what the world would be like if she were someone else. Would those around her also change? When she got back, Luke was very glad to see her. He was real, warm, alive, bulky — and different. Because she had become someone else? Because he sensed the sureness in her now?

If so, was the very sureness that changed him the thing that undid her?

LAST NIGHT SHE'D FOUND him packing his gear. Harold Plank, confident that the negotiations in Florence were falling into place, had agreed to expand the Plank Foundation's horizons and finance Luke's explorations in Turkey. Speed was of the essence, though. Luke was leaving for Ankara the day after next to get all the formalities sewn up. He had held off only for her return.

"It's the chance of a lifetime, Clare. But I sodding need you with me. Please."

The Gift

LUKE CAME STRIDING ACROSS the piazza from the direction of the museum. He lifted an arm when he saw her. "Clare!"

He'd had a haircut. He was wearing some sort of greenish tropical-weight suit with one too many buttons and not enough girth. A narrow leather tie of the sort she hadn't seen for years. If he'd just come thrusting over like the old Luke, handsome and confident and feral, she might still have been able to get up and leave. But the agitation, the tie!

She said, "You're looking very spruce."

"This is an important day."

"What have you done with Sir Harold?"

"I'm picking him up later." Luke paused, gulped. "He agreed to put off the appointment till this afternoon. I wanted to talk to you first, alone."

Luke sat down across from her. He put his big hand over hers. Again he said, "Clare." She said, "Luke." With his other hand he fished into his breast pocket. He said, "I've ..." He pulled out a box. "Well, the fact of the matter is that I've got something for you here."

He edged over a coaster, and carefully set the box on top. He took a deep breath. "For a fine, exceptional woman ..." Eyes fixed on the table in front of him, as if intent on something many times rehearsed.

"… With fine, exceptional qualities of every sort — a small token, to mark our stepping off together into the future."

He pushed the coaster with the box towards her. A small square box, deep blue velvet, with the gold insignia of Cartier of London embossed on the lid. *Jeweller to Her Majesty the Queen.*

"I should have wrapped it," he said.

"It doesn't look like the sort of box that wrapping could improve."

"You can say that again," the woman at the next table said.

Clare reached over and slipped the box back in his pocket, grateful for the intrusion.

"I think we'd better do this somewhere else. Come on, let's take a walk."

They headed down the level street, past the perfume shop, past the shop of the woman who sold leathers, past the office of the notary where she would shortly sign away her peculiar heritage. Across the Piazza Garibaldi, where the same policewoman was directing traffic through that odd backing-and-turning routine. Up the slanting cobbled route she'd driven down to execute that same manoeuvre, ages ago.

Before we step off together into the future, he'd just said. The carefully thought-out words.

For a fine, exceptional woman, he'd said — with fine, exceptional qualities.

They reached the gate where the saint had come into the city. She turned and faced him under the tree that reached over the gate, its leaves parched, its blossoms gone.

The familiar creases on his face. His slicked, silly, short hair. His eyes that shifted from hers. None of the old bracing mockery, the rasping edge of lust. What happened to the lust?

The need to shock him flooded up — and to know him. But finally, above all, to have the true story that had shaped her life understood by someone else on the face of this earth. Maybe, then, stepping off into that future could be a new start.

She went over to sit on the low stone wall by the cobbled track. She said, "Luke, I need to tell you some hard things."

"Clare really — there's no need."

He thought she was about to tell him of Gianni. Of course. He'd been hoping to scrape by without ever knowing anything for sure.

"This is about what happened long ago."

"Oh that." As if he was positive he knew the gist of that already. But this was her chance — his as well — to define that future they were stepping into. She imagined them standing there together making a bonfire of their secret shames, becoming weightless.

Dry leaves. Clacking pods. The plain below seared by the flat iron of the summer sun. The Stations of the Cross leading up the hill. A good man she did not love, waiting with reasonable patience to hear a story he did not want to hear.

But she told him all of it — indeed, more than she'd allowed herself to know. The sense of power that the young girl had been infected with flared up in her again, the need she'd had to make the one who had shoved her away become evil as she was, to make him weep and be evil, too. She didn't dare look at Luke all the time she was talking, feeling the waves of rigidity coming off him, unable to stop peeling back the layers of her life.

"So you see, I'm not fine and exceptional at all," she said at the end. "But there's something I still can never get straight — how all of this had such power over me all these years. I was just a kid, Luke. No matter what, I was just a kid."

In the silence where her words had fallen she realized she was waiting for him to say, *Jesus yes, you were just a kid.*

He was scuffing a pebble, worrying it with the toe of his shoe, trying to get it to turn over. He finally shrugged. "Yeah, well I always figured the old guy had diddled you, and that's where you got those moves from, you dirty little girl."

His shoe was brown. It had nail-hole dots. A thick-soled walking shoe. She reached down and picked up the stone he'd been kicking, clutched it tight until her palm hurt.

Imagine revealing herself like that. Imagine having taken herself seriously enough to have made a drama of herself like that. Her bones were melting with the shame of it. She pictured the bronze mirror from the tomb, the way the metal had blistered, bubbled, changed, turned green and in some parts actually replaced the cloth that once had covered the reflective surface.

How many lifetimes to learn a trick like that?

What had she imagined she would accomplish? She had never felt so lonely or so squalid, and not only about the story itself, but about the attempt to put it into words, make something of it, spark something with it …

She threw the stone over the wall.

"Yeah, so fiddle-diddle, right? So what!"

There. In truth it only took a moment for the molten mess to chill and harden, start sprouting its own protective layer. She knew what could happen, though. She remembered Luisa di Varinieri explaining how the corrosive elements in the patina could eat and eat away until there was nothing left of the inner metal; but this seemed a small price to pay.

So she stood up. He did, too. Her tone reassured him there wouldn't be any more hideous and embarrassing personal revelations; and she certainly would not be expecting any in return, which could be the very best way to live. So misguided, the urge to merge. She tapped his chest. "Well?"

"Yes. Exactly." He reached into his pocket, if possible even more nervous than before, and justly so. As he pulled out the box, a piece of paper came with it, fluttered to the ground.

The receipt?

He seemed not to notice, preoccupied, working on more words to say? She bent down and retrieved it, but this didn't seem the moment to hand it back. She slid it into the pocket of her skirt.

The box pried open with the snap of a shell. Gold flared in the sun. For a moment this was all she saw, a coil of flashing little links. Then, half-hidden by the chain, she saw a knob of blue. A tiny miracle of blue, just as she remembered, the fullness of it inside the glass bead's skin.

"Oh."

"A small thing that holds the world," he said. "I remember you saying that. You told me if you had something that rare, you would wear it as a secret talisman."

Each sentence dropped into the pit of her amazement, while currents of hot air argued in the branches of the acacia and set the dry pods rattling. Each sentence so unlike anything he had ever said.

What might have happened, now, if the last ten minutes had gone another way — if she'd opened the gift in the piazza, instead of here, without telling him her story? If his reaction to it had been different by even a degree? Would she have followed, intrigued, along this path of who he really was, someone even further from upright than she had imagined, someone sharing her faults and going one better, to conjure up this illicit gift? Would she have fallen for that? Been touched by that? Maybe even welcomed that? Would she have thrown up her hands at some great expectation suddenly released and banished, some enormous weight of personal expectation lifted from the world, from him, from her? Was this always how it was? People coming together, pulling apart? Was it all only a matter of timing?

"You're not saying much."

"So tell me, Luke."

He had mentioned to Sir Harold that Clare had taken a shine to the thing. "Seen the value of a little thing like this, I mean, which not everyone would see. This was when I was back in London, before Sir Harold came out here. He'd taken quite a shine to you of course. I wanted him to understand that you were so much more than just a pretty face."

"You wanted to show the uniqueness of my inner being."

"Right."

Luke seemed to accept her saying this with some relief. She had a surge of sadness at how it must be for him, negotiating his way across this swamp, jumping from one unsure floating thing to another.

He said, "And I gather that later, when he visited the conservation lab, somehow or other —"

"Harold Plank took it?"

"Come on, Clare. You told me you yourself almost took it. And then, you see, he did want to make some gesture."

"Gesture."

"To show how pleased he is. That you and he … And then that you and I …"

"So this is actually a gift from Harry."

"Well, Sir Harold …"

"Let's just call him Harry. Under the circumstances."

"Yes. Well. Harry put the pieces together, true. But you see —"

The big hand went to his heart. The snake eye pooled a tear of ruby light. Oh, and she saw, she really did, how hard it was for anyone to live a life with dreams and ideals and needs all melded into compromise and dross; such a close line we walked. So unfair that someone as dishonest as she was, so tarred, should cast such judgment — or use it as an excuse.

She closed the box. She put it in her pocket, where she heard the rustle of the slip of paper she'd picked up a moment before. The bill from Cartier? Made out to Harold Plank? With Plank's incriminating signature on it, too?

She turned to Luke. She would have liked to tell him that she understood how she'd asked far too much of him just now with her confession — how there was even the possibility, she saw now, that telling him had been a test she'd hoped he'd fail — and that she understood, too, the gamble he had taken with the gift, and that he truly had believed it might please her.

But maybe he saw. She hoped he saw.

She put her hands on his shoulders. "Don't worry," was all she could manage. "I will make sure that everything comes right. I can do that."

She kissed him on the cheek. "So go on now," she said. "Get out of here."

She said, "Send me a postcard when you get where you are going."

༂

THE STORY SHOULD END there.

Watching the woman climb the hill, following the Stations of the Cross, it is obvious what she is planning. She will confront Harold Plank and concoct a deal. She will make certain the bead is returned. William Sands will see his credibility restored and the financial future of his project will be rescued. The name of Plank will become synonymous, in fact, with the archaeology of settlement, rather than the excavation of glamorous tombs. And, though he will accept this reluctantly at first, the very nature of the patient, far-reaching exploration will change him and he will blossom, for he is a good and genuine man at heart — also quick to see which way the wind is blowing. He will back off entirely from any claim to the cliff face in the field across from the famous Tuscan hill town, accepting the wisdom that this remarkable discovery would best be excavated under the co-directorship of former local inspector Vittorio Cerotti and his wife, together with an extensive team of American garden archaeologists, funded by his foundation *sub rosa*. Then, wonder of wonders, the necropolis along that cliff face will reveal surprising evidence of a hitherto unknown Etruscan literary oeuvre, on which the esteemed Contessa Dottoressa Professoressa Luisa di Varinieri will write a long, much-footnoted paper.

All that could have been predicted just from the woman's stride as she climbs the hill, as she crosses the burning stones in front of the basilica, walks the long aisle, stands in front of the glass casket of a saint, says some words that come to her then, though not before. No need to follow her to the next day, and the next.

Ambiguity

CLARE THOUGHT, TWO DAYS later, how simple and straightforward everything had seemed. Harder of course to bring even some of it about — to engage in blackmail, if that was what it was, to stride from one kind of person to another. A process that rarely has lasting results, a voice wanted to say.

She loaded her brush with terra rosa, that rich red of Tuscan fields. The paint was gritty with the substance she had mixed in. She thought how everything important took place very close to the ground, how useless it was to try for perspective at great height. Look how the colour adhered to the copper sheet. Look how the metal surface — in some parts still bright, in others an extreme and gorgeous rotting blue — reflected the three-dimensional quality of paint mixed with flecks of rocky earth; how this broke up the light, so the colour seemed to glow from within. Imagine receiving this surprising gift from the ground, this new idea.

Up in the olive grove, she heard the clatter of Niccolo's cultivating contraption sputter to a halt. Silence rushed in.

Niccolo.

Only yesterday she'd stood exactly here, shaking, looking out across the valley, wondering who she'd imagined she was. This was after she'd returned from seeing Harold Plank. Shaking at that, and at her situation generally, wondering how she would manage. Acknowledging, too, that there was one more essential thing left undone.

She'd opened the makeup case, removed the metal box that held the ashes, wrapped the casket in the beaded shawl, and put the two hand-drawn maps in there, too. She would carry this bundle to the meadow and bury it at the base of the horseshoe cliff near the entrance of the tomb, in a place she hoped would remain undisturbed. The rest would be left up to time and alchemy — whether over centuries the casket would corrode, fall apart, the contents join the soil of Tuscany, or whether the metal would leach into the fibres of the shawl, replace the cloth with a rough and lasting weave. Either prospect would have pleased him, she thought. But if instead the casket were discovered whole, in fifty years or a thousand, the mystery this would present would surely have pleased him most.

The spot she'd chosen, among the fallen rocks, had been hard to dig. The pile of earth beside the hollow struck her as hard-won and significant, and when she'd completed the burial, she'd rubbed some between her fingers. Hard clay in the process of turning itself into limestone, before tightening back into the ball our planet would be again one day, whirling and shining and cold and hard, not the faintest memory in the entire universe that we were once part and parcel of it, formed like this hard matter from the dust of stars. She'd scooped the remaining soil into her pack.

As she was finishing up, from the direction of her olive grove, she'd heard the surprising sputter of Niccolo's cultivating machine.

WHEN THE THOUGHT OF Marta and Niccolo had surfaced over the past weeks, she'd pushed it away, sick at what had happened — at what she'd allowed by negligence at first, and then allowed by not pursuing. What was Niccolo doing back on her place, now?

Simple. He had come to cultivate the olives. He did not think that she would want to neglect the olives, but also he did not think she understood their care. He had promised her uncle that he would give the olives care.

When he saw her clambering down the hill into the grove, he looked straight at her. As she approached, he subjected her to a stare that was round, dark, powerful, scrutinizing, and at the same time hardly personal: as if possessed of much larger and timeless concerns.

Niccolo, an old man and a thief, speaking for the land. Who was she to imagine that any value it held was not his as much as anyone's? The stare did not so much ask the question as make it irrelevant altogether. Any suspicion between them was over now, it suggested. There was no need of explanation on her side, any more than on his. What was important was the matter of the olives.

Important, further, that the house Marta had tended should still be tended; that the niece who had been put in their care should receive that care. Consequently, here was Marta coming, with a bag of greens.

Like phantoms of Clare's first impression of them — their gnarled goodness and kindness, the simple country virtues she had imagined welcoming her here — she saw how Marta and Niccolo would creep back into the supporting edges of her life, unless she put up her hand, said Stop! Right now.

Her eyes travelled over the terraces as this possibility gathered itself up, became thin as air. She saw the scarred, carved, ancient trees with their load of bitter little stony fruit, saw the olives maturing, plumping out, preparing for the chill month sometime in early winter when they would fall or be battered to the ground. How did all of that take place? What was the procedure for turning green nodules into spaghetti with oil and garlic? She was hungry. *Ambiguity.* That word suddenly danced up in front of her, gleamed. Then she caught a further gleam. In the grass, down the hill at the edge of the terrace with the washing lines — a piece of copper, long and partly curled. No, several pieces of similar shape and length, which until now had been hidden beneath the tall green weeds, exposed as the growth turned sere.

How to explain the way things happen? The way at the same time as she was saying to Niccolo, "*Vieni, vieni!* Come on and help me haul this in!" she'd been seeing the transforming purpose it would serve.

Bashing copper drainpipe into sheets was soothing. Bashing it flat, bashing it thin.

When had these remnants been left behind? There was so much she did not know of the history of this house. The shiny condition of the conduits on the roof made her think the work had been done not long ago. He'd left everything in good shape. With forgiveness? Or with a plea for forgiveness, which he could never otherwise express? You could dig and dig, but what could you ever truly hold? Fragments to arrange in one pattern or another.

She found a sledgehammer in the shed, laid the copper segments on the flagstone porch and pounded, raising a hell of a din and sparks. After several hours, this resulted in three mauled, dented, marvellously textured sheets, each measuring about five feet by two.

This morning she had felt very calm. After she had propped the first copper sheet up on the trestle table, she didn't need to search out the illustration from the journal still in her pack: "Figure 5. A section of King Herod's garden taken in the northeast corner." Her hand remembered the image it had traced on white hotel bathroom tile. She was pleased to lay it down again in conté crayon, with strong lines. The stratigraphy took on the weight of her years, in gritty paint mixed with soil. Beyond the window, light rippled across the Val di Chiana. A haze of heat obscured the farther hills. She had climbed a long way for this calm.

SHE WOULD NOT STOP breathing just because she caught the sound of a car coming up the hill, though still very far away. Just because she heard it turning in to her drive, caught snatches of the song on the radio, heard footsteps on the stairs, heard them crossing the stone terrace, then the scrape of the wooden door. No, this did not mean her brush stroke would be any the less controlled. Look at that flare, that burst of colour. Just because the cavity of the human chest was not built to contain such an explosion, that did not mean she would not stand back and squint at her work, deeply absorbed, before she turned.

He said, "I am so glad you have decided not to sell your lovely place. I was very much heartened when your friend Nikki came to tell me. Though I confess I did not recognize her at first, with that shorn hair."

Across the valley, the haze thinned. The saint's town gleamed for a moment, and then was gone, like the meaning of what she had just heard.

"So you will live here," he said.

"Yes. Here."

He came and stood beside her. He smelled of hot sun, water, sand. He leaned in close towards the copper sheet, studied the texture of the paint, then the clutter of squeezed tubes and the little hill of grainy soil she had gouged, the paint-smeared pocks and valleys. She steeled herself for the moment when he would ask what she was doing. But she had forgotten the essential thing.

"This is very beautiful," was all he said. "This is very ... *avant garde*, I would have to say. Yes, this is what they will pronounce, in the galleries where the new work of Clare Livingston shows."

She had forgotten how his foolishness roamed into the deep woods of those that had vanished, how he would work to bring them forth, no matter what, though they insisted their time was past or had never been.

Acknowledgements

WITHOUT LONG HOURS IN a hammock at Molino di Metalliano (gazing up at Cortona's Etruscan walls) this book would either have been written a whole lot quicker — or not at all. So thank you, right off the top, to Dan and Sharon Callahan.

And without generous help from the Canada Council for the Arts, so many books in our country would not have been written, including this one.

ALL WRITING IS TRAVELLING, but with this novel I stepped into spheres I'd previously only glimpsed. Most rewarding on that journey have been not just the detailed help and advice I've received, and the valuable things I've learned from people with extremely demanding lives, but the friendships along the way.

IN THE WORLD OF the Etruscans:

Many thanks to Dr. Greg Warden, Director of the Mugello Archaeological Project at Poggio Colla north of Florence, who so generously, over so much time, has given me not just the benefit of his insight into the Etruscans and the archaeological process as a whole, but also courage --

And to: Sybille Haynes, author of the marvelous *Etruscan*

Civilization: A Cultural History for so amiably sharing her wisdom and knowledge; Dr. Eric Nielsen, Director of the excavations at Poggio Civitate near Murlo, for replies to detailed questions; Nancy de Grummond, for her important works including (specific to this novel) *A Guide to Etruscan Mirrors*; Susan Stock, Metals Conservator at the Royal Ontario Museum, for crucial details including the "raking light" and the "pseudomorph"; Krysia Spirydowicz, Professor of Artifact Conservation at Queen's University, for information about work in an archaeological conservation lab and in the field; Sarah Kupperberg, for insights into Etruscan landscape archaeology; Suzanne Lopez: for the *tombaroli*.

And for illuminations in a broader context: Kathryn Gleason, Cornell University, whose work on the excavation of ancient gardens led Clare Livingston to the gardens of King Herod; the late Dr. Wilhemina Jashemski, for fascinating phone interviews about her life work of excavating the gardens of Pompeii; artist Victoria I, for sharing the experience of working with Dr. Jashemski on *A Pompeian Herbal*; Naomi Miller, University of Pennsylvania, for conversations about art, archaeology, archaeobotany, palaeoethnobotany — and the prime importance of "a high tolerance for ambiguity"; Michelle Wollstonecroft, for sharing her work at Çatalhöyük; Brian Fagan, for the wide-ranging resource of his many books and for cordial replies; Jason Jeandron, of Archaeological Prospectors in New Brunswick, not only for so aptly quoting Winston Churchill, "*The farther backward you can look, the farther forward you are likely to see*," but, in particular, for the gradiometer and its quirks.

And lastly in the world of archaeology — sadly — huge thanks to the late Andrew Sherratt, archaeologist and world pre-historian, for his many seminal written works — and for a generous and lively conversation during which one of my characters got led permanently off the beaten track.

AT THE START I knew little of botanical art, except that I thought I knew what I liked. So I am particularly grateful to the internationally exhibited artist Mary Comber Miles, for her insights into this discipline (which demands sensitivity and acuity both in art and in science) and for her friendship. And to Leslie Bohm for an entire morning of watching her paint a magnolia spray, while she told me about scientific work in the botany lab.

〜

NOW THE IMPORTANT DISCLAIMER: I hold none of the above responsible for glitches, inaccuracies, or infelicities. Nor will any of you find yourselves in this novel. And if I have played around with the topography, here and there, well come on — this is a work of fiction.

〜

DURING THE VOYAGE OF the book itself, I had invaluable feedback from my daughter Shaena Lambert, and from Eva Stachniak, Theresa Kishkan, Jamie Evrard, Jennifer Glossop and Blanche Howard. And thanks to Kathleen Conroy for the little goats.

I owe such gratitude, too, to my children and their partners: Jamie and Alexita Lambert, Shaena Lambert and Bob Penner, John and Marie Lambert, and to all the rest of my family near and far, for the delight and interest of having them in my life. Above all I am so thankful to my husband Douglas, my partner in travel and rest, for his love and support in every way.

Finally, I count myself lucky indeed for the wise, insightful editorial skills of Marc Côté — and for the excellent crew at Cormorant Books in bringing *The Whirling Girl* to light.